surrender

Also by Elana Johnson

possession

surrender

elana johnson

simon pulse

new york london toronto sydney new delhi

SIMON PULSE
An imprint of Simon & Schuster Children's Publishing Division
1230 Avenue of the Americas, New York, NY 10020
First Simon Pulse hardcover edition June 2012
Copyright © 2012 by Elana Johnson
All rights reserved, including the right of reproduction
in whole or in part in any form.
SIMON PULSE and colophon are registered trademarks
of Simon & Schuster, Inc.
For information about special discounts for bulk purchases, please contact
Simon & Schuster Special Sales at 1-866-506-1949 or
business@simonandschuster.com.
The Simon & Schuster Speakers Bureau can bring authors to your live event.
For more information or to book an event contact the
Simon & Schuster Speakers Bureau at 1-866-248-3049 or
visit our website at www.simonspeakers.com.
Designed by Mike Rosamilia and Angela Goddard
The text of this book was set in Berling LT.
Manufactured in the United States of America
2 4 6 8 10 9 7 5 3 1
Library of Congress Cataloging-in-Publication Data
Johnson, Elana.
Surrender / by Elana Johnson. — 1st Simon Pulse hardcover ed.
p. cm.
Summary: In Freedom, where Thinkers rule and Rules should never be broken, Raine, daughter of the Director, is expected to spy on her roommate, Vi, and report back to him in case heavy brainwashing is not enough to prevent Vi from remembering the secrets he is anxious to keep hidden.
ISBN 978-1-4424-4568-0 (hardcover)
[1. Science fiction. 2. Rules (Philosophy)—Fiction. 3. Brainwashing—Fiction. 4. Insurgency—Fiction. 5. Fathers and daughters—Fiction.] I. Title.
PZ7.J64053Sur 2012   [Fic]—dc23   2011040177
ISBN 978-1-4424-4570-3 (eBook)

To my children,
who I hope will never give up, never surrender,
in the fight for what they think is right

Gunner

1.

Someone is always watching. Always listening. Freedom doesn't exist in the city of Freedom, what with the glinting silver surfaces recording thoughts everywhere and the surrounding walls keeping everyone and everything in—or out.

On the east, the ocean hugs Freedom, but no one knows how to swim. That's against protocol, and all Citizens follow protocol.

Identity also doesn't flourish in Freedom. Which was why, on this crap Monday, I escaped the confines of the Education Rise amidst a stream of other students, hopefully unnoticed by Raine *she'd be easier to ignore if she wasn't so gorgeous* Hightower.

Up next: snacking and flying.

Or so I thought.

Raine materialized out of nowhere, her stark-as-snow hair falling over one shoulder. She adjusted her hat as I cast my eyes around to see if anyone was watching us. We seemed to be as alone as two people could be in a city where Thinkers monitored everything, from what job I'd do for the rest of my life to who I'd marry.

I wished They'd chosen Raine for me.

"Hey, flyboy," she said. Her voice made my insides flip. She stepped off her hoverboard and fell into stride beside me.

I fought the urge to look behind me, see if any of my buddies saw me talking with this amazing girl. I managed to stall the smile before it gave my feelings away.

"Hey." I pocketed my hands against the February afternoon chill. I could've mouthed Raine's next words.

"We really need you, Gunner."

I didn't respond. Not a sigh, not a shrug, nothing. Now, if she'd say "*I* really need you," I'd probably reconsider everything. But she never did.

I'd heard her recruitment speech before. Raine belonged to a group called the Insiders, and apparently they were working to enact some "governmental change."

I was pretty sure that meant she snuck out after hours to

2

drink contraband coffee with either her match/best friend Cannon Lichen or her tech guru Trek Whiting.

She wouldn't tell me anything about the Insiders until I joined, and I wasn't joining until she told me something.

The conversation felt stale, but this was the first time she'd approached me in person. The other petitions had happened over my cache. I'll admit, I liked this way better.

I snuck a glance at Raine and admired her sea-foam-green eyes. Immediately afterward I heard her voice over my cache. *Are you even listening to me?*

Every Citizen in Freedom is implanted with a cache when they're born. In childhood, they were more of a nuisance, as they took special concentration to use. I couldn't hear every thought someone had—I'm not a Thinker or a mind ranger. Those people can hear thoughts and read minds—and so much more.

No, a cache was a mental communication implant. After I learned to focus my thoughts, thanks to the introductory course we all took as first-year primary students, caching was dead useful.

I could talk to my buddies on the hoverboard track without yelling. I could send a friend a message without my mom knowing. Over time—and a few more caching lessons—sending and receiving messages became as easy as thinking.

My friends and I exchanged conversations mentally while together. After we went home, messages were easily transcribed just by thinking and could then be sent as electro-communications. E-comms could be kept in the cache's memory and accessed later.

The Thinkers could monitor a cache stream, but They maintained a very exclusive Watched list. And trust me, you knew if you were on it. Saved e-comms, however, could cause problems if they fell into the wrong hands.

I'd deleted all of Raine's, some of the most recent ones without even reading them.

Of course I'm listening, I chatted back to Raine, trying not to let her proximity derail my annoyance at her for asking—again. This issue was nonnegotiable. *It's just that I can't join.*

Raine fidgeted with the fingers on her gloves, her agitation thinly disguised under a layer of frustration. I could feel it coming from her, though she didn't know that, and I didn't want her to find out.

Not everyone appreciated an empath.

"Your mom," she said out loud.

"My mom," I repeated. I couldn't leave her. She and I, we'd always been there for each other. I didn't want to get her in trouble. She had a good job in the Transportation Rise. Sure, she worked until five, but no one needed to be home to monitor my afternoon snacking and flying sessions.

Besides, Director Hightower—that's right, Raine's father—did all the monitoring in Freedom.

Raine paused, one foot on the grass of the green area across from Rise One and one foot still on the sidewalk next to me. I looked at her properly, almost flinching with the beauty I found in her face.

"So," I said, working hard to keep my voice from breaking.

"So, I'm worried about you, Gunn," she said. A secret flashed in her eyes; her words held more than concern. I realized how little I really knew about this girl, despite my crush on her.

I frowned. "Worried?"

"My dad . . ."

Now, her dad I knew all about. Technically he was a Regional Director, presiding over many cities in the nearby area. Not that I'd been to any of them. I didn't know how close they were or what they were called. I just knew that Van Hightower owned a lot more than Freedom.

Rise One loomed before me, making late-afternoon shadows drip across the green area. "I didn't know you lived in Rise One," I said. "I thought you had a student flat."

Raine's mouth tightened at my blatant change in topic. "There's a student section on the second and third floors."

"You have a flatmate?" I asked.

"Yes. You want her picture?" Raine adopted her power stance: left hip out, arms crossed, eyes challenging me to say something.

I held up my hands in surrender. "No, no picture."

Pictures could also be sent over the cache, attached to an e-comm. Everyone in Freedom was fitted with corneal implants, which allowed us to view things on an individual basis on our vision-screens. It wasn't really a screen, more of a movie or picture displayed before our own eyes. Of course, you could forward images through the cache, or you could load them onto microchips and pass them around physically.

See, every Citizen of Freedom also had a wrist-port. This was a simple, inch-wide band of black around the left wrist. On the top, just below the back of your hand, was a slot for microchips, and then you could watch memories on your vision-screen.

We'd eliminated almost all handheld devices in Freedom. It's something Assistant Director Myers was forever bragging about. "We're down to just the electro-board!" he boasted from the roof of the Technology Rise—his beloved home just beyond the taller central Rises.

The e-board was cool; I'd give AD Myers that. It was this

tiny little thing, about four inches long and two inches wide. A screen could be brought up to hover above the device if you wanted to show your buddies a particularly entertaining memory. Other than that, we used the e-boards in school to store class notes. Simply compose a message in your cache and send it to your e-board. Notes: taken.

Educators could send items to their class lists, providing students with an endless supply of study materials. Free-time hours: gone.

"Anyway, she's not a student," Raine was saying. She took a few steps backward, committing fully to crossing the green area to Rise One. "Well, I should go." She didn't seem too enthused about leaving, but that could've been wishful thinking on my part.

"Wait," I called. "What's your flatmate's name?"

She waved her hand dismissively. "Just some chick named Vi."

I watched Raine walk away, wondering why Vi, a non-student, was living on a student floor, with a student. I needed to learn more about the real Raine Hightower, stat.

I glided through the remaining Rises, covering mile after mile easily on my hoverboard. Each Rise—and there were twelve situated in the center of Freedom—took up an entire square mile and created silver canyons, even with all the green areas. On the outskirts of those Rises, more buildings reached for the sky.

My mom worked in the Transportation Rise, and there were others: technology, energy, water purification, protocol enforcement, medicine, and evolutionary development, just to name a few. Each Rise had a Thinker who ran the affairs in that particular area, but only one of them was Assistant to Director Hightower: Thane Myers.

As I drifted through the Rise-canyons toward the Blocks, I forced the Directors from my mind, focusing instead on something more important: my snack selection. On Mondays, my two options included crackers and cheese or raisins. I chose the crackers every Monday.

By the time I made it to Block Three, I'd moved on from snacks and spent a more than healthy amount of time fantasizing about Raine. I swept my palm across the panel on my front door and pushed into the living room, where my mom knelt in front of our safe, a slip of microchips in her hand.

Everything froze, as if the Director had pressed the pause button on my life. Mom stalled with her hand halfway inside the safe. Her face held shock and fear and guilt, all of which I actually felt as my own emotions.

I stared, my mouth still watering over the promise of crackers and cheese.

Just as fast as we'd paused, life rushed forward again. The safe slammed shut, and Mom stood in front of it. Like that would erase the secret she'd just put inside. Like I wouldn't be able to see the hulking black box behind her. It's always been there, and I'd always been involved in the decisions about what we hid inside. Until now.

"Gunner, you're home early."

"Not really." I dropped my backpack and hoverboard and headed into the kitchen for that snack. The safe screamed at me to *look at it!* but I kept my eyes on the floor. "Why are you home?" I called to Mom.

I pulled a bottle of water out of the fridge and ordered up the crackers from the food-dispenser. Mom didn't answer and she stayed in the living room, her frustration about my slobbish behavior a thin veil of normalcy over my heavy curtain of anxiety.

"No reason," she said when she came into the kitchen. "You're going flying?"

"Yeah, be back for dinner." I ate on the way to the hoverboard track, but the crackers held no taste. The icy air I sliced through at the track felt just as restrictive as the rest of the city. As the rest of my life.

All I could think about was that blasted sleeve of micro-chips, what they were, why my mom had hidden them without telling me.

I flew my regulated hours, returned home at the appointed time. Just like always.

Bedtime couldn't come fast enough. At exactly ten o'clock, I plugged my cache into the mandatory transmissions, closed my eyes.

Like I slept.

After an hour that felt like forever, I unclipped my transmissions and crept downstairs to the safe. I had four minutes to plug back in, but it shouldn't be a problem. Like I said, my mom and I didn't used to keep secrets, so I knew the combination to the safe.

Three minutes later the sleeve of microchips lay under my pillow and the transmissions reblared in my head.

I needed time to think. So I lay awake, trying to imagine what I might see.

I couldn't.

I popped the first chip into my wrist-port. My vision-screen filled with my mom's remembrances. My past birthdays and, as I got older, my performances at the hoverboard flight trials. The second to last one held my victory last year. Mom was hiding her fondest memories of me, almost like she couldn't hold them in her head anymore. Why would she secure these without telling me?

I slid the last chip into the port and nearly choked. Director Hightower sat at his desk; the surface glittered with clouded glass.

He leaned forward to speak, and while he looked kind and fatherly, his voice came out full of steel and sternness.

"Hello, Ms. Jameson. Our records indicate that the child we entrusted you with, Gunner, has considerable talent. The Association needs to begin his training as soon as possible. He will be summoned next Saturday, at six thirty a.m., for a personal appointment with me. His afternoon classes will be moved to Rise One to aid in this new academic direction."

Director Hightower paused as he sipped clear liquid from a tall glass. I couldn't work up enough saliva to swallow. He'd called me "the child we entrusted you with." What the hell did that mean?

When he looked into the camera again, I felt like his eyes burned through the lens, the microchip, my vision-screen, and right into my soul. Like he could see and hear and feel everything and I was utterly exposed.

"You will not be able to see him again, Ms. Jameson. But know that he will be of great service to the Association of

Directors, not only here in Freedom, but throughout the entire union."

I dug my fingers into the pillow in an attempt to escape from his penetrating eyes. Numbness spread from my fingers into my arms, but the Director wasn't finished yet.

"You've done a superior job with his upbringing." He bowed his head for a moment, then raised his chin again. "You will be notified of his new address no later than Sunday evening. Until Saturday at six thirty. Good day."

The image went black, but I still felt the Director's eyes lingering on me.

My hands shook, and my head buzzed. The Director's words raced through my mind. *You will not be able to see him again.*

The last person who'd left her was my father. I didn't want to put her through that again. I knew what had happened, even though we'd only spoken about my dad once.

She'd forgotten him.

Once I moved out, would she forget about me too?

"Tell me everything," I whispered to Raine Hightower the next day before genetics class began. Briefly, I thought about my mom. We'd always protected each other, and I was more determined than ever to keep her safe, even after my forced relocation on Saturday.

Raine pushed her ice-colored hair over her shoulder, focused her eyes on me. I didn't know what she saw there, but her expression softened. "What did you find out?"

I shook my head in a universal gesture of *it doesn't matter*. Like I wanted Raine to know I'd fallen apart over a memory.

"You're on the list, aren't you?" She leaned closer. So close, I smelled something warm and sweet coming off her skin.

I cleared my throat and moved away. "Just tell me what to do." Maybe if I joined the Insiders, I'd be able to breathe without this band of tension constricting my chest.

"The Director has his new recruits coming in on Saturday morning," Raine whispered. "Friday night, one a.m. I'll forward you the coordinates later."

Then she turned away.

On Friday night I unplugged from the mandatory nightly transmissions so I could sneak downstairs. In four minutes an alarm loud enough to wake the dead would fill the Block. I couldn't have that, and since I wasn't planning on coming back, I clipped my transmission feed into the e-board I'd configured to simulate my sleep patterns.

Then I slipped down the stairs, knelt in front of the safe. I took a deep breath, not sure I could handle the contents of this thing again—not after that creepfest recording of the Director.

An invisible weight lifted as I replaced the sleeve of chips I'd "borrowed" and pressed my thumb against the scanner to close the door.

That's when I saw the single chip at the back of the safe. Jabbing my hand into the gap to stop the door from latching, I could only stare. That chip hadn't been there on Monday night. My mom had told me about the approaching appointment with Director Hightower on Wednesday afternoon. She'd been leaning against the safe during the conversation, and no tears were shed, though I'd felt her profound sadness.

Quickly, I eased the chip from the slot, slipped it into my jacket pocket. When the safe closed, the beep echoed so loud I squeezed my eyes shut. But no one stirred upstairs. My mom's transmissions would block the sound; she never slept without plugging in.

It'd be so easy to simply go back to bed, plug in, show up for my appointment tomorrow morning at six thirty.

But I couldn't go back. What I'd learned had changed me, and the old me was gone for good. I felt like I should mourn him, and in a way I did. Sure, he'd known his world wasn't perfect, but he'd been happy. Or at least willing to go with the flow.

With my backpack shouldered and that one new chip resting in my pocket, I had a feeling any semblance of contentment lay solidly in my past. I stepped toward the front door. My mother had locked it down last night at ten, just like she always did. Beams of light swept from one side of the entryway to the other. Nothing I couldn't handle.

Step-step-shuffle. Pause. Step-back-pause-leap. I stood at the door, wishing I could say good-bye to Mom the right way. I'd tried last night, but it pretty much went like this: "Night, Mom."

"Good night, Gunn."

And then I'd stood in her doorway while she'd linked into her transmissions and closed her eyes. I didn't get to hug her or tell her I loved her or anything. I buried the troubling good-bye; I couldn't go back and change it.

With one click and one scanner sweep, the front door hissed open. I'd barely melted into the shadows when someone spoke over the cache and straight into my head. *Nice to see you.*

Trek Whiting = Raine's tech genius. Every muscle in my body tensed. I was really doing this. Whatever *this* was. But I'd finally made my own choice. And it felt wild, dangerous. Perfect.

First rule out here, Trek said over my cache, which echoed inside my mind because he'd used my personal cache code. I'd given it to Raine after school, secretly hoping she'd be the one to contact me. My dreams crashed and burned, even though Trek's reverberating voice over the cache meant the code had worked. He'd insisted that a coded cache wouldn't be as detectable, and I had no experience to argue.

No names. Do you know your location?

Yes, I chatted over the cache to him, completely ticked at his condescending tone. *Are we secure?*

Yeah, but there are always seeker-spiders lurking somewhere.

And he spoke the truth, even if he wasn't my favorite person on earth. I shivered at the thought of meeting a seeker-spider in the dead of night. Truth be told, I didn't want to get in the way of a seeker at any time. Programmed by the higher-ups in the Tech Rise, seeker-spiders had a fourfold mission: find, detain, record, report.

If I was found, well, I didn't want to think about the "detain" part. I'd seen a few too many projections detailing exactly what the fist-sized spiders could do to a human body.

As if the seeker-spiders weren't bad enough, I could meet Enforcement Officers or trip some silent alarm or throw too many thoughts into the air. Any of those could bust me before

I'd even begun. I couldn't afford that. Director Hightower wanted me—but he wanted me clean.

His daughter wanted me too.

I wish she wanted me in more ways than one, I thought. But Raine just wanted me to join the Insiders. Earlier today she'd sent her instructions. She'd take me to the Insiders and make sure I got hooked up in an Insider-monitored flat.

And I'd get a few hours to enjoy my life before it belonged to someone else. I seriously hoped Raine had something amazing planned for the night.

Just then I picked up on her emotions. Wisps of feeling flitted across my awareness, telling me of her confidence and calmness. I shivered, but it had nothing to do with the freezing temps.

I allowed Raine to fully form in my imagination. She rarely smiled, but when she did, my heart pulsed in my throat. She could wait, though. I had one more thing to do before I joined her rebels.

I extracted the chip I hadn't watched. With the tiniest of clicks, I slid it into the port on my wrist. My mom's face filled my vision-screen, brightening it with her pale skin, dark blue eyes, and strawberry-blonde hair. Something like a sob gathered in my throat.

I should've said good-bye the right way, whatever way that was.

She looked at the camera for a few seconds without speaking. She swallowed. Then she said, "Gunner, I've loaded a letter onto this chip. It's from your father. He instructed me to give it to you when you were ready."

While she paused, my mind raced. Letter? My father = a man I'd never met. A man who'd been dead since before my birth.

Mom jerked her head toward a sound only she could hear. She leaned forward; her voice hushed. "Compare it with the journal. I love you, son."

Then the memory went black. A second later a scan of the letter filled my v-screen. The writing looked faded, but I could still read all the words, decipher all the numbers. It made no sense, but since it'd come from my father, I longed to feel it in my hands.

I watched my mom's recording again. And again. Every time, part of my being leeched out when she said "son." At some point during the viewing, I'd slid to the ground. Cement-cold crept into my legs, my lungs.

What journal? I wondered. The only answer came from the glow of crimson seeker-spider eyes. An intense fear pounded in my veins. I leapt to my feet and turned quickly down an alley, only to see additional pinpricks of red. More recordings being made.

In six short hours the Director would own me.

I wanted to own my last six hours, dammit.

I knelt, reached down to my ankle, lifted the cuff of my jeans. Four sets of lasery eyes moved closer. I kept my chin pressed to my chest so they couldn't capture my face and beam it back to whoever would dispatch the Enforcement Officers. The wide-brimmed hat helped conceal my identity. For once I was glad protocol dictated hat-wearing at all times.

I extracted a small canister—a scrambler—from my shoe and set it on the asphalt. *Just a little closer . . .*

I felt the eyes behind me, above, below, on all sides. Claustrophobia pressed in unexpectedly. After all, I felt like this everywhere. In school. At home. On the hoverboard track.

So many cameras watching. Always watching.

The scrambler vibrated under my fingers. I traced over the two looping figure eights on the top to control the shaking in my hands, waiting one—more—second.

When the metallic legs of a spider touched my elbow, I smashed the scrambler with my fist.

An electromagnetic pulse sent the seeker-spiders flying backward, their eyes winking into oblivion as they—and everything they'd managed to record—shorted out.

Then I ran.

Raine

2. My new flatmate has nightmares every stinkin' night, which creates a mountain of work for me. Not that she knows that, but still. I sorta wished her dreams would dry up already.

The first couple of nights I'd jerked awake to her anguished cries and muttered words about someone she'd forgotten.

I'd knelt next to her bed, careful not to touch her while I tried to wake her up.

Fact 1: Violet Schoenfeld is a very deep dreamer.

My brief-sheet hadn't said anything about her violent midnight behavior. Instead, the b-sheet provided a detailed analysis of Vi's personality—uh, quirks—and included more than I should ever know about someone else's match.

Zenn (the aforementioned match) came and collected Vi every morning, and most days I didn't see her again until lights out. Because of their identical rings, I knew Zenn had a checklist of responsibilities regarding Vi too. Jewelry is forbidden in Freedom, but rings like Vi's and Zenn's screamed of monitoring. They meant my dad was simply waiting for either of them to slip up. Then the ring would record everything he needed to know.

My responsibilies re: Vi included filing a report if she had a nightmare. Now I prepared the form every night before bed. When she started thrashing and calling out, I recorded the time. Sent it off to Thane Myers, the man who loved to make my life more difficult if he didn't wake up with his precious report.

Fact 2: Violet can't remember anything of substance. I made sure that detail made it into all my reports. Whether it was true or not remains to be seen.

I tried not to dwell on Vi. She wasn't my problem, even though my conscience nagged me in my quiet moments. The way Thane kept her brainwashed for so long (over eight months now) just didn't sit right with me.

Of course, that was one of my responsibilities too: Keep Violet close. Close and under the influence. Thane said it'd be better that way. I was still trying to figure out what *it* was.

Fact 3: Violet did not attend genetics classes—at least not in the Education Rise—though it was clear she had talent. And all Citizens with talent were required to enroll in genetics classes. In fact, anyone suspected of maybe-possibly having talent was required to take genetics.

I'd been in the class for ten years, yet I hadn't formally registered any talents. Several of my classmates had. I'd watched them go from suspected to confirmed to registered. Then my father put them on his list and moved their afternoon classes to Rise One.

They still attended genetics in the morning. We endured lectures and projections about the superiority of talented Citizens. We took field trips to the premier Rises—the Evolution Rise, the Technology Rise, and the Medical Rise—to see which jobs our talents could benefit the most. We learned to control those Citizens without talents.

I'd seen people go from hunched over in desks to avoid eye contact, to waving their hands to control the wind (or detecting passcodes, or commanding the Educator in powerful voices), to looking everyone straight in the face and flying to Rise One after lunch.

I'd seen people go from the Education Rise, to Rise One, to a job in one of the premier Rises, where they continued to brainwash the general population.

I didn't want to be one of those people. I didn't want Gunner to be one of those people. I was thrilled he'd agreed to meet, agreed to learn more about the Insiders.

I watched Violet's chest rise and fall, rise and fall. Lines of exhaustion marred the (once sunburnt) pale skin around her eyes. *I should do something*, I thought. But I didn't know what, and even if I did, I'd never get away with it. So I filled in the time on the form—12:13 a.m.—and blitzed it off to Thane.

Then I slipped out the door into the darkness.

Gunn had agreed to meet me at oh-one-hundred, which worked out perfectly with Vi's nightmare schedule. Convincing him to join the Insiders took for-freakin'-ever. Even for me, and that's saying something. And not something good.

Now, outside in the dead of night, I leaned against a medical kiosk across the street from our agreed-upon location. I thought of him, of the careful way he'd avoided me at school today. He'd been hiding something. Something more than his voice talent. I mean, I'd heard him use that many times on his ~~victims~~ admirers.

Other girls are such suckers for a nice voice and a sexy smile.

But not me. I'd known Gunn for practically ever, and while he had all the right stuff in all the right places, he

23

wasn't really my type. I mean, who likes the dark, silent type anyway?

Not me, I told myself, even though Gunner's face came to mind every time I thought about my match. That boy—Cannon Lichen—had these freaky eyes that saw way too much.

Cannon was perfect for me—as a best friend—because I had a freaky habit of wearing gloves all day, every day, no matter the season. Cannon and I have never held hands in a romantic way. I don't allow people to touch me, and besides, it's *Cannon*.

Neither one of us dreams about kissing the other. It'd be way too weird. No one knows me better, though. Not my father, not anyone. Cannon knew I went out after hours, but he'd never tell. Our loyalty to each other bordered on insane.

"Raine," someone hissed, out loud, not over my cache. I hated all the talking in my head, but I couldn't very well have this convo out in the open street—especially after hours.

"No names," I whispered through clenched teeth. I straightened, embarrassed (and irked) that I'd been caught with my guard down.

Encode the cache, I chatted to Trek Whiting, one of the best technicians on the Inside. I peered into the darkness, unsure of which direction Gunn's voice had come from.

"There're spiders. It's me, Gunn—"

"No names," I repeated, annoyed. Gunner was already screwing things up, and had he seriously brought spiders with him? "Come on." I slipped into the darkness, sure he'd follow. I pulled my coat closed at my throat, protecting myself against the bitter wind blowing in from the ocean. My gloves hid my talent, and while I never went anywhere without them, they didn't provide much in the warmth department.

Gunn fell silently into step beside me. He never says much. People with voice power are sorta like that.

I'd joined the Insiders almost a year ago in a (possibly lame) attempt to make my own choices. Because in Freedom, no one makes choices. My dad—the Director—does that for them.

I played his game. I let him think he owned me—and in many ways he did. He didn't know about my midnight activities, and I wanted to keep it that way.

Where are we going? Gunner chatted over my cache.

I tugged at my gloves, trying to keep the chill out. *Problems leaving?* I asked, ignoring his question. *Last good-byes and all that?*

He cast me a sidelong glance and shifted the hoverboard he carried. Leaving his mom behind wasn't my fault. He'd have been shipped off in the morning anyway, and that was the real problem.

Instead of living in a student flat, Gunn still lived at home. I didn't really get that (okay, I didn't get it at all), but he'd told me once that his mom didn't have anyone else, and hey, he liked living off-site.

If she knew you joined the Insiders, she'd have to report it, I chatted him. Protocol dictated it, and everyone living in Freedom follows protocol.

Everyone except the Insiders.

I did what you said to do, he messaged, his thought-voice tense, angry. *There were still a dozen spiders at my place.*

Did you pulse them? I asked as we turned down another alley.

Had to. Gunner grabbed my arm when a particularly nasty gust of wind threatened to unseat our hats. I yanked my arm away, even though I wore a thick coat. He didn't touch me again, and he didn't speak.

Disabling the spiders would buy us a few hours at most. My dad employed technicians round the clock. Sooner or later, they'd know their seekers had been destroyed and send Enforcement Officers to investigate.

Definitely not good.

I ran through the hideout possibilities. We needed to go off-grid for the next six hours, and we only had about three before the city would be swarming with EOs.

I led him through the Blocks, turning whenever I felt like it and striding through random alleys in case we had a spider tail. Trek would've warned me, but Gunn didn't know that. He didn't know anything—as per the rules of the Insiders. No information is given until commitment is confirmed.

Gunner trailed behind me, his body heat a slow, familiar burn. At least he knew how to move silently.

Unbidden, I thought of the two of us, matched and assigned to a town house in the outer Blocks. I stopped short, and Gunner stumbled into me. He caught me across the shoulders to keep both of us from falling. When he didn't let go, I turned and looked up at him.

The moonlight shone on his pale face. His eyes held the same secret I'd seen at school today. My feelings spiraled up, down, and around. First from the intimate way he touched me (against protocol), then to how I'd fantasized about him being my match (*totally* against protocol).

He ducked his head, concealing his face in murky hat-shadows. But I held his features in my mind. I knew the way his lips curved. The slant of his shoulders. The way his pulse bounced in his throat. How he chewed on his fingernails when he didn't know an answer in calculations, how he lingered near the back of the class on field trials. And, seriously, the guy can *fly* a hoverboard.

27

Why did I know all that? I thought of Trek, my technician for the last year. I knew just as much about him. More, maybe. Cannon flitted across my mind. I could definitely name everything about him too, right down to the ridiculous boots he wore. All. Winter. Long.

Gunner Jameson wasn't special.

Sure, he had inky hair. It sometimes curled from under his hat because he let it grow too long—a direct violation of protocol. His eyes were the color of tea, deep and dark, like looking into the middle of a storm.

I have to tell you something, he messaged, using the encoded cache so his voice seeped into my mind. He stepped closer. I inched toward him. We stood, mere breaths apart, studying each other. I traced the strong edges of his face with my eyes.

I swallowed hard, trying to regain my composure. Crushing on him in his last hours of freedom wasn't great timing. I employed the tactics I taught the Insiders and folded my feelings into a neat box inside myself. That way no one could use them against me.

We need to get off the street, I chatted back, forcing a measure of nonchalance into my message. *You can tell me then.* I stepped away from his touch and took another random turn.

What's going on? Trek asked. *Your vitals are vibrating.*

Nothing, I grumbled, Gunner's intense stare still burning my senses.

Doesn't register as nothing. Trek's chat carried a frown, as if his equipment wasn't telling him the truth.

Look, techie, I said it was nothing. I moved faster, trying to put more distance between me and Gunn.

Whatever you say, Rainey.

Don't call me that. Only my dad used that nickname. I hated it, and Trek knew it.

Left at the corner, and then the alley on your right, Trek said. *I have coffee.*

Halfway down the appointed alley, I opened a door and motioned Gunn inside. He raised his eyebrows, something I pointedly ignored, and stepped past me.

The darkness was twice as thick inside the hallway. "Am I supposed to grope my way forward?" he asked out loud.

A soft chuckle escaped my throat. Not a giggle. Not a laugh. I don't do stuff like that. I'm cool and calm and not crushing on this Gunner guy. "Ten steps, flyboy."

He counted off the steps and waited. I came up behind him, stopping just as he turned. "Now what?" he asked.

"Open the door already. I'm freezing."

He grumbled but groped the wall for the latch. Thankfully, he found it after only a few seconds and opened the door to a brightly lit café. I squinted into the tech lights and blinked away the spots from my vision.

Two dozen people loitered at the crowded tables. They all wore winter hats and gloves and nursed cups of coffee. The oldest one was eight years older than me—twenty-five. Their eyes, sharp and focused, swung toward me.

I pushed past Gunn and settled at a table across from Trek, in all his mousy-hair and hazel-eyed glory. I grinned at my tech handler and the leader of this group, the Lower Block Insiders.

"Close the door!" someone yelled from a table in the corner. I rolled my eyes as I removed my hat and peeled back the fingers of my gloves. Gunner stood in the doorway like he'd never seen a café before. He pushed the door closed with a little too much force, then cringed when it slammed.

"Newbie," someone nearby muttered. But playfulness lingered under his grumpy expression. Most Insiders were very good at being two different people. We had to be. We lived one life during the day and a completely different one at night.

"Yup, someone new," Trek said, standing up to address the entire café. "Guys, this is Gunner Jameson, Raine's newest recruit, and number one on Director Hightower's list. Voice candidate."

The Insiders shifted. None of them had voice talent. And, seriously, it's a pretty freaky talent. Very rare. My dad's been looking for voices for a while now, which was why I'd been trying to get Gunn on the Inside these last few months.

"Thanks for that smashing intro," he mumbled to Trek as he slumped into the chair next to me. He scoffed in a way that said *Really? A coffee shop?*

Trek simply grinned, pocketed some piece of tech that kept this location and all its inhabitants off the radar, and settled back in his seat. I ignored them both and drummed my navy fingernails on the table.

Protocol fact: Nails are to remain unpainted. We can't have piercings either.

Raine fact: I paint my nails every Friday night. Usually blue. Sometimes purple. Never pink.

Gunn studied my discolored nails, a mix of disbelief and something else I couldn't identify on his face.

"What?" I snapped.

He cleared his throat. "Your nails are tight."

I squinted at him, trying to decide if he was going shady on me or not.

"I like them," he added, a hint of amusement seeping into his expression. I watched his smile form, thinning his lips and revealing his perfectly white teeth.

31

I squeezed my eyes shut when I realized I'd been staring too long. "Coffee?" I asked Trek as I opened my eyes. He got up and moved toward the counter in the back, poured coffee into three cups, and returned to the table.

Trek dumped an obscene amount of sugar substitute in his and frowned at me. He flicked his gaze to Gunn and then back to me, raising his eyebrows. For a moment, a flare of embarrassment shot through me. But it's not like Trek knew why I'd gotten all flustered outside.

"So Raine's gonna be your trainer on the Inside, your main contact," Trek said after a long swig from his mug. "That cool with the both of you?"

"Fine by me," Gunn mumbled into his drink. I stirred my coffee without speaking, without even looking up from the curling wisps of steam.

"Check-in is at six thirty, Raine," Trek said. "There's a spidered flat in Rise Nine. Your dad is expecting Gunner." He looked at Gunn, who didn't react.

"Done deal," I said, wishing I'd brought my hoverboard so I could fly to Rise Nine, get Gunn all set up, and then spend the rest of the night on the track. Six thirty seemed impossibly far away. "Gunn used the scrambler."

"I had to," he said again, this time with a major dose of *not my fault* in his tone. He shot me a glare before relaying the details to Trek.

When he finished, silence settled over the three of us. I nursed my coffee, feeling very un-rebellious. While Trek messaged Gunn the hideout possibilities, I daydreamed about the flight trials. My feet itched to be out flying, and I replayed Gunn's performance at the competition last fall. He'd—

Did you have to bring him here? Trek's voice came over an encoded cache signal—I could tell from the high-pitched whine in the background.

Annoyance swept through me. *He has a top-notch voice. He's on tommorrow's list. He gets his one night of freedom.*

Trek leaned so close I smelled the fabricated jelly dough-nut on his breath. "This is one of our last unknown locations," he whispered—so loud it wasn't a whisper at all—as the encoded cache collapsed. "And he's . . . dangerous."

Trek had no idea who was dangerous and who wasn't. Even with his feared voice power, Gunn had nothing on me. But Trek didn't know that. Only Cannon did, and he'd die before he told anyone.

Everyone with talent could be labeled as dangerous. Everyone in this café. Everyone in my genetics class. If Trek meant "dangerous" in the way the Insiders did, then anyone with talent was a threat.

We wanted the government to ease up. The Great Episode had happened a long time ago; the fires were a distant memory; the sun shone again; the Earth was renewing itself. Those in power wanted to keep their power, and They were using the talented to do it. I glanced around the room at all the talent/danger within. None of them looked like they thought Gunn would be a problem.

"I'm your top recruiter," I hissed back. "We need him a whole freakin' lot. He just wanted some freedom before his check-in tomorrow."

Trek cut a glance at Gunner, who acted like he couldn't hear us. "Just get him hooked up and outta here."

I waved him away before meeting Gunn's gaze. No doubt he'd heard the venom in Trek's last statement. Instead of noticing the accusation on his face, I saw him flying with the wind hitchhiking in his hair, the concentration riding in the lines across his forehead.

"How's Cannon?" Trek asked me, interrupting any thought I had of talking to Gunner like a normal person.

"Fine. How's *your* brother?" I countered.

Trek made a noise of disbelief, but anger shone in his eyes. He didn't like talking about his brother. He and Trek didn't see eye to eye on a lot of things, one of which was the level of control the Thinkers currently held. His brother worked in the shining jewel of the Rises: the Evolutionary Rise.

The Evolutionary Rise employed the best scientists. They worked on genetic manipulation, trying to fabricate environmental conditions that would produce talented people. So far, all we got from their experiments were clones. They served in the most menial jobs, if they survived at all.

"Cannon's *not* your brother," Trek said, practically growling.

"He might as well be," I said in a cool voice, but really a rumble of anger grew in my stomach.

Gunn watched us, keeping up with the conversation, which only made me embarrassed on top of furious. He shifted toward me a tiny bit. "Raine—"

"I saw you win," I blurted out, tearing my gaze from Trek's. "Last fall, in the flight trials. I used to watch your memory every night."

Gunn just stared at me. I could tell his brain was working hard to catch up. To think of something to say.

I picked up my mug, my hand shaking—how ridiculous was that?—and gulped my coffee. A slow heat crawled up my. neck and settled into my cheeks.

"Raine's real into flying," Trek mocked, like it was today's megaheadline. Ignoring him—and the surge of anger—I turned back to Gunn, who now wore that winning smile all mindless girls love. I wasn't mindless, but that smile still made the coffee in my stomach boil.

"You won first in the girls' league," he said. "I should be watching your memories. Got a spare?"

"She'd love that." Trek volleyed his gaze between me and Gunn. *Now I know why your vitals were all screwy.* He all but laughed over the cache.

I choked and coughed, causing the fire in my face to intensify. I leapt from the table and clicked off my cache. "Let's go, flyboy. No copy, Trek," which meant *Try to message me or turn my cache back on and you might die tonight.*

I moved toward the back room without waiting for Gunner. I grabbed a fistful of pills and stuffed them in my pocket. When I turned, Gunner stood there, watching. "I've got the hideout coordinates," he said. "What's with the pills?"

"You'll need them to stay awake in school. You take the lead with the coordinates." I stepped carefully around him so we wouldn't even be in breathing distance. Trek watched our every move, almost like he was cataloging the exchange to review later. He probably was.

With Gunn behind me, I headed toward the door, glaring

at Trek as if to say, *Pills, check. Spidered flat in Rise Nine, check. Anything else?*

Trek simply shook his head, a tiny grin not quite concealed behind his coffee mug. Just because he was currently in charge of the group didn't mean he had to be a high-class jerk. We usually got along fine; Trek just didn't like Gunn because of the whole flight trials loss. I'll admit, that's why I brought it up.

Once out in the pitch-black hallway, I groped my way along the wall to the door. I pushed it open to find bright tech lights illuminating the alley. Several seconds passed before I could see the three men standing there. Two of them held tasers at the ready. The third wore his *I'm very disappointed in you* face.

Time slowed as I tried to process the scene. Words raced through my mind. Excuses tripped over each other—what would he believe this time?

"Raine, this is wrong," my dad said, taking one parental step forward. "You shouldn't be out this late."

"Dad, you gave me permission to *fly* at night." My voice verged on panic, but Gunner had to be right behind me, and he didn't need to get caught mere hours before reporting for his training. And Trek and the other Insiders . . . our last unknown location was now known.

With my cache off and my dad blocking my only exit, I gathered my raging emotions and tightened them so he couldn't read how I felt.

"Yes, you and your flying." Dad pinched his lips together in a way that screamed disapproval. He looked at the ground, searching for something. "Well, where's your board?"

Damn.

Gunner

Van Hightower—the Director—had eyes and ears everywhere. Which was the biggest reason I'd kept my distance from his daughter over the past twelve months.

That's right. For one solid year I'd been watching Raine from my peripheral vision. Sure, we'd been friends for years, we ate lunch together sometimes, whatever whatever. But at some point she'd become more than whatever to me.

For a minute there, back in that alley, I thought maybe I'd graduated into more than whatever for her too. But she held everything so close, kept her emotions so boxed up. Somewhere secret, where I couldn't see and feel.

Which showed her intelligence. Of course she'd know

how to protect herself from Thinkers. From people like me.

I had another reason to keep my distance from Raine, and her name was Starr Messenger. We'd been matched since I turned fourteen—for almost three years now—but she couldn't stomach me and I didn't like her much either.

Starr hung with the tech-science geeks, even though she clearly possessed some high-class mind control. Her goal was a job in the Evolutionary Rise, and I had no doubt she'd run the place one day. No one has eyes as sharp as Starr. She'd spotted my near-obsessive crush on Raine after a single genetics class period. She sent me an e-comm, commenting that I might want to "take the staring down a notch."

We never talked, never spent our time together falling in love. But that hardly mattered.

Starr held natural beauty in the bones of her face, and her hair fell in waves as dark as the night. Her eyes blazed with power, almost violet instead of blue.

Maybe I could love her—eventually.

But she'd never be Raine Hightower. That much I already knew. I'd always wanted what I couldn't have.

I'd been stewing about coffee—*coffee!*—when Raine spoke. The way she emphasized "fly" didn't escape my attention. Neither did the fear/panic/desperation pouring off her. At least until she controlled her emotions and swallowed them whole. The girl could really tame her feelings when she wanted to.

Plenty of other feelings buzzed in the alley. And they weren't pleasant. More like *I will control you* emotions.

I did the only thing I could with that much fear screaming through my senses: I stumbled back into the café.

I burst through the door, only able to say two words— "Director Hightower"—before all hell broke loose. As I exhaled, the lights in the café were extinguished. Someone grabbed my arm, yanked me back inside. The door banged closed behind me, and the darkness blazed with the blue spots of guard-spider eyes.

No one pushed past me. I heard footsteps, moving as if they'd evacuated this space many times. My own panic mixed with the elevated emotions of the other Insiders.

"Let's go," Trek said as he moved in front of me. "Those beasties'll buy us some time. Gotcher board?"

"Yeah," I managed to wheeze. "But Rai—"

"No names," he interrupted. "She'll be fine. It's her old man."

She didn't seem fine, even if it was her dad. Trek pressed something round in my hand just as fluorescent rings burst to life on the floor.

"Throw it!" he shouted over the other voices in the room, all issuing locations to their ascender rings. "Catcha later!" He launched his ball straight at the floor, where a blue ring grew. He stepped inside and said, "Camp A, tent seven fourteen."

And then he winked away in a shower of royal-blue light. Around me, people disappeared in red and orange sparks.

I pinched the disc between my fingers, then chucked it at my feet. A vibrant green circle appeared. Once inside, I tucked my board under my arm and simply said, "Roof."

I hated traveling in any way besides flying and walking. But now only green existed in my world. Blinding, dizzying, puke-inducing green, as my particles disassembled and reassembled on the roof.

Finally the cold winter air pierced my lungs. I dropped my board, saying, "Unfold. Power level ten." I used my most authoritative voice. Before I could draw another breath, the hoverboard grew to its full length, vibrating with the best tech complete obedience will buy.

The alley below burned with the brightest tech-lights I'd ever seen. Raine bathed in them, clearly in need of help.

Fear almost forced me onto my waiting hovercraft. I couldn't fly away, but I couldn't afford to get caught out after curfew five hours before reporting to "fulfill my duty" either.

Raine shifted, taking one tiny step backward, while I seriously considered leaving her.

The barely contained worry filtering from the alley told me that Raine wasn't as calm as she looked. One more step backward . . .

I couldn't just turn tail and leave. I swallowed hard against the memory of the Director's words on that blasted memory—*you won't be able to see him again*—wishing I'd never watched it.

Raine took another step backward. "I think I left my board in the alley."

She needed a hoverboard, and I had one.

"Slow descent," I whispered, urging my board over the shallow lip of the roof and down into the alley. "Hover, six inches."

Raine had mad skills on a hoverboard, so she'd be able to fly mine, even with its tricked-out features. Below me, her sheet of blond hair spilled over her shoulders. She hadn't put her hat back on, another black mark on her record. When my board sliced the tension between her and the Director, I ducked, using the shallow wall on the roof to conceal myself.

Raine's almost maniacal laughter interrupted the hysteria gathering in the back of my throat. "Here it is. So, can I go practice?"

I didn't hear Director Hightower's response, but the lights below me dimmed as he packed up his goonies and left.

Raine leapt onto my board and became a smudge against the winter sky. I ran along the roof and jumped the narrow gap between buildings, following her. She couldn't have my board, no matter how beautiful she was.

I almost took a header into a flight of stairs watching her navigate, though she did seem to be having a bit of trouble steadying my board. In order to keep from maiming myself, I focused on the obstacles on each rooftop.

At least until Raine slipped from the board.

Gravity. Super.

My board hovered there, as if she'd given it a command to remain unresponsive. She raked her hands across it, shedding her gloves in an attempt to stay airborne. I launched myself over the rooftop wall, groping for her hands as she slid off the board completely.

She actually pulled her hands away. Our eyes met before the distance between us widened as she dropped.

"Rescue!" I shouted to her retreating form. My hoverboard zoomed down, obeying my command, and managed to catch Raine, slow her fall. But she still crashed into the ground with enough force to render her unconscious.

"Rise, half power." I stepped onto my board and descended

to Raine's still form. She wouldn't wake up. She looked peaceful, the lines around her eyes smoothed with the release of her cares. Her mouth hung open a little, and I imagined—not for the first time—what she might taste like.

Listen, voice-wonder, reign yourself in when you're on the cache, all right? Trek said in my head. *Raine's like, my sister or something.*

Raine's no one's sister, I chatted back, my fingers itching to touch her hair. But I kept my hands to myself.

Aren't you matched to Starr? Trek didn't wait for me to answer before he continued. *You have maybe five minutes before spider surveillance arrives at your location. Wake her up.*

I shook her shoulder, said, "Raine, wake up." Nothing.

I've located a spare board. You guys pretty much have one choice—the sky. Wake her up!

Where's the board?

En route now, flyboy. Trek didn't even try to hide his annoyance.

Shut the hell up.

Trek laughed and chatted, *Use your voice.*

But I didn't want to. I absolutely hated using my voice to get what I wanted. Even when what I wanted was right, needed, essential.

I nudged Raine again. She didn't wake up. Calling her

name repeatedly just filled the sky with words, creating a deliberate target for the spiders Trek had said were coming in, what? Five minutes? My pulse bounced in my throat; my hands shook as I all but slapped Raine, trying to get her to wake up.

Incoming spiders, ninety seconds. Trek's laughter had disappeared. *Use the damn voice, Gunner.*

Ninety seconds. Super. Sighing, and with no other choice, I employed my voice. "Wake up immediately."

Raine

4

Vi's hair had grown in the past few months. It almost brushed her shoulders now and fell in filament-straight layers of plain brown. I'd never told her about hair enhancements and how she could have blue or green or so-black-it's-blue (like she used to) with a simple word and the right technology. In this case, a hair enhancement wand. Mine currently sat mostly unused under my bathroom sink. Because of this, my choice points were multiplying.

In Freedom, students earned points for hard work and good performance, compliance, and respectful behavior in school. We used our points to get coffee on the way to class, change our hair color, or sometimes, if points were saved long enough, students could skip a class period, no questions asked.

I almost had enough points to get out of calculations for one day, and that was only because I hadn't changed my hair color in eight months.

But I didn't tell Vi about choice points, let alone the enhancement wand. Not because I didn't want her to have freakishly cool hair. I remembered marveling at hers when she'd been brought in. No, I didn't tell her because my brief-sheet said not to.

And I follow all protocol concerning Vi, even the items that would've been easy to break. Following protocol gave me power. And the Insiders needed as much power as possible when it came to Vi.

My dad wanted her. Even without any empath genes, I could see the hunger in his eyes when he looked at her. Which meant one thing: She could help him get what he wanted. Dad didn't like anyone. He only liked what they could do for him.

Since my dad wanted her, the Insiders monitored her closely. My reports had been nothing but "still brainwashed" for months. Whatever Dad wanted Vi for, I wasn't any closer to finding out.

Another problem with the inability to share hair enhancements with Vi was that I was stuck with the enhancement

I'd had the day she became my flatmate. So I've had hair the color of snow, cascading down my back like some stupid frozen waterfall, for the past eight months. It could've been worse—the day before she came I'd set my hair on lime green, and it clashed horribly with my normal not-neon-green eyes.

I also didn't tell Vi about advanced meal planning. She ate the same thing—limp veggies and protein packets—every single day. Sure, Zenn brought toast and hot chocolate in the morning, but my reports said he had authorization to deviate from the meal plan.

I did not.

So I didn't say anything.

She caught me eating once, about a month ago. I'd usually eaten and had moved on to schoolwork before she returned from her session with Thane. But that night I'd been running late. I'd just shoveled a forkful of food into my mouth when she said, "Raine?"

After swallowing, I looked up. "Yeah?"

An invisible layer peeled away from her face. She stared at my plate. "What are you eating?"

"Mashed potatoes and ham."

"Ham?" The word sat in her throat the right way, like she'd said it before. Vi screwed up her mouth, like she'd tasted ham in the past.

But she hadn't.

According to my brief-sheet, Vi was a vegetarian. Had been her whole life.

She didn't say anything else, but that layer, that thin film of control, had been erased. It never did come back.

The voice commanding me to wake up filled my soul, my limbs, my very existence with sound. I had no choice but to comply. Even though I wanted to stay in the endless darkness, I simply couldn't disobey a direct order when it was spoken with that kind of control.

And so I opened my eyes.

To the stunning beauty of Gunner Jameson's face. Worry clung to his eyes, and he held me with his piercing gaze for three agonizing heartbeats.

"You okay, Hightower?" he asked, his voice back to normal. "We've gotta jet."

I reached up to touch a stinging spot on my head. My fingers came away sticky, but that wasn't the real reason for the balloon of panic swelling inside. "Where are my gloves?"

"You lost them," he said, and I couldn't tell if he was more upset about my injuries or his hovercraft. Probably the latter, especially the way he was now examining it.

He cast a glance over his shoulder and his mouth moved, but all I heard was, *You lost them.*

No gloves. *No, no, no.* "I—need—" I sat up, trying to reason through the rush of sound in my head.

Gunn put his hand on my shoulder as if to push me back down. I recoiled violently. He couldn't touch me. I didn't want to see the consequences of that.

"She's all freaky," Gunn said out loud, though it was clear he had a cache-convo going on. "She said she needs something."

"Gloves," I blurted.

"Gloves," Gunn repeated, skimming his gaze down my covered arms to my very bare hands. Then he reached into his back pocket and pulled out a pair of black gloves. He held them out to me, and I snatched them by the dangling fingers so my skin wouldn't touch his.

He watched me put them on with this ultrashady glint in his eye. "Looks like you've got something to tell me too," he said, standing up and offering me his hand.

I let him help me. "Thanks for the board. That thing is tight."

Gunn glanced at it hovering next to him. "I'll spill first, if you want. But we only have about thirty seconds before spider arrival."

"Did you trick that thing out?" I asked, eyeing his hover-board. "Because I don't think it knew what to do with me. I don't usually fall."

"Once we're in the air, we can talk." He handed me a hemal-recycler from his backpack.

I pressed the recycler to my forehead and felt the sooth-ing coolness of advanced medical tech as it absorbed the blood. "Are you going to ignore everything I say?" This time his smile was easy to overlook.

"When you start listening to me, I'll start listening to you."

"I listen to you."

"Sure you do." Gunner watched me with an emotion I couldn't quite place. Wonder? Frustration? Something. "You're welcome, by the way. I'm glad you could use my board to pacify your dad. And yes, I tricked it out myself. What else did you ask? Am I going to ignore what you say?" He took a step toward me. "I hear every word."

Looking into his eyes, I lost myself a little. I told myself it was because of his voice control, but he hadn't used it—at least, I didn't think he had.

"Hearing is different from listening," I finally said, my voice hardly more than a gasp.

"Not to me," he said. "So we each have some secrets. But our hideout—"

Get in the sky! Trek ordered, finally coming over the cache. *And you two need to go mental. Incoming Officers down the alley behind you in, like, ten seconds. Gunn, the hoverboard is waiting at the corner.*

Gunner was already sprinting toward the streetlight on the corner. I fell into stride beside him, thankful we'd met in the Blocks and not the tech canyons of the Rises.

Nice fall, he chatted, doing that sideways lookie-thing. *Really graceful.*

I smiled as wide as I could under the circumstances. *I've been practicing that move for months.*

He returned my grin, and the sight of that rare smile sent a ~~strange~~ warm tingle through me.

That's when Cannon's face bled behind my eyes. Even though he didn't want to be my boyfriend, he wouldn't be happy about Gunner's involvement in my life. A forbidden relationship with a non-match meant trouble—for me and Cannon both. I'd send him a message tomorrow; he could help me construct my cover story. I'd helped him half a dozen times so he could sneak off and kiss other girls. He'd help me this one time with Gunner.

Before tonight Gunner was a prize the Insiders needed desperately, if only to keep him from doing too much damage once my dad got his hooks in him. But something new and weird had flowed between us back in that alley. And he'd saved me by sending his hoverboard. Another thing he probably shouldn't have done.

He already belonged to Starr. So I casually stepped away from Gunner, just so he'd have to reach for me if he wanted to touch me. Which, of course, he didn't. He always did the right thing. Well, until tonight.

The white beam of a surveillance scanner swept the street in front of us. We both stopped short. I held my breath, hoping against hope.

Then, "Citizens must surrender to search after curfew!" screamed through the empty streets. Footsteps pounded and spider legs scuttled on the pavement behind us.

Gunner

5.

"You look so much like your father," Mom had said from the kitchen doorway a couple of months ago—our first and only convo about my dad. I hadn't even turned around, since I'd felt her loitering behind me for the past ten seconds. She was feeling all nostalgic. Super.

I scanned my meager meal plan. An apple or an orange. I'd rather eat my dirty socks than a piece of fruit. But I ordered the orange. While it generated, I decided to push Mom a bit. "Tell me more about him."

A large skylight in the ceiling let in plenty of natural light. She gazed up, as if my dad would somehow materialize there. Not that I would recognize him; I'd never met the man.

"He had hair the color of midnight," she said, a dreamy tone in her voice. "And eyes like a sandstorm, filled with browns and golds." She focused on me. "Just like you, Gunn."

I peeled the orange, waiting for her to continue. When she didn't, I said, "And?"

"And because of his brilliance, he was needed elsewhere."

"Elsewhere?" I tossed the peels in the recycler, hoping.

"The Director sent him to the Western Territories." Her gaze rested on my hair. "Your hair is too long." The light in her eyes was fading fast. She took a step away.

"Have you seen him since?"

She gazed at the skylight again. "You have his voice too."

"What's his name?" I asked, something I've never dared to bring up.

"His name . . ." Mom's voice trailed off. She shook her head as if the name lingered there, but she couldn't quite make it come out. Her sad smile confirmed that she didn't know. Or had been made to forget.

When Raine had approached me about joining her Insiders, I'd declined because I didn't want to leave my mom the way my dad had.

I didn't want to be erased.

*   *   *

As Raine and I ran, the warning echoed around us, ricocheting against the pavement, the teched walls, my brain. The scratching of spider legs didn't erase the words *Don't get caught, don't get caught* streaming through my head.

At the corner, Raine leapt onto the waiting hoverboard just as I dropped mine. She disappeared into the night before I could holler, "I'll catch up!"

"Activate, level ten," I said. I cinched my pack as the hoverboard grew to its full length, vibrating and ready. Trek's instructions were to get in the air and stay there. Any ground hideouts were out of the question—too easy to track.

We'd be spending the next five hours on ten-inch-wide hoverboards. I didn't care. Those five hours belonged to me, and that's all that mattered.

"Fly," I commanded, jumping onto the board before it shot upward. I climbed to maximum height, needing to get the smell of coffee out of my nose, the color of Raine's fingernails out of my eyes, the severity of my situation out of my mind.

Behind me, a perimeter of light marked the area the Enforcement Officers would search. Raine and I had already crossed the line. We wouldn't be found. Not in the next five hours, anyway.

I aimed my board toward the camps, as per Trek's coordinates. Four winter camps blanketed the western side of

Freedom. Orange flags in the center of each camp marked the inner oval of the hoverboard track.

It held a streak of white-blond hair. Blurred green lights crested the northern curve and headed south—fast. I kept my board high in the air, unwilling to intrude on her late-night/early-morning practice session.

"Half power," I whispered to my board, and the fans quieted. "Stay at this altitude. Don't drop me."

I settled into the most comfortable position possible on the unforgiving hoverboard, deactivated my cache to fully disconnect. As a technopath, I could go dark periodically without penalty. With everything finally silent, I watched Raine's green lights go around and around.

My thoughts wandered to the flight trials, which were held every September. The girls had flown first. When Raine had won, I couldn't stop applauding.

My hands itched to start clapping again. I smiled just thinking about flying next to her. "I can't believe she watches my memory," I said. "What does she see on it that she likes? The flying? Or me?"

"You always talk out loud to yourself, flyboy?"

I swung around, my smile fading at the sight of Raine hovering ten feet away. How much had she heard?

"You went flying?" I asked.

"You think you can sleep on a hoverboard?" she asked, playing with her gloves and ignoring my question—something that was becoming a Raine standard.

"Sure."

She sat on her board and pushed a button to accommodate for her shift in position. "It's beautiful tonight."

I looked up into the black expanse. I lay down, cradling my hands behind my head. "Do you know the names of many stars?"

"No. I have astronomy next term." Her breath puffed out in bursts of fog.

I pointed up, as if that would be accurate enough to show her which pinprick of light I meant. "That's the north star. The brightest in the sky." I moved my finger a fraction of an inch. "That's actually a planet. Mars, I think." The tension radiating from her cut me off. I turned to look at her. "What?"

"Have you had astronomy?"

"No, I have a brain."

Most girls would've scowled and then thrown something at me. Or giggled. Raine simply studied me for a moment and then inhaled real slow, like she wasn't sure she should. "Who taught you?"

"My mom." I made my voice strong so it wouldn't crack. An ache throbbed in my chest, something my mom used to ease. I didn't think I'd miss her so much, so fast. I focused on the stars, remembering lectures from my genetics classes. After the Great Episode, sunlight didn't reach the Earth's surface for years, and almost everything died. Humans were all but extinct, and those that remained sheltered themselves inside walls. Thinkers—anyone who had some measure of advanced genetic ability—established ways to clean the air and water. They ensured the survival of the human race.

After many years the stars had reappeared. Democracy had not. And that's just the way we wanted to keep it, if my genetics Educator was to be believed. He often said that our mutated genes were what had saved humanity, and we ought to take advantage of any ability we'd been given. When Starr had asked him how our genes were mutated, this predatory glint had entered his eyes.

"No one knows for certain what happened in the Great Episode," he'd said. "There were fires, and nuclear explosions, and war on a global scale. Our top scientists are trying to re-create those environmental conditions in the Evolutionary Rise. In very controlled situations, of course."

"There's been no success there, has there?" Raine had asked.

"Not yet," the Educator said. "But I have full faith that there will be soon. Every clone they make is one step closer to finding the exact formula to create a powerful voice, or someone who can feel and read technology, or someone like Chrome, who can make the wind obey him, or even . . ." he trailed off, this creepfest look on his face, "the ability to read thoughts."

Some people in the class shared his joy at controlling others. They actually bought into the whole superiority thing of the Darwinians. I wasn't sure what I bought into, but I didn't like controlling others simply by speaking.

"I know all about the different animal kingdoms." Raine peeled back the fingers of my gloves, showing me her illegal fingernails again. "Animalia, fungi, plants, protists, and monera. Go on, test me."

"I haven't had bio yet."

"Just name a living thing, and I'll tell you which kingdom it belongs in."

"But how will I know if you're right or not?"

She played with the frayed ends of her bootlaces. "I believed you about what'sit? Mars?"

"Yeah, Mars. It's a planet. Have you had bio?"

"No."

"Ah, so you have a brain too."

She pressed a button on her board and moved closer to me. So close, her board nudged mine.

"You're interesting, Gunn." She reached out and swept

her now-gloveless fingertips from my wrist to my knuckles, where she paused.

I sat very still, waiting and watching her. Her touch left a path of fire on my skin, and something wonderful flitted to the front of my mind. A memory, one I couldn't quite grasp, one that made me the happiest I'd ever been. Raine was there, inside the memory I couldn't really see.

My mind blanked as more feelings than I could identify rushed through me. I stared at Raine's fingers on my mine.

"Right," I said, moving my board away from hers. With the loss of Raine's touch, the joy/wonder/peaceful feelings vanished.

Holy mind control power. I'd often wanted Raine to touch me, but I wasn't superexcited about her controlling my mind.

"That's tight," she said mildly, nodding to my board and holding out my gloves.

"Yeah," I said, trying to figure out if we were really talking about my hoverboard or not.

I took the gloves, and we hovered there, watching each other. I couldn't stop thinking about her skin against mine. I almost felt physical pain from experiencing it, from being so close to that memory and not being able to see and feel it completely. I craved her touch, but I clenched my fists and kept my hands to myself.

Raine

The dining room is all chrome and glass. Dad called it sanitary. I thought of it as prison.

He expected me to eat in there with him every Sunday night. Because I pretend to be a good daughter who makes the right decisions, I did.

In fact, while eating in the dining room, I'd found out the most information about my mom.

"So tell me," Dad began one night in December, spearing a perfectly cooked piece of asparagus. "Have you talked to Cannon this weekend?"

I hadn't talked to him since Friday, at school. Dad would already know that. He knows everything.

"No," I said.

"Who have you talked to this weekend?"

His dark hair glinted in the tech lights. I looked him dead-on in the eye. "No one."

He nodded, a tiny smile pulling at his lips. He kept track of who I talked to. And I'd passed his little lying test.

I contemplated my next words while a clone entered the dining room carrying a bowl of cherries.

"Tell me about my mother," I said as soon as the clone left.

Dad jerked his head up, his eyes filled with razors. A few moments passed. He always closed down when I asked about Mom.

"You know the story, Rainey," he said.

Case closed, I thought. *And I hate that nickname.*

"But I want to know why she breached the city walls."

Dad's nostrils practically stuck together he inhaled so hard. "She was seeking happiness." He bit into a cherry and removed the pit. "In places it cannot be found. You get that, right, Raine? All you need is already inside these walls. Me. Cannon. Keep the protocol, and you'll be happy. Your mother, she . . . well, she thought she could find something out there."

If Dad thought all I needed was him, Cannon, and the protocol, he lived secluded deep inside his own dreamworld. Problem was, that's exactly what most people needed. Someone to love. Someone to love them. Someone to keep them safe by telling them what to do.

"Out where?" I asked.

"It doesn't matter. She left the city, and when she came back, she carried more sicknesses than we have cataloged." Dad wiped his cherry-stained fingers on his napkin. "It was mildly embarrassing for me as Director, as you can imagine."

I shoved a piece of bread in my mouth so I wouldn't scream at him. He selected another cherry, as if that would end the convo.

I swallowed, my Perfect Daughter act dropping. "So she died of embarrassment?"

Dad cut me a hard look. "She died of three diseases that exist in the wild. My physicians could do nothing for her. And that"—he jabbed his red-stained finger at me—"is why you never get near the wall. Ever. Am I clear?"

I nodded, too stunned to even speak. He'd never told me how she'd died. He'd never even told me she'd come back. Simply that she'd breached the city walls (somehow), left Freedom (for some reason), and died (quickly) because of it.

Through the rest of dinner, he didn't speak, but I saw the calculating in his eyes. My dad never does anything without a specific purpose. I hadn't quite figured out what the Sunday dinners were for, but I knew he had his reasons. And they weren't good.

After I escaped, I flicked my way through various projection screens until I found an image of the walls of Freedom. Made of gray slate, the walls stood 150 feet high. An invisible tech-barrier extended hundreds more feet, arching over the city to create a dome of protection. Workers wore special suits while working on the wall to ensure their air supply remained uncontaminated.

In the image I found, the tech-barrier shimmered in the sunlight, making the wall feel sinister and intimidating.

I'd always thought it interesting that our city is called Freedom when we have towering walls to keep us in. I'd never considered the walls existed to keep something out. I clicked off the p-screen and punched my pillow. I also hadn't considered my father to be right, at least not in a very long time.

I plugged into my transmissions, thinking that I needed a mom in a situation like this. She'd know what to say when Dad went all razor-wire with the "who are you talking to?" crap.

If only she hadn't died.

"But she did," I said out loud. I shuddered, trying not to think about what bacteria lived out there, trying not to imagine what could possibly infect a person in a matter of minutes. The closest we came to discussing sickness came in genetics—and even then it was always about genetic mutation and how amazing that was. I'd never been sick; disease didn't exist inside the walls of Freedom.

I let the images fade into the voice on my transmission. *You can never leave Freedom. You will not survive. Diseases we cannot cure exist out there. The air you breathe inside is purified, enriched with nutrients. The wall must not be breached. You can never leave . . .*

Good thing I'd had a lot of practice tuning things out. My dad? The transmissions? Hardly worth listening to.

Gunner knew. He'd seen or felt something when I'd touched him. I had too, but the shapes were black and blurry. I needed to hold on longer. My fingers ached to touch him again, but I kept them tucked under my legs so I wouldn't impulsively reach out and manhandle him.

Jeez, the guy can stare forever. I finally tore my eyes away and looked into the city.

The Rises stretched up to meet the sky, with Rise One towering the tallest. It took up an entire square mile and functioned as a minidistrict inside the megacity of Freedom.

All the Rises did. They had their own Thinker, their own cafés and kiosks, their own solar power grids. The other eleven

Rises radiated around Rise One, all operating at maximum efficiency, with perfectly compliant Citizens.

Mandatory green areas filled the gaps between the Rises, a waste of space if you ask me. It's not like Citizens have permission to lounge around on the grass. Yet it's there, according to my father, "making our city beautiful."

Special-use Rises lay beyond the residential Rises, maintaining things like transportation, education, medicine, tech production, evolution, and compliance. Just as expansive and only slightly shorter, the special-use Rises provide employment for the millions of people who call Freedom home.

Because I was Raine Hightower, I'd been in almost every Rise. My favorite was the Medical Rise, because it offered me two of my favorite things in one place: sleeping and eating. The entire bottom floor alternated between juice bars, yogurt shops, coffee joints, and nocturnal lounges where physicians slept on soft cots.

Growing up, Cannon and I often spent our Saturday leisure hours alternating between doing homework while sipping peach nectar and dozing in the dark recesses of the nocturnal lounges.

Now that I'm older—and on the scientific track at school—I had a shot at a job in the Medical Rise. Cannon often teased me that then I could sleep in the lounges without the fear of getting caught. We both knew I'd be doing something for the Insiders, something covert, in the Medical Rise—if I could keep my biology marks high enough. And that was a big if.

Every building, except the Education Rise, has dedicated its bottom level to providing the workers with what they need to function in their assigned duties. Students have similar facilities in their housing Rises. Clothing, shoes, food, and medical equipment were all provided at quick and convenient kiosks on the first floor. While we slept, clones took stock and sent requests for replenishment.

Beyond the skyscrapers, the buildings shorten into smaller levels, smaller zones of control, where families live in a more suburban climate. Blocks. There are hundreds of those, extending north to the city limit, east to the ocean, south to the orchards, and west to the camps.

I turned away from the city center, having seen enough for a lifetime. Gunn and I hovered above the camps, the dimmest part of the city. The four camps housed three types of people. Those who were having upgrades done on their homes lived in Camp A.

Camps B and D were for vacationers. I'd been there twice with both of my parents and, every summer since my mom had died, with only my dad. He often got called back to work, and we usually missed our weeklong mandatory vacation time in the camps.

I wasn't complaining about that one.

Camp C sheltered only clones.

Trek lived in Camp A voluntarily, claiming to have found many people sympathetic to the Insiders. If that was true, I couldn't tell. None of them had joined, and I suspected he lived in the camps so his protocol-keeping, junior-assistant-status brother couldn't find him, but I'd never say that to his face.

I swept my gaze over the camps briefly and looked into the distance. Past the wall.

Darkness bent over everything, concealing anything that might be lurking. It didn't matter. I'd seen it all before. In the summer, a smear of green clashed with the sandy landscape of the wild.

Trees. The trees in Freedom are only a meter or two taller than me, and they all produce apples, oranges, or peaches. In the spring, the air swims with their amazing fragrance.

But now, in February, only shades of brown and gray existed. Drab sky met dirty earth.

I tried not to look into the wild too much. I tried to stay away from the walls of Freedom. I tried, despite what Dad thought.

"What are you thinking about?" Gunner asked. I jumped, and the hoverboard whined and shimmied to the left.

My heart pounded in my throat as I opened my mental cache to him. *What do you think is out there?*

With a murmur, Gunn maneuvered his board to face the same direction as mine. *I don't know. Sand and sickness.*

Carefully, so I wouldn't plummet to my embarrassing near-death for a second time, I brought my knees to my chest and wrapped my arms around my legs. *Maybe.* Other people's hoverboards freaked me out. Combined with Gunner watching me, I was just as unsteady now as I had been when I'd fallen earlier.

Maybe? Gunner turned toward me. *What do you think is out there, Hightower?*

I smiled—involuntarily. Gunner's voice carried an edge I liked. And the way he called me by my last name? Sexy.

Have you ever thought about leaving Freedom? I chatted him.

No. Yes. Every day. He drew in a deep breath. *You?*

No. My mom died because she breached.

Wrapped up in the memories I didn't have of her, I didn't notice Gunner had moved closer until he touched my arm. Through the wool of my coat, I couldn't feel anything but the weight of his hand.

"I'm sorry," he said, his voice floating on the wind.

"I was seven," I said, as if that made her absence now

less painful. I switched off my cache, worried about what he might be able to hear inside my head.

A long silence followed, disturbed only by the sighing breeze and the winking stars. ~~Exhaustion~~ Sadness seeped into my very bones. My shoulders drooped.

"Well, my dad left, so it can't be all bad," Gunner finally said.

"Your dad left?" I asked, looking at his profile. The pale moonlight cut deep shadows across his face.

"Yeah. There're other cities out there, other places to survive." He yawned and settled back on his board. "You didn't tell me we'd be sleeping seven hundred feet up, Hightower."

I didn't know, but I didn't say so. Instead, I said, "We have to wait for morning to report in at the Rise. Trek hacked into the files and assigned you to a unit we have spidered for the Insiders. That way, even though you'll be training with Thinkers, you'll have some way to counteract their surveillance."

"Training with your dad has me freaking."

"You probably won't work with him. Whoever you're assigned to will just report to him. And you can gather intel on whoever you're assigned to for the Insiders."

"You guys didn't set up who I'll be working for?"

This guy didn't miss much. I especially noted the "working for" when I had said "working with."

"We only arrange for housing," I said. "Every time we go into their system, we could get caught."

Gunner didn't respond. Had he already fallen asleep? For some reason, that annoyed me. Mr. Perfect could fly, rescue me (twice) with his hoverboard, and sleep on the stupid thing?

"I'm awake," he said.

"Oh, great," I said. "You can read minds. I thought your talent was in your mouth."

"It is."

"But you—"

"I guessed."

Yeah, right, I thought, hoping to lure him into a mental argument with my cache off. If he heard me, he didn't take the bait.

"You work for your dad?" Gunner asked.

"Sort of," I said, annoyed that he couldn't seem to grasp the concept of being an Insider and sickened at what I actually do for my dad. "I do as little as possible for my father to gain as much power as possible. Just like all Insiders do. Just like you will."

He watched me silently, as if I had more to say. When I didn't speak, he said, "Okay. But this isn't how I expected to spend my last six hours of freedom."

"Oh?" I asked. "You were expecting something different? After-hours frozen yogurt, maybe?"

"No—"

"Maybe a projection?" I continued before he could fully protest. "We could've caught the latest propaganda flick in the Entertainment Rise. I hear they serve vitamin water and don't issue dietary citations when you drink too much."

Gunn's cheeks colored, adding to his boyish charm. I immediately wished I hadn't teased him into such a strong reaction. That fluttery tingle zipped along my extremities, unwelcome and thrilling at the same time.

"Sorry, I—"

"It's fine," he said roughly. "I don't know what I was expecting."

I didn't know what to say to erase this new awkwardness between us. Luckily, I didn't have to suffer long; Gunn settled down on his board with his arms folded behind his head.

"'Night, Hightower."

Sexy.

I chased that thought away real fast, wishing I had something witty to say in return.

Dawn took a long time coming. I'd never slept on a hoverboard, and what happened that night could hardly be classified as sleep. Gunn tossed and turned, and his high-tech wonder adjusted to everything. An alarm sounded just as the sky started to lighten. An on-board wake-up call.

I hated him for a moment when I realized how much I wanted that hoverboard. Then he opened his eyes and found me staring. He grinned, and my hatred melted into something wrong. A smile.

The kind I should only give to my match, if my match and I were more than best friends.

I folded my mouth into a frown and nodded at his hoverboard. "Do you have breakfast in that thing too?"

"You didn't tell me I'd need breakfast."

"Yeah, well."

"You'd think you had a voice, the way you keep information to yourself." He sounded beyond irritated. That crease in his forehead only appeared when he was annoyed.

"You're on a need-to-know basis until we're secure."

He stood up, straightening his backpack and rubbing his hands together to ward off the early-morning chill. "We've been floating seven hundred feet above the ground for hours. How much more secure do we need to be?"

"You don't need to know that," I quipped. I tried to get to my feet too, but the combo of my stiff joints and the lame regulation hoverboard almost made me take another nosedive.

"I could make you tell me," he threatened, a sparkle in his eyes.

I brushed my hands on my pants after I finally regained my balance. "You could. But you won't."

Incoming Enforcement Officers, a male voice came over my cache. It sounded too low to be Trek, but before I could register who it belonged to, my watch beeped. We needed to exit this airspace, quick.

"Incoming EOs. And check-in for new recruits is in twenty minutes. Let's fly." I nosed my board toward the ground. Two seconds later my watch beeped again. I frowned even as dread settled over me.

Then my watch beeped a third time. A fourth. The beeps became one steady alarm. Dammit. "Try to—"

"Enforcement Officer nine-seven-one-two," a voice boomed above me in the sky. "Open both eyes as wide as you can." A man wearing a silver suit descended slowly, his hoverboard emblazoned with the symbol of the Association: the olive branch.

A red laser bloodied the murky morning light. An iris recognizer.

"What's the charge?" I kept my eyes trained on my boots.

Gunner hovered nearby, his fists and his jaw clenched.

"Stolen property," the EO said, his voice filled with flint.

When I looked up, I expected to find him glaring at my low-class hoverboard, but he had his eyes glued to Gunner.

7.

I met Trek Whiting when we were thirteens. That year we both applied for extra flying hours. We'd both been approved.

We saw each other on the hoverboard track every day. He had decent skills. Speed? Not a problem. His parents worked in the Tech Development Rise. They had tons of hookups. His board was as tricked out as they come.

His balance? Superb.

His training ethic? Unmatched.

No, his biggest problem was the bulk of his shoulders.

I'd fixed that for him when I showed him how to contort his body into a more aerodynamic shape. I'd only told him because my transmissions droned on and on about sportsmanship, and I'd felt guilty.

We'd become friends by then anyway. We were fifteens, eligible for the flight trials, and two of the best upcoming flyers in Freedom.

Enforcement Officers began to monitor our training, recording their observations for our possible recruitment to the squad.

Trek found the idea of becoming an EO unappealing but, secretly, I thought there'd be nothing better. As an officer, I could (a) fly without restrictions, (b) be curfewless, and (c) learn how to block the power of someone's voice.

Sure, the life of an EO sounded just about as perfect as a pawn living in Freedom could get.

Too bad I got (d) disqualified from the trials for "encroaching on another contestant's airspace."

Two other people got tossed from the tournament too. One of those people was Trek.

He actually crashed when I got nudged and sort-of-maybe bumped him. He broke his right leg and three fingers. My lip got busted open, but only because my face got in the way of his boot as he fell.

Besides the injuries, I couldn't figure out why he was so

upset. His file disappeared from the list of possible Enforcement Officers. If anything, I'd done him a favor.

The next year I entered the flight trials again—and won.

For half a second I wished I had a microchip with the victory. Then I remembered who did. Something sharp bit through my insides. I hated that I'd watched my mom's memories.

Sometimes not knowing is actually better.

The Enforcement Officers wouldn't touch Raine. Instead, they pulled on thick gloves and skirted around her.

My earlier suspicion about her talent solidified. Something really had happened when she'd touched me. No wonder the girl wore gloves all the time. I'd thought she was just making a fashion statement in the limited way she could. We'd been in genetics class together for years, but I'd never matched the gloves with a talent. I'd just assumed anyone that came from Director Hightower had to enroll in genetics.

While the EOs bound her hands together with tech cuffs, I let my board drift lower and lower. Like that worked. Two EOs followed and one of them said, "You're the stolen property, son."

Super. Stolen property? How could a person be *stolen property?*

I thought about the chip resting in my jacket pocket. Would it be considered stolen property? I didn't want to give the letter up to anyone, especially Director Hightower. So I kept my mouth shut as the sun bathed the city with early-morning light and the EOs programmed our hoverboards with their destination. After that, all I could do was enjoy the ride.

But it so wasn't enjoyable. The streets below me lay silent and empty, mirroring the way I felt inside. Raine never turned, never looked at me.

We left behind the orchards on the south side of the city, bypassed the outer Blocks, turned away from the ocean on the eastern border. I'd lived my whole life in Freedom and had never touched the water. As we headed toward the Rises, I wondered if I ever would.

We flew past the outer Rises, on a straight course toward Rise One. Director Hightower's lair.

My pulse grew heavier and quicker in my chest. In imitation of Raine, I squared my shoulders and tried to pretend that I didn't give a damn what he did to me. She didn't know it, but I could feel her fear. And it settled in my stomach, amplifying my own.

As soon as we landed in the street, a swarm of officers surrounded Raine, effectively blocking her from view. She said something I didn't catch, so I called, "What?"

Raine swung wildly, and an Enforcement Officer fell down. I saw the panic written all over her face when she met my gaze. "Don't watch—"

And then the EOs tackled her, and the rest of what she said was mumbled into asphalt. Shock didn't allow me to move. She'd said not to watch, but I couldn't look away. So I just stood there like a raging loser while they hauled her back to her feet, watched as the blood trickled over her alabaster face, stared as she succumbed to their threats and let them lead her into her own freaking home.

I remained in the street, hatless, with the two EOs. Uncuffed. Stunned beyond words. If the Director let them do that to his own daughter, what would he do to me?

"Let's go, Gunner," an officer said. "Director Hightower would like to speak with you about last night's events." He sounded stern but tired. His left eye drooped a little bit, making his face asymmetrical. The other officer sported shoulders so broad he could probably block an alley by himself.

"I'm not leaving my board with anyone." I stepped to the ground, pushed a button to make the hovercraft fold up. I tucked it under my arm and tried to act carefree. Too bad I trembled.

The two EOs exchanged a glance, their emotions smoth-ered under years of service. I thought I could make out a hint of confusion. Along with that, a vein of . . . of *unknowing* swept between them.

That's when I realized they were just doing their jobs. They didn't know who I was. Sure, they knew my name, but not what I could do or that I topped Director Hightower's six thirty check-in list.

I decided to play it right. "Look, I've never been here before." I glanced into the sky, trying to see the top of the Rise. I couldn't. "Where do I go?"

"We have strict orders to accompany you," Droopy Eye said. He'd obviously been appointed as the spokesperson. Maybe the other guy was all brawn and no brain.

"All right, then," I said.

Droopy Eye stepped in front of me and moved to the door, where he swiped his palm across a reader. The black glass slid to the side, revealing nothing but glaring white light. I followed him into the Rise with Brawny behind me.

I'd never been inside any of the Rises, except for the Education Rise, where I went to school, and the Transportation Rise, where my mom worked. And neither looked like this.

Oh, no. This place was all tricked out. And by tricked out I mean, tricked. Out. I paused in the foyer—a foyer!—just so I could take everything in. The furniture glared back at me with geometrical, white faces. Not a spot or a dent to be seen.

Did people really sit there, waiting to see Van Hightower, Director Extraordinaire?

No way. Those couches were unsittable.

And surely no one could relax while in the near future they'd be face-to-face with the man who decided every aspect of their lives.

The glass tables sparkled with the bit of sunshine trickling in from the slanted windows far above. P-screens covered the walls, switching between luxurious pictures of waterfalls, white lilies, and brightly colored fish.

The whole ensemble was supposed to say "Welcome!" but all it did was make cold prickles erupt over my neck and down my arms.

Brawny prodded me with his elbow, jerked his head toward the other EO, who stood in front of a silver wall, waiting. I started walking again, tripping over the insanely white rugs before quickly stepping back onto the stainless, silver floor.

But I'd left a dirty footprint on the rug. I closed my eyes in a long blink. Great. Here for two seconds and I deface the place. As soon as I thought it, anger settled in my stomach. What did I care if I muddied up a rug in the foyer of Rise One?

Someone brainwashed would care. Last week—yesterday— I would've cared.

I took a deep breath and whooshed it out in one breath.

"Man, I'm sorry," I said, laying on the gush real thick. "Look what I did."

Brawny didn't even look, just poked me with his elbow again. "Doesn't matter. Keep moving."

I maneuvered around the throw rugs to the silver wall and Droopy Eye, catching a glimpse of a wide corridor beyond. The smell of coffee mixed with an antiseptic scent mixed with a hint of conversation. I wondered what kind of people worked in Rise One, and did they really go downstairs for a latte to unwind?

"Mr. Jameson."

When I turned around, I saw a spider scurry under the couch closest to where my footprint used to be. The carpet gleamed. Spider maid service. *Scary.*

A faint glow on the floor drew my attention. A rectangle large enough to house several people pulsed with blue light.

"Inside the ascender box, please," Droopy Eye said. The box. The lines. Always stay within the lines. I suddenly felt trapped. And inside Rise One—with the promise of meeting the Director face-to-face—the walls were so thick I'd never escape.

"Now," Brawny said. Remaining motionless, I contemplated the ascender box. I really, really hate ascenders—and I'd already used one to get out of that diner. I didn't want my particles accelerated again, not up or down or anywhere.

"Mr. Jameson?" Brawny asked, and it sounded like a threat.

I joined the two EOs inside the lines, gripped my hover-board, held my breath.

"Laboratory seven."

My only thought: *Please, not a laboratory.*

And then I blitzed away into a million + one particles.

Raine

8 The first time I met Violet, she didn't even know her own name. Thane— whose hatred of me was only matched by my blatant distaste for him—brought her to my room. I lived alone in a student flat—and it had taken a lot of whining to get my dad to agree to that. *And* I had to compromise by attending the torturous Sunday evening dinners in the glass-and-chrome prison.

I'd told my dad that I needed space, that other fifteens got to leave their families to finish secondary school. I told him I didn't need clones serving me breakfast anymore, that I had to learn to take care of some things myself. Dad was all about right and fair—and I got my own flat.

In Rise One. But, hey, being on the third floor—in a flat of my own—was better than living in my dad's lavish apartment on the nineteenth.

I lived alone for two years until Violet arrived. I'd never heard Thane speak so gently or look so kind. He led Violet to her bed, her feet going *wisp wisp wisp* on the metal floor. She couldn't even lift her legs onto the mattress until Thane said, "There you go, V, raise your right foot now."

Now *that* was extreme brainwashing. Once Violet lay prone on the bed, eyes closed and barely breathing, Thane turned toward me. His face shifted from almost parental to *I really don't like you*. I pressed my back against the wall in an attempt to put maximum distance between us.

"Raine." Thane advanced slowly, as if trying to make sure I couldn't escape. "I need to know everything."

I shook my head, tears already flash-flooding my face. I opened my mouth to protest, but only a strangled whimper came out.

Thane nodded as vigorously as I shook, silently mocking me. "Everything, Rainey."

And then my room held half a dozen physicians and I was strapped to Violet's bed before I could scream. When I finally released the rage, Thane slapped a silencer on my throat and leaned across me to soothe his precious V.

The physicians attached live-streaming stickers along my forehead. Thane activated the projection screen in my room and linked the streaming to the right frequency.

"Everything," he repeated, all the kindness gone from his expression.

Violet's drain tormented me. Not only because the safety of my flat that I'd worked so hard to secure had been shattered, but because Vi had some freaky stuff going on in her head.

And I got to see it all. *Everything*, just like Thane said.

The show always starts with what the drainee wants most, broadcast through my touch to the live-streaming stickers to the projection screen.

This girl had it bad for some guy. I never judge what I see inside someone's head, but I sure didn't want to witness much of this relationship.

Thankfully, her memory of the guy was broken. No name, no face, only a feeling. The most powerful feeling: love.

I didn't understand that all-consuming emotion. I'd never felt it choke in the back of my throat and burn behind my eyes.

Soon enough, Vi's want morphed into something bigger and far more dangerous—freedom.

She craved with every fiber, cell, and quality of her body, mind, and soul to be free. No wonder she couldn't walk on her own power. If she could, she'd be running—and telling everyone she met to do the same. And they'd all obey, because Vi possessed some heavy-duty mind control.

Tears slid down my cheeks and pooled in my ears. I desperately wanted to stop the drain, but I couldn't.

So I suffered in Vi's cesspool of want until her mind had been emptied of it.

Hers was my longest drain ever. I've never experienced that level of desire before, and never want to again.

But the show didn't stop there. After I see what the person wants most, I'm, uh, privileged to see what will happen if they get it. My father adored this part of my ability. He used me to discover the innermost secrets of those he deemed dangerous.

In Vi's drain, I smelled oily smoke and wet cement. I tasted the triumph as it mixed with fury.

I saw what would happen if Vi gained her freedom. I saw Thane weeping into his hands. I saw the sky flashing with fire, the wind howling with my father's screams.

I saw Freedom fall.

And standing next to Vi, watching it all from a hoverboard, I saw myself.

Someone flew up behind me, and I turned at his touch. He kissed me, and we surveyed the chaos with our fingers entwined.

"About time, Gunner," Vi said, her voice a mix of sarcasm and power.

That's when I started screaming, both in the vision and in real life.

Later, I got an official e-comm with Thane's name decorating the letterhead. I could never tell anyone about what I'd seen during the drain. Not Vi. Not Cannon.

And especially not my dad.

That was eight months ago, and I'd been watching Gunner Jameson ever since.

The Enforcement Officers acted all jumpy around me, and they'd put on those thick gloves before cuffing me. It's not like I can physically hurt them. But no one wants their deepest secrets exposed.

Not even me.

Once inside Rise One, I kept jerking to a stop in the sterile halls. Then I'd get a bump in the back along with a nasty word, and I'd take a few more steps. I knew where they were herding me.

Laboratory seven.

My throat seized, and I stalled again. This time, the bump became a push, but still I couldn't move. I dropped to my knees, shaking my head. "I can't. Please. Don't make me."

"Get up, sugar." Rough hands gripped me under my arms and hauled me to my feet.

Tears streamed down my face. "No. Please." My voice came out childlike, full of desperate fear. I dropped to the ground again.

"I'll carry you if I have to," an unfriendly officer threatened.

"No!" I screamed. "No! I won't!" With my hands cuffed, I couldn't do much but lie flat on the ground and roll away from the officers brave enough to get close. I kicked at anything that came near. My head pounded; my wrists ached from the cuffs.

But I absolutely could not go in that lab without a fight. Perfect Daughter be damned. I just couldn't.

Finally everyone backed away. I knew someone had e-commed my dad. Sure enough, he teleported right next to me.

He smiled, genuine, fatherly. An act for the officers, all of it. "Raine, honey." He crouched next to me.

"Shut up!" I shouted in his face. "Just shut up!"

He put his bare hand on my cheek, and the gesture was so parental my heart squeezed. Fat tears formed in my eyes, and I sobbed and sobbed, because he wasn't wearing gloves. He wasn't afraid to touch me.

Just as the images began to form in my head, he removed his hand.

"Please, don't. I can't. Please, please don't make me."

"I need you, Raine. You know how much I need you." His eyes stared into mine, sharpening, yet pleading at the same time. My mind slipped away as we breathed in and out . . . in and out.

"Let's go, daughter." Dad gently placed his hand under my elbow and helped me stand. I sniffed, unsure why I'd been crying.

"Daddy?" I swiped at my nose, and both my hands rose. Cuffed. Confusion clouded my mind.

"Here, Rainey." Dad removed the cuffs, letting his fingers linger on mine for just a second longer than necessary. "Right here," he said, opening a door with a silver 7 frosted on the glass. "Your seat is over there. Which projection would you like to watch?" He gestured to a black ergonomic with a slip of microchips sitting on a table next to it.

Daddy-daughter time, I thought. I smiled, and the dry tears on my cheeks cracked. I quickly scrubbed my eyes, trying to get rid of the evidence of my bad behavior. Daddy didn't like it when I cried.

"You choose," I said, hoping to make up for whatever I'd done before entering this room.

Dad smiled and selected a projection without examining the chips. I settled into the ergonomic as four EOs took positions against the wall near the door. The p-screen in front of me blared to life with Dad's choice. Everything seemed great—no, everything was finally right.

I turned to see where Dad had gone, only to find a table had been positioned next to my ergonomic. My breath caught in my throat. Silver tech filaments hung from the table—restraints.

Something roared inside my head. He'd done it again. I couldn't believe he'd brainwashed me *again*. I leapt to my feet, or at least I tried to. At some point I'd been chained to the chair. A tech rope encircled my waist and kept me in a seated position.

My hands were lassoed to the armrests and my feet secured to the base of the ergonomic. Something tugged at my temples: live-streaming tech stickers. I couldn't reach up and yank them off.

Hatred burned in my veins. The EOs sensed a change in my attitude, because they slowly withdrew tasers and activated them.

"Let me go!" I cried.

But they weren't looking at me. I craned my neck to see the door they were watching.

It opened, and two EOs entered, tasers out and on. My dad followed, murmuring with Thane, who frowned in my general direction. Not enough to even acknowledge my presence, just enough for me to know I was always and forever beneath him.

Behind them came another man. Maybe three or four years older than me, heavily cuffed and wearing two silencers, one on each side of his neck.

He surveyed the room, barely acknowledging the armed officers or the playing projection. He zeroed in on me, and I gaped at his abnormal skin.

His rashed and bumpy skin.

The anger inside fled, replaced by an unknown horror. This guy wasn't from Freedom; he wasn't right or wrong. He was something else.

He looked like he'd been through hell, with bruises surrounding his dark eyes and blood oozing from the wounds on his wrists where the cuffs had torn the skin. But he didn't fight as they strapped him to the table next to me.

I already knew what came next. His left hand was secured, palm up, waiting for me to hold it. To reach out and suck his deepest desire from the recesses of his mind. The projection screen would soon show those scenes, through my touch, through the live-streaming tech stuck to my forehead.

At least his hands didn't carry the same disease as his face, though further up his arms, red splotches disfigured his skin.

"I'm sorry," I said to the outsider. No matter his medical disorder, he didn't deserve to have his mind raided and splashed across a screen for all to witness.

He moved his head from right to left, just once. I got the message. Not my fault. The restraints I wore made that obvious. But it didn't make me feel any better.

Dad switched his gaze to the outsider's face. "Just stay still." He looked at me, the power and hunger clear in his expression. "You too." He put up with my outburst simply to use my power, and now his eyes clearly said, *Do this. Or else.*

A physician released the restraints on my right hand and painted it with a thin layer of clear perma-plaster. Before I could yank my hand away, he cemented it to the outsider's.

And then the show began.

Gunner

Before I even opened my eyes, someone spoke. I couldn't hear their words
through the whine of the tech screaming
in my ears. I stumbled when someone bumped me, and by
the time I gained my equilibrium, a man stood in front of me.

Not just any man.

Raine's dad = Director *oh my hell* Hightower.

I inhaled sharply, the desire to step away completely overwhelming any other impulse. I stumbled over my own feet.

Director Hightower didn't wear a hat, and his dark hair
was clipped short, as per protocol. His dark, fiery eyes seared
into mine. His smile stretched across his milky-white face,
pleasant yet utterly predatory.

"Hello, Gunner. So glad you could join us this morning."

I opened my mouth to speak, but nothing came out. Another man joined the Director, his lips bent into a smirk. His brown hair followed protocol in cut and style. His flecked eyes studied me with open fascination.

I knew this man, if only through reputation. Everyone knew Assistant Director Myers. He inspired fear with a simple look.

I lowered my gaze when a stream of hostility echoed from AD Myers. I took another step back, bumped into the two Enforcement Officers. Director Hightower looked from me to his AD, and I detected a slight glimmer of smugness.

Which was totally confirmed when the Director's creepy smile extended into his eyes. I couldn't think past the paralyzing horror at being in the same space as him. I felt an overwhelming need to get out of there, stat.

"Gunner, this is Thane Myers, my second-in-command." Director Hightower made a sweeping gesture with his hand toward the-man-who-needed-no-introduction. "Come, son. You'll need to get checked in before you can begin with Dr. Myers."

Right. Like I wanted to begin anything with the freaky Thinker who stared too much. Yet somehow my feet moved down the hall, slapping the silver with enough force to create an echo. I wanted to walk lighter, but I didn't know how.

And then it didn't matter. At the end of the hall, a windowed wall stretched from floor to ceiling. Through that glass I saw Raine. I had time to see the restraints and suck in a breath before the glass frosted, effectively blocking her from view.

I glanced at Director Hightower, and the twist in his lips made my blood flow faster. I wanted to be anywhere but here. Things around me felt surreal, foreign. The air smelled medical, sharp, too clean. It stung my skin, giving me goose bumps.

I heard every sound as if I were the only person alive, yet everything blurred together into one streak of whirring fans and voices and footsteps.

A door creaked. A blast of warm air hit me in the face, bringing a hint of flowers mixed with coffee.

Somehow I sat down. The Director stood near the door like a guard, while Thane settled behind a very large glass desk. The supports were made of the same stainless steel as the floor and seemed to merge seamlessly into it.

The chair I sat in forced my back into a curve, making me feel small and childlike. Folded. Subservient.

"Welcome, Gunner," Thane said, his voice smooth as warm water yet completely unwelcoming. "We're pleased you've accepted your summons for training." He held his hands unnaturally still in front of him, his gaze never wavering from mine. He wore a thick gold ring on his left hand, a fact I found odd. Jewelry is against protocol.

He caught me staring at his ring, and he slid it off and placed it somewhere on his side of the desk. Maybe in the leg?

"I'm going to send you several files." Thane focused on me again. "You'll have time this weekend to review them, and then we'll meet on Monday afternoon for your first session."

Before I could respond, my cache alerted me that I'd received a file called "Welcome Packet" from "Assistant Director Thane Myers."

He didn't ask me if I'd have time this weekend. He told me.

He didn't ask me if it was okay to beam over several files. He simply did it.

Thirty seconds later I had nine new files and a major headache to accompany the growing rage in my gut.

"That should suffice for now," Thane said, standing. "Come, I know how tired you must be. Who gets up for an early flying lesson on a Saturday?" He chuckled, but his face didn't move. He didn't believe I'd been flying any more than I believed he could exhibit kindness.

"My daughter sometimes does the same thing." Director

Hightower's low laugh met my ears. "You kids and your hover-boards."

I looked down at my lap. My board lay there, and I still had one hand curled around it in a protective grip. "We went super early."

I shouldn't have spoken. Neither of them expected me to. I had barely inhaled when the Director stood in front of me, towering impossibly high over my bent body.

"You should not have been with her at all, Mr. Jameson. If you're going to work for me, we'll need to get that clear."

I leaned back to get away from the power, the harshness, in his voice.

"You will do well to remember who your true match is."

"Y-yes, sir," I said.

"Van, watch yourself," Thane warned Director Hightower, but I couldn't look at him. I felt utterly pinned by the Director's gaze, just like I had while watching the memory of him.

I simply wanted him to look somewhere else. Anywhere else.

When he did, I sucked air into my lungs. I'd never felt such a strong wave of relief. How in the world had Raine survived growing up with this guy? I trained my eyes on the floor and kept them there.

Through the rest of Thane's yammering, I never once

looked up, never spoke. We walked down the hall, descended to the lobby, stepped into the street.

"Ah, here's your flatmate," Thane said, causing me to contemplate raising my chin. I still didn't.

"Gunner," the Director said, "meet my junior assistant over Rise Nine. He'll assist you with whatever you need."

The words came as a command, not an invitation, and my head snapped up. I stared into the blazing blue eyes of a guy no older than me. His hair spiked in the front, exactly at protocol length, and was very, very white. His face held only amusement, as if he knew a secret and might burst before he shared it.

He'd spent some time in the sun too. But the color in his skin was fading, I could tell. I wondered briefly if he was reformed.

"Hey," barely escaped my throat.

"Gunner," the guy said. "My name's Zenn." His eyes darted to Thane and back faster than I could blink. "Zenn Bower."

Zenn pressed his thumb to the scanner outside a door that looked like every other door on the tenth floor in Rise Nine. After a single beep, an iris recognizer activated on the door panel. Zenn stood stock still while his identity was confirmed.

Then he threw me a small grin and lifted the latch. The flat had four rooms: a bedroom, a bathroom, and a common living area with two ergonomic chairs and two p-screened walls, which connected to a kitchen equipped with tech devices: food-dispenser, recyclers, the works.

Zenn let me explore while he ordered something to eat. I wanted nothing more than to e-comm Mom as I prowled in the posh bedroom. She'd love this place: the high ceilings, the natural light simulators lining the walls like shelves.

Zenn's bed had razor-sharp corners from the protocol-perfect way he'd made it. I sat on his pristine blankets, my feet resting on the plush carpet. Heavy drapes covered the windows. Two e-boards sat on the bureau. I could project anything onto the bare walls, anything at all.

My stomach twisted. What would I put up on the walls? Pictures of me and my mother? Maybe a snapshot of my long-dead father? An image of Starr, someone I was destined to marry but barely knew? I certainly couldn't display the Director's daughter. An ache blossomed inside, an unknown hurt I couldn't stop.

As the air filled with the scent of warming bread, I put the memory chip containing my father's letter in the safest place I could find: a slot in the light simulator meant for an energy panel.

I'd just sat on the edge of my bed when Zenn flopped onto his. "Heavy digs, yeah?" He folded the fabric of his shirtsleeve up and over, up and over, revealing skin that still held the hint of a tan.

I swallowed back something that felt curiously like loneliness. "Do I have to stay here?"

"I already programmed the spiders. So, yeah."

"I gotta charge my board." The air in the bedroom seemed too heavy with expectations. I got up to leave.

"I already clipped it in." Zenn handed me a stack of toast, and I focused on his hand, not daring to look into his face. "Look, man, I know it's a lot to take. Trust me, I do. You'll get used to it; you just need to sleep."

Answer me, Zenn chatted over my cache when I said nothing. *Play along*.

I nodded, bit into the toast, said, "Yeah, I have some files to go over from AD Myers first."

"Yeah, you wanna make sure you get on Thane's good side." Zenn chuckled, and it came out so effortlessly, so real.

I tried to copy it, but knew I'd failed when Zenn cut his eyes toward the ceiling in a quick eye roll.

"So, where you from, Gunner?" Zenn sat easily on his bed, as if he didn't have a care in the world. His unprotocol bare arms settled loosely on his knees. The dude was one cool cat.

Or else he'd had a lot of practice pretending to be something he wasn't.

"Block Three."

"In the Lower Blocks?"

That's what Raine had called her Insider group. His question made me wonder what he was really asking. I had to be careful with what I told him. After all, he was a junior assistant to Hightower.

"Yeah," I said. "My mom works in the tech department in the Transportation Rise." My chest felt collapsible at the mention of my mom.

"And your dad?"

I shrugged, suddenly unable to force words past the burning in my throat. I'd never been much of a crier and I didn't want to start now. Especially over a man I'd never met. I crunched through two pieces of toast while Zenn busied himself on his e-board.

A chime sounded, signaling the hour: eight o'clock. Zenn knelt in front of me, words hissing out the side of his mouth.

"Gunn, we'll protect your mom—and find out what happened to your dad. We will, I promise you that. Right now, you need to get—and stay—on Thane's good side. Do everything he says, immediately when he says it. Obedience will buy you power. My job is to free Vi. You know who she is, right?"

The chiming stopped, I blinked, and Zenn stood back at his e-board. He turned, his gaze sharp and focused. "I've got training this morning, but Thane has cleared you for a mandatory rest period until lunch." He tucked his e-board in his back pocket. "I'll see you during afternoon leisure hours, okay?"

Something more passed through the air between us, something unsaid yet understood. I nodded and said, "Yeah, see you then."

He left me alone in the flat, alone with my thoughts. I felt hollowed out, as if everything that mattered to me had been scraped away, leaving only a Gunner-shaped skin behind.

"Mandatory rest period," an electronic voice said, "please lie down."

Obedience will buy you power. Zenn's words echoed in my head, and I complied. The room darkened to simulate nighttime. I thought about the girl Zenn had mentioned: Vi. I recognized the name—she bunked with Raine. The non-student. I didn't know more than that, but if she was Zenn's whole job, she must be pretty important.

I lay there, regulating my breathing, keeping my eyes closed, but I didn't sleep. I couldn't, because I'd never been able to sleep away from home.

Raine

10.

Leave Freedom at dawn, head into the sun for five hours, nudge south, keep flying. My name is Cash, I am Cash; Cash, Cash, Cash.

The name echoed through my head, because it's the only thing this guy could think about. I wanted to scream at him to stop already. I wanted to do a lot of things, including rip the tech sensors from my temples and grind them into Thane's eyeballs.

I hated seeing what other people wanted most. I hated feeling their desperation, their desires, their absolute longing. And this guy only wanted one thing: his identity. His name carried power, and he was determined not to forget it.

My name is Cash, I am Cash; Cash, Cash, Cash.

I closed my eyes, hoping to speed the drain. The images still flashed through my head, and the bright lights from the vision-screen flickered on my eyelids. Watching inside my own mind was much worse, so I opened my eyes again.

Every second became agonizing. My skin felt like a prison, a fiery barrier I couldn't escape.

A scream welled in my throat, but I didn't let it take flight. It wouldn't help, and I'd only come off looking weak. I ground my teeth together, praying the drain would end before I broke.

Finally, someone wearing filament-thin gloves ran their hands down my arms to my wrist restraints. I didn't have the energy to raise my head, even though I knew I should. Because, above all, I had to pretend to be in love with my match.

Cannon applied the dissolvall to remove the perma-plaster, and my hand came free with a terrible squelching sound. Tears streamed down my face at the tender way he touched me, as if I were made of glass and might shatter at any moment. I was eternally grateful protocol said matches could touch each other; if I didn't have Cannon to hold on to after a drain, I didn't know how I'd survive.

"Don't cry," he whispered, wiping my tears. "They'll think

you're weak." He slipped a pair of gloves over my hands and smoothed my hair out of my face.

"Maybe I am."

He smiled, and kindness and sympathy shone in his eyes. He shook his head, almost imperceptibly. I didn't deserve a friend like him. More tears coated my cheeks now, mostly because I didn't have to hide anything from him. Cannon has known about my touch-and-see talent for years. An overwhelming sense of gratitude filled me.

"Cannon—"

"Later, okay? Come on." He wrapped his arm around my shoulders—something he always did after a drain—and led me toward the door.

Cash-my-name-is-Cash watched my every move. I tried to look away, but something in his gaze held me captive.

Pleading.

"You cannot help him," Cannon said, his voice taking on that weird quality it did just before he spoke Seer. "No one can help Cash Allan Whiting."

The full name of the diseased man rang in my ears. I stalled in the doorway, shock coating my other emotions.

"Trek's brother." I turned back in time to see a physician release his hands. He shot to a sitting position, turned toward the EOs raising their tasers, and held up one hand.

Even voiceless, he rendered them absolutely still. Without a verbal command, they sat, their faces blank, angular planes. No wonder he worked in the Evolutionary Rise. He probably labored to find that exact mutation that created such exceptional mind control.

Cash turned back to me, rubbing his throat along the silencers. He ripped them off with a gurgled yell.

I took a step back into the lab. I tried to remember if I'd heard an alarm recently signaling a breach in the tech barrier surrounding the city. Cash's skin disfigurement could have only come from outside the wall. Wouldn't I remember those screeching alarms? The warning to stay indoors? The long hours waiting to be notified it was safe to go outside again?

That's what always happened after a barrier breach. Protocol dictated it.

Cash found my gaze and held it steady, as if we'd had this little staring contest before. I wanted to ask him what had gone wrong. Why he—Trek's straight-laced older brother— had tried to leave the city. How long it had taken for the rash to form once he'd breached the wall.

I realized there hadn't been an alarm. Which meant Cash knew how to get beyond the wall without setting it off. "Cash," I said, desperate to say more but not sure how.

"Who?" Cannon asked, glancing at me as if he'd only just realized we weren't alone.

"Don't," Cash rasped, looking at Cannon now. He wiped at the blood trickling down his neck. The rash disfiguring his skin came off.

Time slowed into thin ribbons. Both Cash and I stared at the redness now staining his hands, unable to speak or move. The scene split into an array of images, all competing for my attention. The crimson trickling down his neck; his skin the color of snow beneath the rash; his dark eyes blinking as if he couldn't believe what he was seeing.

I couldn't believe it. Cannon pulled on my arm, bringing me back to the present. "Raine, let's go." He sounded terrified.

My legs wouldn't move. Cash scraped his fingers down his face, leaving pure white tracks in the rash. Slow understanding registered in his eyes at the same time I realized the cold, hard fact: The rash wasn't a rash at all.

Cash zeroed in on me again. "Don't believe everything you hear, okay?"

The room unraveled, each piece spinning into splintered fibers and colors. Everything felt so cold, and all I could hear was *"Don't believe everything you hear, okay?"* over and over again.

"Get her out of here." Thane's heated voice made the

room refocus. I hadn't seen him enter or materialize; he was suddenly just there. He stood over Cash, who was now crumpled down on the table. Blood oozed over the non-rash from a fresh wound on his forehead.

"Raine, please." Cannon pulled on my arm again, and this time I let him lead me out of the lab.

Thane's eyes—full of anger and . . . sorrow?—haunted me no matter how many steps I put between us.

The fury I could deal with. But seeing Thane exhibit anything that leaned toward human? It didn't mesh.

Cannon squished onto the cot next to me, and I finally felt safe again. We were alone in the corner of the nocturnal lounge in the Medical Rise. Darkness covered my shame and kept Cannon from speaking.

That hot feeling eating at my insides—that guilt—was what kept me from telling anyone else about my ability. It's why no one in genetics class knew what I could do. It's why I could never touch Gunner skin-to-skin.

After a drain, Cannon always waited for me to start the conversation. This time wouldn't be any different. That's the best thing about Cannon. His steadiness. His unwavering friendship.

I inhaled deeply, finally calming the last tremor inside my belly. "Thank you."

"Any time," he murmured. He sounded half-asleep.

I nudged him with my shoulder. "Are you asleep?"

He flailed like I'd shoved him with all my strength. I laughed, and he laughed, and everything that had happened back in the lab didn't matter.

"I was almost asleep," he said in a playful voice. "Then you went and ruined it by speaking."

"Oh, so sorry," I said. "Go ahead and take your afternoon nap."

He pushed himself up, sighing. "Can't. Your physicians are wondering why you're not home to take the post-drain meds."

My smile faded as quickly as it had formed. I hated the post-drain haze. Sometimes it lasted a few hours, and sometimes a few days. But I let Cannon pull me off the cot. I clung to his hand with my gloved one as he wove through the nocturnal lounge.

He stopped short before exiting the Medical Rise. "It's raining."

"It's pouring," I responded automatically.

"Don't melt," he said, finishing our childhood game. He signaled to someone, and a clone came forward with a selection of rain slickers and umbrellas.

* * *

113

Back in our room, Vi slept with her back to me. Her shoulder gently rose and dipped with every breath. I wanted to kneel next to her bed and tell her everything, make her help me riddle out the pieces I couldn't make sense of.

Of course, I didn't.

Instead, I sat on my bed with my back against the wall, every blanket I owned tucked up to my chin. Because of the two vials of icy meds the physicians had poured down my throat, I couldn't get warm. My vision blurred along the edges. Every noise sounded amplified. All this combined into the typical post-drain haze.

Outside, the rain streamed down in sheets, separating my world into neat compartments of wet and dry. Right and wrong.

But nothing in my life could be so organized. The line went down the middle, with my dad (right) on one side and the Insiders (wrong) on the other. That much was true. But I crossed over the line every night, sometimes further than others. Sometimes I felt like I was walking on top of the line.

I wished I was strong enough to ignore the line completely. Never go back to the glass prison for dinner. Never let my dad tech me up and use me to suck wants from other people's heads.

But the truth is, he protects me. Outside his small circle

of physicians—and Thane, of course—he's never told anyone, not even the General Director, about my ability. And that's a direct violation of protocol. All talented Citizens have to register.

And I'm unregistered.

My mother begged my father to keep my talent a secret. At least that's the story he tells. I like it. I like imagining my mom as my biggest champion. As the one to stand up to my dad—and win.

Because I haven't figured out how to do that yet.

The rain pelting the glass reminded me of myself. Always beating against something, trying to find a different way to accomplish the goal. Dad believed in brainwashing to achieve peace and ensure survival. Centuries of success had proven him right.

Humanity emerged from the Great Episode as changed beings. Brainwashed beings, fighting against other brainwashed beings, with Thinkers at the helm. When the General Director—one step above my father in the hierarchy of union government—set up the Association to prevent the extinction of mankind, he began a whole new movement: the Darwinian Episode.

Darwin was an ancient scientist, but he taught a principle the General subscribed to: natural selection. No one could argue that some people who remained in the fragments of society possessed great talents.

The General Director believed those select people should lead the talentless. They had the means to do it. Mind control, voice power, adaptability to tech, even the ability to control the elements. Some people had evolved; others hadn't. The General's motto: "The strong lead the weak."

The system worked. Under the leadership of the Thinkers, water supplies have been somewhat replenished. Forests are regrowing, leaving the charred remains from the fires beneath canopies of leaves. Air quality is on the rebound. People don't travel anymore (and when they do, it's with clean methods), instead remaining in the cities where they were born. They're educated, classified, and expected to contribute to their society.

The Insiders' main argument was that the human population had bounced back enough to take some control back from the Thinkers.

The Thinkers, naturally, disagreed. And therein lies the conflict of the Darwinian Episode. Regular people want some measure of power returned. The evolved Thinkers want to keep it all.

I wanted . . . I wasn't exactly sure what I wanted. Something different. Something less controlling.

A city without walls. Cannon told me once about his parents. He wasn't supposed to tell, and he'd received a citation for it. But I'd just completed a particularly taxing drain. We'd gone to the Medical Rise, like always. Protected in the nocturnal lounge, he'd whispered secrets in my ear.

Words like, "My parents said the filters do nothing for our air. That if they went down, we'd be fine. That those suits the maintenance crews wear are just for show."

Later, after he'd been cited, he'd told me that he'd made it up. That leaving Freedom was impossible. He didn't quite go Seer, but almost.

I'd believed him. Leaving Freedom *was* impossible. It would kill me (if the drains didn't do the job first). My mother had breached and died—providing all the proof I needed.

Yet Cash hadn't died. He wasn't even sick.

Which led to one question: Could I leave Freedom . . . and live?

11.

Life seemed to move around me, independent of my body or my thoughts. I couldn't remember telling myself to get up and shower, but I did it. Zenn and I ordered mountains of toast, as if bread and butter were the only items on our meal plans. Maybe on his, but by Monday morning I'd received three dietary notices. I'd have to file copious exception forms if I kept it up.

I forced my vanilla yogurt and granola with no nuts down a too-narrow throat so I wouldn't get a citation. Zenn ate toast. And more toast. The guy probably went through two loaves of bread every day. I wondered what kind of clearance I needed to get a meal plan like his. When I asked, he said,

"I'm a junior assistant." He swallowed. "Informant status."

Just like that. Like it meant nothing. Like he wasn't turning in people left and right and up and down.

"It's not what you think," he said, reading my disgusted-yet-surprised expression. "It just means I have no privacy."

"Big deal," I said. "I have no privacy either. Do you know how many notices I got this weekend for eating thirty-two pieces of toast?"

Zenn licked butter from his fingers. "Thane'll help you with your meal plan today."

"You didn't answer my question."

"Which was?"

"Oh, come on, Mr. Junior Assistant. Informant? No privacy?" I gestured between the two of us, as if we were exactly the same. But we weren't. Not even close. Zenn had an easy charm about him, what with his sleeves rolled up and his hair all spiked. He'd been playing the protocol much longer than me—and winning.

"My voice wins me some points in the meal plan department too."

"Your voice?"

Zenn stacked his plate in the recycler. "As I said, I don't have any privacy. My friends don't know that, but the big boys do."

I opened my mouth to tell him he still hadn't explained when sudden understanding bloomed in my mind. Zenn was a plant. By "friends" he meant "people They want me to monitor."

"I'm sure you get it now." Zenn checked something in his pocket and headed for the front door.

The yogurt wouldn't slide down my throat, and I choked. "Are you—? I mean, am I—?"

He leaned against the doorframe. "Don't worry, Gunn. We already know everything about you. And you're right. You have no privacy either. The difference between you and other people is that you know it." He pointed to my hoverboard, charging on the balcony. "Are you coming? School starts in ten."

I stumbled after him, leaving the rest of my breakfast on the table. Privacy—I used to think average people had some measure of it. Of course, I hadn't been average for a while, what with my genetics classes and winning the flight trials. It was only a matter of time before Director Hightower came calling. I guess I just didn't realize that being nonaverage meant I had to live with a *junior assistant, Informant status.*

I couldn't stop thinking about the message behind Zenn's words. The guy never spoke without every word meaning something completely different from what he said, another talent he must've picked up from his years of playing both sides. Whoever was listening just heard idle chatter; I heard more. Much more.

When he told me not to worry, I worried.

When he told me They knew everything about me, he meant he was gathering intel for Them. On me.

When he said I had no privacy, I knew They wanted me to turn Informant in exchange for a few minutes of unmonitored time to myself.

The stigma of that bothered me. Part of me wanted a dietary plan of my own choosing. The other part wanted nothing to do with luring people into a false sense of friendship just to rat them out.

And there was the nasty question of who They could possibly want me to Inform on. Who did I know worth monitoring?

Thane's office under the Monday noon light felt suffocating. I didn't spend any time basking in the sun—a direct violation of protocol—but Thane had his curtains thrown open. This time the cabinet beside the door flickered with projections. Thane stood with his hands buckled behind his back, looking out the window at the city of Freedom. The gold ring glittered on the middle finger of his left hand.

The air here went down like dirty water—and smelled just as stagnant.

I paused just inside the door, not sure if I should speak or tiptoe back out. Interrupting Thane's power trip didn't seem like a good idea—especially after I tasted the blatant disdain emanating from him.

"Ah, Gunner," Thane said, without turning. "Sit, and let's go over your new schedule."

I sat. Thane turned and slithered into his desk chair. "You'll have two training sessions each weekday. One right here in my office, in which we'll discuss voice practicalities and useful ethics, and one—"

My mind stalled on "useful ethics." What did that mean?

"—in the field, where you'll demonstrate what you've learned here."

I immediately forgot about ethics as the word "demonstrate" filled my ears with a roar. I stared at Thane, who wore something between a frown and a smile.

"Let's get started, shall we?"

Uh, hell no, I thought. But "sure" came out of my mouth.

"Your first task is very simple. I want you to compel me to hurt myself."

I folded myself further into the ergonomic, fear/shock/denial working its way through my bloodstream. Okay, and maybe a little spark of excitement. Thane could use some bloodying up.

But compel him? That sounded so strong. So forceful. I'd always used my voice to get perks, like girls' private cache codes and extra flying hours on the hoverboard track.

"I—I . . . can't—"

Thane swept away my stammer with a jab of his hand. "You can. And you will. Just do it."

A voice always knows when another voice has employed their power. And Thane hadn't. I didn't even know if he possessed voice control. Not all Thinkers did.

We stared at each other, unmoving, unspeaking, barely breathing. A thousand possibilities ran through my mind, all of them ending with Thane bloody and me shackled and on my way to the modification chamber where my memory would be purged.

He blinked. I swallowed. The projections played inside the cabinet, a cacophony of background noise.

He leaned on his desk. "The Director needs to know the scope of your abilities."

Like I wanted to show anyone the "scope of my abilities." Especially Director Hightower, the man who restrained his own daughter behind walls of glass.

Just as Thane opened his mouth again, I said, "Punch your way through that window." I inclined my head to the sheet of glass behind his desk. I'd employed my most powerful voice, and strangely, I felt the need to smash something, stat.

Thane's gaze deadened, and he stood up mechanically. His legs barely bent as he stepped to the windows. Clonelike, he cocked his fist back and slammed it as hard as he could into the glass.

Cracking noise filled my ears, my eyes, my mouth. He punched again and again, even through the warnings and shrieking alarms, until the window-wall came shattering down. Shards of glass spilled onto the floor, rained into the street far below. An alarm spiked the air with a shrill *beep-beep-beep!* Thane turned around real slow, as if made of gears and tech.

Bits of jagged glass stuck in his knuckles, blood flowing thick and free over his ruined hand. It dripped onto the silver floor as three clones, a physician wearing a blue lab coat, and Director Hightower burst into the office.

He wore a look of amazement and a triumphant smile. His gaze swept me from head to toe, satisfied, yet terribly terribly terribly hungry.

The door to my flat jerked open before I pressed my thumb to the portlet. Good thing too, because I felt like I didn't have enough energy to push hard enough.

"Holy—Gunner!" Zenn grabbed my arm and hauled me into the flat. "How did you do it?"

I collapsed at the kitchen table, my stomach gnawing at me for something to eat. I didn't check my meal plan before I said, "Toast first."

The smell of browning bread revived me a little, and I raised my head just as Zenn set the buttered slices—six—in front of me. "Spill, Mr. Voice Talent."

"Spill what?" I asked around a mouthful of bread—and another dietary notice in my cache.

"How you got Thane to smash his hand through a plated window. Through the tech barrier of Rise One." Zenn studied me like I had untold knowledge, the secret to the universe, or some other huge factoid.

"Um, the same way you would have." I moved to the food-dispenser and ordered orange juice. I gulped it, trying to steady the shaking in my hands with the burn of the citrus in my mouth. Zenn pressed in next to me, too close for comfort, yet neither one of us moved.

He ordered something on the dispenser, and while it generated, he whispered, "Really? Just your voice?" His words didn't hide a secret message this time. They didn't conceal his fear either.

I nodded, still guzzling the juice, wondering what about my voice could make Zenn afraid. Didn't he have a Gunner Jameson brief-sheet? He should know everything about me.

"That's the most powerful voice I've ever heard of." He angled his body toward me just a bit. "Planning session, midnight, okay?"

I searched his gaze for some hint of how we'd trick the sensors, the spiders. Them. I found nothing. Zenn collected his own stack of toast and sat at the table.

"I'm so glad your first day went well, Gunn. Welcome to the team!"

Again, I marveled at how seamlessly he moved from *I'm terrified—you only used your voice?* to cheery Informant flatmate in under two seconds.

At least I now knew the food-dispenser was good for concealing three seconds of whispered conversation.

And I wanted more.

After stacking my plate in the recycler, I lifted the front cover of the dispenser. The flat area where the food materialized needed to be cleaned.

Like I did that.

Instead, I turned the dispenser, removed the cover on the back. A flashing green light on the inside showed its functionality. I rested my hands over the tech inside, imagined that I wanted the dispenser to take longer to generate the food.

Maybe seven seconds instead of three. Then Zenn and I could talk in sentences longer than two words.

I adjusted the timing portlet, nudged it along until the tech zinging up my arm translated to seven seconds in my head.

Satisfied with the juiced food-dispenser, I ordered a glass of water and turned back to Zenn. His shock permeated my senses in a quick jolt. "Technopath. Sweet."

If he said so. I flashed him seven fingers before settling back into my chair at the table. "So . . ."

"So now the Director knows the extent of your voice." Zenn took the water from the dispenser, ordered another glass. "Be careful, Gunn. He collects people with talents as if they were trophies." He put the water in front of me. "You just made my job harder."

I picked up the glass, cold dread creeping down my throat as I gulped the water.

"Your job?"

"He'll want to know everything now."

"What will you do?"

"Feed him in small bites."

I nodded before heading to bed for my mandatory rest period, wishing those seven seconds of stolen conversation could be erased from my memory.

I had no doubt Director Hightower would swallow me. Slowly. Painfully. But completely.

* * *

Midnight arrived with Zenn shaking me awake. He pressed his finger to his lips, then stole across the rug and into the living area. I scraped my hair off my forehead, followed. I caught a reflection of the moonrise in the glass as he paced on the balcony.

When I joined him, there wasn't much room for either of us to move. And it was holy cold. My teeth knocked together, and I cursed the fact that I hadn't grabbed a heat stick first. "Wh-what's up?"

"One of the perks of living in this flat is the spider surveillance," Zenn began. When he drove his hands deep into his pockets, I didn't feel like such a wimp. "Our spiders scramble the Association's feed every day for twenty minutes. When the time changes, we're notified on our way home from our last session."

Anything I said would come out garbled, so I kept my mouth shut. Everything about Zenn glowed too-white in the light of the moon; his hair, his skin, his teeth. He freaked me out a little, and I wanted to return to the warmth and comfort of my bed. Then the exhilaration of living, breathing, talking freely washed over me. "Can't They just record our cache?"

"Not all the time. And besides, spoken conversations aren't cached." Zenn waved one hand before repocketing it. "Just be careful with your thoughts when you're around

Thane. Disguise the information among the other mundane details of your daily life. I mean, even Thane is human."

My lower jaw shook in response. Despite the blood that had dripped from his hand, I wasn't so sure of that. I shifted back and forth from foot to foot in a lame attempt to warm up.

"Spoken convos can be recorded," I said, just to have something to argue about.

"That's why we have technicians," Zenn replied matter-of-factly. "It's why we have a scrambler in our living area. And why the spiders give us these twenty minutes."

He waited for me to say something else. I opted to let him talk.

"We want to gather as much intel on Thane as we can, and we haven't had anyone in his office for over a year. So you'll be our main contact there. I—"

"Our?"

"The Insiders. I run a group in the southern Blocks, just above the orchards. Each group has separate yet synced directives." Some annoyance drifted from him. Maybe I should know all this already.

"Oh, right, course." I made a mental note to send Raine a nasty e-comm as soon as I could.

"Raine provides us with the necessary info about her father. And I'm with Vi, so I can bring in her status as well."

"Who is Vi, exactly?" I asked.

"She's my match," Zenn answered. "She could control the entire Association—if she wasn't kept completely brainwashed. I'm working with her."

"Doing what?"

"They think I'm implanting new memories. Or at least keeping her sedated. She trains with Thane too; he's her dad."

"Her dad?" The words sandpapered against my tongue. I noticed that Zenn didn't say exactly what he did with Vi.

"Yeah, her dad. But Vi's useless to us in her sleepwalking state. She rooms with Raine, but Raine's brief-sheet forbids meaningful contact. Raine's forced to comply so she can keep her position of power. Remember that obedience buys power. It buys freedom."

"Got it. So, what next?"

"Notice anything in Thane's office today? Before you had him punch down the security system, that is. Anything we can use?"

Thane's office was as undecorated as they came. Unless he had secret compartments in the silver floor, I didn't see how my presence in his office was going to help at all. "He's got a desk, a chair, and a cabinet. That's it."

Zenn leaned on the railing. "He must have an e-board. Probably two or three."

"There were a couple projections playing inside the cabinet. Could've been from e-board data."

"Did you see what they were broadcasting?"

"No."

"Well, that's where we'll start. Tomorrow night, midnight."

I groaned. "Do we ever sleep on this job?"

Zenn laughed, the sound almost ringing with happiness. "You'll get used to it after a while. And you've got those pills for school, right?"

I grunted, which passed for a "yeah."

"Hit the coffee kiosk first thing in the morning," he added. "I'll stall the Director if I can. But try not to do anything else with your voice for a while, okay?" He went back inside the flat, leaving the sliding glass door open for me.

I hesitated out on the balcony, even though the cold pricked at my fingers, ears, and nose. The city lay dormant at night, and I felt a strange sense of power at being up at a forbidden hour, viewing it.

Taking strength from the ink-stained sky, I drew in a deep breath full of frost and zero expectations before returning to bed.

All I could think about was my head on the Director's wall. My voice = his trophy.

Sleep didn't come. I ended up retrieving my chip from the light generator. After clipping my feed into my e-board so whoever was monitoring me tonight would think I was asleep, I brought up my father's letter. I studied it, trying to make links between phrases like, *reverse coordinates of incoming reports—91, 112—Green River,* or *shut down tech generators—123—Harvest,* and then, *olive branch will amplify—118—Goodgrounds.*

Apparently punctuation was optional in my father's world. Capital letters were rare, and periods even more scarce.

As the night wore on, my eyes grew as heavy as my memory. Both filled with line after line of nonsensical instructions.

The next morning I stood in the shower, thinking about the letter. The numbers suddenly clicked into place.

"Page numbers," I whispered into the steam. "Stars alive, those are page numbers in the journal."

Time passed in blurs of purple, navy, and black. Gloved hands touched my bare skin. Doors opened and closed. People talked. Through the medical-induced, post-drain haze, Cannon's voice said my name. Thane's too. My dad. But Vi's voice was the one that sliced through the loudest. When she traced her fingers over my forehead, she wore no gloves.

She sang to me, her voice as beautiful as the birdcalls in the spring. Her words didn't register, but they didn't need to. The fact that she was there spoke volumes.

Several times I felt like I was falling, and always Violet stood ready to catch me. She soothed me when I shook; she stroked my hair while I wept.

But when I finally woke up on Tuesday morning, she'd already left with Zenn.

Our room felt stale, as if no one had been there in days. The air barely moved, and I turned up the circulation portlet to clear the place out. My hands shook as I pulled on a long-sleeved shirt and light-blue jeans (total fashion crime).

My cache held several messages from Cannon, which I flipped through while the food-dispenser made my breakfast. He'd sent the standard *Hey, Raine! It's raining, it's pouring . . . Hope you're not melting* messages, mingled with the more serious *Hope you're feeling better*s I received after every drain. I managed a weak smile at his humor. I wished he was here right now to escort me to school. A pang of loneliness accompanied the thought.

As his messages continued, they grew shorter, more afraid. One even said, *Your dad said not to message you again, so this'll be my last comm . . .* He'd sent it on Sunday night.

I answered it with a quick *I'm fine, and I'll be at school today* while I nibbled on a breakfast burrito. My stomach ached on the way to school.

I longed to hear Vi's voice singing that lilting melody. As I hurried through the streets toward the Education Rise, I thought I could hear it echoing off the buildings.

But I'd forgotten the words.

* * *

The Education Rise was like a mini indoor city. It spanned an entire city block, but only stretched six stories.

Level One housed the primary school. Children from five to twelve attend classes in one of four Squares inside the Rise. An administrator presides over each Square, which consists of twelve classrooms.

I'd hated primary school. Forced to endure the same group of students for seven years was not my idea of fun. Friendships established, and that was it. The only class that changed was genetics. We were grouped by age, so no one ever joined the class, but over the years many stopped coming. I was ten years old before I realized why: Those of us who remained had some sort of talent. A genetic mutation that allowed us to do something regular people couldn't.

Gunner stayed in my genetics class. In fact, we still had that class together. We didn't have to reveal our talents unless we wanted to, and Gunn had told the class about his ability to control tech last semester after he won the flight trials. He revealed it as part of a report we'd had to do on what profession we were training for. Gunn wanted a spot on the Enforcement squad.

He'd been on my radar for a couple months at that point,

and as soon as class ended, I e-commed Trek with Gunn's name for a possible recruit for the Insiders.

I knew if I didn't get him, my father would. Because I knew Gunn had voice power too, whether he'd said it explicitly or not. The geneticists in the Evolutionary Rise would kill to get a sample of his DNA.

All my friends came from my genetics class, because no one else wanted to be friends with the Director's, uh, creepy daughter who wore gloves all the time.

Except for Starr Messenger, the girl with freaky eyes who sat on the back row in genetics. I didn't get the impression that Gunn liked her all that much, but I couldn't figure out why. Guys fawned over Starr. They signed up for the tech geek classes in droves, even if they didn't have any ability, just to be closer to her.

As children, we spent our time playing vids and projection puzzles. I knew she had killer mind control. She could Think over an entire Rise or sit on my dad's advisory council. I liked her; she didn't judge me. I didn't judge her.

But we went our separate ways right about the time we moved up to Levels Two and Three for secondary school. That's when you're sorted into talented and untalented.

And Starr had lied. Hidden her talent. Talked way too fast for someone with advanced mind control.

But I'd heard her speak just fine. I'd felt her control more than once. She was still in my genetics class. I knew she was a control freak of the highest degree.

She faked it, blew it, failed. On purpose.

As a twelve-year-old, I didn't understand that. We've always been told to do more, be better, work hard. You could be *this amazing thing* or *that leader of whatever*. Never *be yourself*, or *who you are is good enough*, or *it's okay, maybe you'll do better next time*.

With my dad as Director, there often was no next time.

So when I heard Starr blatantly lie, when I watched her get assigned to the lesser mind control track, when my dad crossed her name off his list, so did I.

Fortunately, he never made me drain her.

Unfortunately, I'd never found a way to repair our friendship. Once I smartened up, I realized Starr had things figured out long before I had. I've been playing catch-up with her ever since.

And I'm still not winning.

But at least she's not talking. She's never ratted me out to anyone, never told anyone about my ability.

Thirteens and fourteens attend classes in what the Administrator called "in between education." I made it onto the athletic and scientific track, which meant I could use my leisure time to fly and would be assigned classes like the human body and tech production. Once I turned fifteen, my classes were moved to Level Three—that's where I still am. Next year, after I turn eighteen, I'll move to Level Four: specialized training. If I could keep my marks up in biology, I'd be on the path toward that job in the Medical Rise.

Level Five of the Education Rise housed the administration. Administrator Cage didn't allow students on the admin level, and the reason why anyone would want to go there escaped me.

Level Six was a mystery. Students weren't allowed up there. I often wondered when I saw an Educator or an Administrator use the ascenders if they were going to the unknown Sixth Level. Of course I never asked. I did everything I could to avoid scrutiny at school.

After grabbing a coffee at the kiosk and ascending to the third floor, I found Trek leaning against the wall across from my first period class (environmental studies). He wore a look of discomfort, as if he could anticipate the questions building in my head. For once, I appreciated the strict cache-off protocol at school.

"Hey," I said casually, pretending I hadn't drained his fake-rash-wearing brother over the weekend and then missed an entire day of school.

"Morning." Trek sounded normal. But the lines around his eyes told a different story. And when he broke school protocol by sending me a file over my cache, I knew he'd been radically changed. As Insiders, we keep protocol during the day. Outstanding Citizens, we are. Except when we aren't.

I stared at him a moment too long before flicking my eyes to the other students walking in the hall. They whispered, as per protocol. They didn't touch, as per protocol. They were the picture of calm, quiet, and controlled. As per protocol.

"Good weekend?" Trek asked as I flipped open his document.

"I guess," I murmured. At the top of the list sat the word *Aliases*.

My eyes slid over the columns of names, searching. I found Cash's name halfway down on the third page. *Insubordinate* sat next to it. And beyond that, *Deceased*.

The world spun too fast. He'd been alive after the drain. I hadn't killed him. Thane had been there. *Not my fault*, I told myself, as the word *Insubordinate* burned its way through my body.

"Time for class," Trek said, but his voice echoed as if from very far away. I'd seen everything I needed to, and I should've closed and deleted the doc. Yet I didn't. I kept skimming name after name, thinking I'd see someone important. Someone useful.

Someone life changing.

That's when I saw *Kyla Hightower—Unmodifiable—Deceased*.

My blood raged in my ears, drowning out Trek's urgings to get to class. I blinked, but the hall stayed dark even after I opened my eyes. The floor shivered under my feet.

I was going down; I felt it. My knees hit the ground before strong fingers gripped my bicep.

Another protocol-breaker.

It was Gunner. His voice, his strength, pulled me back to my feet. I couldn't make sense of anything he said. Everything looked soft around the edges; everyone seemed to be watching us.

Somehow I made it to my seat, my arm aching where Gunner had practically squeezed it off. I closed my eyes and took a deep breath, getting only a lungful of Gunner. He smelled like buttered toast.

Cannon met me at the door after environmental studies and accompanied me to genetics. His hand hovered near mine under the table, and he shot furtive glances my way.

I was about to open my cache when the Educator said, "No caching, Starr."

She glowered, but the Educator rubbed his ear, as if he could hear the whine of her cache in his head. Which, of course, he could. As a technopath, his sensitivity to tech made it impossible to skate under the strict no-caching radar.

After class, Cannon grabbed hold of my gloved hand. I clung to him, scared I couldn't move without his help. Our friendship provided me with the anchor I desperately needed. He pulled me around the corner.

"Raine, we must speak." His eyes searched mine as if he could convey his concerns telepathically. "What did I say in the lab over the weekend?"

"What? I don't know." I could barely remember what day it was.

"I think I said something I shouldn't have. I got a citation from your father." He swallowed hard. He raked his hands through his hair. "I have to meet with him later today."

Fear flowed through my body with my blood; each breath felt heavy with it. Cannon didn't know a fraction of what my father was capable of, and a meeting didn't sound good.

"Did you get a citation?" Cannon asked.

"Only for missing school yesterday, but my father waived it. What was yours for?"

"Behavior unbecoming a Citizen."

Which could mean anything, even simply that my dad didn't like him.

The ring around Cannon's iris sharpened. His pupil grew wider. I knew that look: Here came a Seer statement. He blinked at me. "You will have to decide how much to share with your father. And when. Every person has a season for knowledge."

I stepped backward to escape the penetrating tone of his voice. Like a single step would help me riddle out his words, or build a shelter from those who don't have to be present to see, feel, smell, *know* everything.

Cannon squeezed my hands quickly, something he'd always done to reassure himself as much as me. "See you later, Raine." And then he blended into the stream of students on their way to lunch. I remained with my back pressed into the seamless wall, watching him walk away. Everything I'd heard and seen in the past two hours swirled together until I had no idea what to focus on first.

This marked the third time in two weeks that Cannon had skipped lunch. But I wouldn't tell anyone. Just like I wouldn't tell anyone what I'd seen when I'd touched Violet.

I kept my talent a highly confidential secret. Anything with the Insiders was carefully concealed, buried deep, and never thought of in the wrong places.

Gunner rounded the corner. He saw me and hurried forward. "There you are. You all right?" He scanned my face, and I tried to compose it into my usual *I don't give a damn* expression. I don't think it worked, because he leaned closer.

"Why weren't you at school yesterday?" He edged in a little farther. My breathable air disintegrated.

"I was ill," I lied in a whisper.

Gunn cocked his head, his eyes never leaving mine. *We don't get sick* echoed in my head, over my nonactivated cache.

"How—?"

He shook his head. *I'm a technopath. I can use your cache even when it's not on.*

Embarrassment crept up from my stomach. He could hear me all the time, no matter what? I didn't know that was part of technopathic ability.

Don't worry, he chatted. *I can't hear you with the cache off. I can simply connect to your cache if I want.*

Instead of worrying about what he had or hadn't heard, I activated my cache. *I have something important to tell you,* I chatted.

So tell me, Hightower.

It's about Trek—

A sharp cough cut me off. I looked over Gunn's shoulder to see his match—yes, the same Starr Messenger—glaring her pretty little eyes out.

Catch you later. I inched along the wall as Gunn turned toward Starr. I was halfway down the hall before he responded: *Tonight, Rise Five, two a.m.*

Gunner

13.

My stomach settled in my shoes at the sight of Starr. She'd enhanced her hair into this funky purplish-brown color, and her eyes cut as sharp as ever. More than one guy glanced at her as she pressed in closer to me.

"Gunn." Starr linked her arm through mine and steered me toward the dining hall in the corner of the building. Other students turned to stare at us, mostly because of the way she was touching me in public, even if we were matched. I felt like I had a blazing *I* stamped on my forehead and a spider screaming "Informant!" from my shoulder.

I'd figured out that the only person I knew worth spying on was Starr. Even I knew she should be on a higher track than she was. What I didn't know was why she wasn't. I felt sick. Not that I was in love with Starr, but still. She didn't deserve to be ratted out for everything she told me.

So much in my life had changed in only three days, and I felt light-years away from the classmates I used to laugh with.

My flying buddies grinned openly at Starr's possessive grip, probably interpreting it as some sort of romantic thing. They couldn't feel her dagger-nails piercing my flesh. I winced when we rounded the corner. "Ease up, Starr."

She cocked her head, placed her hands on her hips. "I don't like the way Raine was looking at you."

"She wasn't—"

"Oh, please. She was too. Don't lie."

Starr was the only one who could really get me riled up with a simple look. Her harsh tone didn't help. "I wasn't going to lie. I was going to say it isn't what you think."

"Really? And what do I think, Gunner?" My name sounded so sharp on her tongue. Her eyes blazed violet with anger.

I sighed. "You think . . . well, you know what you think," I finished lamely. My shoulders knotted with her tension. I simply wanted this conversation to end. "I'm sorry. It won't happen again."

"You think I don't know about your obsessive crush on Raine Hightower?"

"I do not have an obsessive crush on Raine."

"Then what just happened?"

"She was trying to tell me something about Trek, that's all. We're both friends with Trek. You're freaking out over nothing." I almost choked from describing Trek Whiting as a friend.

Starr appraised me like she might rip my heart out and eat it for lunch. "You know I can confirm this with Trek, right?"

I held her gaze, internally begging her to drop this. "You have nothing to worry about," I continued, carefully lacing my fingers through hers. They felt cold as ice, bony, and fragile. "You're my match, Starr. I don't think about anyone but you."

I closed my eyes against the glass forming in hers. So I'd used my voice, tase me. When Starr's lips met mine, they felt just as frigid and frail as her hands. I'd never felt so low. Who brainwashes their match into a kiss, just so they'll forget what they were mad about?

She pulled away first. With her cool breath skating across my neck and Raine watching from the doorway of the dining hall, I whispered, "Sorry."

"Be careful how much you tell Raine Hightower. That girl is keeping secrets." Starr stepped away and looked down the hall toward Raine, the ice returning to her eyes.

I straightened with difficulty. The weight of pretending to be the right match, the right Insider, the right guy, pressed on me so hard I thought my legs would give out.

How could I keep up the act for Thane every afternoon?

How much could I trust Raine?

How could I keep Director Hightower satisfied?

I felt like each of them expected a different Gunner, and I didn't know how to be any of them.

"Oh, and Gunn?" Starr leaned in close, close enough for me to kiss again. "Don't use your voice on me again. Ever again." She wiped her mouth before walking away.

Midnight came before I'd fallen asleep. I dressed in the traditional garb of sneaking out: black from head to toe. Even the silver rivets on my boots had been coated with black colorall.

Zenn came out of the bathroom, his newly dyed hair as dark as his clothes. He tossed me a tube, mimed rubbing it on his face.

I examined the label. Toner. When I glanced up, Zenn's white-toothed grin gaped back at me from a heavily tanned face.

He gestured for me to get toned up. I wanted to ask him where he got it, but we'd agreed to keep our conversation to a minimum, even over the cache. Our feeds were plugged into our e-boards to simulate the mandatory eight hours of transmissions.

The white cream squeezed out in smooth curls. It warmed as I massaged it into my face. The chemicals stung the corners of my eyes, tasted like filament powder against my lips. In the time it took me to walk into the bathroom, my skin turned from white as milk to dark as dirt.

Zenn mimed washing his hands and nodded vigorously, so I washed my hands before the toner could stain my palms.

Zenn led me through the bedroom. *We might have to bleach before school.*

Super, I chatted as we went out onto the balcony, merged into the night on silenced hoverboards.

Flying fast at night was amazing. The air felt lighter, unweighted by thoughts and emotions. Sure, it practically froze my lungs together, but I decided I'd take that over suffocation any day.

Instead of landing and entering Rise One through the unsittable foyer, Zenn zipped up to the roof. I touched down silently beside him; we stowed our boards in a tech generator closet.

I paused with my hand on the latch, remembering the line in my father's letter that read, *shut down tech generators—123— Harvest.*

I cataloged the location of this generator, hoping it would help me find the one in the city of Harvest—wherever that was. Suddenly, the task of finding the journal seemed insurmountable. The list of cities in the letter went on and on. The journal could be in any of them. Even if I managed to get my hands on the journal, to carry out every line of instruction in the letter would take me months.

You're not alone, Zenn chatted over the cache.

I jerked my head up. Had he heard my thoughts? Had he seen the letter? I flexed my fists, unsure if I could trust this guy I'd only known for four days.

He shook his head in a *we'll talk later* gesture and strode to the edge of the roof. He launched himself face-first into the air.

I followed him. He hovered a few feet below the lip of the roof, his hand extended to me. Throwing all caution to the wind—literally—I took Zenn's helping hand and stepped onto the cushion of invisible air under his control. This shady "plan" had formed during seven-second conversations at breakfast and then dinner as we'd ordered toast and more toast. He'd told me he could control the wind. "Speak to it," I think were his exact words. "Trust me. It won't be a problem," he'd said.

But it was. Holy hell, it was. Because flying with a very solid hoverboard under me is exhilarating. But flying with nothing under me? Terrifying.

Zenn held his arms straight out to the sides of his body, and we slowly descended until we reached Thane's ruined window.

I pushed aside the useless tech filaments and leapt from Zenn's air cloud into Thane's office. The solid silver floor was the most comforting thing in the world. Zenn whispered something that sounded strangely like, "Thank you. Wait here," and joined me at the cabinet.

The locked cabinet.

He glanced at me, and I got to work. Three minutes and one major tech-buzz headache later, and the cabinet swung open. Zenn handed me the first e-board.

I held my hand over the top of the e-board, closed my eyes. My fingers vibrated. The tech surrounding me grew into a living, breathable thing. I felt it enter my bloodstream, smelled the ashy-ness of it.

A moment later the number-letter combination of the passcode flowed to my cache. I entered it into the first e-board and handed it back to Zenn. He nodded toward the cabinet, where three more boards waited. I had them all up and operating in five minutes.

Okay, so my genetic ability to control tech was as freaky as Zenn talking to thin air. Whatever.

We pored over the boards for a few minutes. I didn't see

anything worth mentioning. Daily task lists, supply forms, dozens of reports. None of them had a name I recognized.

Zenn waved his hand, and I joined him at his board, where he had the docs up on the screen. He'd hit the jackpot: a file full of reports with two names we both knew well—Raine Hightower and Violet Schoenfeld.

He forwarded them all to his cache, grinning. I returned to my board, discarding it a minute later. The second board brought up some files that looked promising. At least, they all had Vi's name on them.

And another name I didn't recognize—Jag Barque. I raised my hand to motion Zenn over when the alarm sounded.

"Get it all," Zenn said out loud, which rocketed my rising panic into full-fledged *are you kidding me?* mode.

I inhaled and held my breath as I sent myself every file on the e-board. I shut it down and chucked it back into the cabinet with the others as shrill sirens joined the chorus of wails.

Zenn seemed to be faster than me at everything. He already stood on the pillow of air, gesturing wildly for me to join him.

I ran, jumped, caught his hand. He was already moving up before I could release the stale breath from my lungs.

* * *

After we arrived back at the flat, Zenn showered while I pulled up the Jag Barque reports. During the regulated five-minute bathing time, I'd seen more than enough to know that this Jag guy was a huge problem for the Association.

As Zenn dressed and gestured wildly toward the bathroom as if to say, *Your turn*, I discovered that Jag was a major inconvenience for him too.

Because this Jag Barque guy and Violet Schoenfeld were Chokers—not that she could remember. I glanced at Zenn, sure he wouldn't want me to know this.

I wanted to delete all the files, forget I'd seen them, and, for Zenn's sake, hope like hell that Jag would stay lost forever. I seriously considered it for one, two, three seconds.

Then I forwarded everything to Zenn, went to shower so Raine wouldn't freak when I showed up for our two a.m. "appointment" with a toned face.

Raine

14.

After school I watched Cannon's brown-haired head flop back against the ergonomic in my living area. He exhaled loudly, as if today had been the longest of his life. I knew exactly how he felt.

I ordered my snack (one half cup of strawberry yogurt) from the dispenser. By the time I turned around, Cannon already had his e-board out, reading something on the screen for one of his classes. That's all he did lately. Work.

After depositing my e-board in my bedroom, I sat cross-legged on the floor across from him. Neither of us spoke. He turned off his e-board, leaned forward, and gathered my gloved hands in his, instantly erasing my exhaustion.

His touch provided me with what I needed most: safety.

His skin felt warm through the thin filament gloves. Cannon massaged my fingers and down over my wrist while I puzzled over his prophetic words from earlier that day.

"Cannon?" I said, trying to keep my voice casual. "Do you remember what you said at lunch?"

His eyebrows bunched into a crease. His blue eyes held nothing but confusion. "No, I can't. What did I say?"

We used to share everything, but I still hadn't mentioned Gunn. Or the Alias list and Cash's death. And Cannon hadn't told me why he'd been skipping meals. I hadn't decided what to say when he continued.

"Everything I say is important." He pinched harder against my gloves, as if he could somehow impress upon me the severity of his warnings.

"I don't remember anything I say when the Seer takes over. I hate that part the most." He cleared his throat, and when I looked at him, I was surprised to see his bottom lip trembling. "I hate being a Seer."

Fear blazed through my veins. "Cannon, don't say tha—"

"But I do." He gripped my fingers now, painfully. "What if I say something hurtful? What if I cause someone to do something they normally wouldn't? Do you understand how heavy that burden is?" He leaned forward, squeezing my hands harder. But when he spoke, I could barely hear him. "Your dad reamed me for letting you see Cash."

The breath solidified in my lungs. "But I—I was in the lab with him. Of course I saw him."

Tears (real, genuine tears) filled Cannon's eyes, and he turned away. "My job was to get you out of there as fast as possible. But you saw him control the EOs, heard him speak . . ." He shook his head, dodging to wipe his face. He inhaled deeply. "It doesn't matter. It's over."

It doesn't matter? It's over? "Nothing is ever over with my father," I whispered.

Cannon met my gaze. Naked fear lived in his eyes. "I know."

The silence that followed felt so heavy. So full of nightmares—all of them featuring my father.

I moved closer until only a few inches separated us. "It's okay. Everything is okay. We just have to play smarter than my dad."

"What if—?"

I pressed my finger to his lips so he couldn't finish that sentence. He'd be Watched, then I'd be Watched (as if I wasn't already), and then my dad could do anything. Anything at all.

After a few moments of tension, Cannon exhaled. He released my hands and nodded. I hugged him quickly, just enough to reassure him that we were okay. He felt thinner than I remembered. And he'd just skipped his snack too. I wondered when he'd last eaten.

"We may have more trouble," I said, moving to sit in the ergonomic across from him. What I needed to tell him required distance.

He caught my eyes with his. Suspicion and surprise resided in them simultaneously. "What?"

"Well, I need a cover story." I fiddled with the fingertips of my gloves.

He rubbed his right hand up his left arm the way he always did when he was preparing for bad news. "For?"

I dropped my gaze to the polished floor. "A guy."

The silence that followed wasn't angry or awkward. When I chanced a look at Cannon, I found him leaning back, resigned. Something registered in his expression—fear? Maybe. But it dissolved quickly into concern.

"Who?" he asked. That was our policy. We got to know who we were lying for. I'd helped Cannon sneak out to meet Flare Riding more times than I could remember. Too bad she got so jittery a few months ago. Cannon hadn't seen another girl since.

"Who?" he repeated.

I hated the cool note in his voice but appreciated his steadiness, his willingness to help.

"Gunner Jameson," I said. "I'm meeting him tonight."

Cannon stood up and turned away, sighing in a way that said I was more trouble than I was worth.

"Do you really think you have time for another guy in your life?" he asked.

Another guy? Cannon was, well, Cannon. My best friend. A guy, sure, but not a *guy*.

"I can help you too," I said.

He spun around. "With what, exactly?"

I hesitated at the flicker of resentment in his eyes. Maybe I'd crossed a barrier—except Cannon and I had never had any barriers before. "You're skipping meals."

He looked like he might argue, then his shoulders sagged. "I can't talk about it."

My brain couldn't process those words, not from Cannon. We talked about everything. I'd just revealed my crush on Gunn! If that wasn't proof enough, I didn't know what else Cannon needed. But I found myself nodding. "Okay."

He moved toward me and gathered me into the comfort of his arms. "Be careful here, Raine. You mess with Gunn, you're taking on more than a guy."

So many things jumbled in my mind. Cannon was right. If I started acting differently, my dad would suspect something.

"You've done it lots of times," I said.

"Yeah, but you haven't," he said. "Promise me you'll be careful. Like, really careful."

"I promise. Will you do the same?"

Cannon inhaled slowly, as if the extra oxygen would bring him to his senses. "We can keep each other safe." His hands quivered against my back. His arms trembled, and a strangled note escaped his throat.

I leaned out of his arms to find him squeezing his eyes shut and clenching his jaw. "Cannon?" I ran my fingers down the side of his face.

"You control the information," he declared in a voice that was hardly his own. "No one can keep secrets from Raine Hightower. Secrets hold power. Raine holds all the power."

After Cannon spoke, the room fell silent. But the prophecy echoed in my soul in time with my heartbeat.

Pow-er, pow-er, pow-er.

I felt it—the power—coursing through me. I'd lived my life in a way so as to have access to as much power as I could. Power to recruit those whose names sat on my father's list, power to keep the most talented from truly helping him.

And then Cannon said, "Every person has a season for knowledge."

Again.

I knew he meant that I held the power to reveal the secrets I kept when the time was right. Information was power in Freedom. And I had information no one else did. But now that I had an idea of the measure of influence I could have, I wasn't sure I wanted it.

Scratch that. I didn't want it. Not even a little bit. Who was I to decide what someone needed to know, and when? Who was I to see the innermost desires of someone's heart?

"And Raine?" Cannon sounded like a little boy about to cry. "I don't want you to leave Freedom."

I jerked backward as if he'd branded me with his words. I wasn't going to leave Freedom. Thoughts of my mother's name on that list and warnings from the transmissions blended with images of Cash and his fake rash.

A tiny, quiet voice asked, *Can I?*

I forced it into silence. The very thought of crossing the wall terrified me. No, I wasn't going to leave Freedom. Ever.

At precisely two a.m., Gunn separated from the shadows at the base of Rise Five just as I melted into them. My breath quickened at the simple sight of him, and in the next heartbeat he walked next to me. We both wore long coats and scarves to keep the nasty wind snaking through the Rises from searing our skin.

"Cold," Gunn murmured, edging back into the darkness—and closer to me.

I nodded, something he couldn't see, because I didn't dare speak yet. During the walk from Rise One, I'd battled with myself about what to tell Gunn. What did he need to know? What did he *want* to know? Were they the same? Did that matter?

"Sorry about this weekend," he whispered.

I shrugged, bumping him with my shoulder. We felt our way along the edge of the building toward an outdoor stairwell. I ducked under the steel beams and finally drew a full breath when Gunn joined me in the confined space.

"You look like hell." Gunn spoke so softly I had to lean forward to hear him.

"Thanks," I hissed. My desire to share everything with him evaporated.

Several minutes passed in icy silence. I opened my mouth to speak half a dozen times, each time snapping my jaw shut again, unsure what to say.

Then Gunn surprised me by wrapping both arms around me and pulling me into his chest. "Tell me," he said, his whisper tickling my ear. He stroked my hair, and his heart beat against my cheek, calm and slow.

For some stupid reason, I started crying. Before I knew it,

I'd spilled everything about Cash, that I'd seen his name on the Alias list Trek had cached me.

I didn't tell him about my ability. I just couldn't. The shame of it welled up in my throat and blocked the words. I kept the horror of my mother's name on the Alias list to myself too.

When I finished, he still held me, his fingers entangled in my hair. "I wonder if my dad's name is on that list."

I read the hurt behind those words. Saw it fly across his features, even in the navy darkness. "I'm sorry," I said.

"I think I already knew." Something grew in Gunn's eyes I didn't like. Something sharp. Something dangerous.

My suspicions solidified when he said, "I'd like to leave this city."

Arguments flew from one side of my head to the other. I didn't say anything. While I couldn't stomach the thought of leaving Freedom, Gunn was already planning his escape.

Incoming Enforcement Officers, a voice said over my cache. One look at Gunn and I knew he'd heard it too. We separated without speaking, moving as far away from each other as possible.

The voice sounded slightly like Trek, but a little deeper and with more echo behind it. *How long?* I asked, hoping Trek didn't have his full system hooked up. I shouldn't be mixing Insider work with my personal life. A flicker of embarrassment warmed my cheeks.

Before the voice could answer, my watch beeped. Not long enough.

"You go," I told Gunn. "You can't get caught out here."

"What about you?"

"I'll work it out with my father," I said, hoping I actually could. How far could I push him before he decided I wasn't worth the trouble?

The beeps became a constant alarm. "Stay here. I'll distract them." I dodged under the steel supports, already running away from Gunner and the stairwell. Amplified voices demanded that I surrender to search.

I had to lure them away from Gunn. I knew why they were after me. Dad always sent for me in the middle of the night when he needed a shady drain.

I sprinted toward the corner and headed down the next street toward Rise Six. And then Seven. Flashes of light, sirens, and voices followed me.

I slammed into an invisible barrier and flew backward. My coat smoked with tech sparks, and I slapped them away before true fire could start.

Behind me, footsteps crashed against the ground. Tasers whined. "Citizens must surrender to search after curfew," blared from about forty sources.

No less than eight EOs advanced toward me. I squared my shoulders and remained silent, even though I felt like exploding. When they tech-cuffed me twice, I didn't flinch. When they flew me back to Rise One, I didn't give them the satisfaction of knowing I was about to wet myself.

But when we ascended to laboratory seven, I freaked out.

With so many of them, I couldn't do much. I screamed and kicked, but that only made them back up so they wouldn't get hurt. While I paused to inhale, one EO's gloved hand wound around my throat while another two pressed my shoulders into the wall.

I thrashed my head from side to side. "Stop it! Let me go!" I spit in the officer's face, but he didn't remove his hand from my windpipe. The world went soft around the edges. I drew a shallow breath and screamed as long and loud as I could.

I stopped when Thane's furious face swam before me. "Release her," he barked.

Immediately the EOs removed their hands from my body. I slumped to the floor and refused to look up at Thane.

"Stand up, Raine. Stop this infantile behavior."

I stayed on the floor, hot tears signaling my infantilism.

Thane crouched in front of me. "Let's try this again, shall we? Stand up." When I didn't, he said, "I'd really hate to have to brainwash you into that room. We both know I can—and I will. Your choice."

I hated him so much it infected my bloodstream. It pounded through my body with every heartbeat, every breath. "I hate you," I choked out.

"As if I didn't know," Thane retorted coldly. "Now let's go."

I drew my knees to my chest and locked my hands together around them. "You can go to hell." I glared up at him. "I'm not entering that lab."

His face sharpened into jagged angles of rage and hatred before he smoothed it back. "Yes, you are."

"You'll have to brainwash me." *Help me,* I thought to Trek, desperately hoping he'd been the one who'd assisted me earlier.

Thane leaned down, closer and closer, until his face hovered only inches from mine. "I need this, Raine. Please."

I closed my eyes against the fire in his.

I woke up strapped to the ergonomic in the lab. The only sound was air forcing its way through vents in the ceiling. I smelled nothing but pasty perma-plaster and metallic tech.

When my vision cleared, I found the lab empty. No EOs standing guard along the wall. No doctors prepping me. Panic boiled in my stomach, working its way up my throat to my mouth. I swallowed hard but couldn't help vomiting down my front.

That didn't help the stench in the room. Being in the lab alone was infinitely worse than being surrounded by physicians. Where was Thane? Who did he need me to drain in the dead of night? Where was my father?

"Hey!" I wanted them to know I was awake. "What's going on? Where are you?" I shouted myself hoarse before Thane appeared again.

He entered the room from the back, where the doctors usually congregate. He strode forward, each step full of purpose and self-confidence. I expected a team of physicians to follow him, but they didn't.

The only person who did follow Thane made my skin tingle, and not in a good way. His was tanned deeply. He walked forward stiffly, as if his whole body hurt from the movement. He didn't glance right or left but simply stared straight at me with icy-blue eyes.

His mouth had been secured with, get this, tape. *Tape.* So low class. As if the six silencers (three on each side of his jaw) couldn't keep him from speaking.

My eyes lingered on his dark, matted hair before returning to his familiar face. I recognized him. When I remembered how I knew him, a strangled sob caught in my throat. I shook my head and helpless tears splashed my cheeks. "No," I sobbed. "No, please, no."

"Stop it, Raine," Thane commanded. He eyed the sick all down the front of my shirt, puddling in my lap. "I'll take care of that."

The kind words didn't make sense, not coming from Thane. But I didn't have the energy to answer as he secured the leader of the Resistance to the table. Still, the guy looked at me, forever looked at me. I couldn't escape that penetrating gaze of his.

"There you go, Jag," Thane coddled, like he would to a toddler. "Just lie nice and still now."

I can't drain Jag Barque, I thought. *I can't, I can't, I can't.*

Help me, I pleaded to Trek, to anyone listening. Someone had offered assistance before, why not now?

Only silence answered as Thane reached for my gloveless hand.

Gunner

**5.** I ran faster than I ever had in my life, each footstep filled with guilt. *You left her, you left her* echoed in my head. Trek's voice also bounced around in there. At least I thought it was Trek. He'd warned us about the EOs the night I'd left home, with the exact same words. His voice had sounded slightly off, but that could've been because of an encoded cache.

I hated that he was in my head, monitoring my activity, when all I wanted was a little time alone with Raine. Our meeting tonight had nothing to do with Insider business.

Everything has to do with Insider business. Now the voice

sounded warped, half-high and half-low. *You should try to be a little quieter,* it warned.

Crimson spider eyes awakened in each doorway I passed. I didn't care. Ignoring Trek, I didn't try to be quieter, didn't care who saw, listened, knew.

They all knew anyway. Someone had a record of every breath I took. I didn't believe for a single second that Zenn and I could sneak out at midnight, toned faces or not. Just the fact that the window had been opened was recorded, monitored, corrected.

Zenn didn't normally shower in the wee hours of the morning. That would be investigated too. He would probably even get cited for it. Except Zenn didn't seem to receive citations for anything. Not the mountain of toast he ate every day or the casual way he rolled his sleeves up.

So I wasn't all that surprised when I burst into our flat to find him awake and dressed— in all black. He sat in an ergonomic reading on his e-board.

"Raine," I panted. "Let's fly."

Without a word, Zenn abandoned his e-board in favor of his hoverboard. We launched from the balcony and set our sights on Rise One. Below me, I imagined alarms wailing and the scuttle of a thousand seeker-spider legs cobbling against the cement. But flying through the sky, all I heard was the wind whispering *Coward* in my ears.

Every second seemed to hold that word, weigh it, toss it back in my face. Even the brine in the air assaulted my nose with the smell of shame.

As I sliced through the night, I didn't have a single thought that belonged to me. My mom's last words—"I love you"—haunted me. Raine's sadness still lingered in my nerves. When she'd said "I'm sorry" about my dad—

EOs en route to Rise One, Trek said. *Raine's there, in—*

"Lab seven." Zenn's spoken voice sounded so foreign against Trek's weird reverberations in my head.

I leapt off my board while it still hovered a few feet above the ground. "Half size. Follow." I didn't wait for the board to collapse before I stepped up to the front door of Rise One.

Tech vibrated under my skin, rattled in my teeth. A moment later the glass door slid to the side, allowing Zenn and me to enter the shiny foyer.

I strode past the gleaming-with-moonlight carpets and never-been-touched couches. The glowing ascender boxes in the back of the foyer provided an eerie backdrop to our breaking and entering.

From the barely lit hallway beyond the foyer, someone came forward. Their footsteps landed heavily, and Zenn shot me a look. A clone emerged into the light, his head cocked to the side. "Hello. State your business, please."

"You didn't see us," Zenn said, his voice strong and powerful. "Go back to your station. Do not log this encounter."

The clone pivoted and retreated the way it had come. Zenn and I continued toward the ascender box in the corner.

Something buzzed in my head, zinged along my bones. I'd never felt this level of anger before. Anger at myself. At Raine. At Zenn. At everyone I could think of. But mostly at my crap-controlled life, and how I'd let myself be told what to do and what to believe for almost seventeen years.

"Laboratory seven," I barked as soon as my board cleared the glittering lights in the ascender.

We need stealth. Settle down, Zenn instructed just before I shot upward.

When I landed, I was anything but settled. I stumbled forward, unable to see but determined to do something.

Zenn's footsteps landed nearby. When I heard him curse out loud, I knew we were in big trouble.

Panic spiked, making my throat constrict. "Wh-what?" I choked out, my vision still blurry.

"I don't believe it," Zenn breathed.

I blinked furiously, willing my eyes to work again. As soon as they did, I thought for sure they'd malfunctioned.

Behind a wall of glass, Raine slumped in an ergonomic. Blood trickled down one corner of her slack mouth.

Raine

Thane didn't wear gloves. Just that gaudy golden ring that flashed under the bright tech lights. His right hand bore a row of bandages across his knuckles. His skin against mine set every cell on fire. I tried yanking my hand away, but he held me fast.

"Play nice, Rainey," he said.

I didn't respond. I let my hatred of him explode into something more powerful than anything I'd ever felt. The injustice of it all twisted my insides.

"I can't do this," I said, desperate now. "If you make me do this drain, you'll kill me." I knew it, felt it deep inside.

"Raine." It wasn't Thane who answered, but Jag. The sound

of his voice, raspy and weak, felt like a slap across the face. I looked at him, and he pleaded with those cold eyes. He hadn't spoken; he couldn't have, not through all the tape and silencers.

Yet I'd heard him say my name.

Don't believe everything you hear. Cash's warning could apply to almost every situation in my life. And I hated that more than injustice. More than Thane.

Trapped inside my bubble of hopelessness and hatred, I vaguely felt Thane paint my hand with perma-plaster. I barely felt the chill of Jag's skin.

"I won't do this," I growled through clenched teeth.

"Like you have a choice." Thane slapped two live-streaming stickers on my temples and turned to fiddle with his gadgets.

He was right. I had no choice. Already, dark shapes danced in my head. They darted across my vision-screen, taking on distinct colors and forms.

I locked eyes with Jag again. *I won't do this,* I thought, sending it to him hard, even though he didn't have a cache implant and couldn't hear me. He closed his eyes in a long blink as if to say, *Then don't do it.*

I don't have a choice. Tears accompanied this thought, because it was so, so true. I had very few choices in my life.

Something inside me roared. I grasped for that strong part

of myself, the part that could choose, the part that wouldn't sit idly by while I completed another drain. While I died.

A face flashed across my v-screen.

A face I knew well.

Vi's face.

I snapped my attention back to Jag, who was watching me. A raging fire burned in his eyes.

"I won't do this," I said, hardly more than a whisper. I pushed against the image of Vi's face. It withered into a curl of indigo smoke and disappeared, leaving my vision-screen blank.

More shapes formed, hooded and dark. I caught hold of the strong part of myself and pushed and pushed and pushed. I thought I'd closed my eyes because everything in the lab turned black. But when I blinked, I couldn't tell the difference between open and shut.

Far away, Thane yelled my name. He put his slimy hands on me. I jerked away, still fighting against the images coming from Jag's drain. Every muscle in my body begged for release. But I sat straighter and clenched my fists tighter. My jaw felt on the verge of breaking.

"I won't do this," I said through my teeth. I would not be bent. Not to drain Jag—someone who held valuable secrets, maybe even some of mine.

"You must," Thane said, his foul breath billowing against my cheek. "You stop whatever it is you're doing and let those images come up on the screen."

"I won't—"

"You must!" Thane pinched my chin between his fingers, yanking my head upward at a sharp angle. I snapped my teeth and came down on flesh. Blood flooded my mouth, the dark walls crowded closer, and Thane's scream filled the void.

"I won't do this!" My words covered up Thane's fury, bounced off the silver walls I couldn't see, battled against the caging glass.

"I won't do this!" I pushed and pushed and pushed against Jag's deepest desires until I couldn't see anything. Couldn't hear anything . . . Couldn't feel . . .

"I won't do this," I murmured through sluggish lips. My body felt limp. Darkness blanketed me, and I gratefully sank into it.

Gunner

17. Someone gripped my hands, pulled them behind my back. I heard a voice, but I couldn't form the sounds into words.

All I saw was Raine. And the blood. So much blood.

My throat hurt, and I realized it was because I was shouting her name.

Thane's face slammed against the glass, all rage and wild abandon. He looked unhinged, and that scared me into silence.

Zenn's words penetrated the numb feeling spreading south from my mind. "Look at his hand."

He'd used his voice, and I allowed myself to feel the power of it. So I looked at Thane's hand. In less than a second I took in the hemal-recyclers he held against a series of puncture wounds. I felt a flash of triumph. *Good fight, Raine,* I thought. Now Thane had two damaged hands.

"She's okay. Let's go," Zenn said, releasing my wrists. He looked through the windowed wall at Thane and said, "I'll take care of it."

It = me. Zenn was going to play Informant here.

"She's okay? Let's go?" My voice squeaked. "You'll take care of it?"

Zenn tapped my shoulder. "We really have to go." He cast a long glance at Thane before striding away.

You really do, the voice of assistance came over my cache. *Officers have landed. Use the roof.*

I hated Trek then, more than ever. He surely sat, safe and secure, in his crap-hole tent, eavesdropping on my life. And then bossing me around. I didn't need an assistant. At least not right now.

I had hundreds of words piling up inside me, but none of them formed into sentences. Somehow my legs followed Zenn to the descender rings. But he wasn't standing in the box to go down.

We took an ascender—up—to the roof, left Rise One via hoverboard, and climbed into the sky. With each passing foot, the air got cleaner and colder. Soon it had cleared away the numbness clouding my head, but nothing could erase what I'd seen in that lab.

Even beaten up and strapped to a table, I'd recognized the guy featured in at least two dozen reports.

Jag Barque.

Neither Zenn nor I wanted to disturb the silence in the sky. I rode sitting down, thinking back to the night I'd lingered up here with Raine. That night I'd left my (somewhat) secure life. That night I'd left my mom.

I inhaled slowly, trying to capture the same smell that had been present that night. But this high up, there was no smell. So much had changed since Friday. I'd held Raine in my arms, stroked her hair. She'd let me. And stars alive, I never thought I'd see Raine Hightower cry.

As if Zenn had been following along with my thoughts, he said, "You better watch yourself with Raine. And we need to talk about Jag."

I didn't want to. I wanted to drift above the city forever, not thinking, not doing anything. "You talk about him." Anything I said to junior-assistant-Informant-status Zenn was sure to be repeated to Hightower in bite-size pieces.

Zenn leaned back on his hoverboard. He looked relaxed, as if he spent hours lounging around in the sky. "He's the reason you got recruited."

I tried to hear the hidden meaning behind his words. "I don't get it. I've never even heard of the guy."

"The Director couldn't have him." Zenn cleared his throat. "So he recruited you."

"Super," I said, thinking it was anything but.

"Yeah, super."

This time I turned to study Zenn. He gazed at the horizon, a frown etched into his eyebrows. "You don't like him."

"It's not that. He and I—we—it's not that." Emotions battled across his face. I felt them pouring off him: loyalty, friendship, anger, hatred, desperation, brotherly love. Jag made all kinds of warring things take place inside Zenn.

"Then what is it?"

"He . . . complicates things."

I exhaled, pushing all the air out of my lungs. I took a cleansing breath. "Uncomplicate it."

"Jag is the leader of the Resistance. I was his spy in my homeland a couple years back. Thane found out, and he threatened to take away what mattered most to me—his daughter, Violet—if I didn't turn Informant." He looked at me, and now I felt his shame, sadness, love.

"I did it, and Jag was furious. He lost a lot when he lost me." Zenn cleared his throat, and it was the first time I'd seen him look anything but 100 percent collected.

"When Jag left, he put his second-in-command in charge. A girl named Indiarina Blightingdale." He took a deep breath. "Indy and I have been communicating since I arrived. She's following Jag's plan, and since I've been here, I've implemented everything she's told me."

My brain spun, working hard to keep up. "So you're . . ."

"I'm Freedom's liaison to the Resistance. I also lead the Insiders."

A maniacal laugh threatened to escape. "No wonder you don't have time to sleep." Now I knew why he could act the part of Mr. Cool As Ice, Mr. Oh So Right, and Mr. Don't Mess With Me. It also made sense why he never attended school. I wondered what exactly he did during his "training sessions," but didn't ask.

"Trek does what I can't." Zenn settled his gaze on me, and I felt the weight of it deep inside. "He's a genius with tech. He's the reason we can talk right now without anyone hearing."

I couldn't help the scoff of annoyance that escaped.

"You don't have to like him," Zenn said. "But he's the one who gets my messages out of Freedom. He's the one who keeps the communication open between the groups of Insiders. And he can scramble almost any form of communication."

With every word, my dislike for Trek grew. Zenn had said I didn't have to like Trek—and I didn't.

"How many groups of Insiders are there in Freedom?" I asked.

"Seven," Zenn said. "I'm surprised it took you so long to join."

"Why's that?"

"Your match has been in for years."

If anything, this revelation only deepened my annoyance. "Yeah, well, she and I aren't exactly close."

"So I've noticed."

I didn't answer. Instead, I reran everything he'd told me about the Insiders. I tried to make it fit with what I knew about the Darwinian Episode and our current form of government.

In our genetics classes, we were taught that all evolved people—like me, like Zenn, like Raine—had a responsibility to lead the general population. Our current brand of "leading" included brainwashing through transmissions and complete force. Those who didn't comply simply didn't belong.

The Association's motto went like this: "The strong lead the weak."

The Resistance was something I wasn't sure I believed existed until Zenn had spoken the word. Rumored—I guess now confirmed—to be run by evolved people who didn't want to use their talents to compel others to live a certain way. Like Jag Barque.

Now that I'd had a taste of living life my own way, I had to admit I didn't want anyone telling me what to do, how to live, who to love.

Zenn shifted on his board, drawing my attention back to him. "I haven't mentioned my allegiance to the Resistance to anyone else, especially Vi. Because when Jag met her, well, let's just say they clicked."

"Clicked?"

"They're Chokers." The words clipped out of Zenn's mouth, like they'd make him sick if they stayed unsaid too long.

"That sucks for you," I said, and I meant it. I didn't know this Jag guy, or this Vi chick either, but I knew Zenn.

"Yeah." He turned away from me, his words cutting through the sky. "When he met her, he realized how important she was. I think he finally understood why I turned. He'd do anything to keep her safe, just like I will."

Like I could argue or agree. "What now?" I asked.

"I've never seen Jag controlled before," Zenn said, so quietly it took me a minute to piece the sounds into words. "This is cruel of me, but I don't want him and Vi to get back together."

"I get that," I said. I thought of Cannon's friendship with

Raine, and I wished I could have that kind of relationship—
and more—with her. "I get it," I repeated.

When Zenn spoke again, his voice bowed with sadness.
"I can't get Vi's memories back. If I do anything too drastic,
the Director will know it was me." His breath shuddered on
the way in. "Maybe if she saw Jag again . . . maybe that would
wake her up. But if she sees him and remembers, I'm nobody.
In more ways than one."

"You think she'd pick him over you?"

"Yes." Zenn didn't hesitate, not even for a fraction of a
second.

"Okay, so we don't let them get together."

"But if it'll help her, then we should. She's vital to the
Insiders. The Director wants to use her talents for his own
plans."

"Which plans are those?"

Zenn sighed. "Same as for all of us. Me, you, Raine, Starr.
He wants to use us to control people."

"But he already controls people." A lot of them. He was
a Regional Director. Only one person held more power than
him—the General Director.

"More people." Zenn looked at me, and I recognized the
worry in his eyes. "So what should we do about Vi?"

"I have no idea." I yawned, feeling the winter chill seep

into my bones. "But I know one thing: with Jag here, I'll be a nobody too."

"Voices are never nobodies," Zenn said. "At least that's what the Director keeps telling me."

Raine didn't show up for school the next day. I wanted to convene an Insider meeting immediately. We had to rescue her.

Trek denied my request. Four times.

I couldn't think anything but *jerk. Jerk, jerk, jerk.*

Wednesday bled into Thursday, and still Trek wouldn't meet.

When I cornered him in the Education Rise during Thursday's lunch period, he said, "We only meet on weekends. Deal with it."

"But Raine—"

"She's fine," Trek snapped. "We have people on the Inside everywhere. Our intel indicates that she's fine. Back off, voice wonder." He straightened his already pristine school uniform. "We meet tomorrow night. I'll have one of my people send you the coordinates."

One of his people, right. As if he didn't have the time to e-comm out coordinates. I glared at him, almost wishing he'd hit me so I could feel the physical pain. So I could bleed out some of this anxiety over Raine.

He smiled, but it looked more like a scowl. "Pay attention to the arrival time. We can't interfere with other people's airspace." Then he walked away. I watched him go, angry that he'd mentioned airspace. I'd been *bumped* in the flight trials; I hadn't deliberately encroached on his airspace.

My anger/shame/guilt/impatience turned into desperation. How could Trek go to class every day and tap out reports on ancient civilizations?

How did he stand it?

I couldn't.

I felt trapped inside my own life, the normalcy of it burying me deep within folds of unbreathable air, the hours until the Friday meeting mocking and eternal.

I sat in genetics class, staring at Raine's empty seat, even when Starr glared so hard I should've had new holes burned in my head.

Preoccupied as I was, I still noticed that Cannon's seat remained empty all week too.

Worry gnawed at me, until I felt empty and limp.

Friday at one a.m. finally arrived. Without Raine, I felt naked in front of a group of strangers. The younger Insiders watched me from the corners of their eyes. The older ones stared openly.

I ignored them all, found a shadow in the back of the warehouse where we'd met, and hid.

Ten minutes later Trek emerged from a half-lit room, lines of exhaustion already carved around his eyes. I knew how he felt. Raine occupied my every thought, and sleep had eluded me.

Trek scanned the waiting group. "Did the voice-wonder show?"

I wanted to fly across the room and punch him. Too many witnesses, I decided. "I'm here," I said unnecessarily. Everyone was already staring at me when I stepped out of the pool of shade. "What's the news with Raine?"

Trek made a guttural noise that meant *what a lame question.*

He didn't answer it, instead crossing his arms over that too-big chest. "Assignments for tonight include caching in everything learned over the past week." At least while he talked, the other Insiders weren't staring at me. "Some of us have had exciting discoveries. We need everything pooled for the other groups."

I ground my teeth together at the way he emphasized "some of us." Like I had nothing valuable to contribute.

Trek half-turned away from me. "Some of you may know Zenn Bower. He's the leader of the Insiders here in Freedom.

He's here to take a select group of you on an exciting field trip."

I sidled up behind them, waiting until everyone had moved on to their next task. "What about Raine?"

Trek turned, the dislike streaming off him like dirty water. "She's fine. Word is she's back home, still sleeping. Hightower has his personal physician attending to her."

Somehow that didn't comfort me. I'd seen what Director Hightower made his physicians do to his daughter.

"Gunn, I hear you have some hidden talents," Trek said.

I didn't respond. I was afraid of what I might tell him to do. I felt Zenn lingering just behind me.

Trek lifted his mouth into a half smile. "A technopath, I've heard." His eyes flicked over my shoulder to where Zenn stood. Point taken. Zenn was Informing on me—to both sides.

"Can't you access the database to find out whatever you want?" Trek asked.

I remained silent. I could, but I didn't. So much surveillance in there. So many seeker-spiders. More bugs existed inside the system than in the streets.

Trek looked me up and down. His eyes radiated coldness. "And Raine thought you were useful." He stepped around me toward his office. "Zenn, see if you can't teach the voice wonder something tonight," he said before shutting the door with a bang.

"Come on, Gunn," Zenn said. "You brought your board, right?"

I nodded, still staring into the office where Trek gestured to an e-board screen and spoke with a blond girl.

"We're flying to Rise Twelve." Zenn shrugged into his coat, waved a few others over to us.

"Whatever," slipped out of my mouth. Life in the Insiders sans Raine sucked.

I barely felt the chill in the air on the way out to Rise Twelve. I didn't notice anything about the people with me and Zenn. A fishy smell came off the ocean, and I turned away from the water after we landed in the street just outside the Rise.

I stepped forward, assuming my technopath services would be needed. But the door was unlocked. Everyone had already gone in except for Zenn. He pinned me with a stare unlike any I'd ever seen from him. "You're going to see things in here you might not understand."

"What kind of things?" I peered through the doorway, but only darkness stared back.

"It'll be easier to show you." Zenn stepped through the door. I followed.

Rise Twelve had a foyer, just like Rise One. But this one was completely sittable. Well-used couches lined the walls.

Bright rugs covered the silver floors. The projection screens broadcasted everything from wavy neon lines to billowy clouds to ocean waves lapping the shore.

Lights strobed in the background, illuminating the people lounging on the chairs. Some held e-boards, some ate sandwiches, and some chatted—chatted!—openly with each other.

All of this was happening at one o'clock—one o'clock!—in the morning.

Nobody looked tired. And they weren't wearing the typical clothing of the controlled. Bright colors assaulted my eyes from shirts and hats and ties and shoelaces.

The idle talk faded into the background. All I could hear was the drumming of my heart. The pulsing of my blood through my veins.

I blinked, expecting the crowd to morph into silver-suited Enforcement Officers who'd raise tasers and shout, "Freeze! Come with us so we can wipe your memory clean!"

No one even looked in my direction. More people entered the fray from the hallway. They carried fresh cups of coffee, or tall glasses of juice, or bags of snacks. A sign near the hall directed people left, toward the bank of ascenders.

The rest of Zenn's crew had disappeared. He stood at a desk at the back of the foyer, speaking to a woman seated there. She kept flipping her long black hair, like that might entice Zenn to lean closer and kiss her.

She was *flirting* with him. My mouth dropped open.

These people, *these people*, they weren't controlled. Not controlled. Uncontrolled. I rolled each word around in my head, trying to make it fit into my vocabulary.

"The Thinker in Rise Twelve is sympathetic to our cause." Zenn's "explanation" snapped me out of the freaky place I'd entered. Somehow he wasn't flirting with Desk Girl anymore. She looked at me sourly.

"Sympathetic?" I squeaked.

"He runs his Rise a bit differently. He allows for free choice."

I scanned the foyer again. This time I noticed two people in the corner of the room, dancing.

Dancing. I'd learned in ancient civilizations that dancing contributed to the downfall of our society. Well, that and music. Too thought-provoking.

"They think for themselves," I said, as if the concept was completely foreign. In many ways, it was.

"And they choose many things for themselves too," Zenn added.

"But, but how?" I asked. "How—I mean, who's the Thinker here?"

"Whoever he or she is, he doctors his reports, obviously." Zenn motioned me forward. "Come on, I'll show you the market. I like to come here when I can't sleep. Rise Twelve is perfect for insomniacs."

I couldn't stop staring. This place felt easy and light, like I could flop down on that completely normal couch and strike up a convo with those totally normal guys sitting there sipping perfectly normal coffees.

Easiness and comfort aside, nothing about this place was normal.

After we ascended to the fifth floor market, Zenn babbled about how the students here *chose* which tracks they wanted to study. How they trained for professions they *liked*, that they *wanted* to spend their life doing. How they shopped for the food they *enjoyed* to make their meals—they made their own meals!—how they chose clothes in colors they wanted to wear.

In the market, my eyes flew from one uncontrolled person to the next. I'd been to the Transportation Rise with my mom, and I'd gotten milk shakes from the kiosk while the clones tuned my hoverboard. The waiting room held metal furniture and an e-board docking station.

This market was something completely different. People—real people, not clones—worked in the shops, wearing aprons and asking people if they needed help. It seemed to be meal time, as many people were ordering sandwiches and soups and salads.

Further down the row, the shops gave way to booths. Each one provided a space for people to create. My mom would've loved to live in Rise Twelve and dye cloth or mold pots or bake pies or paint sailboats.

I continued thinking of my mother when Zenn showed me the greenhouse on the roof. So many plants, some with broad leaves, some with flat branches, some with tiny little buds. Trees towered in the corner, contained in enormous wooden tubs. I'd seen trees like this in the green areas. I had no idea they'd come from the roof of freaking Rise Twelve.

Zenn fingered the leaf on an unknown type of flower. "I like coming here, but sometimes . . . I don't know. Sometimes I wonder if it's worth it."

I wandered down the neat rows of plants inside the greenhouse. The flowers gave way to vegetables, the delicate stems just poking through the soil. Suddenly the air turned cold; Zenn had moved to the edge of the roof.

I joined him in the winter air, gazed out at the ocean the way he did.

"What's 'it'?" I asked.

"What?" Zenn asked.

"You said you wonder if it's worth it. What's 'it'? What's worth it?"

He swept his arm across his body. "You know. This. Rise Twelve. Is it worth going against Director Hightower and the Association? Does it really make a difference?"

A million more questions lurked behind the ones he'd voiced. Could we implement the culture of Rise Twelve into the rest of the Rises? Into the entire city of Freedom?

The entire union?

Could the Darwinian Episode come to an end? They had a lot of talent on their side. The Evolutionary Rise had a team of dedicated scientists, all searching for a way to tweak exactly the right genes in exactly the right way at exactly the right time to produce more talented beings. So far, all we got for their hard work were clones.

So much for natural selection, I thought. It didn't seem natural if we were scientifically engineering it.

"I think it's worth it," I said, softly, almost to myself.

"Maybe," Zenn said. "Maybe not." He exhaled hard, his breath steaming out of his mouth and into the night. He yanked his attention from the city, stepped toward the descender—which did not require a passcode to use.

"They don't get caught, because most of their activity

takes place at night, contained here in the Rise, where the Thinker manufactures the reports sent to Director Hightower," Zenn said after all the Insiders had reassembled in the foyer. I could barely keep my eyes off the group of people dancing in the corner.

"The Insiders do the same thing," Zenn continued. "Trek falsifies our feeds, providing Director Hightower with pre-recorded conversations and old projections. Of course, that's if he's watching at all. Often, he relies on his reports. That's one of Director Hightower's flaws. He doesn't believe his subjects will defy him."

For good reason, I thought. Because if Van Hightower knew about what the people were really doing in Rise Twelve, they'd all be dead.

Raine

 *I'm running. Fast. Faster than I've ever run before. I'm trying to keep up with Vi, and man, she's fast. She pauses every now and then, chest heaving, searching.*

We dodge into the doorway of a building that feels too small for two people. Vi can't seem to get a proper breath, and if she can't, then I'm screwed.

I wheeze while she touches the bricks real careful, like they might whisper secrets to her if she caresses soft enough.

Before I can ask her what's going on—or where we are—the doorway disappears and we're walking in the desert. The sun beats down too hot. The craving for a cool drink of water starts immediately.

Next to Vi walks none other than Jag Barque. He holds her hand and rubs cream into her sunburned shoulders.

She looks at him. No, through him. She says, "Why can't I remember your name?"

"Vi," I say, trying to get her attention.

She turns her head to look at me. Right at me. "Raine?"

I glance over her shoulder at Jag, but he's gone.

"How did you get here?" she asks. "Where's—?" She gropes for the name and comes up silent.

Even though I'm trapped in this ridiculous dream, I know I shouldn't tell her. My brief-sheet said not to tell Vi anything.

I shouldn't tell her, but "Jag" comes out, strong and sure.

Vi halts, her eyes wide. "Jag." The name fits inside her mouth. "Yeah, that's it. Jag." She grips my shoulders, and I see the desperation in her eyes. "Where is he?"

The words flow out before I can censor them. "Thane has him."

"No." Vi shook her head, as if that would make what I said false. "No, he can't." Tears fall down her face, and she doesn't move to wipe them away. "I saved him."

"I saw him here in Rise One."

"No!" Vi shoves me away, and I fall into a void so deep and dark that nothing exists except the echo of those two letters.

* * *

197

The dream looped. Over and over. Always the same. I ran. Caught Vi. Walked in the desert. Told her Jag's name. Fell.

Four times. Five. Six. Ten.

Forever.

"Wake up," a hoarse voice croaked. "Come on now, Raine, wake up." Hands that felt like liquid ice brushed over my forehead and smoothed back my hair. Then Violet started to sing. The haunting melody wrapped around me, realigning my senses and stitching all my broken pieces into a cohesive whole.

With difficulty, I sat up and opened my eyes. Faint light filtered through the drawn blinds in my bedroom. Not quite morning yet. Vi knelt next to my bed, still singing in that soothing tone.

"Thanks," I whispered.

"You entered my dream," she said, cutting right to the point. "How did you do that?"

I regarded her in the semidarkness. Her ordinary brown hair fell across her forehead in jagged bangs. But her eyes radiated with an inner light I'd never seen before. Her entire existence seemed to hinge on my answer.

"I don't know," I admitted.

She nodded with understanding, a strange sort of acceptance in her upturned mouth. "I've done that too. Entered dreams, I mean."

"Um, okay." I wasn't sure if this dream-viewing thing was a talent or not. "Do you—do you remember your dream?"

"Yeah." She sat back on her haunches and sighed. "I'm always running."

"But you saw me, right?"

"Yeah, this was the first time I've ever seen anyone."

"Did you hear what I told you?"

She pressed her eyes closed and cocked her head to the side. I waited, hardly daring to breathe. Minutes passed. Vi didn't move, and I didn't dare to even breathe too loud lest I disrupt her.

As time clicked by, I realized how much my body ached. I had little half-moon scabs on my palms from where my own nails had dug in. My back felt like I'd taken a beating, and my head throbbed.

The light coming around the blinds was just beginning to brighten when I received an e-comm from Cannon. I opened it, since it didn't require any movement.

It's raining.

That's all the e-comm said. He always messaged me when it rained; it was a tradition of ours. I smiled to myself and returned his lame message. *It's pouring.*

He didn't answer with the traditional *Don't melt*. I fiddled with the hem of my shirt, twisting the fabric harder with each passing second. When he didn't respond, I checked the time stamp on his e-comm. It was several days old.

I looked toward the window. Sunlight pooled on the floor just behind the curtain. It wasn't raining. For some reason, this made me miss Cannon with a fierceness I didn't think possible.

Where are you? Comm me so we can sneak over to the Medical Rise later, okay? And yes, you can afford to take a break.

I composed and sent the e-comm to Cannon, desperation mixing with worry. What if—?

"Jag," Violet said suddenly, and I jerked my attention back to her. "His name is Jag."

"Yes!" I cried. "You remembered. What else do you remember?"

"Nothing. I can't—"

An alarm cut off the rest of what she said. Before Vi could get to her feet, my father's physicians entered our bedroom, needles drawn.

Behind them came Zenn.

And then Gunn.

Over the next few minutes I broke protocol about ten times:

1. I leapt to my feet and put my arm protectively around Vi. Touching: not allowed.

2. I ordered the doctors to "get the hell out." Swearing: against protocol.

3. I opened my cache to the physicians and tried to tell them that *nothing is wrong and hey, can you put down the giant needles?* Now, technically this isn't against protocol (I can have cache convos with whomever I want), but asking them to go against their orders? Definitely a problem.

4. After one doctor ordered me to surrender, I grabbed his face in my bare hand. He shrieked and fled the bedroom. Terrorizing government officials: frowned upon.

5. I may or may not have kicked two physicians. I wasn't sure which protocol law that broke, but I'm sure there was one. Side note: Vi has a wicked short temper. And a really tight right jab.

6. When Gunn used his voice and ordered the doctors away, I yelled, "And stay out!" I immediately received a citation. Behavior unbecoming a Citizen: not allowed.

7. Zenn scurried into the living area with Vi, and I eavesdropped on their hurried conversation (totally

against protocol). I couldn't hear much, but I got the gist. Vi: angry. She felt betrayed that Zenn hadn't told her about Jag. Zenn: apologetic, yet firm. As per his usual.

8. Zenn used his voice and told Vi to go to sleep, which she did instantly. "You beast!" I screamed, launching myself at him. "You've been keeping her under all this time!" My fingers raked across his neck before he shoved me away. Attacking another person: not allowed.

Okay, so that's only eight, but I'm sure some of those held double charges. I'd have to meet with my father.

Do not cry, I commanded myself. *You will not cry in front of Gunner. Not again.* I sat in the ergonomic in my living area while Zenn bustled over to the food-dispenser and ordered coffee.

Gunner perched on the other chair, his face pinched with ~~worry~~ exhaustion. "Good thing we arrived at the same time as those doctors."

"Yeah, good thing," I murmured. "When's the last time you slept your mandated hours?"

He gave a laugh that held nothing funny. "Last week?" He scrubbed at his face. "Yeah, last week, the night before you got caught and taken to lab seven for the drain."

"I didn't—wait a second. Last week? That drain"—I cringed at the word (and wondered how Gunn knew to use it)—"that was last week?"

His eyes came open bloodshot. "You've been out for eight days. You missed a boatload of school." A wry smile curved his lips. "Rumors are flying, Hightower. Cannon's been gone too."

The earth seemed to spin faster. Sudden fear gripped my heart, and squeezed. Where was Cannon? Was he okay? Maybe he hadn't responded to my e-comm because—I cut the thought off before I could finish it with something horrible. I couldn't bear the thought of seeing Cannon's name on the Alias list. Everything twisted upside down and backward.

Zenn pressed a hot mug into my hand, and the world righted itself. "Drink up, Raine. We've got some plans to make." He handed Gunn a cup and settled onto the floor, nursing his own drink. "Gunn, their dispenser is wonky. I ordered coffee and got milk."

Even as I watched, steam tendriled from Zenn's mug—clearly not milk in that thing. His neck bore the battle lines of my fingernails, but he'd smeared some techy cream on it and the redness was already fading. I should apologize for accusing him of keeping Vi brainwashed deliberately. But I couldn't, not yet.

"Milk?" Gunn and Zenn looked at one another for a moment too long before Gunn nodded. I didn't have the energy to ask about the creepy starefest and coded convo.

I drank so I wouldn't have to speak first. Apparently my ability was out in the open. The coffee went down hot, and I was glad for the burn. It felt like shame. Tasted like it too.

"So," Zenn said, glancing up. "What's up with Vi?"

As if he hadn't seen the spectacular fight she'd put up against those needles. I'd never heard such profanity or such anguished screaming. I checked the ceiling too, noticed a flash of blue indicating a scrambler, and immediately knew we had a few minutes of unmonitored conversation.

Thanks, Trek, I thought. He was always one step ahead of the game, always assisting us when we needed a few minutes to talk.

Ten minutes, he warned, his voice over the cache garbled and too low, probably to avoid detection.

"Raine?" Gunn reached for me but yanked his hand back before touching me.

"She remembered Jag," I said carefully, watching Zenn for his reaction.

He gave none. Instead he watched me back, waiting for more. When I didn't offer anything, he said, "And you remembered him too, yes?"

"When I saw him in the lab, I knew who he was. I didn't—I didn't drain him."

"I know," Zenn said. "Your father is rather interested in how you can suddenly control your ability."

"I don't know how," I said. The coffee felt like slush in my gut: cold and heavy. Zenn wasn't merely making conversation. He was asking, and not because he cared. Because my dad did.

"I just couldn't," I said. "I'm never going to do another drain."

At that, Zenn grinned. He cut a glance at Gunner, and I followed his gaze. Gunn was leaning forward, his jaw set. "You better tell her now, Gunn."

"Tell me what?" I asked.

Gunn threw Zenn a glare and went into my kitchen.

"Tell me what?" I repeated, suddenly cold all over. Gunn kept his back to me, and Zenn kept right on sipping his coffee-milk like nothing was happening. "Zenn?"

He drank from his mug, maddeningly silent.

I watched Gunn in the kitchen instead. His shoulders were so tense; his movements jerky. What could he possibly have to tell me? Had he seen the Alias list? Was his dad's name on it, with *deceased* next to it?

I already knew about his voice ability and his genetic ability to control tech. We'd spent enough time together in genetics class.

Maybe his secret was something else entirely. Starr's face floated in my mind. "Someone better tell me something," I said. "And fast."

"I have a special ability too," Gunn said, turning around and leaning against the kitchen counter. "I can, well, let's just say that I can tell you were embarrassed a few minutes ago. And now you're . . . defiant? Yeah, I think that's it."

"Don't you dare tell me how to feel," I snapped.

"That's just it," Zenn said. "Gunn *can* tell how you feel. He's an empath."

Before I could fully process that, Gunn murmured, "And now she's mad too."

"I'm not mad," I argued. How perfect. The guy can talk to me in my head *and* detect how I feel about him. About everything. No, I wasn't mad. More like furious. Here I thought he'd been in genetics all this time because of his voice. But no—the guy had two major talents!

I squinted at him, as if I might be able to see his DNA that way. I couldn't help wondering what else he could do.

"She's *really* mad," Gunn said to Zenn, like I wasn't sitting a few feet from him.

"It's a very useful skill," Zenn said, as if that would make it all better.

"How long have you known?" I practically spat at Gunn.

He shrugged. "My whole life."

That didn't make me feel any better. All this time he'd been emotionally eavesdropping on me. Humiliation made me hang my head so I wouldn't have to look Gunner in the eye.

Zenn set his mug on the floor. "So let's get back to Jag. What do you think we should do about him?"

"Well, he was the leader of the Resistance," Gunn said, his tone somewhat softer now. "We can't let Thane keep him."

"I agree," Zenn said. "But what I meant was: Should we reintroduce him to Vi? Or send him back to his rebels in the Badlands with a new weapon?"

Those words fizzled some of my anger and embarrassment. "A new weapon?"

Zenn inclined his head toward Gunner. "He's willing to accompany Jag out west. It might be our only chance to get them both out."

With everything else going on, I'd forgotten about Gunn's desire to leave Freedom. I looked back and forth between him and Zenn, trying to formulate a response.

"She's stunned," Gunn reported.

"Stop it," I spat. "It's getting really annoying."

"As if I couldn't tell," Zenn quipped. "Do you still think I'm a beast, Raine?"

I focused on my coffee, the apology I owed him pooling

in my mouth. "No," I murmured. "It's just that Vi—she—well, how come she can remember stuff when she's with me but not with you?"

Sad silence filled the living area. I didn't have to look up (or possess a special ability) to know how Zenn felt.

"Because I haven't really been trying," he said simply. "We all have our roles here, and I'm the only one playing both sides."

"That's not true," I said. "What do you think I've been doing?"

Zenn leaned his elbows on his knees. "You really think your father doesn't know what you've been doing?"

"Have you told him?"

"Of course not."

"Then, no. He doesn't know." My dad gave his permission for my midnight flying sessions, but if he knew about the Insiders, he'd put a stop to that. Immediately—and probably with my death. "He allows me clearance to be out after curfew. He thinks I'm flying. I promise you he doesn't know about anything else."

I raised my eyes to meet Zenn's, and we had a conversation without speaking. Without using the cache. Without special talents.

I looked at Gunn as if to say *so there*.

Gunn cleared his throat. "About Jag?" he asked. "Do we get him out and send him back? Let him and Vi"—he did that awful grinding in his throat again—"hook . . . I mean, remeet? Do you guys need me more here, or can I, you know, go with him?"

I appraised Gunn. As much as I hated to admit it, he couldn't stay here. I wanted him to, wanted it deeply, but I could tell he felt caged here. He kept running his hands up and down his arms, like he had an itch he couldn't scratch.

So I told them everything I knew, everything about Vi's dreams and how she'd remembered Jag.

A few exhausting minutes later, I concluded, "So we've got to bust Jag out of high-security confinement somehow, and get him and Gunn over the wall, which we don't know how to do, and past the barrier, which, when breached, alerts every Citizen over their cache *and* raises an alarm. They need hoverboards, which we have, and food generators, which we don't." I swallowed my now-cold coffee. "Sounds easy."

"By Monday," Zenn added. "Thane's ordered a trial for Jag on Monday morning."

"What day is it today?" I asked, suddenly feeling very weary.

Gunn blinked, checking his cache. "Thursday, 6:42 a.m."

"Is it Thursday already?" Zenn asked innocently.

"Like you didn't know," I grumbled into the last drops of my coffee.

Gunner

Zenn left on his hoverboard while I turned back to Raine's food-dispenser. I could feel her eyes on me as I worked, and I shifted so my body blocked her view. "Zenn said this isn't working right," I said.

"Is that what he said?"

I allowed myself a small smile. "Zenn's language takes some getting used to, that's for sure. But I can fix the dispenser for you. You'll be able to have longer conversations."

I set the timer to seven seconds, just like my dispenser. I noticed another tic in the gadget. I paused, letting the tech stream into my bones. The codes twisted, danced away from me, so I couldn't get a clear view of what that portlet was set to do.

Raine's gaze became a laser, so I deactivated the portlet, hoping the girls wouldn't get ice when they ordered ice cream.

"You shouldn't have a problem with that now," I said, turning toward her. "Seven seconds." She nodded her understanding.

I wanted to order something—anything—just so I had seven seconds to apologize for not telling her about my empathic ability.

Then I'd order whatever, whatever just so I could kiss her without anyone knowing. Instead of doing any of that, I leaned against her counter and watched her settle into the ergonomic.

I wanted to stay in her flat until she fell asleep. Because no matter what she said, she wasn't fine. When she stood, her legs shook. Her eyes sunk into her skull despite eight days of "rest." She seemed on the brink of dying.

I couldn't feel anything but exhaustion from her, and my welcome was officially worn out. So I mumbled a good-bye and ascended up to Thane's office. Since the break-in, new passcodes generated every hour. Unbreakable windows and fingerprint portlets had been installed on Monday. Security cameras monitored both sides of the door.

Like any of it mattered. He must know who had broken in. Everyone should've known. But I had yet to receive a citation for staying up too late or deviating from my schedule. My sessions with Thane had produced no conversations about my new sleeping habits, my new diet, my new flight plan. He acted like he didn't even know.

As the first week of classes had worn into the second, I realized he didn't. Someone very high up was on my side, making sure of that. I'd spent a sick amount of time speculating about who was assisting me. The logical assumption was Trek, but he was still a student, whether he lived in a tent full of convo-canceling equipment or not. I puzzled over how he'd get clearance to cache during school, during all hours of the night. Then I'd remember that the voice didn't sound exactly like Trek. Maybe he'd teched it up so he wouldn't get caught.

I dismissed Trek Whiting and strode to Thane's foreboding door and pressed the portlet. "Dr. Myers?"

He didn't answer. I felt the lenses on the cameras zoom in, catching every wisp of breath, every bead of sweat collecting along my forehead.

I shifted to the side to block the view, and held my thumb above the fingerprint console. Tech streamed between my skin and the pad, electrifying my cells until I thought they might catch fire.

When I pressed my finger down, the door unclicked. I

entered the office quickly-but-not-too-quickly, so I wouldn't look like I was breaking in. With my back pressed into the wall, I said, "Unrecord." The four security cameras in the room powered down.

I didn't know what I was looking for, only that I'd find it here. The cabinet gaped open, totally gutted. That didn't matter. During my training over the last eight days, there'd been no discussions about "voice practicalities" or "useful ethics," but I had seen where Thane hid the important stuff. I crossed the room, slid into his desk chair.

There, on the steel support leg of his desk, a series of slots had been carved. About half of them housed a microchip. I took a deep breath and started at the top.

My thoughts churned with Jag, his powerful voice, and what that meant for me. With Raine, her debilitating ability, and what she might see if she ever touched me skin to skin. With Zenn, his not really trying with Vi, and what instructions from the Resistance he was following. With Starr, and my mom. Would she be notified of my absence? Did I have time to sneak back and say good-bye the right way?

And I'd been dreaming about life in Rise Twelve for eight days. Asleep, awake, didn't matter. There wasn't a minute that passed that I didn't wonder about that place.

It's raining. What would a gardener do when it rains?

Do they have spider maid service? Or do they clean their flats themselves?

How many pots were thrown today?

Are those people dancing tonight?

Finally I put my head down on the glassed desk and pound-pound-pounded out the thoughts.

When I received the citation for missing my first class, I pulled myself together. That would be forwarded to Thane, and who knew when he'd start caring about me keeping protocol. I slipped another chip into the port on my wrist and waited for the material to come up on my vision-screen.

I flipped through it all and found nothing useful. Nothing on the second chip. Or the third. Or the fourth. I received a second citation for missing another class; I expected Thane to come roaring over my cache, demanding an explanation. He didn't. My assistant must be screening my citations too.

My stomach clenched. I squeezed my eyes shut, saw white lines on the backs of my lids. *This one,* I thought. *This one will have something.*

I inserted another chip. And another. *This one, this one, this one.*

I was flipping so fast through the docs, I almost missed her name. I flicked back one, two, three screens. Violet Schoenfeld.

In family tree style, the branch above her name read *Thane*

Myers with another leg leading to *Alias: Lyle Schoenfeld*. The branch below Vi's name was labeled with her mother's name: *Laurel Woods*. All the names were clickable.

I went straight to the alias, Lyle Schoenfeld. His picture came up on my v-screen, and the first thing I noted: Thane Myers ≠ Lyle Schoenfeld.

But I recognized myself in the real Lyle. The sloping jaw. The flecked eyes. The long nose.

I couldn't scan the information fast enough.

Born in the mountain region, before it had been split into the Goodgrounds and the Badlands. Political activist. Opponent of the Association. Writer of books. I cataloged "Badlands" as the first possible place to search for my father's journal.

Under Lyle Schoenfeld's "Family Information" I found two more branches: *Elise Jameson (match) and Gunner (product)*.

The sound of my blood rushing in my veins became the only noise. I'd discovered my father's name, but immediately wondered why I had my mother's last name. I decided to ask her when I went to say good-bye.

I downloaded the document and replaced the chip in the desk support. I wiped my face, squared my shoulders. I had one easy thing to accomplish before I left Freedom. Hug my mom.

But I also had one very hard thing: Rescue Jag Barque.

* * *

I didn't bother with school. I'd missed most of my morning classes anyway, so I went back to my flat and ordered anything I wanted to eat. We got to choose from holiday menus exactly twice a year: on my birthday and on my mom's. First I ordered her favorites: Mashed potatoes with pork roast and gravy. Baby carrots with spicy green beans. Then I ordered mine: Rich honey wheat bread with butter and raspberry jam. And soda. Lots of soda.

Briefly, I felt like a resident of Rise Twelve. The thought made my food taste that much better.

My cache alerted me that Thane had canceled our afternoon training session. I took the opportunity to fly above Freedom. I worried briefly at the cancelation, since Thane hadn't missed a session yet. But I decided not to dwell on it. Instead I nosed my board away from Rise One and toward the Confinement Rise beyond the southern orchards.

Inside, I felt restless, conflicted. Dangerous.

The branches of the trees seemed to reach for me, trying to claw me back to earth. I imagined how they looked in the summer: full of the sweet smell of flowers and dangling red apples. Now they only held the emptiness of death.

Two guards stood outside the Confinement Rise. Before I considered what I was doing, I landed and commanded my board to fold. We all waited as it flopped and bent into a square the size and thickness of my palm. I picked it up, put it in my back pocket.

Then I leveled my gaze at the guards.

Don't do it. Thane's voice roared in my ears, not over my cache, but as a brainwashing message.

I suddenly realized I'd been listening to his voice every night over the transmissions. I'd been obedient. And I didn't want to listen and comply anymore. I took a step forward.

What are you doing, Gunner? Thane sounded dangerous.

The truth was, I had no idea. I knew I was sick of genetics and engineering classes and begging for extra flying hours. I hated eating oranges and apples and yogurt without nuts.

I wanted toast. Lots of toast.

I wanted Raine Hightower all to myself.

I wanted to do something wild, something spontaneous, something that wasn't planned, calculated, predictable.

Making my own decisions, I replied, calmly striding within taser-firing distance. The guards pulled out and activated their tasers.

You can make your own decisions, Thane broadcasted. *That's why I'm training you.*

No, you're training me to make decisions for everyone. I don't want to do that.

You're going to ruin everything. His thought held an edge of . . . panic? Or was that rage?

I didn't know what he meant anyway. And I didn't care. Both guards had just taken a step forward.

"Stand down," I commanded. "Deactivate the tasers." With my most powerful tone, the guards didn't stand a chance. They relaxed, stuffed the now-useless tasers into their pockets.

"Tell me where Jag Barque is."

Inside my head, Thane roared with rage.

One guard blinked, probably checking his cache. "Floor nine, cell one," he monotoned.

"Get me in this building," I ordered. The two guards punched in the codes, and the door hissed open.

I remembered to say, "Thank you," before ordering them to "Make sure Thane Myers doesn't set foot in the Confinement Rise."

Then I did something I swore I'd never do. I e-commed Trek and asked for his help. *How much time can you buy me?*

Ten minutes, came his instant reply. *If that.*

Getting to floor nine required no skill. No ability. Just an ascender ring, which I took in a blaze of yellow stars. I landed in a sterile hallway with four sealed doors lining one side. On the other wall, high-up windows let in stale winter light.

I walked past four, three, two, to door number one. A smear of dark red marred the latch. Blood.

I blinked, hoping it would disappear when I opened my eyes again. Instead, the crimson-black splash superimposed over everything I looked at. The door was locked, of course.

Like that stopped me. I clutched the steel latch in my hand, felt the tech warm at my touch. It zoomed around inside, bolting into my palm, my fingers.

Then it clicked open.

I entered the room, expecting (a) a fight, (b) a shout, or (c) an acknowledgment.

I got (d) none of the above.

The great leader of the Resistance, Jag Barque, lay secured to the bed, three silencers attached along each side of his neck, blood dried across his face, fast asleep.

So I got him cleaned up.

Which sounded easy, but so wasn't. For one thing, silencers hurt real bad when removed without the right tech. And I couldn't seem to get a feel for this tech, because these silencers weren't Freedom made. I did the best I could and pried them off.

The first time, Jag screamed, the absence of sound filling the tiny cell and making me slink into the corner. He looked at me with wild eyes, fresh blood trickling down his neck into the bedclothes.

"Sorry," I said. "I'm sorry." I repeated it over and over as I removed the six silencers. By then the guy was a huge mess. Crying and bleeding and trying to get up so he could punch me out, probably.

I took off my shirt and ran it under the dripping faucet in the corner. He pressed it to his neck while I unhinged the tech-tethers from his ankles, removed the restraints across his thighs, waist, and chest.

"Who are you?" he croaked as I worked on the cuffs on his hands.

I looked up. "I'm Gunner. I think we have a friend in common. Zenn Bower?"

I *beep-beeped* the cuffs off Jag's hands and helped him stand. He rewet the shirt and mopped up his face. I rummaged in my pack and handed him a tube of med-gel for his wounds.

While he rubbed it in, I wadded up the soiled sheets and flung them into the corner.

"Tight security here," I quipped.

"I only get fed once a day," he said. "And that happened this morning. I get ten minutes to eat, and then I'm strapped down for the rest of the day. Guards come at dark so I can go to the bathroom. That's it."

I swallowed hard, trying to imagine what life would be like to be that caged. Physically controlled, not just mentally.

"How do you know Zenn?" Jag asked.

"He's my flatmate." My eyes had adjusted to the dimness pretty well. Even having been confined, I could see why Jag was the leader of the Resistance. The guy had some strong will, some blazing fire in his eyes.

"He's been working with another friend of ours," I continued. "I think you know her too."

"Oh?" Jag tossed my wet and bloody shirt on top of the sheets and turned toward the bed.

"Yeah. Raine Hightower. Oh, and Violet Schoenfeld. They're flatmates."

He spun around, his face taut with what felt like panic and fear and anger and at least five other emotions I couldn't separate fast enough. "Vi's here?"

"In the flesh." I leaned against the wall near the doorway, trying to get a lungful of air that wasn't full of the scent of Jag's blood and sweat.

"But . . . how?"

"She's been here for eight months, man. Same as Zenn."

He shook his head, tears falling. Maybe he wasn't so tough-Resistance-leader after all. He sank onto the bare mattress. "She didn't mention that."

"She? She who?"

"Indy." Jag sounded more angry than sad. Zenn had mentioned an Indy. "She's the one running things for you, yeah?" I asked Jag.

"She should be. So is Vi running the Insiders?"

"What? Vi? No," I said. "Zenn's doing all that."

Jag didn't say anything, but I felt his disbelief. Just like Zenn, Jag felt a multitude of warring emotions when discussing Zenn. Weird stuff there, and I didn't want to be involved in it.

"Well?" Jag asked. "Why are you here?"

"Okay, well, I'm just sort of making things up as I go," I said, an uncomfortable feeling oscillating in my stomach. "Thane will probably be here soon. I bought us some time to talk, but let's face it. He can brainwash anyone. We need to work out a way for us to escape."

"Us? You mean me and you?"

"That's what I mean, genius." I pulled on my coat since I couldn't put on my wet and bloody shirt. "Raine and Zenn have an intricate network of spies here in the city. We need to get your rebels and regroup. Then we'll come back and help with the overthrow here."

"Overthrow? You mean—"

"Yeah, that's what I mean," I interrupted. "I need to find a journal. You're going to help me with that."

"A journal?"

Apparently being a great leader meant repeating everything someone said in the form of a question. "A journal. My father wrote it."

Jag opened his mouth, but I cut in. "Don't say it. Yes, my father. I've never met him, and he died a long time ago. But his name is Lyle Schoenfeld. Not the Alias version—not Thane. The real Lyle Schoenfeld."

Jag paled, if that were possible. Wracking coughs shook his body. I didn't think he'd make it five steps down the hall, let alone out of the building and into the wild.

When he finished, he said, "I know who he is. I've read that journal."

I pushed into a standing position as the ascender ring filled the hall with golden light. "You have? Where is it?"

"Yeah, Lyle wrote a lot of things before he died. I've got a couple of his published books. His journal is invaluable."

"And? Where is it now?"

Jag shrugged, casually lifting one shoulder. "Indy should have it. The Resistance has had it for years."

"Where's Indy?" I asked.

"What month is it?"

"February."

"Winter." He shuddered, as if he could feel cold tendrils

223

of wind. "If things have gone according to plan, she'll be in the Badlands."

My desire to go there tripled. I needed that journal.

One minute, Gunn. A tremor of fear ran through me. This voice was decidedly not Trek. It pitched too high, almost feminine. But it couldn't be—the voice had always been masculine before. And I'd just asked Trek for assistance.

"I—"

"I recently found out who Lyle really is too," Jag said.

Well, I couldn't leave now. "Who?"

"The reason my parents were killed." He didn't look away from me as a loud pair of footsteps sprinted closer.

A girl appeared in the doorway. "Come on, Gunn. We've gotta fly." She glanced at Jag. "Now. Thane's on his way."

Jag and I stared at her. "Starr?" we asked at the same time.

Raine

20.

As soon as Gunn finished with the dispenser and left, I started an e-comm to Cannon. He'd been gone for a whole week, same as me. We'd missed our ritual of sneaking through the nocturnal lounge of the Medical Rise after my drain.

Of course, I hadn't completed the drain. Part of my mouth smiled; the other half shook with fear.

Cannon, where are you? I really need you to respond. Please. I'm worried about you.

One minute became ten, and he still hadn't answered. So I roused Vi. Or at least I tried to. Zenn had put her down deep, and it took a few minutes to get her to even open her eyes.

When she did, a milky film smothered the fire I'd seen in them just a few hours earlier. I wondered if she could remember anything that had happened.

"Hey," I said gently. "How do you feel?"

She groaned. "Where's Zenn?"

"He went to meet with Thane."

Vi's body stiffened. "Without me?" A moment later relief painted her features. "Oh, I'm . . ." She met my expectant gaze, wearing confusion in hers. "Excused?"

She said it like a question, and I nodded. Trek was doing a bang-up job of keeping us in the clear. "I'm free all day too," I said.

Thank you, Mr. Assistant, I thought. Trek deserved major props for rearranging my day. I'd need to get his board tuned up to thank him properly.

"Free," Vi repeated, running her fingers through her hair in a rough attempt to be presentable.

"Free," I said. "We're free, Vi. So, you wanna talk?"

My brief-sheet said not to talk about anything specific. So I went right for something specific. "What's your favorite color?"

Vi gazed at me as if she didn't understand English. "I don't get it."

"You know, red, blue, purple. Which one do you like best?"

"I don't know. They're all fine."

I sighed. "Yeah, they're all fine, but which one do *you* like?"

"I like them all."

I suppressed the desire to roll my eyes. She'd been brainwashed into a complete clone, devoid of even so much as a favorite color. "Okay, let's try foods. What do you like to eat?"

She blinked. "My meal plan says I can have toast and hot chocolate for breakfast."

"Forget about the meal plan. What else do you want?"

"I don't understand. Why would I want something else?"

This was going to be harder than I thought. As I searched my brain for something to talk about with Vi, I realized how little I knew about her. I could pick her out of a crowd and describe her physically. That's it. I didn't know what she liked to eat, her favorite color, how she'd like to wear her hair—

"Want me to show you something?" I asked.

"I guess."

I stood up and waved for her to follow me into the bathroom. "Okay, so some of us have the option of hair enhancements. I can make mine whatever color I want. Maybe my favorite shade"—I found the discarded wand under the sink and smoothed it down over my snow-colored hair—"of pink."

I watched my hair turn a shocking shade of pink, but I really saw Vi's astonishment at the change.

I smiled at her in the mirror. "Or blue." I ran the wand over the pink streak. It melted away into a brilliant navy that matched my weekend fingernail polish. "You wanna try?"

She took the wand, but then just stood there staring at it.

"You have to say what you want, and then start at the scalp and pull out or down or whatever," I offered.

She thrust the enhancer toward me, but I pushed it back. "No, try it. Maybe, hey, maybe you'd like to have darker hair." I thought of her old dye job, hoping to use it to reawaken part of her.

She swallowed hard and gripped the wand harder. "Isn't this against protocol?" Her question reminded me of the scared girl she was, but the force of it told me she didn't care.

"No. I have enough points." I felt a slight pang at losing the points. In another week, I could've skipped a class, no questions asked. "Besides, you used to break the rules all the time."

A wicked grin graced her mouth, pulling her skin tight across her high cheekbones. "I did, didn't I?" Then she set the enhancer against her scalp. "Black, with a hint of blue." She ran the wand over her head, deftly changing the color of her hair in a few minutes.

"Do we have scissors?" she asked, turning back to me.

With her snow-white skin and ultra-black hair, she looked dangerous.

Pieces clicked around in my head. No wonder my dad wanted her. No wonder she'd been kept in a brainwashed haze for months.

No wonder I was her roommate. Dad knew I'd follow protocol, keep him informed about his little pet, anything so he'd keep looking the other way.

Suddenly I wondered what my dad wanted most. And how Vi played into that.

How I played into that.

With my mind churning, I retrieved the scissors for her and sat on the closed toilet seat while she cut off the six inches of growth she'd accumulated since she'd arrived.

"That's better," she said, shaking her head. She wet her hair by running her dripping hands through it. "I just need something to make it spike."

Leaning down, I pulled a bottle of freeze spray from the cabinet. Vi wrinkled her nose. "No, not that. Something else. Do we have something else?"

I moved bottles of shampoo out of the way. "Like this?" I tossed her a tube of clear gel.

She opened it and took a whiff. "I guess this'll do." As she pulled the sticky stuff through her hair, I watched her eyes.

The foggy layer lifted off, leaving behind brilliant aqua eyes that sharpened with every passing second.

I hid my satisfaction and thought about asking her another question. But I needed more information first. I needed her file. Suddenly, I wanted to touch Vi, really press my hand against her bare arm and find out what I'd see this time.

Before I could muster up the nerve, she turned toward me. "Raine, is Gunner your match?"

I wasn't expecting that. I turned my embarrassment into a cough.

"Ah, okay. He's not. But you like him."

"How can you tell?" Horror snaked through me at the obvious transparency.

"Let's just say I know what it's like to be in love with someone other than your match." She went back into our bedroom, her back straight, her movements sure. I'd never seen her like this before. I liked it.

"I'm not in love with Gunn," I said, following her.

"Yeah, okay. And I'm not in love with Jag."

Before I could respond, an alarm sounded. Three things happened at once.

1. A voice that slightly mimicked Trek's came over my cache. It said, *Stop saying that name.*

2. Starr Messenger barged into my bedroom.
3. Vi took a step back and slid her hand into mine.
   Palm to palm. Skin to skin.

Five seconds passed. Then ten.
I saw nothing.

Starr was talking, but I couldn't hear her. I clung to the nothing, to seeing nothing, feeling nothing, smelling nothing.

This *nothing* had never happened before. Is this how normal people live all the time? Able to touch without consequences? Without seeing what they'd rather not see?

It was beyond amazing. I never wanted the nothing to end.

But it only took Starr about four seconds to realize I wasn't paying attention to her. Her freaky eyes zeroed in on my hands.

"Raine," she said, stepping forward and gently breaking the contact between me and Vi. "Snap out of it."

"I can't see . . ."

"I know," Starr said. "Come on, sit. We have to talk. You have to listen."

I sat. I listened.

Man, Starr can talk fast. It's like the words were already strung together and all she had to do was exhale. They streamed out of her in rivers, and I only caught some of what she said.

I got the gist. Gunn had busted *into* prison (what the hell?), found Jag (Vi inhaled sharply; Starr didn't even pause), and was now in session with Thane (who was pretty freakin' mad).

The conversation lasted about three minutes, her sharp gaze shredding me the whole time. She stood and walked toward the door. "And I'd appreciate it if you stayed away from my match."

I wanted to defend myself, say that there wasn't anything going on between me and Gunn.

"Don't even try it," she said, her voice barely above a hiss. "Surely you haven't forgotten how much time you and I spent together in primary school."

I hadn't. I swallowed the lies I'd been about to say. "Right," I said instead. "I'll stay away from your match."

Starr narrowed her eyes as if to say, *I doubt it*, but didn't vocalize anything else as she swept her palm across the reader.

"And you should stay away from my father," I shot back. Her Thinker-ness was so obvious.

Fear flashed across her face, only present for a single blink. "I can't. My name appeared on his list at the end of last term." She paused. "It's good to have an *inside* connection."

I stared at her, unblinking. An inside connection? I couldn't believe I didn't know, on both counts. Her name hadn't come up on my list, but there were several Insider groups in Freedom. I didn't know everyone.

The fear belonged to me now. The air circulators whirred to life. "Then be careful," I said.

Starr nodded. Then she turned and left my flat.

Just after midnight, Gunn and I flew side by side (so I lied to Starr, cite me). I had so much to ask him, yet at the same time it felt good to say absolutely nothing. The silence felt clean and comfortable. I didn't want to ruin it by opening my cache. So I pulled my hat lower over my ears to keep the chill out, and just flew.

After a few laps, Gunn moved in close and brushed his hand against my gloved one. "What's up?"

I took a deep breath. "Okay, what I'm going to tell you will sound stupid."

"As stupid as breaking *into* prison?"

Laughter burst out of my mouth, free and loud. Gunn ended up joining me, and I liked the way the tension seeped from his shoulders when he let it. All too soon, they bunched back up, holding the weight of the world.

"Thane was pretty pissed." Gunn said. "But it was weird . . .

almost like he wasn't mad about me breaking in, but about something else."

"What?"

"I don't know." Gunn bumped me again. "And we met in a sterile office, not Thane's regular digs. He kept running his hands through his hair and glaring at me. I didn't get cited, but I have to research a bunch of crap about the Confinement Rise and the Association's imprisonment guidelines. I spent the rest of the afternoon doing that, and I have to complete extra sessions after dinner for the rest of the week."

"Wow, sorry. But hey, at least you didn't get cited."

"Yeah. But enough about that. What's eating you?"

I cast him a glance out of the corner of my eye. "I think I might have partial voice power."

Gunn chuckled again. "Be serious, Hightower."

"I am being serious."

"That's not possible. Voices don't work that way. If you have voice power, you have it all the time, over everyone."

I didn't like the superior edge to his tone. He almost sounded like he thought he was better than regular people. Like he subscribed to the Darwinian ideas. I knew Gunn, though, and he didn't feel that way.

I frowned, thinking of how I could erase the barrier in

Vi's mind, allowing her access to her memories. "So says you."

Gunn cast me a wary glance. "What did you do today? Besides streak your hair blue."

I looked up into the sparkling, star-filled sky. I contemplated telling him about my little convo with his jealous girlfriend. Wondered what he'd say then.

"I helped Vi remember," I finally said.

He made a noise of disbelief in his throat but didn't answer otherwise. Annoyance swept through me, and when he cocked his head in my direction, I remembered that he could feel my emotions.

Which only made me angry on top of annoyed. I leaned into my board, urging it to go faster. Flying with Gunn had lost all its appeal. He left me alone for a few laps, just long enough to cool down.

And, of course, he would know when that happened.

But I couldn't blame him for his abilities. I certainly didn't choose mine. So when Gunn floated next to me, I reached for his hand. He let me take it between my gloved fingers, and then he squeezed.

Flashes of Freedom burning stole through my head. Images from Vi's drain—especially the one where Gunn flew up behind me and kissed me—filled my mind.

My throat felt too narrow and too hot. Just one glance

toward the wall reminded me of my dead mother. *I don't think you should leave Freedom*, I chatted, because it felt safer to say it in my head than out loud—even if it could be monitored easier this way.

I have to.

He didn't, but I couldn't say that. He thought he did, and nothing I could say would change his mind. Which reminded me . . . "Is Trek in your mind, helping you?"

"Someone is. Not sure it's Trek all the time. Or at all."

"That's just because you don't like him," I said.

"No, I don't like him, but sometimes the voice is . . . weird. Too high or too low."

"Yeah, but it's nice to have our own personal secretary."

Gunn did that sideways-lookie thing, and my heart rate picked up. "I call him my assistant."

I liked that. "Good one."

But we were skimming the surface of what really needed to be chatted about.

"Once, I though the voice was Starr," Gunn said a little too casually.

I cast him a glance, thinking—again—about his match, and how I wasn't her.

"Sure, it could be Starr," I said, forcing casualness into my voice too. "Zenn could be helping too. Maybe he's the lower voice." I'd never heard a voice that sounded like a girl, let alone Starr.

"Let's just call them a collective assistant," I said.

"Sounds good."

We lapped the track in silence, each second bringing us closer to the convo neither one of us wanted to have.

"I—I've seen the end," I finally said, finding the strength to say it out loud. "And it's here, Gunn. Not in the Badlands. Here. In Freedom."

He raised his eyebrows at me.

I nodded, and fear from several scenarios (Gunn dying in the wild, my role in the end battle, how to help Vi get her memory back) boiled upward. "Please don't go. I have a bad feeling about it. You're needed here, in Thane's office. I'll unbrainwash Vi, and then we'll proceed with, well, whatever."

For half a second he seemed like he'd concede; then his jaw tightened again. "I can't, Raine. You do what you have to, and so will I."

"What do you have to do, Gunner?"

I'd rather not tell you, he said over the cache. *Then if anyone asks, you won't have to lie for me.*

I took a deep drag of frosty midnight air. *I want to lie for you.*

There. I'd laid it all out. I let my feelings for him surface, let them dance across my face, let them infiltrate the air around us.

He nudged his board closer again, and this time I didn't move mine away. His eyes, deep pools of black glass, searched mine. I put my hands on his shoulders to steady myself; he wrapped his arms around me. Our boards flew side by side, barely an inch between them.

When his lips met mine, the oxygen in my lungs ignited. I expected dark images to form from the contact, and when they didn't, I relaxed into him even more.

By the time he pulled away, my whole body vibrated.

"I'm sorry, Hightower," he whispered out loud. "That wasn't right. Or fair."

I didn't know how to respond. I wanted to kiss him again, wrong, unfair, whatever. So I did. He let me for a few seconds, long enough to make me want to kiss him forever and short enough to make me miss his mouth when he moved away.

His lips caught mine along the edges as he whispered, "I'm still leaving."

I laid my head on his chest and listened to the slow thump of his heart. "I know."

Gunner

21.

I could've stayed in the air holding Raine forever. But all too soon she whispered, "The meeting's about to start."

And so we separated and flew to what I hoped was my last Insider meeting. I'd been cached the coordinates, but I let Raine lead so I could admire her flying one more time. Okay, maybe I admired more than just her sick flying skills.

I had one more day of school. One more weekend in Freedom. *One more, one more, one more.*

Inside the warehouse on the edge of the western orchard, I lingered in the shadows. Like that worked. As soon as

Trek emerged from his dingy office, he searched the crowd. "Where's the voice-wonder?"

I wanted to ask, "Where's the jackwagon?" But of course I didn't. I simply stepped next to Raine.

"Ah, there you are. Your petition to leave the city has been filed and approved."

All undercurrent whispering ceased. Every eye volleyed back and forth between Trek and me, like he had the power to banish me from sheer dislike. "Thank you," I murmured.

Trek filled the group in on Jag Barque and why I was leaving with him. He didn't mention where we were headed. He snapped his fingers at Raine. "When's the breakout?"

"Monday, nine a.m.," she responded, annoyed at what I assumed was the demeaning finger snapping. "His trial is set for ten, and we can't afford for him to attend."

"That's three days, people. We'll all need to work around the clock to pull this off." Trek glared at me, as if I'd determined the date and time of Jag's hearing. I stared right back, daring him to say something stupid so I could deck him. He didn't. Instead, he started issuing orders.

Things like, "Saffediene, make sure the beams on the floodlights are set as low as possible on Sunday night." And, "Dammit, Suri, I need you to make sure the barrier is down for inspection at 8:45 a.m. Can you do that or not?"

She glared at him. "Dammit, Trek, I'm working with our contacts on the maintenance crew."

I almost started laughing. *Suck on that, Whiting,* I thought.

"Just make it happen," Trek said. "The fifteenth sector needs to be down at 8:45 a.m., Monday morning." He blinked before barking more orders. I listened but didn't really take stock of much. Trek would forward the complete plan to Zenn and we'd live, breathe, eat, dream about it for the next three days.

But when Trek said, "Raine, your petition to view Violet Schoenfeld's file has also been approved." I stood straighter. "Gunner, before you go, I need you to retrieve it from Thane's archives," Trek continued. "Get it to Raine, stat."

Every nerve in my body screamed for me to *look at Raine!* but I didn't. I blinked as if Trek and I were discussing homework. "Super," I said out loud. Would it have killed him to say please? I mean, seriously.

"Super," Trek mocked, and I wanted to punch him so he'd stop glaring at me. What had I ever done to him? Well, aside from the whole flight trials thing. Surely all his hatred didn't come from that; it'd happened almost two years ago.

Below his vein of dislike rode another emotion. It took me a moment to identify it as apprehension, but when I did, I knew where it came from.

Raine.

Now it poured from her in waves, and I employed every ounce of willpower I possessed to keep from turning toward her so we could have a private conversation. I didn't know she'd requested Vi's file. She could've just asked me for it. She didn't have to go formal and request it from the jerkiest jerk alive.

I stuffed my hands into my coat pockets while Trek finished his orders and everyone shuffled away. When Raine slid her hand into my pocket and twined her fingers with mine, I couldn't help but look at her.

"Don't be mad," she whispered.

Even with her gloved touch, all the madness drained out of my body. "I'm not mad," I said.

She smiled and looked like a frightened child doing it. "I don't need a special ability to tell," she said. "You stopped breathing when Trek asked you to get that file. And then you wouldn't look at me, even when I chatted you."

"My cache is off," I said, then I lowered my voice. "You could've just asked me."

She squeezed my hand inside my coat pocket. "I know. But I didn't want you to have to do me any favors. This way, it's an order."

I studied her face, trying to figure out what she wanted me

to say. Because this conversation? Strange. And the way she watched me with that hopeful glint in her eye? Even weirder. Which meant there were words to say here that would be correct, and words that most definitely would not be.

Her face fell just a bit as the seconds ticked by. Finally I got it.

"Raine, I want to do favors for you."

She grinned. "You do?"

I put both hands on the sides of her face, feeling her skin, her bones. I wanted to memorize her so I could see her while I flew away. So I could picture the way she'd smile when I came back. So I could always have her with me, no matter where I went or how long I was gone.

"Yeah, I do," I whispered, wondering when doing favors for someone = loving them.

I slept maybe two hours after the meeting, mostly because I was trying to figure out a way to get Vi's complete file from Thane. I didn't think he'd give it up willingly. And the thought of using my voice on him made me feel shady inside.

Zenn hadn't been home last night—had he gone to Rise Twelve? I seriously needed to stop thinking about that place. When I got up, Zenn sat at the kitchen table behind a giant stack of toast. We didn't speak. We didn't have to. I clicked through my cache and found the information.

In the southwest corner of Freedom sat an expansive peach orchard. The wall towered 150 feet over the trees, just like it does around the whole city—except for the ocean on the east side. Each sector of the wall burned with tech surveillance, and it only went down for inspection once a week.

On Monday at 8:45 a.m., the fifteenth sector—beyond the peach orchard in the southwest corner—would be down for approximately twenty-three minutes.

Above the city, a tech filter cleansed the air we breathe. This invisible barrier created a dome that encompassed the city wall and never went down. When it needed to be replaced, it happened at night. All Citizens are required to stay indoors during dark hours, and back-up filters pump in oxygen while the new filter acclimates and ensures we don't asphyxiate in the morning.

The barrier can't be shut off. Jag and I will breach it, which will raise the alarm, dispatch the Enforcement Officers in their special oxygen-generating suits, and force everyone else into their homes for a minimum of two hours.

Director Hightower will have to make up a lie to tell his Citizens, because Jag and I aren't planning on getting caught.

Lying should be easy, since Director Hightower's been

doing it for years—if my dad left, the air must be just as breathable outside the barrier as inside. Maybe-hopefully. I pushed the images of the suited maintenance workers out of my mind.

The details of how to get Jag out of the Confinement Rise were still in the beginning stages. Zenn wondered why I couldn't just voice-order the guards around like I did yesterday. He had a valid point.

Perhaps that's what I'd do. I purposely didn't have a game plan; then I wouldn't freak when it didn't work the way I'd envisioned. I read through Trek's list of preparations and thought he'd done more than enough planning for both of us.

He had people stationed outside the Director's office to slow him down. People sending incorrect breach locations. People to unclip all the EOs' hoverboards the night before.

"If you can pass that test in ancient civ today, anything is possible," Zenn said.

"Yeah," I said, hearing the hidden message in his words. What he meant: *If we can bust Jag out of prison, we can take down the Association.* "Yeah."

That afternoon I entered Thane's office for my training session, still stewing over how I'd get Vi's file. I froze. The sight of him staring out his newly installed windows did little to calm me—nothing new there. But today he wasn't alone.

Director Hightower also loitered at the glass, looking down his nose at the city below. Immediately I thought, *Rise Twelve, Rise Twelve, Rise Twelve.* My heart rate doubled as I tried to bury those two words under something else.

All I could think of was kissing Raine while we flew outside after hours.

If the Director was here, it could mean anything. He could know about the midnight sneak-outs. The dietary citations. Kissing Raine.

He might know I was responsible for the break-in at the Confinement Rise.

Because even though nothing had been said, nothing over the transmissions last night, nothing at school today, surely the Director *knew.*

I swallowed hard and tried to wipe my sweaty palms dry in my coat pockets. I thought about school, about ancient civilizations, about engineering, about my strict genetics Educator who wouldn't let me leave class five minutes early so I could make it here on time.

"Come in, Gunn," Thane said without turning from the window.

I wiped my mouth, as if the memory of Raine's lips would

somehow be visible to her father. He turned as I lowered myself into the ergonomic and, stars alive, he could see everything. His gaze lingered first on my kissed-by-Raine mouth, then traveled to my *please don't kill me* eyes, my too-long hair, and landed on my clenched-into-fists hands.

"Hello, Gunner," he said, pleasantlike but with a river of ice underneath. He pulled the curtain closed, eliminating all sunlight.

"Good afternoon, Director." My voice came out hollow, yet still veined with fear.

"I invited the Director to sit in today," Thane began. "He's always taken a special interest in our voice students."

I bet he has, I thought. I somehow managed to arrange my mouth into a close-lipped smile.

The silence that ensued drove my already frayed nerves into a frenzy. The Director didn't look away from me as he settled in a second chair that had been positioned behind Thane's desk. He steepled his fingers. "So, Gunner, how's Starr Messenger?"

My throat dried up. "She's fine."

"My reports say you haven't spent much time together lately."

My stomach sank. His reports? Of course his junior assistant would have to send him something on me. "I've been busy here over the past few weeks," I said. "Starr understands."

"Does she?" The Director clasped his hands together, gazed at my mouth. I rubbed my hand self-consciously over my lips, expecting my fingers to come away black or something.

The all-knowing Director smirked. I made a mental note to log some hours with Starr, stat.

"We believe some recreational activity sessions might help," the Director said. "Beginning next weekend, you and Starr will have mandatory free time together."

"Super," I said, half-believing myself and wholly knowing I wouldn't be here next weekend for "mandatory free time."

The Director's smile faded. "So, Gunner, I have a few questions."

"Okay." I did my best to keep the tremor out of my voice. I felt pinned by his gaze, the same way I had when he'd spoken in my mom's memory. I tried to imagine how Zenn would play this. I leaned back, swept something invisible from my shirtsleeves. "Shoot."

The Director's lips thinned into a smile while I contemplated my word choice. "As a voice, can you manipulate clones?"

I almost scoffed. "Of course." What a weird question. Anyone could manipulate a clone.

"What about Mechs?"

"Yes and no," I said, again surprised at the question. "Robots don't have a brain to be affected by the sound of my—a voice. But they generally do whatever a human tells them."

"Unless?" the Director prompted.

"Unless otherwise programmed," I answered.

"What about Enforcement Officers?" the Director asked.

"I believe they undergo extensive training to block voice power, sir."

He cut a quick glance at Thane, who took a chip out of his wrist port and deposited it in the slots carved into his desk supports, seemingly bored by the convo.

"Very good, Gunner." The Director leaned forward, and the brown in his eyes seemed to deepen into shades of gray and black. "What about Confinement Rise guards?"

My tongue felt too heavy for my mouth. Saliva pooled because I couldn't swallow. "I don't know, sir," I managed to say. "I've never encountered any Confinement Rise guards." I purposely kept my eyes on the Director so I wouldn't look at Thane. Apparently he hadn't told the Director about my escapade in the Confinement Rise. Or had he?

"But you've met EOs?" The emotions coming from the Director bordered on aggressive, yet he put forth the picture of passivity.

My foot bounced about fifty times a second, and I worked to calm it. "Well, yeah. They've come recruiting at my house. You know, because of the flying."

The Director nodded. "Yes, of course. What kind of voice do you think it would take to brainwash an Enforcement Officer?"

"A pretty powerful one."

The Director looked at Thane again, who acted like he hadn't heard the line of questioning. "What about a Thinker?"

I breathed in, smelling something in the office I never had before. Antiseptic. I shook my head, not sure what the Director was getting at or what the new scent meant. "I don't understand."

"He doesn't understand." The Director aimed his words toward Thane.

"He understands fine," Thane retorted before focusing on me. I couldn't figure out what game he was playing, but I felt like I had a major role.

With both of them glaring in my direction and my barely contained fury covering all other emotions, I stood up. The Director relaxed into his chair, but his jaw muscles twitched.

The tension in the room settled in my shoulders, along my back. I waited one, two, three breaths before saying, "Are we done?"

"Hardly," Thane answered. "Sit down, Gunner."

The power in his tone slammed into me. I could withstand the control, and to prove it to him, I took my time returning to my ergonomic.

"See? He understands fine." Something came through in Thane's words. Annoyance? Sure enough, I watched it pass through his eyes as he looked at the Director. And something like pleading shone in his irises when he locked on to me again. I wished he'd unlock his feelings so I could get a better read on what the hell I was supposed to do. But he kept them boxed up tight-tight-tight.

Interesting.

"Tell me what you understand, Gunner," the Director commanded. This time the control tactic came in my mind, not my ears. The Director possessed no voice power, but he made me think I'd been waiting for ages to tell him what I understood.

"If you're asking me if voices can brainwash Thinkers, then the answer is yes." My explanation came out in clipped syllables.

"Can you brainwash me?" His question sounded like a challenge.

I thought of Thane punching his way through the window. I looked at the silver floor and found myself mirrored there. Angry lines shadowed my eyes, and my mouth was set in defiance. No matter how hard I tried, I couldn't erase my fury.

I didn't want to.

I met the Director's gaze. "I believe I can, sir."

Everything in the room stilled. The awkward staring contest was broken by the Director's words. "I believe you can too, Mr. Jameson." Half a heartbeat passed. "Why don't you try it right now?"

This was my chance to get Vi's file. I narrowed my eyes at Director Hightower, willing all other distractions to fade into the background. With my—and his—cache off, I connected to him. *Forward me Violet Schoenfeld's complete file.*

His nostrils flared; his eyes glazed. From somewhere beyond my awareness, an alarm sounded. But in my realm only the Director existed.

You didn't say please, Thane coached over my cache. I didn't dare look at him, but was he mocking me?

Please. I kept my gaze locked with Director Hightower. *Forward me Violet Schoenfeld's complete file. Please.*

A moment later I received a holy-huge doc from Director Hightower. I shouldered my backpack and left Thane's office—for good.

Thane let me go, no questions asked.

Very interesting.

* * *

I went to the one person Thane and Director Hightower wanted me to: Starr. I had no idea how long it would be before they came looking for me. I wanted to get rid of Vi's file as soon as possible, and even if she didn't want to, Starr would help me. When I knocked on her door, I realized I'd be telling her good-bye too.

"Gunn," she said after she opened the door, her eyebrows so high I couldn't see them through her super-yellow bangs.

"Hey." I leaned against the doorframe, suddenly exhausted. "Got a sec?"

She recovered nicely by painting a perfect smile on her somehow-already-glossed lips. She shrugged into her coat and hat. We strolled down the street without speaking, the sky swirling with snowflakes.

I knew she was waiting for me to explain myself. After all, I'd never shown up at her flat before; I was as surprised as she was that I even knew she lived in Rise Six.

But I needed her. Desperately. She was an Insider; she would understand. "Starr," I started.

"Shut up, Gunner." She stopped suddenly in the middle of the sidewalk. "How could you kiss her?"

I remained silent as Starr's anger assaulted me. And once she started lecturing, she couldn't stop. "You're really messing things up. And not just you-know-what stuff, but breaking into prison? Kissing other girls? You could get into some serious trouble. This is more than citations. This is major protocol-shattering stuff, Gunner." Her tone increased in both volume and pitch until I thought my eardrums would explode. None of it mattered anyway. I wasn't going to be around long enough to shatter protocol.

"Starr, stop," I said, without using my voice.

She stopped. Finally.

"I need you, okay?" I said, feeling like the world's raging-est loser. "I'm going to send you a file that you can't show to anyone. You can't delete it, and if anyone asks—especially AD Myers—about it, you have to lie for me. I need you to give it to Raine as quick as you can. Okay?"

She nodded, her bottom lip quivering. I hadn't realized she was crying during her tirade. It didn't make sense. "Why are you crying?"

She wiped her face and glared. "You make me so mad. Whether we want to be or not, we're in this together. When you get in trouble, so do I."

She was right. Raine's friendship with Cannon made much more sense now.

She sighed. "Send me the file," she said just as I asked, "Who would you pick?"

"What?"

I loaded the file into an e-comm. "Who would you pick?" I sent the message, deleted the e-comm from Director High-tower. Now, no matter who asked, I had no evidence Thane could use against me. Of course, I'd put Starr in danger until she could unload the file, but she had more experience with subterfuge. She'd be fine.

She shifted her weight from one foot to the other.

"Who?" I asked.

"You won't like him," she warned.

"You don't like Raine."

She sighed. "It's not that I don't like Raine. It's . . ."

"It's what?" I was totally confused and obviously missing something.

"You're mine," Starr said, shrugging.

I shook my head. "But you don't even like me!"

"I told you you wouldn't like it."

"No," I said. "You said I wouldn't like *him*."

A half smile lifted her lips. "Trek."

"No," I said automatically. "No way. No way *in hell*. You're mine."

"You're both mine."

I froze at the sound of that voice.

"AD Myers," Starr said cheerfully. She slipped her arm into mine. "We were just taking a walk. Care to join us?"

Raine

**22.** I watched Gunn stride out of Rise Nine, his hands fisted inside his coat pockets. An overpowering want sang through me. I caught myself just as his name threatened to leave my mouth. I ended up biting my lip to keep the sound contained.

He moved with purpose, heading north. Curiosity nagged at me, and I almost followed him. But I didn't want to go stalker on him, and I wasn't supposed to care where he went, so I ascended to his flat instead.

Zenn let me in without a question or even so much as a raised eyebrow.

"Wow, your place is clean," I said, noting the spotless

surfaces—and the sweet scramblers in the ceiling.

"For a while," Zenn replied easily. He settled into one ergonomic and gestured to the other one as if to say, *Sit, tell me everything.*

I sat. I told him everything in bursts of breath and words. Where Gunn had immediately dismissed my ideas about partial voice control, Zenn leaned forward, his eyes sparking with energy.

"Interesting," he whispered. "Talents are as wide and varied as the earth—which is why I personally believe we'll never be able to clone them. Maybe it has something to do with your . . . other ability."

Worry seethed beneath my muscles, making them tight. When I'd touched Vi and then kissed Gunn, I hadn't been able to see anything. But I didn't dare tell Zenn that.

"That's a seeing talent," Zenn mused. "But I have to agree with Gunner. I've never heard of partial voice power." He looked at something on his vision-screen, making him seem unreachable.

I said nothing. I needed Vi's file to really be able to awaken anything useful. An old hairstyle couldn't help the Insiders—or Gunn and Jag. I knew Vi possessed considerable talent, otherwise she wouldn't be my flatmate.

"If I understand this correctly, you can see what people

want most, right?" Zenn asked, glancing up to the ceiling. I followed his gaze and found the scrambler blinking with blue light. Even as I inhaled, the frequency increased. We only had a few minutes without surveillance left.

"Quickly, Raine."

"Yes. And then I see what will happen if they get it." Something dawned in my mind. "So what Vi wants most is to be free," I said slowly. "And I'm able to help her with that because . . ."

"You're there to listen," Zenn supplied.

"Yeah, but you've been there too," I argued. "This makes no sense." Another glance at the blue light showed it pulsing so quickly it was almost solid.

"But I—" Zenn started. He leaned forward, his eyes hot and scared. "I'm Informant. I've done very little. I taught her some songs her mother used to sing. That's it."

"I'll work with her," I whispered, disappointed Zenn hadn't been doing anything for eight solid months. A faint whining sound filtered down from the ceiling. "She doesn't sleep well, and after Gunn and Jag leave—"

Don't say that name! The assistant's voice crashed over my cache, eliminating the rest of my spoken sentence.

Zenn jumped to his feet, so I did too. The blue light in the ceiling had vanished, and so had Zenn. As an insistent knock came on the door, I saw his silhouette as he stepped from the balcony onto a hoverboard.

I'd taken one step to follow him when the voice spoke.

Get the door, Raine. And please stop saying that name. You're not supposed to know who he is.

All right, all right, I mumbled back to the assistant. *You could've warned me his name was flagged.* I knew this person was risking everything. His family, his job, his life. For me. For the Insiders. But still. His patronizing monotone annoyed me.

Hello? I did warn you.

Which was true and only served to further ignite my anger. I flung Gunn's door open. My rage fled, replaced by a cold fear. A gasp escaped my lips. Then I pulled myself together, packaging every emotion deep inside.

"Hey, Dad. What's up?" My voice hardly shook at all.

"I rescheduled our family dinner for tonight." Dad glanced over my shoulder and scanned the empty flat. "And you're late."

The trip to the glass and chrome ~~prison~~ dining room passed in silence. Dad hadn't said anything more at Gunn's before I slunk behind him with my head down.

The air in the dining room suffocated me. Tech lights glinted off the silver platters and crystal goblets. Dad settled at the head of the table and fixed me with a hard glare until I slumped into my chair opposite him. Clones served the first course: a rich, earthy soup.

Dad ate slowly, as if to prolong my punishment by keeping me in this wretched room. "Eat, Rainey."

He didn't say it in kindness, but as a command. My hand automatically moved to my spoon, and I dipped into the pumpkin curry soup. It burned all the way down my throat. After one bite, I deliberately replaced my spoon on the glass tabletop.

"Just say it, Dad."

"You should not have been in that flat tonight."

But that's not why he practically busted the door down.

He laid his silverware down with angry clinks. "You must be more careful about where you're seen, who you're seen with."

"Seen by who?" I asked. "This is ridiculous. People only see what *you* want them to see."

"Well, someone saw *you* flying last night."

The perfect excuse stuck in my throat, and a strangled squeak came out instead. Cold dread filled my stomach. My hands trembled. I pressed them firmly against the glass to quiet them.

"I have permission to fly at night," I said. "*Your* permission."

"That Jameson boy left the track just before you. Did you happen to see him?"

"Gunner?" My voice came out too high. I took a quick drink and managed not to slop water down the front of my shirt. "No, I didn't see him. He has an ultrasweet hoverboard. That thing is dead silent."

Dad nodded and waved his hand. A clone entered with the main course. The roast duck gleamed a golden brown under the bright lights. I pushed the wild rice around on my plate, hoping the conversation had ended.

Five minutes later Dad launched into the worst lecture of my life. I hadn't spent enough time worrying about Cannon; I hadn't filed any reports re: Violet for the past week (apparently being unconscious isn't a good enough excuse); I'd let myself get distracted by Gunner.

Each word seared into my mind. I felt naked before him, his razor-wire voice cutting through my every defense. I kept my eyes on the table in an effort to close the one-sided discussion.

"You might find Gunner strangely absent if you can't pull yourself together," he said, and I jerked my head up. Dad's expression remained steely.

"Your actions have consequences, and not only for yourself. Other people are influenced by your choices." He wiped his mouth with his napkin. "Zenn could probably use a reminder of his responsibilities as my junior assistant. I'll speak to him in the morning."

He folded his arms on the table and leaned forward to drive his point home. "And you know, Raine, a boy should be able to properly motivate his match. I'll schedule *another* chat with Cannon." He said "another" like it would be the *last* meeting with Cannon.

"No." I shook my head, conceding. Horror snaked through me at the thought of my dad hurting Cannon. "Please don't do that, Dad. You're right."

"Of course I'm right, Rainey. I always am."

An hour later I'd e-commed Cannon again. I was bordering on stalker status with the comms. But he still hadn't answered. Guilt twisted in my stomach. He'd had to meet with my father about his citation, and I hadn't heard from him since.

I took a deep breath and composed a message to Flare Riding, Cannon's last crush. Maybe she'd seen him while I'd been out of commission. Her reply came less than thirty seconds later. *Haven't heard from him. Sorry.*

I lay in my dark room listening to Vi mutter in her sleep. Gunn was leaving in three days, yet I could still feel the gentle pressure of his mouth against mine. I smelled the toasty, male scent of his skin. My hand felt empty without his.

I'd definitely gone too far with my Gunn fantasy. I forced him from my mind, and in the blank space Zenn's face came forward. He didn't deserve to be punished for my mistakes, even if he wasn't doing anything for Vi.

And if he didn't, Cannon certainly didn't. After everything went down on Monday, I'd find out why he hadn't been at school. I'd play the perfect best friend, the perfect match.

Tears filled with helplessness splashed over my cheeks. *I have no choice. I have to comply.* Because my dad was right about one thing: My actions had consequences for everyone I knew.

So I stuffed my wants into the dark space in my soul until I couldn't feel them anymore.

Then I commed Cannon again.

Gunner

People talked around me, but I couldn't construct the noise into meaning. Flowers and fresh-cut grass and the scent of rain filled the air. My flat didn't smell like this, yet I lay in a bed; the squishiness of blankets and pillows cradled my body.

I couldn't remember the last thing I'd been doing. I struggled to sit up, to open my eyes. When neither of those things happened, I tried to call out, but only managed a hoarse cry.

Then warm hands brushed my forehead. "Settle down, Gunner."

Starr? I thought, hoping I still had an operating cache.

Yes, it's me.

Where am I? Why can't I get up?

A shuffling of feet sounded somewhere to my right. "No, he's not awake," Starr said. Something in her tone convinced me that I needed to feign sleep. I immediately tried to even my breathing, lie still. No one spoke, but the footsteps exited the room.

We don't have much time, Gunner. The bed shifted as Starr sat down and fidgeted.

Time for what? I asked, more afraid than I wanted to admit. Starr wasn't generally nervous/scared enough to squirm.

Thane is insisting he accompany you back to your flat. I told him you needed to sleep for a couple of hours.

I felt like I could heave at any moment. The heat of her body contrasted with the icy veins of sickness snaking through my body. *What does he want?*

He asked about a file. I told him to search your mind. That's why you can't get up. He . . . well, he really dug deep.

Starr—

I didn't tell him. I sent the file to my e-board and erased the e-comm. You just need to rest. You haven't been sleeping much, have you, Gunner?

I didn't answer, because the deep shadows under my eyes had already said everything.

I have a couple of things I need to tell you, Starr chatted.

Her trepidation swirled with the lilac scent in the room. The bed moved as she stood up.

I know you're looking for a journal. Even in thought, her voice sounded strange. Controlling. *We're all counting on you, Gunner.*

I turned toward where I thought she sat; only a black space stared back. Starr hesitated. I felt like she was hovering above me.

"I made a memory chip for you." Her spoken-out-loud words burn burn burned in my ears. Her breath breezed across my cheek, blazing hot. "Don't watch it until you're gone. Don't tell anyone. Okay?"

An army of questions marched across my mind. Who else knew I was leaving? Did Thane? She'd said he'd read my mind . . .

"Gunner? We're in this together, right?"

Yeah, I chatted her.

"Good." She placed her burning palm in my jeans pocket, leaving a microchip behind with the memory of her voice, her smell.

Her delicate footfalls echoed back to me. As did her voice when she said, "He's all yours."

I lay limp on my hoverboard. A high-pitched whine emanates from it: a warning to recharge the power supply, stat. But I can barely lift my head, let alone worry about my now-plunging hoverboard.

My throat scratches with each breath. Every muscle in my body aches. The little patch of sky I see holds only the unforgiving chill of winter. My bones throb with the cold, my teeth clench.

The whining increases. The board pitches downward. If I'd had anything to eat, I would've jacked it up. My angry stomach rolls as the ground nears.

I crash, hard. But it's just another layer of pain on top of a mountain of hurt. I close my eyes, knowing I need to get up, run, hide.

I can't.

Someone says, "It's an outsider," and I want to protest. He has it all wrong. I'm an Insider, and I need help—in more ways than one.

"Don't touch him," someone else says, a girl.

I manage to open my eyes in time to see a gold-ring-wearing hand holding a needle and plunging toward my neck.

I woke up yelling. "Stop! Wait!" I thrashed, finding my jean-less legs tangled in blankets. And not mine. The smell in the room was the same as it had been earlier, when Starr was here with me. The only thing missing was her floral perfume.

I shoved the blankets away, panic fully rising. "What's going on?"

"You're nightmaring," a robotic voice said.

"Where am I?" My voice power coated my tongue, reverberated in the still, unscented air.

"Rise Twelve, room two hundred thirty-seven."

Rise Twelve! Wait. Rise Twelve?

"Lights." Soft tech lights breathed some life into the room. Sterile from wall to wall, at least I could see I was alone in a chrome room with only a single bed for decoration. "Whose room is two hundred thirty-seven?"

"Gunner Jameson's."

I suppressed the urge to shout profanities at the useless computer. "Whose room was it before it was mine?"

"Empty."

"Super," I muttered. "Where's Thane Myers?"

"Asleep in his flat. Sixteenth floor."

I opened my mouth to ask another question, but I stopped short. My heart slap-slap-slapped against my rib cage. Asleep in his flat on the sixteenth floor? Asleep in his flat on the sixteenth floor—of Rise Twelve?

Thane knew what was going on in Rise Twelve?

Impossible.

"Thane Myers is asleep on the sixteenth floor of Rise Twelve?" I asked.

"Yes."

"Is he . . . is he the Thinker of this Rise?"

The wall remained silent. The room held no dressers, no clothes. I stood up, wearing only my boxers, and activated my cache, intending to infiltrate the database and find out as much as I could about Rise Twelve. A red band streaked across the middle of my vision-screen as it came to life.

"Watched," I whispered. I checked the time: 3:49 a.m., and immediately shut down the cache. Someone would know I'd woken up, manually turned on my cache to check the time. No way I could hack into the database now, techno-path or not.

The assistant had been protecting me since I'd joined the Insiders. Yet the red band burned behind my eyes. I wondered where the assistant was now. Did s/he know I was here in Rise Twelve, being watched?

I couldn't sit around and wait for help. The only entrance/exit was a white door opposite the bed. Two vents poured breathable air from the ceiling.

I paced to the door and back to the bed, trying to quell the desperate need to get—out—of—here. With every step, the walls seemed to press closer, smothering, choking, caging.

I swallowed hard, tried to breathe. The air filled my lungs like sludge, heavy and dark. Fury mixed with panic mixed with fear, and my own skin felt too restrictive.

I had to get out of the confining room. I couldn't live another second in—

The door clicked behind me. I spun, my chest heaving. I expected Director Hightower to saunter in, tech scalpels and microchips at the ready.

Nothing happened. The air swirled. My heartbeat pulsed in my neck. My palms dampened.

After one, two, three agonizing minutes, I strode toward the door and lifted the latch.

It opened. Just swung right in, leaving me to face a long white hallway.

I was alone in Rise Twelve. I'd taken two steps when I dismissed the idea of Thane being this building's Thinker. For one thing, he wouldn't be asleep when his uncontrolled people were awake.

And the Citizens of this Rise had the opposite schedule from the rest of us. I didn't want to meet any of them now, though, wearing only boxer shorts. I hurried toward the end of the hall, where a slight bluish glow seeped under the door there.

The latch lifted easily, allowing me to slip into a room filled with blazing lights on the floor. Ascenders to go up. Descenders to go down.

"Which one to get to the sixteenth floor?" I asked.

Instead of responding verbally, the lights on the floor dimmed until only one remained: a bright orange box.

Super, I thought. A box = the embodiment of my life.

One ascender ride later, I stood on a posh carpet that ran down the center of a shiny, silver floor. Instead of the traditional doorways lining the hall, the sixteenth floor only had one door, way down at the end.

Without thinking, I moved toward it. Like I could get in the flat. Like I *wanted* to get in. I stood outside it, listening.

I don't know what I expected to hear. Thane's snores? The pad of his feet against the luxurious carpets as he got up to use the bathroom? The scuttle of guard-spider legs?

I heard nothing.

The door had a simple latch. No iris scanner. No fingerprint portlet. None of the same security that existed in every other building in the city.

I put my fingers on the latch, lifted it.

The door swung open. The smell of an engineering lab hit me full force. Chemicals and smoke and metal and tech. The scent didn't mesh with the fancy fluted mirror on the wall. Or the vase of flowers on the side table just inside the door.

My feet seemed to have a mind of their own, because the next thing I knew, I'd entered the flat and gently shut the door behind me.

Whoever lived here either (a) took extreme care of their home or (b) had some serious spider maid service. Not a spot of dust existed anywhere. The latest tech gadgets filled the kitchen, which I could see from my position just inside the door. Every surface flashed with a yellow light, which meant they were equipped with p-screens.

Three doors and two hallways led out of the main living area. I didn't dare take a full breath for fear it would make too much noise. I stood rooted to the spot, trying to figure out how I'd come to be in this place. Wearing only my underwear.

The tech in the flat zipped through me, spicy and alive. I reached out and touched the mirror. Instantly, a two-columned menu popped up. My finger automatically went to an item labeled *Citations*.

Three options appeared: *Waived*, *Addressed*, and *Pending*. Each one had a number in brackets, indicating how many citations had been processed that day.

I touched *Pending (15)*.

Three things happened at once.

One, I stumbled backward into the door because fifteen citations came up on the mirror. They all had my name on them. *They all have my name on them.*

Two, the mirror said, "Identity confirmation needed to

execute citation options." Beneath the list, twelve names appeared as pushable buttons. Twelve names = one Thinker for each of the Rises, including this one.

Thane's name was listed at the bottom. *Thane's name is listed at the bottom.*

Three, a series of loud thumps sounded from somewhere down one of the hallways off the living area.

I fumbled with the latch and scrambled out of the flat. "Direct me to the nearest hoverboard," I breathed through unmoving lips, desperate to leave without getting caught. "On quarter sound."

"Tenth floor," the wall whispered.

When I reached the descender and turned back, a man stood in the hallway, frowning in my direction. I couldn't tell if it was Thane or not. It could've been, but a lot of men have dark hair and pale skin.

Right? Yeah, totally, a lot of men have dark hair and pale skin, especially in Freedom.

The man raised his hand as if telling me to *come back,* but I said, "Tenth floor," and descended the hell out of there.

After three turns, endless white hallways, and entering a coded room, I stood on a hoverboard, ready to launch through a portal.

The frigid February night sliced at my bare skin as I flew. I felt it, felt it deeply, and crouched on the board in an attempt to preserve body heat.

Like that worked.

By the time I arrived on Raine's balcony, the only part of my body I could feel was my barely beating heart.

Raine

24.

Through the thickness of sleep, something tapped. And tapped. And tapped. Which was strange, because I was walking through peach-scented orchards in my dream, and tapping shouldn't exist. Still, it lingered, beating against my subconscious.

I didn't wake up until I felt the pressure in the room change. Someone had opened the sliding glass door to the balcony.

"You're a boy," Vi said as I came back to full awareness. "Lights. Why aren't you wearing any clothes?"

As the lights came up, Vi stepped back. She cried out and covered her mouth with her hand. "Raine, get over here."

Gunn had dropped to his knees, shivering violently, wearing only his underwear. His skin looked a ghastly gray, rough and textured like cement. I fumbled out of bed, dragging my quilt with me. I flung it around Gunn before yanking the sliding door shut.

"I know him," Vi was chanting. "I know him, I know him, I know him."

"He's come over before," I told her. "It's my friend—"

"Jag," she said at the same time I practically yelled, "Gunn."

A sharp hiss sounded over my cache, but no alarm came to life. No EOs started beating down the door.

"Don't say that name," I whispered, rubbing my hands over Gunn's shoulders in a futile attempt to warm him. "And this isn't—him. This is Gunner."

Gunn raised his head when I said his name. His eyes looked vacant. "I'm s-so c-cold."

Vi knelt in front of him, stroking one hand over his face. She explored his cheekbones, his forehead, and down his nose. Both Gunn and I stared at her, and I'm sure I was putting off some serious *what the hell?* vibes.

Finally Vi looked at me. "You're sure he's not—"

"Don't say it," I cut her off. "That name is flagged." I pulled Gunn to his feet and supported his weight. "Come on. Get in bed."

He collapsed on my bed, wrapped in my blanket.

"I'll get the warming blanket," Vi said.

I watched him shiver and shake, unsure of what to do next. I pulled the quilt off Vi's bed, wrapped it around myself, and snuggled in next to him.

His breathing came quick and shallow at first. It sounded like my mind felt. Sharp. Frenzied.

Vi returned with the warming blanket and covered both me and Gunn with it. She hummed the same melody she had for me. It vibrated through her throat, rising and falling, finally forming into words.

I closed my eyes, allowing the comfort in the words to seep into my pores. I'd never heard the song before Vi had voiced it; music wasn't meant for the masses. Too thought-provoking, Dad said. But listening to Vi, I wanted to hear the lullaby again and again.

The lyrics calmed back into a throaty hum, and Gunn seemed more relaxed. But I couldn't shake the way Vi had looked at him. How she'd called him Jag. Sure, the last time I'd seen Jag he'd been beaten up pretty bad, but I didn't think he and Gunn looked that much alike.

Certainly not enough to be mistaken for each other. For one thing, Gunn's lighter brown hair hung longer—"No way."

"What?" Vi whispered from her position on the floor.

In answer, I reached up and ran my fingers through Gunn's hair. His enhanced—and trimmed—hair. If I had to guess, I'd say it was about the same length as Jag's had been last week.

"What happened to your hair?" I asked him, pressing my face into the cocoon of blankets enveloping his head.

"I—I don't know. I woke up in Rise Twelve."

My eyebrows shot up. I searched his face and found the confusion residing in his tea-colored eyes.

Except they weren't tea-colored anymore. I jerked away and almost fell out of bed.

"What happened to your eyes?" I felt like a broken e-board, repeating the same questions.

"What's wrong with them?"

"They're—they're not the right color. Did you get enhancements?" I blinked, and the icy blue of his new eyes beamed on the back of my eyelids.

When I opened my eyes, his stared back in that unnervingly wrong color. His jaw trembled; I felt the tension in his body from throat to toes.

"What else is wrong with me?" he asked.

Absolutely nothing, I wanted to say. Yet everything. I liked Gunn as Gunn, not teched up as Jag. "You're not wearing any clothes."

Something akin to total freak-out crossed through his eyes. "My jeans."

"No jeans," I whispered.

"Starr gave me a microchip. She put it in my jeans pocket." He rolled a bit closer to me, moving his lips until they hovered a few inches from my ear. "She has your file."

I nodded as his lukewarm breath dripped over my neck. I didn't like how "She put it in my jeans pocket" sounded. But I didn't say anything. As we lay there in silence, Gunn's breathing steadied and deepened, sending shivers over my shoulder every few seconds. All the nerves in my body stood at heightened alert despite the thickness of the blankets that separated me from Gunn. The thought of Gunn leaving brought a squirm to my stomach.

I wondered if I'd ever see him again. I immediately recalled the thought as I remembered what I'd seen in Vi's drain.

Gunn would be there. At the end of the world, he'd held my hand. He'd kissed me. And now that I knew what his kiss felt like, my lips yearned to meet his again.

As if he could read my mind, he dislodged his hands and pulled me close. With his eyes closed, he murmured, "Don't worry so much."

Then he kissed me, and his lips seemed as excited as mine to be reunited. I saw nothing except my own fantasies where

Gunn and I could live a life where we could kiss each other whenever we wanted.

Half an hour later my brain still buzzed with unanswered questions and anxiety I couldn't smother. Gunn's steady breathing indicated he was fast asleep. I needed to clear my head, and surely Gunn would sleep for at least an hour. I could get to the hoverboard track and back before he even knew I was gone.

I'd slipped out of bed, bundled myself in my winter coat, and stood on the balcony before I heard Vi say, "Wait for me."

Fact: Violet Schoenfeld has never flown on a hoverboard. And if she has, well, she hasn't.

The girl swerved all over the place, all yelping cries and flailing arms. At this rate, the entire squad of EOs would find us before we even made it to the track.

"Bend your knees." I flew in close to her, whispering. "There, like that. Feel the center? Shift your feet back a little. Yeah, good." I edged away. "No, keep your arms down. Better, better."

At least she was a fast learner. We circled the track in silence. I needed time to think, to sort through what to do next. So many people around me seemed to be coming to a crossroads.

I felt like they were all looking to me, judging how to proceed by watching my choices. This thought weighed heavy in my mind. I analyzed each person whose life was somehow entwined with mine.

Starr: She had Vi's file. I didn't know what Gunn had told her to get her to keep it. More than that, I wondered if Gunn knew all her secrets by now. Or if she knew his. No matter what, she wasn't my biggest enemy.

No, that role belonged solidly to my dad. My jaw tightened at the mere thought of him. If he told me I needed water to survive, I'd never take another sip just to spite him.

A penetrating sadness filled me when I thought of Cannon. He'd nursed me back to health so many times. He played his part without flaw so many times, which left me feeling guilty that I hadn't done the same.

He'd warned me to be careful with Gunner, and I'd failed. And now Cannon had disappeared. My last e-comm to him was still unanswered. Worry seethed with my guilt. If anything happened to him—

I silenced the thought. My throat burned. I inhaled, and my breath entered in icy shudders.

Jag: I didn't know him personally, but everyone on the Inside received a lesson about the Resistance—and thus Jag Barque—early in their training. My success, the Insiders' success, depended largely on getting Jag out of Freedom. Which meant I had to risk losing everything and everyone to do that.

Including Gunn.

That's what it came down to. Losing Gunner to ensure Jag's escape. Losing Gunner to get my dad (and Thane) off my back. Losing Gunner so Starr wouldn't tell the world about my ability. Losing Gunner so I could finally understand the depth of loss Zenn must've felt when he spent every day with the brainwashed version of Vi.

Why did I have to lose the one person I loved most?

"I loved Zenn once, didn't I?" Vi's question brought me out of the dark trench inside myself where I was drowning in unrealized want.

"Yes," I answered. "I think you did."

"He loves me." She said this simply, as if she might be commenting on the weather.

"Yes, he does."

"Like Gunner loves you."

I sucked in a breath. "Gunner doesn't—he and I, we're not—well, I mean, he's matched to someone else."

Vi tossed me a quick look. "They can't dictate who you love." She nosed her board closer to mine. "And I can feel something just under the surface of my skin. Like I know things about people I shouldn't." She paused, and I held my breath. She shook her head, her newly dark hair flopping slightly. "Besides, I don't have to be a Thinker to know. The guy flew straight to you when he needed help. He could've gone to someone else. His match, for example. He didn't. He came to you."

I didn't answer. Instead, I let my hoverboard float aimlessly, mirroring what throbbed in my heart.

"I don't know how to help him," I finally whispered, more to myself than to Vi.

"Sure you do," she answered. "Who knows more than you, Raine? No one I know."

That wasn't saying much. Violet didn't know anyone. But suddenly, I remembered something Cannon had said: "You control the information."

And: "No one can keep secrets from Raine Hightower. Secrets hold power. Raine holds all the power."

And the real kicker: "Every person has a season for knowledge."

Right then, with the stars twinkling overhead and the city of Freedom slumbering beneath, I decided it was Vi's season for knowledge.

No matter the consequences, I had the power (and responsibility) to do two of the hardest things of my life.

1. Give up Gunn.
2. Unbrainwash my flatmate.

One of those would cause a slow internal death. The other might get me killed in a much more efficient way.

"Who taught you that song you sang earlier?" I asked, trying to remember the words, trying to grasp onto something to anchor myself.

Vi's eyebrows creased. "I think . . . I think Zenn did." She shook her head. "No, he just reminded me of it. I think my mom used to sing it to me."

"Music is against protocol." I lowered my voice with each word until I couldn't even hear myself.

"I know," Vi murmured. "Zenn and I do a lot of things that are against protocol." She frowned again. "At least, I think we used to. Now we just watch projections, usually. We used to walk on the beach, I think . . ." Her voice trailed into uncertainty, and I let the winter air infiltrate my lungs to prove to myself that I was still alive.

"Who's that?"

I twisted to find Vi pointing at a crouched figure zooming toward us.

"I don't know," I said. "It's not an Enforcement Officer, they'd have lights—"

Raine, a girl chatted over my cache. *I figured you'd be here. It's me, Starr.*

Gunner

Everyone wants a chance to express who they are, their individuality. That's why Zenn ate toast for every meal, rolled up his shirtsleeves. It's why Raine painted her finger-nails blue every weekend, kissed me in the sky.

It's why Starr lied, joined the Insiders years ago.

That's why I grew my hair too long, tricked out my hover-board with unique voice commands.

So when three pairs of hands grip my shoulders and face, holding me still, I thrash. One silencer skids across the floor, but the other two snake their way to my vocal chords and disable my only real weapon.

My muscles burn in protest as I try to get up. I can't see anything, but I know what a pair of shears sounds like: Incarceration.

Tiny shards of hair itch my neck, tickle my nose. A slow fire builds in my stomach. It's just my hair, but dammit, that takes time to grow back. And time is something I don't have.

But I sit helpless. Someone wipes a cold cloth clumsily across my neck. Clatters and shuffles fill the air, but no voices. They're probably all cache-convoing so I can't identify them.

Fear strikes me hard in the chest. If they're afraid I can ID them, then I know them.

Clawed fingers grasp my hair and pull back, making me tip my face toward the ceiling. My eyes are forced open, but only darkness stares back. Cold drops sting my eyeballs, and I twist my head to the side. Enhancements.

Immediately, gloved hands shove me back into position. More drops. Endless blackness.

Coiling,

    waiting,

        rising fury.

I woke to Raine's timid smile. "Hey," she said. She knelt next to her bed, using her arms as pillows. A loud, angry noise carried in from the bathroom. The balcony door gaped open, filling the room with the sound of driving rain.

"Hey." Everything that needed to be said lived in that word. She searched my face as if trying to decide something important. I knew because she kept licking her lips, which was super distracting.

"You look beautiful." Her hair—still white as ice with that one blue streak—was pulled back on the sides. Her pale skin looked almost translucent.

"Well, you look like . . . him," she said just as softly. "Why is that, Gunn? Why do you look like him?"

The dream flashed across my vision-screen. "Because someone wanted me to."

"Is there a new plan I don't know about?" Raine asked, a dose of resentment creeping into her tone.

"Not that I know of," I said. "What's your plan?"

She regarded me with a lazy cloud of *I could stay in this moment forever* between us. "I'm hoping to distract my dad on Monday by being where I should never be. We think it will buy you some additional time."

"We: you and Vi?"

Sourness puckered her mouth. "No. We: me and Starr."

The hope I held deep inside dangled by a thread. "So did you get . . . ? Did she give you . . . ?"

Outside, thunder shook the sky. Raine closed her eyes; a shiver trembled in her hands. "Yes." She breathed, and I felt like I could lie next to her forever, just breathing together.

"Okay, Gunn, I just have to say this," she said, her eyes still pressed shut. "You won't like it, but I can't let you . . . I mean, you can't . . . well, I just have to say it."

She paused so long, I wondered if she'd changed her mind. The buzzing noise continued in the bathroom, the rain pounded down. *Smart,* I thought. *They're using the weather and tech to cover the conversation.*

"I have a very bad feeling about you leaving. It just—well—it doesn't feel like the right thing to do."

"That's exactly the point, Hightower. It isn't the right thing to do."

She opened her eyes, and I found a secret lurking within.

"What did you see?" I asked.

She jerked as if I'd slapped her, straightened so we didn't share the same breathing space. "Nothing. I didn't touch you."

I thought she may have emphasized "you" a little strongly. I wasn't sure, but in this moment, Raine = a big, fat liar.

A sting of disappointment pricked at my mind. Why didn't Raine trust me? What other secrets did she have locked up?

"Starr left this for you." Raine held out the microchip. "But you still don't have any clothes." A hint of pink flushed her cheeks. "Vi messaged Zenn, and he's bringing some of your things. He should be here in a few."

"Sorry," I said, taking the chip from her, flipping it over and over. "I'm still piecing together the events from last night." Quiet relief grew inside me now that I had the chip back.

She cleared her throat. "It's fine. Nothing I haven't seen before."

Laughter exploded out of my mouth. "Right, because here in Freedom, we get to choose our own clothes! Our own meals! Our own—" I cut myself off before saying "matches!" but Raine heard it anyway.

Now a knot of tension filled my throat, and I coughed it away. "So, Raine, did you, uh, see anything when we, you know, when you kissed me?"

"I kissed you?" A barking laugh came out of her mouth. "I think you kissed me, Gunn."

And I wanted to do it again. "Yeah, okay. So did you see anything?"

Her playfulness disappeared. "Promise you won't tell anyone?"

"For sure," I said, hoping we were playing the same game where we said we wanted to do favors for each other, but we really meant *I love you*.

"When I refused to drain *him*, I haven't been able to see anything since." She lifted one hand toward me slowly. Both of us trained our eyes on the motion until her skin met my cheek.

"I think I'm broken," she whispered. She was beyond broken. More like conflicted into so many pieces, I couldn't separate them into recognizable emotions.

"I'll put you back together," I whispered back before leaning into her touch and forming my mouth to hers.

Raine

26.

Starr Messenger had been matched with Gunn when they were fourteen. They both got placed on the science track (like me), and the machines track (unlike me). Because only students from the science track have the opportunity to work in the Evolutionary Rise, all of us had that option. Only Starr wanted it. No big deal.

What was a big deal was how much she knew.

The conversation in the sky had me buzzing. Starr knew about the Insiders. She knew I was an Insider. She'd joined a week after her fourteenth birthday. Another win for her; she always figured things out first.

She knew about Gunn—about everything.

And damn, the girl talked so freakin' fast. I'd barely had time to process anything before she was a streak against the horizon. I'd been left with Vi's file in my cache, a memory chip in my hand, and a new theory about the identity of the assistant racing through my mind.

She had the tech to do it.

Because she had access to my father.

I kissed Gunn with the rain lashing the balcony and Vi tech-drying her already bone-dry hair so no one (Thane) could monitor the way my heartbeat spiked, no one (my dad) would log the moan of longing that emanated from Gunn's throat when I trailed my fingers across his smooth shoulders, and no one (and I mean *no one*) could tell me who I may or may not kiss.

For those few minutes my life belonged to me.

Then the tech-dryer switched off, Vi marched into the room to pull the sliding glass door shut, and Zenn buzzed into our flat through the front door.

I left my bedroom so Gunn could get dressed. My body ached to be close to his in a way I'd never experienced before.

Vi served a stack of toast to Zenn and scrambled eggs to me.

"Morning, Raine," Zenn said around a mouthful of bread.

I grunted a "morning" and wondered how long it took someone to pull on a shirt and some jeans. A few minutes later Gunn joined us at the table, his skin the color of old oatmeal.

"What's wrong?" I asked him.

"I look like—"

Silence pressed down. I glanced around the flat with the same jerky movements as Zenn and Vi.

Vi shot Gunner a glare. "You guys better fly."

Zenn stood, kissed Vi on the forehead, and disappeared into our bedroom. Gunn sat there until the alarm sounded and the scarlet lasers of spider eyes beamed under the gap in the door. Then he scampered after Zenn real quick, leaving me and Vi to deal with the insects.

I didn't get it. We hadn't even said Jag's name.

While Vi allowed the spiders to search our flat as part of their routine inspection, I stepped into the shower. I barely had time to wash my hair, because I'd opened Vi's file. It started with easy things—school (algae collecting? Really?), her match (Zenn, since age fourteen), and her rule-breaking episodes (eight in all).

Her obsession with her hair was noted on page two. Her tendency to skip rocks in the lake and visit off-limits areas was fully detailed on pages four through eleven.

Her trial in the Goodgrounds and her subsequent escape with one Jag Barque took up the next fifteen pages.

All these things helped make Vi into a real person, not the brainwashed shell I'd been living with for eight months. Finally, on the second to last page, I found a list of "Possibly disconcerting items."

1. Seems fascinated by the ocean.
2. Enjoys meat, especially ham.
3. Wishes on stars.
4. Particularly attached to Tyson.
5. Doesn't give up.

The last one made my breath catch. The gasp echoed in the silent chamber, the five-minute shower long since over. I shivered as the circulators forced air across my damp skin.

I left the file open as I dried myself and got dressed. I settled on my bed, chewing on my thumbnail. I wondered about Tyson, and if he meant as much to Vi as Jag did.

Vi had a tangled net inside, with twists and knots of misinformation and brainwashing. I felt a tingling in my gut. I could undo this mess. I could make Violet herself again. She could be free.

And if she could be, then maybe, just maybe, so could I.

"They're gone," Vi announced from the doorway. "I hate the routine inspections."

I swung my head toward her, taking in the scattered hairdo, the slightly baggy jeans, the standard-issue, eggshell-colored, long-sleeved shirt. Her face held no inkling that anything odd had happened here last night.

"Great, thanks." I motioned her to join me on the bed. "So, Vi, what shirt should I wear today? The green one or the red one?"

She crinkled her face and kneaded her fingers on the fabric of her jeans. "I don't understand. The closet just gives you a shirt. They aren't even colored." She looked down at hers, as if to make sure it hadn't been dyed.

I sighed. I didn't understand how she could be so lucid while flying with me, but now didn't even understand the concept of choice. "But if you could choose, which color would you pick?"

"But I don't choose. There's no need to even think about it." Her words could've streamed from Thane's mouth. And I realized that they probably did.

"Turn off your cache," I murmured. I felt certain Vi was on the Watched list, and she probably didn't even know it.

Vi balked, leaning away from me with her pulse bobbing in her throat. "I don't know how."

"Sure you do." My words ghosted across the widening space between us.

Vi stood up, moved toward the balcony, and closed her eyes in a long blink. When she opened them again, I thought they seemed a little clearer.

"Forget clothes," I said. "Which do you like better: Red or green?"

A frown marred her face, and I wanted to scream. So I did. Loud and long, I let my frustration out in one high note.

When I finished, Vi stared at me like I'd sprouted horns in my forehead. I took a step toward her. "Don't think. Just answer. The first thing that comes to your mind, okay?"

She swallowed hard, fear skating through her eyes. But she nodded.

"Okay, good. Red or green?"

"Green." Her answer came out in a rush.

"Blue or yellow?"

"Yellow."

"Eggs or pancakes?"

"Pancakes."

"Long hair or short?"

"Short." Her voice gained strength with this answer.

"Morning person or night owl?"

Her hands relaxed. "Night owl."

"Happy or sad?"

Confusion darted across her face. "Right now I'm okay," she said.

"Right or wrong?"

Another wave of confusion passed through her eyes. "Neither."

"Then what are you?"

"What am I? Or who?" Vi scrutinized me, and I could hear her saying, *"About time, Gunner,"* in my head in that same tone. The one that held a hint of cockiness, of pure authority. I felt the slow burn of Gunner's hand in mine. I saw the individual raindrops on his skin when he pressed his lips to my forehead. I smelled the smoke as Freedom burned below us.

"Who are you?" I amended.

"I'm Violet Schoenfeld. Who are you?"

"I'm Raine Hightower," I said, as if I were someone important.

Vi took quick steps toward me. "You are important, Raine."

"Can you read minds?"

"Yes."

"What else can you do?"

Vi's gaze lasered into me, burning, probing, controlling. "Everything," she said.

I winced, though I tried not to. My next question included the name Tyson, but I bit it back in favor of something more pressing. "Why can't you remember these things all the time?"

She shook her head, like she was trying to dislodge the memories so she could examine them fully on her vision-screen. "I don't know. But with the cache off, it's much easier." She glanced behind her. "What's that whining noise?"

"Our warning," I said. "You'll have to turn the cache back on, Vi. They're monitoring you."

"Who is?"

"Thane, my dad, lots of people."

She nodded, her mouth set into a grim line.

"Just one more question," I said quickly. "Zenn or . . . ?"

She didn't answer.

Gunner

27

Once again, I flew away from Raine when she needed me most. I hadn't detected any frustration from her, or any hurt feelings, but still. What kind of guy abandoned his girl? Once, maybe. But this was, like, the third time.

Zenn navigated toward our flat, but I couldn't go there now. I needed to be out in the open, not confined by walls. So many had sprung up in my life, and not just physically.

Every relationship boxed me in, made me say good-bye when I didn't want to.

Every feeling reminded me that I was someone special. And never, ever alone.

So I nosed my board south, then angled it toward the ocean. I tried to empty my mind, but it filled with pieces of last night.

"He's all yours."

As Starr says those words, a sharp pain radiates through my chest. Not a physical wound, but an emotional gash. What is she playing at? I clutch the microchip in my jeans pocket, desperately willing my eyes to take in some light, see something.

I can't. And that infuriates me. I jump from the unfamiliar sheets and take four steps before someone stops me with a hand to the chest. The air whooshes out of my lungs. I fall to my knees. Silencers are applied.

"Sleep," someone says, someone with superextreme voice power. I know the tone.

Thane.

As I cleared the Rises and saw the windswept beach, the memory ended. I wondered if my hair had been cut, my eyes enhanced, before Thane got ahold of me. Had he done it? And who had helped?

"Sleep," echoed in my head in varying tones that all belonged to Thane. If he'd put me under and then boxed me up in the white room in Rise Twelve, then . . .

Was he the Thinker of Twelve?

If yes, then holy-blazing-hot-stars-alive.

If not, then he at least knew who the real Thinker was. Could he know about the assistant? Could he be that person in my head?

So many things didn't make sense. Like why some of my citations were erased and some weren't. And how I was on the Watched list.

Of course you are, the assistant said over my cache. I lost my balance, fell from my hoverboard.

I wasn't that high, but I still yelled, "Rescue!" to my board. It zoomed down and under me just before I splatted on the sand.

My back cracked against the surface, but I managed not to knock myself unconscious.

My cache was off. No one should be able to use it. Well, maybe a technopath, but neither Trek nor Starr had that ability. There definitely should not be voices on my cache.

But there are, the assistant said. I analyzed its qualities: Robotic, impossible to determine gender, completely unplaceable.

Who are you? I thought it hard, trying to figure out where to place the question. Without my cache to focus my thoughts, I wasn't quite sure where they went and who could hear them.

And the assistant would never answer such a question. In fact, s/he didn't speak again. I sat in the damp sand, staring out over the miles and miles of churning water.

I remembered the only time I'd been this close to the ocean. My mom had brought me during the break between primary and secondary school. I was twelve. We didn't touch the water; that's against protocol. But Mom packed flavored vitamin water and salami sandwiches.

Now, the air held the chill of winter mixed with the birth of spring. My birthday was coming in less than two months. I couldn't help but wonder where I'd be in April, if I'd even be alive.

Rain started to fall; I pulled my hat lower over my face and ignored the transmission telling me to *seek shelter immediately*. Sitting there, watching the water darken into black waves, feeling the relentless thrum of icy raindrops on my shoulders, I allowed myself to open the vault inside.

I let myself miss my mom. Powerfully.

I let myself hold Raine again. And again. And again.

With my clothes thoroughly soaked, I got up and walked toward the spot where the ocean waves licked at the earth. *What's one more broken protocol?*

I crouched, put my hand on the sand, let the glacial water wash over it. Instinctively, my body recoiled from the cold.

I fought against it and moved farther out, my shoes sinking into the wetness. I abandoned all reason and dove under the next wave. Like I knew how to swim. I didn't—no one did.

I let the power in the wave push and pull and tangle me up. I broke the surface, gulped air, and went back under. "I am underwater!" I shouted, gallons of salty liquid muting the sound.

I crashed through the surf, and screamed it again. "I am in the ocean!"

I half-expected EOs to descend from the torrential downpour, or the assistant to acknowledge my rebelliousness. Nothing happened.

So I dragged myself out of the water, my face numb from the freezing temps. I mounted my board and flew home, grateful Thane had canceled our afternoon session—again. I'd seen enough of Thane for a while. He must've felt the same.

I also ignored the three citations I'd received for (a) skipping lunch, (b) logging too many leisure hours on a Saturday, and (c) not reporting to an indoor location within five minutes of inclement weather.

I should've gotten (d) wrestling with the ocean waves.

But I didn't.

Zenn said nothing when I entered through the balcony door, teeth chattering and dripping wet. I managed to store the microchip from Starr next to my mom's before tossing my nearly frozen clothes into the street.

The citation for littering came ten minutes later, while I stood in the shower.

I deleted it and collapsed into my own bed.

After twelve hours of sleep, I consumed a plate of bacon, eggs, and, of course, toast. There's always toast when Zenn's around, even at three a.m. on Sunday morning, which was when we sat at our table, shoveling food into our mouths.

"You want more?" Zenn asked as he stood up and moved to the food-dispenser.

"Orange juice," I said around a mouthful of eggs. I felt like I hadn't eaten properly in weeks. I probably hadn't. Maybe meal plans and dietary restrictions were a good idea. I pushed that thought away as Zenn ordered up the orangey deliciousness.

I'd been doing that a lot: burying unpleasant thoughts.

"I'm going to see my mom tonight," I said, right out loud, while the food-dispenser generated my drink.

"Cool." Zenn set the glass down in front of me.

Conversation over. I finished eating and went back to bed.

In my hands I hold a small, leather-bound book, unremarkable, with nothing stamped on the outside to indicate what lies within.

But I know. I feel it vibrating in my skin, sinking into my pores. It's my dad's journal. I have his page of notes memorized, and I pull up the first one. Northern border friendly—19—Cedar Hills.

Page nineteen will hold the rest of the clue, maybe even a map so I know where to find the city of Cedar Hills.

My fingers shake, my breath quakes in my lungs, as I open the book. The paper feels rough, thick.

The first page is blank. So is the second. I frantically flip the pages, desperate to find all the pieces, see and hear and smell my father's writing.

But I don't.

The book is completely blank. Useless. Untouched by my father.

I woke up panting, the crushing hopelessness a tight knot in my chest. Sunlight pooled on the silver floor, and I sighed. I needed something shiny in my life.

I went to the window and stood in the direct sunlight. I let it warm my bare chest, let it cascade over my face, burn into my open eyes.

A citation for excessive sleep sat in my inbox. I wanted to reply with something that would surely earn me another citation—but that would require me to activate my cache.

And I wanted my thoughts to belong to myself, and myself alone, as I prepared to go see my mom.

I didn't know what I'd say. I didn't know what she'd say. I didn't know, but it didn't matter. She was my mom, and I was her son, and she deserved a better good-bye than what I'd given her a few weeks ago.

I had the flat to myself, and part of me wanted to stay and enjoy the silence of Sunday afternoon. I had a feeling the tranquility coursing through me would be the last time I felt that for a while. A long while.

I slid the microchips into my pocket and stepped onto my board.

On Block Three, nothing had changed. Yet everything felt drastically different. The couple walking down the street arm in arm felt suspicious. Orchestrated.

Two kids whose names I couldn't remember played on the front steps of the building across the street from my mom's house. They laughed, they ran up and down, their happiness pouring into the air.

I couldn't remember the last time I'd felt that happy. Maybe I never had. My internal sensor cried *shady!* and again I suspected that something wasn't right.

And, of course, it wasn't.

A little help would be nice, I cached, hoping the assistant was listening. *I just need an hour or so.*

A few seconds later the garbled voice spoke. *You're in the clear.* I couldn't tell if it was Trek or Starr or Zenn or someone else entirely. And I didn't really care at this point.

Thanks.

The security at my house hadn't changed. I pressed my finger to the sensor portlet, waited for the beep.

Inside, the air rippled in cool waves. The only light came from the skylights, washing the living area in navy shadows and white brights.

I paused when the door clicked closed behind me, trying to locate my mom's emotions. A tremor of fear filtered through my senses.

"Mom?" I called, so she wouldn't think a random stranger had busted into her house.

My mom flew down the stairs, yelling, "Gunner!" and sweeping me into her arms. I crushed my mom in a lame attempt to keep from falling apart.

Like that worked.

She cried. I cried. She stroked my face, saying she couldn't believe I'd come back and asking how long I could stay.

I swiped at my tears and said I couldn't, but that I'd come to say good-bye. The right way.

Understanding emanated from her, but her eyes told a different story. One filled with sadness and fear. Hope and love. Worry and regret. Joy and pride.

When I handed her the chip I'd taken from our safe, she brushed my not-long-enough hair off my forehead. "I've always known you'd finish what your father started." She smiled, but it looked like it hurt. "I protected you for as long as I could. Almost seventeen years."

"You did great, Mom." A lump full of words and secrets and fears gathered in my throat. I swallowed, but that didn't help. "I have one question, though."

She nodded. "I'll answer it if I can. I assume you're secure?"

"Yeah, I've had some help there. So I'm wondering why I have your last name and not my father's."

A faraway look entered my mom's eyes. "Safety reasons, he'd said."

I leaned forward. "Who said?"

"Your father had to leave just before you were born," Mom said. "Director Hightower struck a deal with your dad. If he put his name on an Alias list for the Association, he could leave Freedom, no questions asked. We couldn't use the name Schoenfeld, so we used Jameson."

"What's the Alias list?" I thought of Thane Myers and how he'd used the alias of Lyle Schoenfeld.

"It's a list of names Association officials can use when they can't use their own."

"But what does that mean? Why would anyone in the Association need to use an alias?"

Five minutes, Gunn. I'm sorry, but Hightower wants to know where you are right now.

"Mom, I have to go." I stood up. I didn't want her to be in danger.

She hugged me again. "I love you, Gunner. Be careful. Come home soon."

"I love you too, Mom." That's all I could say. But I think she heard everything else I held inside.

As I hurried away from Block Three, my fear escalated, spreading through my body. The assistant wasn't Trek. He would've never said, "I'm sorry."

Raine

 *Cannon, you have to message me back.* I sat on the edge of my bed on Saturday night, composing an e-comm to Cannon. I'd sent one this morning, adding to the others. He hadn't responded once.

Please, I just need to know if you're okay. I'm sorry about everything. Just message me back, okay?

I sent the e-comm just as Vi entered the bedroom. "Ready?" she asked.

I clipped my transmission feed into my e-board in response. Our plan was to stay up tonight so I could ask her about what I'd read in her file. Zenn had sent Vi a code to program the e-boards to simulate sleep patterns and fabricated dreams.

Vi clicked her feed into the e-board too, and we both lay in our beds. I asked her to tell me about her life in the Goodgrounds. I promised there'd be no questions from me. (Of course, I broke that promise after about three minutes.)

"Wait, wait. You and Zenn snuck into the Abandoned Area?" She'd been telling me about her escape from prison with Jag, and how she'd stayed in the Abandoned Area alone.

"All the time," Vi said. "Once, I dared him to stay out all night so we could watch the sunrise from the attic of this old house." Her voice grew wistful. "We didn't sleep a wink, just talked and drew patterns in the dust and lay in each other's arms."

"Sounds nice," I said.

"Yeah," Vi said. Then she talked of tanned skin, hair dyed without an enhancer, tech facilities that shouldn't exist, the beauty of the desert in the dead of night, and then the reflective quality of the ocean at sunrise.

Fact: Violet loves the ocean. Just listening to her talk about the water could infuse passion into the most dispassionate soul.

She made it through her whole story without once mentioning Tyson. "So, who's Tyson?" I asked.

She recoiled as if I'd slapped her. "Who?"

"Tyson," I repeated. "His name is in your file."

Vi blinked, and her eyes came open a little sharper. "Her.

Tyson is a girl. My sister." Her voice shook with emotion.

I pushed myself up on my elbows to look at her. "Your sister?" Her brief hadn't mentioned any siblings.

"Yeah." Vi turned away from me, but not before I saw the tears in her eyes. "My father killed her."

"Thane did?"

Vi's only answer came in the form of sniffles.

I lay back down and focused on the ceiling. I wondered what it would feel like to have a sister. My relationship with Vi was as close as anything I'd ever had with another girl.

How would I feel if my father killed her?

~~Fury. Endless grief.~~ Terror.

The same way I felt about Gunner leaving Freedom.

Leaving me.

I'd been asleep for a couple of hours when a physician woke me. "Drink this." He held a small glass toward me. The bottom was rimmed in silver metal, and the glass held a thick, white substance.

I clenched my teeth and spoke around them. "What is it?"

"Medicine."

"I'm not sick," I said.

The physician leaned closer, his eyes angry and narrow. "Yes, you are."

"I feel fine," I insisted, though I suspected what this "medicine" was for. My dad wanted to fix my ability to drain. He'd probably tasked this physician with the responsibility to make that happen.

"Drink it," the physician said. "Or I'll force you to drink it."

A pit of desperation formed in my stomach. I didn't want my ability back. But I didn't see how to get out of the situation, especially when the physician pulled a syringe from his pocket.

"How will this bring back a genetic talent?" I stalled.

The physician's mouth tightened. "This will help you relax. Your father thinks it will help."

Relax. Right. I shook my head.

"Fine," he said. "We can do this the hard way."

"No," I said quickly. "No. I'll drink it." I reached toward the glass. It felt colder than ice against my fingers. I shivered when I pressed it to my lips. The liquid inside slid down my throat in one gulp, equally as icy as the glass.

The chill spread through my chest and into my stomach, just like the post-drain meds. The physician left without another word. I watched Vi sleep in the bed across from me, feeling spongy and strangely detached from myself.

Maybe the medicine won't work, I thought, but I'm not great at lying to myself.

* * *

On Sunday night (fourteen hours until Jag's trial, thirteen until the breakout), Zenn knocked on the door. Vi flew out of the bedroom where she'd been painting her fingernails blue.

She shrieked when she opened the door, and his deep laugh reminded me that he loved her.

Zenn poked his head into the bedroom. "Gunn's gonna be a little late. He went to see his mom."

I started to wave him away when I saw his hair. No longer white-blond, he now sported the same spiked black hair as Vi. And Gunn. And Jag.

"Nice, right?" he said, laughing. "So you're gonna be at the Education Rise? Unauthorized level?"

I nodded, unsure how this conversation wasn't being monitored. As if he could read my mind—which he probably could—Zenn held up his hand. "I got a personal scrambler." A thick silver band hugged his middle finger. Every few seconds, a brilliant turquoise shimmer skated over the surface. It reminded me of the ring Thane always wore, but I'd never seen Thane's flash.

I put my e-board aside and crossed over to him. "How'd you get that? Trek's been denying my petition for months."

Zenn flashed a quick smile. "I don't need permission from Trek." His words held more than letters, and I tried to figure out what he meant. Did he know the assistant? Was he the assistant?

"So, the unauthorized level . . ." Zenn said.

"Oh yeah," I answered. "Eight a.m. sharp. I'll be there." I appraised him. "And you?"

"Gunn and I and *him* are look-alikes now. The three of us will fly in separate directions, hopefully spread the officers out. They'll meet up out there, and I'm going to take a little swim."

My heart sped. "In the ocean?"

"Yep." Zenn laughed at the incredulous look on my face. Then he leaned closer and lowered his voice. "I know how to swim, Raine. Vi does too. Water folk are taught to swim before they can walk."

The thought of swimming terrified me. The ocean was strictly off-limits, used only for food, and then only in case of an emergency. And it was February. The air alone froze my lungs together. I couldn't imagine what icy water could do.

"Gunn took a dip last night," Zenn said easily.

"What?" I shook my head, disbelieving. "No way. He would never, I mean, he can't swim. He wouldn't break protocol like that anyway."

Zenn leaned against the doorframe. I wanted to smack—no, punch—the grin off his lips.

"He did."

"Why?" I struggled to understand. I felt like the Gunn who would do something like that wasn't the person I knew.

"Because he can, that's why," Zenn said. "Sometimes, Raine, it's not about right and wrong or keeping protocol. It's about doing something simply because you can."

His last words settled into my very bones, resonating with life. *It's about doing something simply because you can.*

I almost smiled. Until I remembered that this was Gunner doing things just because he could. Illegal things. "Did he get cited?"

Zenn chuckled; the sound of it grated on my nerves. "I'm sure he got cited. He's not exactly opening them anymore."

Again, this bit of information about Gunn surprised me. "So he's just ignoring his citations? Won't Thane notice that?"

"He's not ignoring them. He's deleting them." I gasped, but Zenn continued. "And Thane has a lot of other things landing in his queue right now." His blue eyes twinkled with mischief.

Sudden relief made me smile too. "So Gunn won't get caught."

"Oh, he's gonna get caught." Zenn pushed his shirtsleeves up to his elbows, completing the perfect picture of carefree and casual. "I've heard the alarm for a barrier breach is quite shrill."

I smiled, and it wasn't even forced. "It is," I agreed, and we went into the living area together.

Vi worked at the food-dispenser, and when she turned around, tears coated her face. Zenn ran to her side, cooing to her in a low voice. He helped her sit down at the table, and by the time I managed to force my feet across the room, he'd handed her a hydro-dryer to wipe her face.

I sat across from her, ~~afraid~~ dying to speak. She looked back to Zenn, her lovely eyes filling with more tears.

"It's okay, beautiful." Zenn's quiet voice held only understanding. He wiped her tears and kissed her.

I should've been embarrassed to watch them, but I wasn't. Their love was real, tender, deep. I suddenly wondered if Gunn and I had anything that genuine. I wondered if I'd ever feel like that about him, about anyone.

"I can't remember," Vi whispered, wiping angrily at her face. "Raine and I were talking last night, and I remembered things. Important things. Names. I think I had . . . a sister?" It came as a question, but before Zenn and I could even exchange a look, Vi had gone on.

"And when I woke up this morning, I could still remember all of it. Until just now, when I ordered a glass of milk, and then . . . I can't even remember what I was thinking about." She pinned Zenn with a desperate look. "I don't remember you coming over. The last thing I remember is Raine setting up her e-board puzzles for me."

That had happened an hour ago. I knew what it felt like to lose large chunks of time (a lot longer than an hour too). To not be able to remember what happened, or where, or when.

I reached across the table and placed my hands on top of Vi's. I didn't know what to say to make everything okay, because everything was not okay. And I wasn't sure that what I was doing—what any of us were doing—could ever make our world okay.

As I kept my hand on Vi's, gray shadows began to dance on my vision-screen. Indistinct and void of color, but images nonetheless. I yanked my hands away from hers, feeling sick that somehow that medicine had worked.

Before anyone could say anything, the door buzzed. I got up to answer it so Zenn could have a moment with Vi.

Gunn stood in the hall, his face haunted with exhaustion and grief. I wanted to gather him into my arms, feel his heart beat against mine, and whisper the exact words he needed to erase the sadness in his eyes. But I didn't want to see anything in his head. Based on what I'd just seen when touching Vi, I needed my gloves back.

I stepped back to allow him room to enter the flat. The

door hadn't even closed behind him before Zenn said, "How could you?" and was swinging.

His fist connected with Gunn's jaw, whose head snapped back. Vi cried out and pushed her chair back, scraping it on the floor. But I just stood there, leaning against the wall as my pulse pounded in my temples.

"What the hell?" Gunn held his nose; blood dripped onto the silver floor. The room spun, creating little rivers of crimson among the gray.

"You programmed their dispenser to alter memories." Zenn swung again. This time Gunn ducked.

"Zenn!" Vi yelled, but it sounded so . . . very . . . far away.

The smell of blood hit me hard, and I almost fell. With the floor tilting, I stepped forward. "Stop," I said forcefully, placing one hand on Zenn's chest while I held the other toward Gunn. "Stop it now."

He raised his fist, but I grabbed it with my free hand. Skin to skin, the images came fast and hot. They swam between light and dark.

I saw Gunn, triumphant and glowing, watching Freedom burn from his position high above the city. His desire to be the one to take down the Association flowed through my veins like blood. Underneath it ran a river of love that made no sense with the images in my head.

Most surprising though, was the shifting I felt inside. I'd been working to undo the ties that bound the Association for over a year. I couldn't do it myself; Gunn couldn't do it himself. But together, yes, together we could accomplish what neither one of us could do alone. If we worked together, maybe all the pieces would fit together into a cohesive whole.

"Raine, I have something to tell you," Gunner said. Each word stretched into long syllables.

I swung my head toward him, and it seemed to take years. "I have something to tell you too," I said, my voice quiet and thick. Because for the first time, the picture playing across my vision-screen didn't change. What Gunn wanted, and what would happen when he got it, were one and the same. And if he knew what I'd seen in Vi's drain, we might be able to succeed.

I flung aside the pictures to get to the only emotion in the drain: love. But it didn't belong to Gunn. I swung my head toward Zenn, and found the tips of my fingers pressed into the bare skin of his exposed throat.

I moaned at the spike of unadulterated love. His images were muddy, hard to distinguish, but I didn't have to have perfect vision to recognize Vi.

The floor tilted up; the ceiling slanted down. My knees cracked against the solid silver as my vision darkened.

Then someone cradled my head in their lap. Cool fingers worked through my hair. A voice said, "Her pulse is thready." Lips pressed against my forehead. "Raine, stay with me. I—I want to do favors for you."

Gunner, I thought. *I love you too.*

Then I passed out.

I tumbled down, down, down. Cliffs blanketed me on both sides; voices cried from the crevices as I passed.

I saw faces, pale and tired. I saw flashes of red light, pulses of blue, and a strong beam of white.

Above me, another girl was falling too.

She had my face, my long, white-blond hair. Her mouth stretched into a scream, but all the sound tore through my throat.

She blinked; my eyes closed.

I reached toward her with my bare hand, desperate for someone to anchor me. She responded by stretching her hand toward mine. Our fingertips touched, and she winked into oblivion.

She was me. I am her.

I'm torn, wandering, falling, being pushed and twisted and called to from all sides.

Who deserves to get what they want? Gunner? So he can

hover in the starless sky and watch his homeland burn? So he can watch my father fall?

Or Zenn? So he can keep Vi under the influence of his voice and sail away with her into the far north and love her and make her love him?

I could help them both get what they desired most. I didn't know what to do, so I just kept falling and falling and falling. Vi sang, that same lullaby that she always did. The words bundled around me, wrapping me in a protective layer.

I allowed myself to get lost in the melody, trying to find a path through the maze of music the same way I needed to find a way through the confusion in my life.

I couldn't.

And after a while I realized why Vi couldn't choose between Zenn and Jag. Some choices are impossible.

Gunner

29.

The sounds coming from Vi's mouth confused me. She linked all her words together, holding some out, clipping others short. The melody was familiar somehow, and it infused my soul with peace. It definitely calmed Raine. Her muscles stopped seizing, and she relaxed onto my lap. The right side of my face throbbed where Zenn had hit me, and the shock of witnessing Raine's collapse brought a frustration/hurt/ache so deep, I thought I might drown in it.

So many questions rumbled in my mind. What was Zenn's deal with the dispenser? What had Raine seen when she'd touched me? Because that had been a drain—I knew it. It had sucked the life right out of Raine's face.

"What is that?" I voiced, directing my question to Vi.

She broke the tune off. "It's Raine's favorite song."

"Music is against protocol."

Zenn threw his head back and laughed. Really laughed, like what I'd said was the funniest thing in the world. My jaw hurt too much to join him—and I didn't find anything funny.

"Why'd you hit me?" I asked him.

He leveled his gaze at me, all serious. "Someone programmed the food-dispenser to alter memories."

"You think I did that?" If anyone could've done it, Zenn could have. He played both sides all the time.

"No one else has been in this flat." His voice could've sliced me to bits.

"*You* have," I fired back. "I didn't reset that dispenser. *I'm* the one who fixed it."

Zenn clenched his jaw, then his fists. I braced myself for another blow. But Vi placed one hand on Zenn's forearm. "He's telling the truth. Drop it, Zenn."

Zenn deflated. The angry sparks in his eyes died as he studied Vi.

"Of course I'm sure," she said, answering some silent conversation I wasn't privy to—not that I wanted to be in the middle of that.

"You've done nothing," I said. "Nothing with Vi. Nothing for Raine. Nothing." I gathered Raine into my arms and picked her up. I walked toward her bedroom, her head lolling against my shoulder.

"I've done nothing?" Zenn said, his voice too high and too tense.

"You're Informant. Maybe you needed some information on your little girlfriend. I don't know. But I do know you play both sides," I said over my shoulder, "while accomplishing absolutely nothing."

His anger hit me in the back, propelling me forward. I couldn't tell if he was mad because what I'd said was way out of line, or if because it was true.

Vi said, "Give him space, Zenn," and he didn't follow me into the bedroom.

I laid Raine in bed and tucked the blanket tight around her. She mumbled something, and a strange electric thread pulsed through me. I leaned closer to her. "Say it again," I whispered.

"I have to tell you about Vi's drain," she murmured, her eyes still glued shut.

I glanced at the door. It was open, but Zenn and Vi couldn't be seen. "I'm listening," I said.

"We're there, Gunn. Me and you, at the end, when Freedom falls."

I only kept breathing because it was an involuntary action and required no special skill. I tried to make sense of her words.

Seconds melded into minutes. She didn't speak again.

I smoothed my thumb over her delicate cheekbone. "Are you okay?"

She jerked away from my touch, something wild in her expression.

"The drains, they're hurting you, aren't they?" I asked.

A single tear leaked out of her right eye. She nodded, a sob choking in her throat.

"I'm sorry," I whispered. I knew how it felt to have an unwanted power. More than that, a power that could harm other people.

"It's not your fault," she said. "I have a terrible talent."

"You're terribly beautiful," I countered.

She tried to smile, but it came out more like a grimace. "We work together, Gunn, to overthrow the Association. You'll get what you want."

"Will I?" The words escaped before I could censor them.

"And I can say good-bye," Raine continued, "because I know I'm going to see you again."

She sounded so sure that the ball of worry deep in my gut dissolved. I hadn't even known it was there, or what it signified, until now.

"I'm going to kiss you now," I whispered, since she already had her eyes closed. I wondered what she'd see when my lips met hers. But right now, I didn't care. Would she?

"Okay."

She let me kiss her and kiss her and kiss her, until we finally figured out how to say good-bye without using words.

I recalibrated Vi's food-dispenser before I left, this time encoding it with a portlet to keep it from becoming compromised again. Then Zenn and I cut through the frozen sky toward our flat.

When we landed on the balcony, Zenn paused. "Sorry, Gunner. I was way out of line."

I touched my tender nose. "You suck, man."

He clapped his hand on my shoulder as we went inside. "I know. Sorry. Vi said they had spiders doing a routine inspection. They probably reset it." He settled into his ergonomic, his e-board open, but I went straight to bed.

Like I slept.

Because I wanted my last night in Freedom to last forever, the hours flew by. Before I knew it, Zenn was stepping out of the shower and I was double-checking to make sure I had the microchip from Starr in my pocket and the scan of my father's notes loaded on my cache.

Zenn joined me in the kitchen for our last toast-only breakfast. If he had been two inches shorter, we could've been twins. "Let's fly," he said, exactly as he did every other Monday morning at 7:50 a.m.

Except this time, instead of flying toward the Education Rise, we set our sights on the Confinement Rise.

I thought about all the people doing things this morning to aid the breakout. We had exactly an hour to get in the Rise, get Jag out, and get through the fifteenth sector of the wall.

Twenty minutes later we cleared the orchard. "Voices?" Zenn asked. Below us, two rows of guards flanked the front entrance to the Confinement Rise. Double the personnel—super.

"Voices," I confirmed. We flew in fast, crouching low and dipping our faces behind our hats so we couldn't be identified before we could speak. Without landing, Zenn faced one row of guards, and I squared off with the other.

"Sleep," we said together, short and forceful. The four guards on my side swayed on their feet. Before I could add,

"Now," they fell to the ground, already snoring. Zenn spoke a few more times and accomplished similar results.

"Should we hide the bodies?" he asked.

"No time," I said, dismounting from my hoverboard. "Let's go. Half power, hover—fifteen feet." Both mine and Zenn's boards obeyed my command.

Sending a clean-up crew, the assistant said in my mind. *Target's been moved to room B-12.*

Where's that? I asked, trying to focus on entering the locked and coded Rise.

Basement. Raine and Vi are in place.

Super, I chatted, finally getting the door open.

Zenn and I moved with speed and precision, unrushed but urgent. Inside the Rise, something felt wrong.

I hesitated, glancing around. *It's too dark*, I chatted to the assistant, to Zenn.

Powered down from the weekend, the assistant said. *We've detained all workers who should be in this building. They're at home until nine o'clock. Take the stairs. I'm sending Zenn upstairs to get the hoverboard.*

I met Zenn's eyes and nodded. He wrenched open the door to the stairwell and went up, leaving me to go down alone.

My footsteps sounded muted, timid, even though I took

no care to make them so. In the basement, darkness permeated my senses.

Until the spiders awoke. Then all kinds of red screamed against my retinas.

I held out my hand, palm forward. The tech burned under my skin before shorting out the dozen spiders close enough to receive the blast. The others backed up, crowded around a door in the corner. The unearthly blue glow of guard spiders combined with the red seekers, resulting in a violet glare.

Can you do something about these spiders? I asked the assistant.

That's all you, came the response. If possible, I thought the robotic voice carried some sarcasm. Maybe Trek was behind the voice.

A solid stream of purple lit up the twelve on the door. One touch from a guard spider could electrocute me, or paralyze me, or erase my short-term memory. They were like a mystery poison, their abilities unknown until it was too late.

I had no weapons except for my voice and any tech I could suck from the walls. And that's all I needed. With a primal yell, I spread my arms wide. The scratching of spider legs on the metal floor became the only sound, the smell of my determination the only scent.

My muscles quivered with tech. I clapped, sending a

pulse toward the insects. They flew back in a tangle of shattered bodies and severed legs. A pair of blue eyes leapt, but I shouted, "Deactivate," before it landed on me.

A few more voice commands to power down, and I had the violet mob under control in less than ten seconds.

I stood in the corridor, breathing hard, as the last glow from the spider eyes faded. I felt along the doorframe, searching for a way into the room. The door had been equipped with a series of codes that had to be entered within a certain time frame or an alarm would sound.

Like that mattered—if the door was opened before 8:45 a.m., the same siren would wail.

AD Myers is on the move, the assistant came over my cache.

"Super," I mumbled. I'd been hoping to make it all the way to the barrier before activating any alarms.

No such luck. I punched in the codes as they raced through my nervous system, and when the door clicked open, the first *whoop! whoop! whoop!* nearly knocked me backward.

It was holy *am I deaf yet?* loud. I couldn't help clapping my hands over my ears.

The strobing orange light that matched the alarm revealed Jag huddled on a bare mattress, doing the exact same thing.

Getting him out was not going to be easy. At least a dozen

guard spiders came to life. Their blue eye glow blended with the flashing orange light and painted the silver walls with creepy light.

A spider launched itself and landed on my arm, its legs scuttling against my jacket. A wave of blue attacked my feet while I bashed my arm against the doorjamb. I kicked and stomped, but a sharp prick on my left ankle bloomed into full-blown *ouch!* as it spread up my leg.

Frustrated, I lifted my arms toward the ceiling and pulled strength from whatever tech I could find. The remaining spiders backed up against Jag, their eyes narrowing into slits. Two seconds later I'd stolen their power, and their bodies clattered to the floor, unmoving.

I didn't speak. Neither did Jag. He held out his tech-restrained hands, and I had the cuffs deactivated before another three *whoops!* sounded.

Jag and I sprinted toward the stairs, propelled by that ominous orange light. My left leg felt heavy and stiff, but I forced it to *move!*

Halfway up the stairwell, another alarm shrieked against the one I'd set off. *AD Myers crashed into the Confinement Rise*, the assistant said. It was the most shocked I'd ever heard the voice sound.

I doubled my speed, taking the stairs three at a time.

I paused long enough to check the lobby to see if Zenn was waiting for us there, but the strobing spotlight revealed emptiness.

So I went up another flight, peeking through the window in the door, hoping with every fiber of my being to find Zenn.

I did. But he wasn't alone. Thane Myers stood looking out the window with Zenn next to him, his back so straight he must've been in severe physical pain. He didn't move, not even a twitch.

There went our decoy. Zenn—with his Jagified hair—was supposed to draw officers after him as he flew toward the ocean. Jag and I were going the opposite way.

Zenn had been caught too early.

Fear twisted in my stomach. Then Zenn turned, slow slow slow, and his eyes locked onto mine. He touched Thane's shoulder, and he started to twist also.

Jag gripped my bicep, thrust his chin upward. A row of silencers adorned his neck. As we flew up another flight of stairs, I became the guy who left everyone behind. Guilt raged inside at leaving Zenn—brainwashed—in Thane's clutches. At leaving Raine at the mercy of her father, even if phase B of the plan was to see her soon—outside the wall.

I stumbled over my own feet; my left leg ached. I just wanted this to end. All of it.

When Jag pushed open the door to the third floor lobby, fresh, frigid air assaulted me.

I sucked it in, using it to drown out the terror. I pushed past Jag, strode over to the windows. Splintering lines snaked across the glass = Thane's crash site. I punched once, twice, thrice, four times before the window shattered.

Another alarm joined the two still raging throughout the city. I yelled, "Rescue!" out the ruined window. My blood was falling to the ground below. My wrist port sparked, and a jolt of techtricity raced up my arm.

I turned and dragged Jag in front of me. "Jump!" I said, shoving him out. Two seconds later I leapt too.

After a heartbeat, I crumpled to my knees on my hoverboard, which whined and shook with my impact.

"Up, up, up," I urged in my most powerful voice. I cleared the roof just behind Jag—who demonstrated some tight flying skills—and said, "Sector fifteen. Fly south and we'll meet in ten minutes. Lose your tail." I jerked my head to the few officers—not as many as there should've been—entering the sky behind us.

"Sector fifteen," he mouthed.

"South, southwest, twenty-one degrees," I instructed Jag. Then I pointed my board toward the northwest corner, drawing half the guards after me and my Jagged-up appearance.

Raine

30.

When I woke up, the sky was spitting and flashing. I echoed its displeasure, especially since Gunn would be leaving today. Even so, I welcomed the morning, firestorm and all. At least whatever was going to happen today would happen already.

I e-commed Cannon, though I held no hope that he'd respond. Sure enough, he didn't. My nervous energy skyrocketed.

Vi sat at the table, eating pancakes. I ordered my mandated breakfast (oatmeal, no brown sugar), but couldn't force it down. At the front door we nodded to each other and separated.

She was headed to Thane's personal quarters, pretending

to have a question for her father. We'd rehearsed her lines last night after the guys had left.

I had authorization in most parts of Rise One, and my presence wouldn't be questioned in the remaining areas. Instead, I went to the one place I'd rather never see again: school.

The Education Rise held many secrets, and the list of things students are strictly forbidden to do could take hours to scroll through. If I could cause some mayhem here, EOs would be dispatched. And when their hoverboards failed to power on (as per the plan), the Administrator would call my father (I hoped).

With my resolve as hard as tech filaments, I strode into the Rise. Small clusters of students funneled down the halls or gathered in common areas, whispering.

I switched on my cache—against school policy—and chatted everyone. Four citations landed in my inbox before I made it to the end of the hall—and I was moving fast. Someone else could move faster, apparently. And it wasn't the assistant.

I even chatted Educators as I practically ran to the ascender bank near the coffee kiosks.

Then I committed the dire act: I ascended to the mysterious Sixth Level. No one knew what was up here (not even me), because the entire floor had been prohibited since the dawn of time.

A physical alarm pierced the air as soon as I materialized. I knew it was because of my unauthorized entrance into—

a—

laboratory.

Three white-coated physicians paused in their work to stare at me. I could only gape back. A public transmission covered the shrieking siren. "All students return to ground level immediately."

I imagined the urgent footsteps on the second through fourth floors as everyone rushed to the descenders. But there'd be no pushing, no panic. Responsible Citizens don't do things like that.

I remained frozen in place, taking in as much as possible with quick sweeps of the room. Flat tables, like the one in lab seven, dominated the large room. Dangling tech connectors. Cabinets filled with sensors, medical tools, e-boards. Portlets broadcasted a stream from Rise One on the wall opposite me. Sterile air assaulted me. Bleached surfaces gleamed shiny and silver.

Beyond the main room, three doors led into smaller cells. The lights were off in two of them. But in the third—

I screamed. The sound went on and on and on, filling

every crevice, every pocket in the lab. At some point during my tirade, the building siren had quit, and now the silence rang louder than the alarms.

One physician approached me as the other two turned to look at the reason for my outburst. They immediately stepped together, their shoulders touching, so I couldn't see past them.

But it didn't matter. I'd already seen Cannon.

Restrained. Bleeding. Teched up.

Without thinking, I took a swing at the now-standing-in-front-of-me-talking physician. I hit him hard, and pain exploded in my fingers and up into my arm. "Damn you!" I pushed him to the ground, my chest heaving.

Rage I didn't know I possessed drove me forward. I sprinted toward the two technicians, who wore expressions of ~~shock~~ terror. I snatched a taser from a counter as I ran and didn't hesitate to use it.

Seconds later I stood next to Cannon. Everything floated around me in slow motion. Tech cords bit into his swollen wrists, making them weep blood. I tried to wipe it away so I could release him. The slickness of it made me sick. The smell of it forced me to close my eyes until the room stopped spinning.

"Raine," he croaked.

"Shh." I slashed at the tears coating my face. My breath

shuddered in my chest, but I vowed not to fall apart. Somehow I managed to release his hands, and then I began on the tether across his chest.

"We're getting out of here," I told him. "You'll be fine. Just fine." I kept talking, telling him how everything was going to be okay and that I'd take him back to my place. Anything to fill the silence. Anything to quell the rising fury inside. I feared that if I didn't talk, I'd explode.

Cannon wept, and that only angered me more. No one had the right to treat him this way.

"Why are you here?" I asked him as I shouldered his weight. We hobbled into the main lab.

"They've been bringing students up here for years," he whispered. He trembled with each step; his breath tore through his throat in wet rasps. "They run tests on them."

My chest constricted. "What kind of tests?"

"I don't know exactly. But I'm part of a study. They've been reducing my food allotment for months, putting me under greater stressors in class, making my friendship with you . . ." He trailed off, his voice nothing more than wind.

"Different," I supplied, guilt twisting inside. If anything, I'd been helping them in their sick study.

He gathered a breath and released it. "They've been testing how much I can endure."

"You're almost dead." I remembered how thin he'd seemed last week, how he'd been skipping meals, how he went straight to studying after school, how he hadn't answered any of my e-comms.

He gave a mirthless laugh. "Tell me about it." He leaned against a table, completely winded. "They've been testing you too. Not here, but in lab seven."

I studied him, the cold realization impossible to swallow. "The drains."

Cannon coughed and wiped blood off his lips. "The drains."

Cash-my-name-is-Cash. Goose bumps erupted down my arms. "What about them?"

"I don't know, Raine. I don't know." He sounded so broken. "But I heard them talking about some sabotage in the Evolutionary Rise. Someone wouldn't complete an experiment and actually destroyed the embryos."

I blinked. Behind my eyelids, I saw Cash's name on the Alias list. *Insubordinate* sat next to it. I felt the pieces of my life shatter, taking all certainty with them.

"Cash Whiting works in the Evolutionary Rise," I said.

"He *used to* work in the Evolutionary Rise." Cannon coughed, gripping my shoulders painfully.

Tears flowed down my face. "I'm so sorry."

He shook his head. "I heard something else when they thought I was unconscious."

I pulled him into a tight hug, furious and profoundly sad at the word "unconscious."

"Whoever sabotaged those embryos, they destroyed an army." Cannon's whispered words sent a chill through my bloodstream.

"An army?" I repeated.

"There's a war coming," Cannon said, all Seerlike.

"Oh, no," I moaned. What if Cash's drain had just been to test my ability—my loyalty—in some sick way? What if the wild really did hold nothing but sickness and sand? What if my father was building an army?

What if, what if, what if?

I turned away from Cannon and threw up.

Get it together, the assistant commanded. *Your father is on his way up.*

"My dad," I choked out, still tasting bile.

"Won't help us," Cannon said in his freaky, prophetic tone.

Before I could answer or take cover or anything, my father materialized in the lab. He took in the bodies on the floor before settling his sharp gaze on me. In a fluid move-ment, he raised his hand and held his palm toward me. Then he curled his fingers into a fist and pulled his arm to his body in a sharp, fluid movement.

The air left my lungs; my insides felt as coiled and tight as his fingers. I dropped to my knees, darkness creeping in along the edges of my vision. Next to me, Cannon struggled for breath.

"Naughty, naughty," Dad taunted, looking down at me. "Don't pass out now, Raine. I don't want you to miss anything."

Half an hour later I hadn't missed anything. Not the absolute silence in the Education Rise. Not the total humiliation of Cannon as my father forced him to walk down the hall with blood dripping from his nose.

Not the way Cannon held his shoulders with defiance, straight and strong, and stared down everyone who dared to glance his way. I tried to do the same, and failed.

I didn't miss the Educators stationed at every classroom door. Didn't miss the syringes they held, ready to administer the drugs that would make everyone forget whatever they'd seen or heard this morning.

I didn't miss the lack of EOs. Didn't miss the two dozen Confinement guards. If they were here, maybe Gunn had gotten away. My father didn't miss the tiny curve sitting on my lips.

I didn't miss the urgency in Cannon's grip as we held hands in the transport on the way to Rise One. Didn't miss the raw panic in his eyes when my father's physicians came and told him, "We'll help you get cleaned up, son."

When they led him away, I missed him immediately. My sense of loss was so deep, I wondered what it meant and if it would ever go away. The days where we used to sneak in a nap at the Medical Rise felt like a different lifetime. I ached for those days, that friendship.

Would I feel this empty tomorrow, with Gunn gone? I mean, he was leaving the entire city, not just going down the hall to get medical attention.

And what did these feelings for Cannon mean, exactly? Can a person love someone without being *in* love with them?

I didn't know. But I hated myself for being so wrapped up in Gunn that I hadn't seen my best friend's need.

"Sit, Raine." My dad gestured to the couch in his office. I guess I did miss ascending to the nineteenth floor, where he lived and worked. At least it wasn't the glass prison.

He settled opposite me in a reclining ergonomic, his legs crossed and his fingers steepled under his chin. The ultimate Director, Dad could get inside someone's head without even trying. I'd gotten good at folding everything up and hiding it from him. But today I couldn't. All my innermost secrets lay bare for him to see.

Except he wasn't looking—yet.

I glared at him; he simply gazed back. Not mad. Not upset. Not happy. Not anything. And that unnerved me enough to make me shift in my seat.

The fidget brought a cruel twist to my father's mouth, but he still didn't speak. And I sure as hell wasn't going to start.

The air in the room sharpened. I kept breathing in, exhaling, breathing in, exhaling. The longer my father stayed here, the better it would be for Gunn and Jag.

"I'd like to hear it from you," Dad finally said, dropping his hands to his lap.

"Hear what?" My throat felt caked with mud. Too narrow and too sloppy.

"How you wound up on Level Six in the Education Rise." His gaze flicked over my body and back to my face.

I folded my arms across my jacket and clamped my mouth shut. If he wanted to hear it from me, he'd have to compel me to speak.

Instead, he invaded my mind. I managed to keep the emotions about Gunn and the whole escape plan submerged, but I had to sacrifice Vi to do it.

"You're unbrainwashing her?" Dad had never sounded so incredulous, as if he'd never been surprised before.

I didn't answer. I squeezed my eyes shut against his penetrating mind control, desperate to keep him out, but not knowing how.

"How did you do that?" he murmured, exploring my mind again. He dug deeper and deeper, peeling away layer after layer, trying to find the root of my motivation for defying orders, for helping Vi remember her past.

I'd hidden the visions from Vi's drain at the bottom of the pile. On top of that lay my participation with the Insiders. And then Gunn's escape plans and my role therein. He couldn't see any of those. If he did . . . I didn't want to think about the consequences.

Frigid air washed over my neck. I jerked my eyes open to find my father directly in front of me, kneeling on the floor. His razor eyes hooked me, held me fast. I shook my head and mouthed *Stop*, but he didn't.

He was going to see everything.

Everything, everything, everything.

My late-night flying sessions.

My (forbidden) relationship with Gunner.

The escape—

A shrill (piercing, shrieking, wailing, blaring, ear-splitting)

345

alarm rent the air—and the connection between me and my father.

A moment later the public transmission system broadcasted this message: "The barrier has been breached. All Citizens have fifteen minutes to report to their homes and initiate lockdown procedures."

Dad stumbled backward, ~~astonishment~~ fury washing over his face.

"The barrier has been breached. All Citizens have fifteen minutes to report to their homes and initiate lockdown procedures."

"This isn't over!" he yelled over the siren.

"The barrier has been breached. All Citizens have fifteen minutes to report to their homes and initiate lockdown procedures."

He scrambled into a personal teleporter and left. Twin clones watched me from their positions flanking the door.

I relaxed into the couch, feeling the true weight of exhaustion. Then I opened my cache and focused my thoughts. *The Director is on the move.*

The assistant didn't respond.

Gunner

31.

I ducked low on my board, driving it to go faster. The hoverboard track loomed ahead, the orange flags waving in the morning breeze. A dozen people rounded the curve toward me, and I threw a *thanks* to the assistant.

I joined the flyers as they rounded the curve and headed north. I slowed my board to match their speed. They jostled around me until I was concealed in the center of the pack.

"The fifteenth sector is down," someone said very softly.

"Thank you," I murmured.

Eight officers paused on the fringers of the track, watched us. I tightened my grip on my board. When we were as far from the officers as possible, I said, "Thanks, guys. Split!"

The group broke up, scattering in twelve different directions.

"Drop," I said, and my board fell out of the sky. I sucked in a breath and stayed in a low crouch. The tents of Camp B flapped at my body as I maneuvered through them. Vacationers looked up at me casually, and no one tried to stop me. I turned south and zipped under the cover of apple tree branches, heading back toward the rendezvous point.

Sector fifteen really was down. I could tell even from a distance, because the wild wasn't obscured by the film that covered the rest of the world. Instead, lightning flashed, illuminating something much worse than I imagined. The color of the looming horizon smudged against the dark sky as kohl, like tech gone wrong. Viewed through other sectors of the barrier, it appeared silky and flowing, silver and peaceful.

The real, unobstructed wild felt menacing. Dangerous.

Jag emerged from the orchards, alone. Thank the stars he knew how to handle himself on a hoverboard.

"A quarter mile past the wall, we'll cross through the barrier!" I yelled to him. He flew on his knees, gripping the sides of the board like he thought he might fall any second. Even so, he maneuvered the board over the wall with unfailing precision.

Techtric shocks jumped the gap between the sectors, weaving the barrier back together. I moved in front of Jag so I could shock the barrier before it could regenerate itself. I held my hands in front of me, palms facing the unknown. I gathered the last tech I could feel in the surrounding sectors of the barrier, focused it, and fired.

The alarm wailed in protest; the surrounding barrier shivered; the fifteenth sector crashed completely; Jag and I shot through the weakened spot.

Into the wild.

I held my breath for as long as I could, thinking only of those special suits the maintenance workers wore. In thirty seconds we'd probably gone another mile. Every cell in my body screamed at me to *turn around and look!* but I kept my face forward. And then my lungs were crying, *Breathe, man! Breathe!*

So I did.

The air seemed full of ice, and I almost expected it to shred me to bits. I exhaled. Took another breath, drawing deeper. This time the oxygen tasted like freedom.

I laughed, letting the unrestrained feelings swell inside. I laughed until air wasn't the only thing coursing through my body.

I nudged my board closer to Jag's, handed him the backpack with medtech inside. "I've never felt so alive!"

He tossed me a grin from a crouched position on his

hoverboard. He ripped open a package with his teeth and applied the tech to his neck. A few seconds later the silencers lay discarded in the dirt far behind us.

He applied med-gel to his wounds, ran his fingers through his hair, stood up. I watched as he nosed his board near mine. He ran his gaze from my face to my feet and back, real quicklike.

"Nice hair," he said. His voice sounded old, misused. He pocketed the med-gel.

"You too," I countered. Suddenly I felt nervous, like this guy knew more, had done more, simply *was* more. Which was lame, because I had almost a year on him in age and at least half an inch in height.

I straightened my shoulders. "So, we're headed to the Badlands."

"We don't want to go there," Jag said casually, as if I'd said, "I'd like to go to the hoverboard track, pretty please."

"Why not?" Uncertainty mixed with annoyance. My best chance of finding Indy and the journal was in the Badlands. Jag had been in solitary confinement for weeks. And he'd even said that's where she'd be.

"Trust me, the Badlands isn't safe at the moment."

He spoke in riddles, the same way Zenn did. "At the moment?" I asked.

He cut me a look out of the corner of his eye. "I've got some people working on it."

He had some people working on it? Working on what, exactly? And how did he manage that? He'd been in *solitary confinement for weeks*.

Right when I opened my mouth to bite out, *What the hell does that mean?* a sensor portlet on my belt buzzed.

"Incoming," I said, twisting to look over my shoulder. Freedom lay in the background, a glowing smear against a storm-filled sky. Lightning struck in the clouds, making the tips of the Rises spark white-hot for a second.

I couldn't see anything that would bother my portlet. When I turned around, Jag was flying backward—backward!—next to me.

Show off, I thought, throwing him a dirty look.

He chuckled as if he could hear my thoughts. And maybe he could. I knew next to nothing about Jag Barque.

"Someone's coming," Jag said, barely loud enough for me to hear over the wind rushing in my ears. I didn't like the way the edges of his eyes held fear. I might not know much about him, but I knew enough to know it would take a helluva lot to scare him.

I flipped my board around, partly to show Jag that I could fly backward too, but mostly so I could scope for the threat.

We flew that way, scanning the horizon, for several minutes.

I didn't see anything, but I felt twinges of tech in my muscles, my bloodstream. Every flicker of lightning made me jump. Jag cleared his throat, and I almost turfed it. Thing was, Jag seemed just as agitated as me.

Like that made me feel better. If anything, his nervousness tripled mine.

"Hello, boys."

I spun around, matching Jag in speed, direction, and intensity. I sucked in my breath at the sight of Thane Myers, also riding a hoverboard backward. The immense wave of hostility coming from him was only matched by the cloud of hatred echoing from Jag.

Bad blood there, and I didn't want to get in the middle of it. But I sorta already was.

Next to Thane, Zenn flew with his knees locked, his eyes staring straight ahead. Brainwashed. Or was he? *Junior assistant, Informant status* looped in my head.

"Lyle," Jag sneered, and my breath stalled in my lungs. Of course Jag knew Thane as Lyle Schoenfeld. The alias was well documented.

"Jag." Thane clipped the word out like it had been contaminating him for years.

I kept my face impassive as I regarded Thane with a terrible dislike I'd just begun to develop. I'd always lived in fear of him. Hating him felt foreign, new. Natural.

"I'm sure this has been fun for you boys," Thane said. "But we really need to get back before the barrier is restored."

Jag burst out laughing, but I simply cocked my head sideways, trying to get a better read on Zenn. He still looked like Jag, but I felt nothing from him. How could he be so susceptible to brainwashing? Didn't he have any willpower?

The same mindlessness of a clone radiated from Zenn. Weird.

That's when I noticed the spot of blood on his neck. He'd been medicated *and* brainwashed.

Horror snaked through me, mingled with a profound sadness for Zenn.

"No way in hell I'm going back," Jag said, pulling my attention from Zenn.

I liked this guy more and more with every word he spoke. "Me neither," I added.

Thane's eyes hardened into sharp edges and anger. "Yes, you are. You both are. You're screwing everything up."

Jag didn't even look at me for confirmation before he employed his voice power. "No, I'm not. And you can go to hell, Lyle."

Thane's face slackened, and I seized the opportunity. "You

just head on home, Thane," I said. "You look tired. Maybe you should request a mandatory rest period."

I swear, if Jag and I were in a different situation, we would've grinned at each other, chatted about how easy this game was. But we weren't. So we didn't.

Thane actually reversed his board, lifted over our heads, and started back east. "Zenn, now would be a good time to fulfill your duty."

Zenn arced over Jag stiffly, his expression unchanging. I adjusted my hovercraft to watch him, so I saw the taser in his hand. I would've felt the tech in my bones anyway, and I did, but not before he fired it—at Jag.

"Stop," Jag commanded, but the barbs continued forward and embedded in his chest. Everything slowed into techtricity and Jag and spiked hair and Zenn and voices and Directors and right and wrong. My life spun around me in half time, and I replayed a conversation I'd had a few days ago.

"*Can you brainwash me?*" *the Director asked.*

"*I believe I can, sir.*"

"*I believe you can too, Mr. Jameson.*"

"Leave," I ordered. My voice sounded so loud, so authoritative. Thane swung his head toward me, his eyes bottomless.

One word wouldn't cut it. So I filled my lungs and said,

"Now, Assistant Director Myers. You will return to Freedom and forget this day ever happened."

Thane nodded at Zenn, who released Jag. Blood stained his jacket in crimson rings. Then Thane paused, searching my face as if he'd find a way to ignore my command. I repeated it and said the same to Zenn. Maybe then he wouldn't remember what he'd been forced to do today.

Thane scrunched his lips up, squeezed his eyes shut. He managed to snap his fingers, and Jag's hoverboard whined as it stopped, reversed, and zoomed toward Thane.

Holy technopathic ability.

"I have to take something back. And this will pacify him." By the end of Thane's holy-weird statement, his voice sounded robotic.

But without a board and with bleeding chest wounds, Jag fell, which in my mind, was a much bigger problem than trying to riddle out the meaning behind Thane's cryptic words.

"Leave," I commanded them. Thane complied, his face a smooth plane of nonemotion, and Zenn mimicked him.

"Rescue," I ordered my board. I crouched as it swung in a tight arc under Jag. Once I had him safely onboard, I said, "Half power," hoping to preserve what techtricity I could.

Jag's breath came and went in shallow gulps, his eyes fluttered under closed lids. I pressed my hands to his chest, trying to stop the bleeding with sheer pressure. Then I remembered the med-gel Jag had put in his pocket. I spread the glop over his taser damage, hoping it would be enough to slow the bleeding until I could find proper medical attention.

Time passed as we flew. Breaths. Seconds. Minutes. Hours.

I pulled out Starr's microchip, but when I went to insert it into my wrist port, I found the slot damaged. Dried blood streaked over the back of my hand from where I'd punched a hole through the window.

Super. I replaced the chip in my pocket, applied some med-gel to my wounds, checked the sting on my ankle. My motions felt hollow. The unwatched microchip felt like it weighed fifty pounds—and so did my injured leg.

Hours later the only movement from Jag was the rise and fall of his chest. The med-gel had stopped the bleeding, but he looked bad.

The dead, wintry landscape repeated endlessly. I might as well have been alone.

I was mapless, foodless, hopeless.

For the hundredth time in as many minutes, I wondered how far away the Badlands were.

Raine

I didn't waste any time lounging in my dad's office. I made an excuse to the clones about needing to use the restroom and returned to Level Seven to inquire about Cannon. The physician couldn't seem to do anything but frown.

"Where is he?" I asked for the third time. "He's my match; I have the right to see him."

"That's where you're wrong, Miss Hightower. Citizens don't have rights."

I wanted to stomp my feet and scream. I couldn't read minds, couldn't compel with my voice, but I could do something. I lifted my hand and removed my gloves. I flexed my fingers and watched the physician swallow. Hard.

"I am not an ordinary Citizen," I said, very low. "Now, tell me where he is."

When he hesitated, I reached toward him. He jerked backward. "He's in room seven-oh-four." Panic had replaced the superiority in his voice.

I wasn't sure whether I was satisfied or disgusted by his reaction, so I strode away without thanking him.

Every step echoed off the slick walls, announcing my arrival. I opened the door to room 704 without knocking.

Cannon lay in a bed—the only piece of furniture in the tiny room—his chest rising and falling in an even rhythm. Relief gathered inside me, almost filling the empty spaces.

The p-screen on the wall adjacent to the door broadcasted his medical file and monitored his vitals. Everything appeared stable, and his diagnosis ran across the top: *dehydration, exhaustion, malnutrition.*

I clenched my teeth in anger. People didn't suffer from these kinds of symptoms anymore. Ever. Mandatory rest periods and detailed meal plans made sure of that.

I turned toward Cannon, disturbed by the concave shape of his chest under the thin blanket. The room felt so cold. I tapped the p-screen until the temperature regulations came up. After setting it a few degrees higher, I moved to stand beside Cannon.

His skin, more transparent than ever, stretched over his bones. His shock of dark hair slashed across his forehead, and when I moved it, the clamminess of his skin surprised me.

"I'm sorry," I whispered. His condition was my fault. They'd been trying to get to me through him. And he hadn't broken.

Tears splashed my cheeks. Guilt eased in, filling the hollow places Gunn had left behind. *What do I do?* I chatted him, even though he wouldn't hear me. No one answered, and I had no clue what my next step should be.

Time seemed to stretch endlessly before me. Finally I leaned down and pressed my lips to Cannon's chilly temple. "I will make this right."

After I left the room, I'd only taken two steps before my father materialized in front of me.

"Come with me, Raine," he said, marching toward laboratory seven.

"No, thanks." I wasn't entering that room ever again.

"It wasn't an invitation." Dad flicked his hand across the sensor, and the frosted glass hissed to the side. Dim conversation from the lab filtered into the hall.

"Sorry," I said, not sorry at all. I continued toward the ascender rings, knowing my father needed to pay for Cannon's condition, but unsure about how or when or where. I needed time to think, collaborate, and plan. I needed the safety and quiet of the nocturnal lounge.

"You're not leaving," Dad said.

I ignored him long enough to make it to the descenders, but when he said, "Lock," I couldn't leave no matter how much I wanted to.

"Unlock them," I said. "Now." Rage bubbled in my stomach. I turned back to face him.

He looked ~~disappointed~~ sad. "Raine, please. Don't go." His voice took on a pleading quality, and something strange lilted across my mind.

"That won't work," I said, recognizing the subtleties of his brainwashing. "I'm way past you guilting me into doing what you want."

"I suppose you are." A hard edge flashed in his eyes, but after he blinked, his eyes were round and full and innocent. "It's Friday night; don't you want to watch a projection? Have popcorn?" A genuine smile pulled at his mouth.

Confusion filled my mind. So much of what he said didn't make sense. Was it Friday already? *Yes.*

Had I missed another week of school? *No, you've been*

excused, what with Cannon being in the infirmary and all. I glanced past my dad to room 704 and thought about how much better Cannon looked.

But . . . wasn't there something I needed to do? *Not unless you count relaxing and eating popcorn with your old man.*

I stepped out of the descender ring, unsure where I was. This didn't look like his posh flat on the nineteenth floor. "Dad?"

"Come on, the projection's about to start. You chose something with rainbows on the chip."

Rainbows.

Vi's voice filled my ears, singing her mother's lullaby.

I ground to a halt. "It's not Friday." My words tripped over each other; my voice came out sticky.

Dad clamped his hand on my bicep and began dragging me down the hall.

I thrashed. I swore. I kicked. "Stop brainwashing me! I hate you!"

But he was too powerful for me. Soon, three physicians assisted him, and I went limp.

Help me, I pleaded to the air, the walls, to anyone listening.

No help came. After half a dozen tethers were secure, my dad slipped on filament gloves and advanced toward me.

His lips curled into a snarl. "Let's see what you've been hiding, Rainey."

* * *

Having someone sift through your memories isn't painful. At least not physically. But I felt violated. Deeply.

Dad's hands pressed on the top of my head, and he stood over me, murmuring. Flashes of my memory flew across my vision-screen, each one also landing on his.

When he discovered my involvement in the Insiders, he jerked his eyes to mine. Shock resided in his, as if he couldn't believe his darling daughter would go so far to oppose him. Surely he knew; he'd just been looking the other way because I performed the drains for him. Or maybe because I'd ignored the whole Vi issue.

Until now.

I closed my eyes, grateful for the resulting darkness. I focused on the sound of the air circulators so I wouldn't have to think about what my Dad might see next.

Because I knew what he'd see: Vi's drain.

His fingers tightened in my hair. I refused to cry out, though it hurt.

Bright colors danced in the darkness. My body felt light, weightless.

Fire slashed across my eyelids. Smoke choked the room. My breath shuddered in my chest at the sight of Gunner coming up behind me, of the feel of his hand in mine.

Then the images splintered into a thousand others—memories from my childhood. Things I'd forgotten—or that had been concealed.

The world is fresh and green. Buds perch on delicate limbs, and apple blossoms scent the air. I'm skipping, and a basket bumps into my side with each leap. "Hurry!" I call behind me.

"I'm coming," a woman's voice answers, and it sounds sweet and high and lovely. "Look for the purple vines," she adds, and warmth expands in my chest.

I emerge from the orchard and scour the wall for wisteria. My mother needs the blossoms for her experiments in the bio lab, and she trusts me to help her find them. I used to be afraid of the wall, but now that I'm older (seven is so much better than six), I realize I'm safe on this side. It's the other side that harbors the unknown.

I gather the wisteria flowers for a while. Long enough that my basket fills. I lie down in the greening grass and sigh as I look up into the sky. Helping my mom is way better than any leisure activity, even if it is the weekend and I have more options.

I sit up to find her. The wall towers a few feet to my right. The grassy strip between the wall and the orchard is empty except for me.

Fear rises in my tiny chest. "Mom?" I call.

She doesn't answer. She doesn't come hurrying out of the orchard, her dark hair flying behind her, her pale skin pink from rushing to my aid.

I get up, abandon my basket, and run into the orchard. "Mom! Mom, where are you?"

The trees trap my calls, holding them somewhere no one can hear. I stumble out of the shadows and find my mother in the arms of a man—a man who's not my father.

He kisses her. She leans on him in a desperate way, like she can't support her own weight without him.

Something inside whispers for me to look away. But I can't. Daddy never touches her, except when he's dragging her to Association dinners in the chrome dining room. His touch said I own you, *and the dining rooms were full of men wearing starched shirts and perma-frowns.*

But this man holds her close. Strokes her hair. Wipes away her tears. I inch closer, desperate to hear what they're saying.

"You need to leave," he says.

"I can't," she cries. "He'll kill me for breaching the wall."

"He'll kill you anyway," the man says, right before he spots me with his golden eyes. He murmurs something to my mom, who beckons me forward. Anger flares at my mom for leaving me all alone so close to the wall.

"Raine, this is Gage."

"Touching is against protocol." I'm confused at why she's here with this strange man and who he is and why she's telling me his name.

Gage smiles as he crouches in front of me. "How old are you?" His eyes land on my gloves, and I unconsciously hide my hands behind my back.

"Seven."

"Old enough," he says, and I have no idea what that means. "You should tell her, Kyla."

My mom shakes her head, making the tears fly from her face. She hugs me for the first time in two years. "Go get your basket, honey. We can't be late for dinner."

I don't want to go through the orchard by myself, but I sense that my mom wants to be alone with Gage. So I take one last breath filled with her powdery scent before I go.

I've barely entered the grove when a team of Enforcement Officers descend into the orchard, broadcasting warnings and setting up a protective perimeter. I duck behind the closest apple tree and watch them silence and cuff Gage.

I don't turn away fast enough—I see them tase my mother. I bite my lip so hard, I taste blood. I force myself to look back. They've bound her in black cloth, the symbol of disease. Even her beautiful face is robed—and I know: She's dead.

Gage has been herded a ways off, his golden gaze swirling

with sadness and anger. He catches my eye and lifts his head as if to say, Run! Get out of here.

So I run. Away from my dead mother, who will never comfort me with a forbidden touch again. Away from the golden-eyed man who's not my father. Away from the happiness and safety I've always enjoyed.

I wander the orchards for hours. My feet ache and my throat burns as night settles in. I sit down and cry until finally, my father comes for me.

Gunner

**.** The first city I encountered
squatted on the edge of a
massive river. An equal mix of
shock and relief flowed through me. Another city. The first
I'd ever seen.

The buildings only stood about five stories tall, and I'd
passed half of them in the time it took to blink. Transmissions
jammed in my head. Everything from *Severe weather warning for the next thirty minutes,* to *All Citizens must be tested by
March 1.*

I didn't know what the people needed to be tested for,
and I didn't really care. The city didn't bear a name. Or a wall.

A fence surrounded the central buildings, but beyond

that, fields radiated from the city in sweeping arcs. The whole thing was circular, with only the center hub protected with tech barbs.

The sky threatened to erupt at any moment, which helped me pass the city undetected. But being out in the open with only the threat of driving rain and an endless horizon made my head pound.

When the rains came, I cupped my hands to collect the water and drank until my stomach felt sloshy. Then I leaned over Jag in an attempt to keep him dry. Like that worked. But at least he wasn't taking the needlelike raindrops point blank.

We outflew the weather, but the sky stayed dark with night. I slept as much as someone sitting up on a hoverboard-built-for-one-but-carrying-two could sleep.

At dawn I slowed and stopped near a small stream. I drank again, but my stomach wanted more than calorie-free water. Trees grew thick along the banks, and I commanded my board to take Jag into a cluster of trees while I searched for something to eat. The bushes lay bare this late in February. I'd pretty much resorted to sucking on bark when an animal howled.

Which was my cue to get the hell out of there.

Jag moaned when I shifted him on my hoverboard. The board whined when I stepped on too. "I know, I know," I grumbled as I directed it west. I smeared more med-gel on Jag's wounds, already bone weary from flying.

But I flew all day. Passed another unnamed city. This one had no fence, no barrier, no nothing. But it did have a Thinker broadcasting transmissions. They infiltrated my thoughts, reminding me that other people existed in this world.

I felt muted emotions in the Citizens. Nothing significant. Nothing powerful. As I passed, I pulled on the tech, using it to rejuice my board. The weak sunlight had helped reserve some power, and the tech brought it up enough to fly all night.

All the next day, while I used the solar portlet to power the board, I thought about Raine and Starr, Vi and Zenn, my mom and the Insiders, Thane and Rise Twelve and the end of the world. I thought about my father and his journal. I studied his letter again, recommitting the lines to memory.

My lungs expanded and collapsed, expanded and collapsed. My eyes continued blinking. My stomach tightened with hunger. My throat cried for a drink. My body lived on; my heart kept beating.

As night fell the third time, I approached another city.

This one was much bigger than the previous two, and I decided to stop and recharge my board properly. It shuddered as I landed in what was really a half crash and managed to get Jag wedged between two trash recyclers. More med-gel for him. Another hunger pang for me.

Keep it together, Gunn.

Moving under the stars, I felt the tech tingling in the back of my mouth. I could probably hijack the tech and force it into the board's power chamber, but it'd be great if I could clip in. I slumped next to Jag, my muscles protesting with the littlest movement.

Twinges of tech emanated from the recyclers. I wondered how long I could unplug them before someone would know.

Taking a chance, I removed the recycler from the clip-in on the outer wall and connected my board. I leaned against the wall, my shoulder pressing into Jag's.

My mouth felt so dry. I knew I needed to drink. Eat. But I couldn't move. Couldn't think.

I'm flying over wastelands. City after city blurs by. I know the names and locations of all of them. Cedar Hills. White Cliffs. Lakehead. Harvest. Green River. Grande.

I've been to every city on my father's list. The Association encompasses land from ocean to ocean, has cities from tiny to ginormous. And I have people positioned in them all.

Next to me, Jag points to something ahead of us. A flash of annoyance at his refusal to wear an implant gets overshadowed by the flock of EOs blocking our way into the Goodgrounds.

Jag gains altitude, and I automatically follow him. We work as a team; his success is mine, mine is his. And we desperately need access to the Goodgrounds.

A spike in techtricity hits me as if I'd slammed into a wall. "Damn," I say out loud.

"Maybe we can enter through the Fire Region." Jag swings his board north. Before I can do the same, something crashes into my hovercraft from below. Techtricity shoots through my feet, sending tendrils of blue light rippling along the length of my board. It quivers, slows, stalls.

I'm falling. Jag grows distant, tiny. I close my eyes, all I can think is, So this is how I die, *before someone yells, "Gunner!"*

Blood surges through my body. My heart pulses in my throat. "Raine!"

Her name still burned in my mouth. I said it again—"Raine"— just to make sure I was awake and alive. My voice scratched, but came out. Maybe a little too loud.

I half-expected a spider to come scuttling along to find,

detain, record, report my presence in this unknown alley. When it didn't, I ran my hand wearily across my face.

That's when I noticed the absence of Jag's shoulder against mine.

Seized with fear, I glanced around.

My hoverboard = gone.

Raine

34.

The light played behind my closed eyes and made splintering lines snake across my vision. I existed in between asleep and awake, half-aware of movement in the room but knowing I couldn't quite reach the surface. Images of my mother's peach-colored skin and waves of dark hair swam alongside me. A pair of glowing, golden eyes flashed. Fear flickered inside me.

Daddy lets me sleep for what feels like a long time, but when he wakes me, it's still very dark outside.

"Come on, Rainey," he says softly, guiding me with gloved hands. I cling to him as we descend to a floor with one long

hallway that dead-ends into a wall of glass. My legs quake from roaming the orchards, and the secrets I hold threaten to eat me from the inside out.

Dad takes me through the door and behind the glass wall. My favorite projection puzzle is already broadcasting. The air tastes wrong, though. Too sharp, too clean, like some piece of tech has been working very hard to get rid of all the blood.

The room feels like a laboratory, and I shrink further against my father. "Come now, Rainey." He gently pries my arms off his waist and helps me into a chair that's much too big for my body.

"Play this for a few minutes, okay?"

I don't want to—I want to go back to sleep—but I pretend to solve the projection puzzle. I really watch my dad. He flicks through p-screen after p-screen on the opposite wall, tapping buttons on some and signing his name on others.

A few minutes later a team of physicians enters through the back door. They scurry around the lab, not looking at either me or my father. Another man follows—Thane Myers, my father's top scientist in the Technology Rise. He attends all the dinners, but I force that thought away. The dinners remind me of my mother.

Four Enforcement Officers enter, and fear seizes my muscles.

Tears spring to my eyes, and I can't look at any of the EOs. What if I see the one that tased my mom?

"Dad," I whisper.

And then he's there, rubbing something cold on my bare hand. "I'm sorry, Raine," he says, and I wonder at it. First at the apology—my dad never apologizes for anything—and second at the fact that he used my real name, not that babyish nickname.

Before I can respond, Dad touches both of my temples, securing something sticky there, and Thane presses my hand against another, much larger one. Instinctively, I try yanking away, but my skin's been welded to theirs.

I look up, right into the golden eyes of Gage. I scream, the sound loud and chilling, before the images begin flashing across my vision-screen.

The pictures are blurry, but that's only because I'm crying. Gage enters a Rise, shaking the snow from his shoulders and escaping the chill of darkness.

The lobby bubbles with chatter, with laughter. I see people touch each other casually, a handshake there, a carefree brush of shoulders over there.

"AD Walker," a man says in the vision.

My hand starts to shake, but only because it's connected to Gage's and he's freaking out. I cry harder and try pulling my hand away again.

"Keep going, Rainey." Dad's voice carries a double-edged blade. Excitement and desperation. No concern. "I'll protect you. Just hold on."

The images come faster now. Gage ascends to an office. Reports are falsified. The clock strikes midnight. He retreats downstairs to eat in a café with a horde of people. They wear strange, brightly colored clothing. They smile and laugh, laugh and smile, like they don't have a care in the world.

It's all very strange.

A loud clanking noise accompanies the shaking in Gage's body. Physicians shout. The air circulators can't rid the room of the scent of blood. It comes, thick and tinny, filling the lab, permeating my senses.

For a second everything turns black. But I know the drain isn't over. I've only seen what Gage wants most: a future where people choose for themselves.

A new show starts; now I "get" to see what will happen if Gage's desires come true.

Gage and my father are facing each other. The room is indistinguishable, the walls all white.

"Rise Twelve is the model of the future," Gage says just before he watches my father fall to his knees. The scene ends with Gage standing over the unmoving body of my dad.

I suddenly realize that everything in the lab has gone quiet. Too quiet. Gage's hand in mine feels cold. Too cold.

My shoulders ache from the continued hunching. Tears spill from my closed eyes.

When I open them, I see Gage lying on a silver table next to my too-big chair. He's ~~restrained~~

~~bleeding~~

dead.

"Thane," my father says. "You've just been advanced to Director of Rise Twelve. I'll need a full report."

"Yes, sir," Thane says, glaring at me like his promotion is my fault.

Gunner

35. I leapt to my feet, panic/fear/ anger making my thoughts irra-tional. Something tugged against my elbow. A nourisher. I yanked it out, and clear liquid dripped onto the stones at my feet. Who'd hooked me up?

I didn't have time to find out. The gray beginnings of dawn streamed down between the buildings, and a buzzing sound rattled in my ears.

My heartbeat pulsed in my throat. My hands felt slick. I finally located the noise as a warning to clip in the recycler. So I did, quickly, expecting a horde of EOs or a swarm of spiders to encircle me, arrest me. Something.

Before that could happen, I hightailed it out of the area. *Jag!* I thought, *Where are you?*

No answer.

I couldn't believe he'd stolen my board and left me sleeping in the alley of an unknown city. What a high-class jerk.

Maybe he'd been found, I thought. But that made no sense. If he'd been found, why had I been left sleeping?

Maybe he'd protected me, maybe he'd led the captors away before they found me, maybe he'd used his voice to convince them to nourish me.

There weren't enough maybes for what might or might not have happened. All that mattered: I needed a hoverboard, stat.

I walked straight down the street, growing more nervous as the sky continued to lighten. People would be up soon, going to work, attending their schools, living their controlled lives. A slow anger started in my gut.

Finally a worker—a trash recycler/maintenance/something or other—exited an alley about a hundred feet in front of me.

"Excuse me," I called, grateful the first person I'd seen in this lifeless city was a simple recycler. "I need a hoverboard. Where can I get one?"

Confusion filled the man's face. "A what?"

"Oh, don't tell me you don't have hover tech in this city."

"Of course we have hover tech," the man said quickly. His

expression blanked, his voice deadened. "But it's all kept in the City Center. Nothing this far out."

Super. "How far to the City Center?"

"It's about an hour into the city. The track will get you there faster, but it doesn't activate until seven."

"The track?" I asked, thinking only of the hoverboard oval in Freedom.

"Public transit." He pointed down the street in the direction I'd been walking. "Daily jobs begin on the half hour, so if you want a spot on the seven o'clock track, you'll have to be a bit early."

Using my voice, I asked, "Once I get to the City Center, how do I get clearance for hover tech?"

The man stared straight ahead. "You'll need the right job."

"Thanks," I said, feeling deflated. "Forget you ever saw me."

I took a deep breath just so my lungs wouldn't stick together. The man moved along, continuing his mindless work, leaving me stranded in the streets of who knows where.

I didn't have time for any of this. For some reason I felt an urgency to find my father's journal and get back east. Raine would be waiting for me at the Insider's safehouse.

I sighed—and distinctly heard an unfamiliar voice in my head.

Get off the street. A guy's voice, not full of control, yet overflowing with authority, continued, *Down the alley to your left. Hurry!*

Without overanalyzing, I darted toward the specified alley. Not two seconds later the streets swarmed with people. They marched silently down the streets in the same direction the worker had pointed. Toward the track.

I pressed into the alley-shadows. *Who's there?*

No names, the guy said. *Come farther down the alley.*

The way he said *no names* reminded me of Raine and our Insider rules in Freedom. I strode down the alley, tech itching beneath my skin, making my fingers tingle.

At the corner a man a few years older than me loitered against the building. He wore knee-high boots of black leather with large silver grommets and bulky laces over his jeans. His jacket covered obviously bony shoulders and zipped all the way to his nose.

His eyes shone bright green in the navy darkness. A Thinker. Or at least someone who wasn't brainwashed.

You're not from Castledale, are you? he asked.

No.

You need a hoverboard, right?

Yes. I kept my answers as short as possible.

I don't know you, the guy said, *and I thought I knew all the runners.*

I wasn't sure how to answer. I didn't know him either, and I had no idea what runners were.

I'm from Freedom, I thought, taking a chance. *And I'm not a runner.*

Those green, green eyes searched me, and I swear they saw beneath my skin. *Who's your handler? The one who communicates outside the city?*

No names, I thought back.

The man grinned, not that I could see his mouth. But the crinkles around his eyes made the gesture apparent.

But it's been a long trek, I thought.

The man snapped his fingers, gestured for someone/something to come from around the corner.

A hoverboard appeared. I held my breath, flicking my gaze from him to the board, him, the board. He held out a bottle of water. I took it before mounting the craft, bowing my head in thanks.

Your destination should be the Goodgrounds, the man said. *I'll alert your handler of your journey.*

Super, I thought. I imagined Trek and the grim look he'd have when he got that message. He wouldn't waste a smile on me, even if it was great news that I'd escaped the city. What did Starr see in him, anyway?

Travel safe, the man said, yanking me from the thoughts

of Trek and Starr. He put his hand on the board before I lifted off. His eyes blazed with a need so strong I couldn't look away.

Remember, we're here. And we're ready.

By midday I'd probably relived the weird convo in the alley of Castledale—a city on my father's list twice—a dozen times. I wondered if Jag had left me the message about the Goodgrounds, or if Trek was still assisting me this far from Freedom. I knew he'd get the message from Castledale to Zenn. Hopefully it would help ease Raine's worry. I switched my thoughts to her and what she might be doing.

I thought five days had passed; it must be Friday. She'd probably be sitting in genetics class, ignoring the Educator and plotting her Insider agenda for the weekend.

Starr and I should be participating in our "mandatory free time" later today. Part of me actually wondered what that might entail. A bigger part wouldn't go back to Freedom for anything.

Not even Starr? Or Raine? I thought, and I seriously couldn't answer. The clouds morphed into each girl's accusatory expression as I sailed through the sky.

By evening I wished I'd asked the guy in Castledale for food before jumping on the hoverboard. The water was great and all, but not super life sustaining. I probably should've asked for a map too. A grid. Something.

Though the borrowed hoverboard vibrated, I kept it flying all night. I slept on and off, half-awake when asleep and half-asleep when awake. I wasn't sure if the things I thought/saw/felt were real or not. Sometimes I felt like I'd just eaten a large celebratory meal. Other times my stomach cramped and complained for food.

I alternated between hot and cold, alive and dead, moving and standing still.

I thought I was more awake than asleep when the sun rose. A city glinted under the morning rays. Tall buildings, like the ones in Freedom, blanketed the southern part of the land.

Strong messages entered my mind. Everything had the word "good" in it.

Good Citizens don't go out after dark.

For the good of all, Citizens must labor in their appointed occupations.

Keep the blinds drawn; sunlight damages delicate Goodie skin.

The hoverboard shook now, the whine a constant annoyance. I saw two of everything on the horizon. I blinked, but the images stayed dual.

I tried swallowing, but my throat stuck together and I ended up coughing. When I heard Thane's voice say, *Unauthorized teleporter use is unbecoming a good Citizen,* I choked.

Could Thane have gotten here ahead of me? How long had I been asleep in Castledale?

I didn't hear his voice again, and I couldn't even be sure I'd heard it the first time. Shadows covered my vision, then the brightest light I'd ever seen blinded me.

I saw Raine's face, all curves and soft lips. She said my name, kissed me good-bye. Then Starr crossed my line of sight, her cheekbones as sharp as her eyes. "You're mine," she said before disappearing.

My mom swam before me. And in my hallucination I pictured her standing next to my dad. I placed his flecked eyes and long nose, then invented his hair, his height, taking pieces of myself and inserting them into someone my mom loved.

The sun burned so hot. My throat hurt so bad.

The hoverboard quit.

"Glide," I rasped out, seeing nothing but forest under me. I had a half second to wonder how much damage trees could do before I crashed into one. I fell. Branches attacked my body until at last, I landed on solid ground.

Still, I breathed. Frost covered the forest floor, melted into my jeans.

Hands clawed at me. I opened my eyes and saw that golden ring Thane always wore. His fingers tightened around my throat.

"Get him in here," he said.

Raine

36.

~~Minutes~~ ~~Hours~~ ~~Days~~ A lifetime later the sound of voices pulled me back to the state of nearly awake. My father sounded close, then far, far, then close. Vi's voice stayed in one place—away, probably near the bathroom or the doorway into the living area.

She didn't sound afraid.

Dad sounded angry, but in a seething-under-the-surface kind of way. (I was pretty familiar with this level of fury from him.)

I listened to the come and go of their voices. But when Vi said, "We know there's nothing dangerous past that wall, Director," I pushed toward the surface. What was she doing?

Didn't she know she needed to pretend to be Brainwashed Vi around my dad?

And no way could I leave Freedom. The mere thought of it terrified me, especially now that I remembered what had happened to my mom when she dared to think about it.

And then what I'd done to Assistant Director Gage Walker.

Despair threatened to drag me back down into a hole so deep I would never be fully awake again. I'd lost much more than a mother that day. I'd lost a father too. He'd just brainwashed me so I wouldn't remember.

I remembered now.

"You came from beyond that wall, Violet," my dad said. He didn't even try to conceal the venom in his tone.

"Exactly."

I imagined them squared off, Vi with her arms folded and an expression of *don't mess with me* etched on her face. Dad would be towering, looking down his nose at her, his hands loose and casual, but the jumping muscle in his jaw telling a different story.

When I finally managed to break through the thick water and open my eyes, that's exactly what I saw.

I mumbled something incoherent. Vi pushed past my dad and came to my bedside. "Raine, don't talk, okay? Everything's fine."

But everything wasn't fine. I could never leave Freedom. I knew it, felt it as surely as I felt the hot tears gathering in my eyes.

She placed one long finger on my lips, silencing me and breaking protocol in front of my father. "Just play along."

I nodded, hoping I'd know what to say—and when to say it—to make it through this act.

Vi gave me a tiny nod before she stood and faced my father. "She's agreed to conform."

I couldn't see her face, but I heard the triumph in her voice.

"I told you I could do it," she said next, and I felt like she'd gone shady on me.

Zenn leaned in the doorway of my bedroom, capturing me with his eyes. I wanted to leap out of bed and rage at him. Seeing him here in my flat combined with Vi saying she "could do it," and everything I thought I knew splintered.

Suddenly I remembered something I'd heard in what felt like a different lifetime.

Don't believe everything you hear, okay? Those were probably Cash's last words after he'd defied my father, sabotaged the army of embryos in the Evolutionary Rise, and then got his innermost thoughts splashed across a p-screen.

How could I decide what to believe and what to discard?

"She needs to get cleaned up," Vi said. "Don't worry. I'm in control here."

Dad said, "Fifteen minutes," and left the bedroom with Zenn. The door hadn't completely closed, and I hadn't moved, before Vi flew into action.

"Come on, Raine. Shower." She pulled me from bed and supported me as we shuffled into the bathroom. She started the water and began pawing at my pajamas.

I slapped her hands away. "I can manage." I glared at her, unsure of where we stood. I mean, she was "in control here."

"This is the only secure place right now," she said, so softly that the words didn't echo off the tiled walls. "Bathrooms are unmonitored while in use."

"How did you find that out?"

"Zenn." Her eyes burned with a life I'd never seen before. "Listen, Gunn and Jag got away, but from what we were able to glean from Zenn's medicated mind, Jag's hurt. And Gunn has nothing but a hoverboard. Thane returned with their backpack of supplies and an extra board. You've been asleep for four days, and I've been attending Insider meetings every night." She spoke so fast, I could barely keep up.

Gunn has nothing looped in my head.

"Wait," I said. "Insider meetings every night? Not just on the weekends?"

"Every night. The government is in complete chaos. We're taking full advantage by setting off the barrier alarm each evening." She grinned and pointed at the streaming water. "You're losing your shower time."

I undressed quickly and stepped into the shower as the alerts came up in my cache. Every night the barrier breach message had been sent out. "Keep talking."

"We don't have time to discuss Insider stuff right now. You need to act like you're repentant. On your dad's side. Brainwashed. Can you do that?"

As I scrubbed my hair, I thought about it. I wasn't sure how much of an act it would be. I didn't want to leave Freedom. I didn't want to die the way my mother had. I didn't want to give my dad any reason to make me drain Cannon—or anyone else—and then claim he'd "protect me" when I killed them.

The water turned off, and Vi held up a towel for me. "Well?"

"I can do that," I said, my throat tight and my voice hardly my own.

Vi scrutinized me, her all-knowing gaze as frightening as my father's. "You have great power here, Raine. You know so much about your dad and how he runs this city. We need your strength to survive."

She wasn't a Seer; her voice didn't go all freaky when she said it. But her words still rang true in my heart.

I didn't know if I could be strong enough to help anyone survive. I didn't even know if I could help myself.

I mean, I never had before.

Precisely fifteen minutes after my father marched out of my room, a knock rattled my bedroom door. "Let's go, Raine," he said through the metal.

Vi pulled the enhancer through my hair one more time, dyeing the last strand the color of fresh snow. "Go on. Good luck."

She hugged me before I left, triggering a flash of memory.

My mom hugs me, hugs me hard. I'm tiny, hardly up to her waist, but I cling to her, somehow knowing that this is something important.

"You're five years old now, Raine. A big girl." She wipes tears from her eyes. "You'll have new transmissions tonight, and if you have any questions, you must ask me in secret, okay?"

"Secret?" The word sits on my tongue strangely. There are no secrets in Freedom. Daddy is always watching. Daddy knows everything.

"We can talk near the food-dispenser or in the bathing chamber, okay?" Her eyes radiate the same urgency as her voice.

I nod. "Okay."

That night my transmissions are brand-new, and they loop through, Touching is against protocol for anyone who is unmatched, *over and over again.*

I never approach my mom about the new message. I never hug my mother again—until the day she dies.

Enforcement Officers escorted me up to my father's office. The door hissed open and sealed shut, adding to my anxiety. With the break in my brainwashing block, so many memories were surfacing. Things that had long been hidden from me.

Four e-boards pulsed with green and blue screens, sending colored patterns onto the glass where my father stood with his hands clasped behind his back.

I slunk into the ergonomic across from his desk, partly playing my role, but mostly scared out of my mind.

"How are you, daughter?" My dad pulled the curtains closed, turned from the windows, and settled into his desk chair. He glanced at the e-boards before powering down two of them.

"Fine. Tired, maybe."

He half-looked at me, his eyes hooded and dark. "You've been asleep for days. Surely you're not tired."

"No, I'm not tired," I said automatically. Too fast. He'd compelled me.

He proceeded to grill me with questions from, "When

is Cannon's birthday?" (August 4) to "How are your marks in ancient civilizations?" (uncomplimentary), and then "Have you ever unclipped your cache from the transmission portal at night?" (I hesitated the longest on that one before I admitted that I had).

I didn't know if I passed the session or not, but Dad dismissed me back to my flat unescorted. Vi and Zenn weren't there, but they'd left a microchip on my pillow. When I plugged it into my port, a single message flashed across my vision-screen.

Tonight: your father's office. Get as much info as you can on your mother and Gage Walker.

I destroyed the chip thinking, *Sure, no problem*, even though I had no idea how to get into his office or find the files or pretty much anything else.

Gunner

37. I only woke up because my stomach was severely pissed that I hadn't eaten yet. My head hurt in at least four places, and I couldn't hear out of my right ear.

The room I lay in had no heat. A single tech unit poured light from the ceiling. The wind whistled along the wall where I lay. I forced myself to my elbows and then into a sitting position. My muscles didn't like the movement and told me so.

I scanned the surrounding walls for an exit. There wasn't one. That launched me into a standing position, adrenaline pumping through my veins.

"Let me out!" I slapped the wall closest to me, which

curved in a twisted rocky smile until it met another one. This wall wasn't made of rock, but sounded the same. Solid, caging.

The only thing in the room besides me was the ratty blanket I'd woken up with. I sat on it, pressed my back into the curve of the wall, concentrated on finding the emotions of the closest person. Immediately a buzz of nervousness filtered through the not-made-of-rock wall.

I got up, strode over to it. I pounded. "I know you're there! Let me out!"

Not five seconds later a *snick!* filled the room and a panel lifted from the wall.

A girl walked in, her hair the brightest pink I'd ever seen. Her holy-bare skin stretched from her shoulder to the tips of her fingers in a smooth cocoa color. She should've been freezing, but she simply regarded me with steely eyes the color of coal.

"Who are you?" I barked.

She swept her gaze from my messy hair to my shoeless feet. Which reminded me . . .

"Where's my stuff?" I fingered the loose shirt. The fabric felt foreign, too light. And the color of oatmeal definitely wasn't my favorite. At least I still had my own jeans. I dug in the pocket and sighed when I felt the microchip Starr had given me.

"You're the one Jag left in Castledale, aren't you?" Her words made me take a step back.

"How do you know about Jag?" I asked.

Something weird crossed her face. "How did Jag get busted up?" An even weirder quality hid in her voice. Almost like she had a thing for Jag.

The fact that neither of us was answering questions wasn't lost on me. "Okay, fine. I'll go first." I ran my hands over my face, through my hair. "I'm Gunner Jameson. Jag was with me, but Zenn tased him as we were leaving Freedom. I did what I could, but all I had was med-gel. We stopped in Castledale to power up and rest. When I woke up, Jag was gone."

She took the information without flinching, without any reaction at all. And she didn't offer an explanation for where I was, who she was, or anything. "And I swear Thane Myers was the one who captured me." I glanced over her shoulder to the seamless wall. "He's not out there, is he?"

"No," she said, like I was just supposed to accept her at her word. "I found you."

I must've been hallucinating, because this girl didn't look or sound like Thane. "So?" I asked. "Your turn."

She scowled at me. "I'm Indy. I've been running the Resistance since Jag went missing ten months ago. This is our forest hideout in the Goodgrounds, and it's actually safer here than in the Badlands these days."

Indy! I almost sank to my knees in relief. "I've been looking for you."

If she was surprised, she didn't show it. "Why are you looking for me?"

"You have a journal I need. My father's journal."

She looked away before quickly refocusing her gaze on me. An unsettling feeling crept back into my muscles. "You do have a journal, right?"

"That journal again." Her voice held no power. Her eyes weren't sharp. I didn't think she was a Thinker in any form.

"Do you have it?"

"I don't even know why you guys want it. I've read it, and it doesn't even make sense." She stood so calmly; her gaze never wavered.

"Where's Jag?" I asked. If she wouldn't help me find the journal, I knew he would.

"He stole my hoverboard in Castledale. That's why I crash-landed on that other thing. My board would've made it much faster. He's probably already here." I glanced around as if he'd materialize from the silver wall the way she had. "So where is he?"

"He instructed Fret to tell you to come to the Good-grounds. Did Fret tell you that?"

"If Fret has sick boots and freaky green eyes, then yeah, he said I wanted to be in the Goodgrounds."

She frowned, rubbed her hands over her bare arms as if cold. She should be, because the air in the room delivered a make-my-teeth-chatter chill. "We'll have to evacuate. Welcome to the team, Gunner." She turned and moved back toward the panel.

"Wecome to the team? Wait a second." I leapt to follow her, unwilling to be enclosed in the doorless cavern longer than necessary. I emerged into a much brighter room, filled with old wooden chairs, backpacks, and teenagers.

The floor had been cut from the rock, and the arching ceiling dripped water. But these guys had access to some serious tech. Gadgets covered all available surfaces; people spoke in quiet voices and elbowed each other when they caught sight of me.

"Freakin' freaker," a girl not much older than me said. "You weren't kidding, Indy."

"He looks just like him," someone else said.

"Like who?" I demanded. The faces closest to me emptied.

"Jag," the freakin' girl said, her voice dull.

"Don't talk like that," Indy snapped. "You're not in charge here, wiseguy."

I glanced around, still unconvinced that Thane wasn't here. I swore I'd seen his ring, swore someone had their fingers locked around my throat. I almost wanted to see Thane. Then I could grill him with questions and finally figure out what was really going on.

"Okay, guys, listen up," Indy said, raising her voice enough to make an echo bounce off the overhanging rocks. "This is Gunner. He's the runner from Freedom." She glared at me. "We have to evacuate this space. Pack it up."

The members of the Resistance didn't resist. They didn't ask questions. They simply started loading up their gear.

"Wait, wait," I said, half-turning so my back faced most of the crowd. "Where are we going? And why? And where's Jag?"

"We're relocating to a more secure location nearby," Indy said through clenched teeth.

Like I cared if she was upset. It wouldn't kill her to dole out a few more answers.

"Why?" I prompted.

"Because you showed up, genius. Your little how-to-crash demo didn't go unnoticed. Hovercopters have been scouring the area since midmorning."

"Where's Jag?" I asked for the tenth time. I needed the journal, dammit!

"I'll tell you in the more secure location," Indy clipped out. "Do you want to come with us or not? You're welcome to stay here and find out how outsiders—and rebels—are treated in this city."

The very thought of that made my empty stomach tighten. "Yeah, I want to come with you." I looked around for something, though I didn't know what. "Do you have some shoes for me? And, uh, what can I do to help?"

She rolled her eyes in response, collected some tech from the table, and walked away.

I didn't know pine needles could be so pointed. And for future reference, the forest was filled with sticks. Sharp ones.

My feet felt raw by the time we reached an ancient, abandoned house on the edge of a whole graveyard of dwellings. In the light of the half moon, all the buildings looked foreboding and sad. Trees ran right up to the back of the house. I filed in after everyone else, half-expecting Jag to be chilling inside with my juiced-up hoverboard, flipping through the journal.

He wasn't.

Dust blanketed the table and chairs, the old electric light fixtures, everything. But not as much as there should've been, probably. My suspicions were confirmed when Indy said, "Jag used to conduct business here. We've taken over the area so we can run our meetings."

"What kind of meetings?" I asked.

Indy's only answer was to stroll toward the front door. She motioned me forward, and I reluctantly followed.

Outside, the air held the unmistakable sound of freedom. Transmissionless. Behind me, I could feel the wonder and anxiety of Indy's team. To my right, I felt . . .

. . . a twinge of fear. And then a hard knot of determination. I swung my gaze to the house across the street. The windows stared back, dark and blank.

"What's—?"

"Jag checked in here yesterday, just for a few hours. Then he went to his uncle's house in the Centrals." Indy walked down the crumbling sidewalk with her head held high, her shoulders square. "Over the past eight months I've established a tiny settlement here, consisting of completely free-thinking people."

I couldn't comprehend her words. They seemed to twist and reorder themselves in my head. "What?"

"This region had been under a looser level of control for twenty-five years. A whole settlement of free-thinking people existed just beyond the fence." She nodded further west.

"The Badlands. It's controlled now, has been for about eight months. Thane made sure of that."

I wondered if Thane's reach was global. It certainly seemed to be. We walked silently down ancient streets with houses on both sides. The forest had reclaimed the area; sproutlings and weeds grew through driveways and right up to front porches.

"But we've been smuggling some of the strong-minded into these houses ever since. We hold nightly classes on how to survive without government aid. Tonight we have a seamstress showing everyone how to mend their own clothes."

She paused, as if waiting for me to say something. I didn't. I'd seen this for myself in Rise Twelve, but I'd be lying if I said I wasn't surprised people could fend for themselves in the middle of a forest. I looked around. I wouldn't even know what to eat here.

"If people can take care of themselves, they don't need a Thinker," Indy said. "If you can sew your own clothes and make your own meals, you don't need the government to provide everything for you."

Indy let me chew on that in the silence for a while. This was Rise Twelve in the wild. The Insider goals coming to life.

At the end of the street she crossed to another cracked sidewalk and headed back the way we'd come. "You wanna go in?" She stopped in front of the house, and though it didn't look any different from any of the others, I could feel the emotions of the people inside.

Anxiety. Fascination. Happiness.

"No, I'm good," I said.

Indy crossed the street back to the lair. I followed, and we entered the main living area, where a dozen other teenagers were hanging out. I wondered if the stairs in the corner would bear my weight and if there were proper beds in the rooms above.

Along with a heavy dose of debilitating hunger, worry gnawed at my gut. I needed (a) something to eat, stat, (b) someone to help me find the journal—and Jag, and/or (c) everyone to stop staring at me.

Instead, I got (d) Indy.

She beat a couch cushion against the floor to dedustify it, and then sat across from me. "You hungry?"

"Yes." My mouth watered at the thought of food.

She held out a glass of cloudy water. So not food. I took it. "Um, thanks."

"It's protein," she said, that edge of annoyance accelerating.

I drank it, not really enjoying the fizz as it popped in my throat. "It's super," I choked out.

Indy folded her still-bare arms, as if trying to keep herself from clawing my face off.

I appraised her as I took another long swig of the not-food-but-protein-water. Surprisingly, my stomach stopped freaking out. Indy reminded me of Raine, with that calm collectedness that not many people could pull off. A slight waver of distrust flowed from her, but other than that, she held herself together.

"Can we talk in private?" I said, leaning forward and lowering my voice.

The people loitering in the living area hightailed it out of there when Indy raised her hand and waved them away. "Go for it."

"I need that journal. It belonged to my father, and it has information that will help the Resistance, the Insiders, all covert operations within the Association."

Indy sighed, looked away.

"Jag said you'd have it," I said, trying—and failing—to be patient.

A flicker of resignation flew across her face. "I think . . . no wonder he was so mad."

I didn't have the energy to even say, "What?" so I just waited for her to explain.

"He turned the office inside out. Then he took off."

"So you don't have the journal?"

Indy swallowed, wouldn't look directly at me. "He may have said something like 'I can't believe you lost it,' before he left." She crossed her arms and frowned. "In my defense, I've been running the freaking Resistance by myself for almost a year. And that journal makes no sense."

I didn't care if it made sense or not. I needed it. "Where did Jag go?"

"To his uncle's place in the Centrals. A farmhouse, I think. He needed medical help, and his uncle is a safe contact."

"I need to go there, stat."

Raine

38.

Vi and Zenn didn't return before lights out, so I lay in bed with my transmissions plugged in. The brainwashing messages rotated around and around in my head, but I didn't hear them. I obsessed over every technicality about getting into my dad's office.

Surely my dad would've changed his entrance code.

Surely there'd be reinforced squads of EOs watching the flat.

Surely my mother's files would be floating in the oblivion of deletions by now. I mean, he'd erased her life as completely as possible. And if he did that inside my mind, I didn't think he'd be keeping e-copies of anything Mom-related.

I never made it to midnight. The door to my flat clicked open, releasing the pent-up tension I'd filled the apartment with. I sat straight up in bed, my eyes glued to the doorway.

Cannon leaned against the doorframe, his breathing somewhat labored. I jumped out of bed and went to meet him.

"What are you doing here?" I asked, throwing my arms around him and holding on tight.

"Let's go to the nocturnal lounge," he said.

I didn't hesitate. I slipped into some shoes, donned my gloves, and walked next to him to the Medical Rise. Once we were safely tucked away in the deepest, darkest corner of the most unused lounge, I allowed myself to breathe.

This silence had always been welcome. It had always felt natural between Cannon and I, even when in the next moment he might tell me the name of another girl he wanted to sneak out and see. Even after I'd completed another drain and had so much shame boxed up inside.

We always had the purifying silence of the nocturnal lounge. We always had each other.

"You were right." I broke the silence.

"About what?"

"I'm not as good as you. I shouldn't have gotten involved with Gunner Jameson."

Cannon sighed as he reached for my hand. He held on,

his bare palm to my gloved one. "Doesn't matter. I wish you would've picked another guy, one that didn't have fifteen red flags on his record, but whatever."

I allowed myself half a smile, because Cannon had only allowed his voice to half-tease.

"I'm sorry," I said. "I think I made things worse for you."

Cannon remained quiet. I wondered if he was angrier than I thought, if I'd pushed things too far because of Gunner. We'd never had this awkwardness between us, and I was determined to erase it.

"Cannon, I'm sorry," I repeated. "Please don't be mad."

"I'm not mad," he said. He truly sounded not mad.

I pressed my eyes closed to keep the tears inside. "I didn't know what would happen. I tried to be careful. I didn't mean to make your life harder."

"Let's just call it even," he said.

I pushed myself into a sitting position. "Even? What do you mean?"

Cannon lay still with his eyes closed too. Rain began to caress the window in soft patters. After only a few seconds the rain gave way to snow, the patter replaced with more silence.

"Cannon?"

"It's raining," he said.

"I'm not going to melt," I said, refusing to continue the game. I got up and left the nocturnal lounge. I ignored the clone who offered me an assortment of protective gear. I stood at the glass door, watching the snow fall, wondering when Cannon had started keeping score.

"Raine, I really am sorry." Cannon came up behind me, his voice pleading and soft.

Before I could turn and re-establish our best friend status, something hot pricked my elbow.

I looked down to find a needle sliding out of my skin. Cannon held the other end of the syringe. Tears leaked out the corners of his eyes. "I'm sorry."

Those two words echoed in the resulting blackness. Cannon caught me before I hit the floor, before I passed out.

I'm sorry

    sorry

        sorry.

The smell lingering in the air terrified me. I knew this scent. Bleach and silver polish and tech and lab-coated physicians. The smell that clung to my dad.

To death.

Sure enough, when I opened my eyes, I lay in laboratory seven. The tech lights overhead made starbursts pop in my eyes. I squinted but couldn't see anything. Only the ceiling, which was a new vantage point.

The ergonomic where I usually sat felt harder, unyielding under my back. With horror, I realized I wasn't sitting in a chair.

I was lying on a table.

A long, silver table, no doubt.

The table.

"She's awake," someone said.

"I told you she wouldn't be out long," my dad answered.

Before I could respond—I wanted to scream and rage—several pairs of hands moved over my body, applying sensors and tech gunk.

My arms got stretched out so my body formed a T and were secured at the shoulder, elbow, and wrist.

I tried to lift my head to see more of the lab, but a tether ran across my forehead, and I couldn't look left or right, only eternally straight up.

Panic clogged my throat; fury built in my bloodstream. I unleashed a string of choice words, all meant for my father.

No sound came out of my mouth.

Something cold painted my right palm.

"Lie still, Rainey," Dad said.

As if I could move. I wasn't sure what was happening, but

being strapped to a table, silenced, and then told to lie still didn't sound like party preparations.

Then a warm hand suctioned to mine, and surprise flitted through me. Who was that? Was there someone else like me? Someone cursed with this seeing talent?

Horror shot through me when I thought: Had the scientists in the Evolutionary Rise cloned me?

I didn't know, because in the next second, fire erupted in every cell of my body. Licking flames coated my skin; billowing smoke filled my lungs; hot ash pricked at my brain, my eyes, and my somehow still-beating heart.

My body reacted without direction from my mind. My back arched (violently). My voice screamed (silently). My eyes cried tears of pain and loss (eternally).

Being on the table had never been like this for my victims. They just lay there, unhappy, sure, but not in so much pain they contorted and thrashed.

Except for Gage. Horror snaked through my body. Whoever was draining me didn't have control of their ability. They were going to kill me—just like I had killed Gage. The desire to yank my hand away before I died screamed through my soul.

Eventually the pain faded. My muscles relaxed.

At least until the images came up on my vision-screen. They started murky, obscured by a wavering film of plastic.

But Gunner is Gunner, no matter if he's in high-def or not. A swirl of sound and smell and touch moved around me. But I existed inside the eye of the hurricane, immune to all of it.

Because of Gunn. Across my vision-screen, I saw him standing outside. The sun streamed down; it must've been springtime. The grass was still greening from the winter. Red tulips had just bloomed in the garden along the front of a small, brown-brick house.

The windows were all blinded, but the front door opened, and I skipped down the steps. My hair flowed behind me like white silk, and I wore traditional plainclothes. Nothing special. Nothing to indicate where we lived, or when. Gunn glanced at me out of the corner of his eye and couldn't hide his grin.

Without speaking, we moved toward the corner of the house and around it. The vision followed, as if we had spider surveillance, recording everything. I felt removed from the scene, yet fully immersed in it as well.

On the table in the lab, my heart pulsed quickly with anticipation and fear, just as it did as Gunn and I strode toward an orchard. Once under the cover of trees, he stepped closer to me and took my hand in his.

A stream of tears trailed over my cheek at his gentle

touch. At the warmth and safety of his hand. At the way he smelled like strength and fresh-cut grass and buttered toast.

"That's all there is, sir." The words cut through the beauty of the apple blossoms, obliterating the picture into fragmented shards. I couldn't identify who'd spoken, so strong was the ache to return to that orchard, be with that guy. My vision hadn't changed. What I wanted and what would happen when I got it were one and the same.

"She wants to love deeply." Dad sighed, like this was the worst thing I could want. "I don't think I need to see any more," he said. "Get her cleaned up."

As my father's footsteps retreated, the gloved hands came. They wiped my tears the way they always had. They released the bindings, carefully, with gentleness and friendship, as in the past.

When he finally lifted me from the table, Cannon wore an anguished expression. He pulled me to him, where the soft folds of his shirt would absorb my tears. "I'm sorry, Raine. I'm so sorry."

Gunner

39.

Indy laughed, a sound without humor. "You want to go to the Centrals? Right. I don't think so."

I stood and headed for the front door. "I'll go myself. I don't need your rebels. Or you."

She followed, her anger a swirling cloud around me. "You can't go. If you get caught, you'll compromise us all."

I spun around. "Whatever. How does my getting caught compromise you? You'll still have your Resistance, your—" I almost said "boyfriend," but stopped myself. I couldn't stand to be in the same room with her for another second. But I didn't want to go into the empty forest/abandoned neighborhood alone. So I pushed past her and strode toward the staircase in the back of the living area.

"You have high-class voice power," she yelled, following me. "We risked a lot to get you out of that city."

I spun toward her. "Wrong. We all risked a lot to get *Jag* out of Freedom. And he doesn't even have the journal." My anger matched hers.

She deflated with the mention of Jag, confirming my suspicions of her fanboy crush on the guy. Plus, the air definitely held some weird lovey-dovey feelings. "We need you," she said, softer, but with just as much conviction.

I couldn't find any trace of betrayal in her emotions. I'd almost conceded her point when a loud bang landed on the front door.

I turned toward the sound. Indy took one step before the front of the house exploded into splinters and flames.

I lost three, four, five seconds of my life to complete blackness. A maelstrom of sound assaulted me, but I couldn't see. Indy had landed on top of me, and we'd both smashed into the wall behind us.

When I regained my sight, strong tech lights beamed from the front of the house. A buzzing sound added to the crackle of the flames.

"Hovercopters," Indy wheezed.

I didn't speak as I struggled to my feet.

"Gunner." Thane's voice cut through the hovercopter hype, the sizzling fire, everything.

"They can't have anything in the office," Indy said. She darted forward, grabbed the edge of a burning rug. She dragged it down the hall and into a book-filled room. I watched, astounded by the strength she had to think clearly, and waited for Thane to swoop in and tase me.

Smoke and ash clogged the air. Gray plumes rose into the steaming night.

"Gunner," Thane said again.

I took a deep breath just as Indy emerged from the now-flaming office. "I'll come with you," I said, my voice on high control. "But everyone else goes free. No discussion. No compromises."

Time ticked by in crackles and crashes. Finally Thane stepped through the flames. "Done."

I glanced at Indy, inclined my head in a universal gesture of *get out of here.*

She shook her head just once, forcing me to growl, "Go. I'm fine."

She stepped closer, stood up on her tiptoe, kissed my cheek. As she did, I felt her slip something in my back pocket.

Then she disappeared through a door that led to the back of the house, leaving me alone with the Assistant Director.

Thane led me through the spotlight beams of the hovercopters toward a long, rectangular contraption.

"Get in," he said, lifting a panel on the side of the long box to reveal seats inside. The transport hovered several inches off the ground, adjusting to my weight as I sank into a chair.

Thane got in the other side and barely spared me a glance. "Two passengers to the Centrals."

The craft maneuvered around a cluster of young trees, shot into the night.

"Slow," Thane said, which only accelerated my pulse. The transporter responded, and I felt the weight of the darkness settle on my shoulders.

"Don't talk. Just listen," Thane said. I'd never heard this level of power in his voice. Something strange happened to my throat. It narrowed, making breathing difficult.

"I have to travel a lot for my line of work," Thane began.

"By line of work, you mean brainwashing people?" I choked out.

Thane pierced me with a glance. Something flashed across his face. Something very much like anger. Just as quickly as it had appeared, it fled. "More like unbrainwashing them."

Silence stretched the minutes into thin filaments until I wanted to punch through the windows of the transport just to let some sound in.

"I stayed the longest in the Goodgrounds," Thane finally said, his eyes unfocused as if watching his life play out on the windshield of the transport. "I loved my daughters. I couldn't leave them." He looked at me again. "No matter what anyone says, I loved them." It sounded like a plea.

"But Van Hightower is very demanding. He wanted me back in Freedom, permanently. I'd left Rise Twelve in the hands of someone Van didn't like. When he was killed, I had to return."

I pressed back into the unyielding seat, wishing it would swallow me whole. *Killed?*

But that didn't compare to the realization that I had seen him that night, in Rise Twelve. I'd stood in his flat, touched his fluted mirror.

"It was the hardest thing I've ever done—leaving my family behind in the Goodgrounds," Thane was saying, and I forced myself to pay attention. "Especially Vi. When her talent was finally registered, Van hand selected her, and I was dispatched to bring her in."

"I heard you killed your other daughter," I said, the words a forced whisper.

"If there's one thing Van doesn't understand, it's human emotions," Thane said, spinning the gold ring on his middle finger. "It's his greatest weakness. It's what has allowed me to Think over Rise Twelve, unbrainwashing everyone who comes through the door, for the past ten years. It's why I can work in the office down the hall from him, sending instructions to the Insiders all over the union, and he doesn't know. He truly believes that I would never go against him. I've made sure he believes that by killing my first daughter and bringing him my second."

The thought of living that kind of life sickened me, mostly because I'd been watching Raine do it for a year.

He held up his hand, something that looked dangerously like tears shining in his eyes. "I wear this ring in remembrance of my daughters. One lost, one wandering in the dark. One day I'll pay for what I've done."

He said it so simply that I couldn't respond.

Thane dropped his hand and looked out the window. "Van Hightower also can't see beneath the surface unless he looks," he said. "I brought Vi to Freedom to protect her. My options were to bring her in or kill her." He drummed his fingers on his knee, as if nervous. If he was, that was the only sign.

"He doesn't look under my surface anymore. He trusts

me. I've spent two decades earning that." Thane's last word felt final, like he was done talking.

But at what cost? I thought. I didn't know what to say or how to proceed from here.

He exhaled loudly, like it lifted a burden from him, and turned back to me. "So, Gunner, these last few weeks have been very trying, to say the least. Once Van put you on his short list, I've been doing everything possible to get you Inside."

I stared openly at him now. "You? *You* wanted me on the Inside?"

"Or assigned to me. I accomplished both." He sounded so pleased with himself. A momentary flash of annoyance mingled with the raging disbelief I had storming inside my chest.

"See, if you were my student, I'd have access to your cache. Then I could guide you, help you . . ." He let his words hang there, screaming with implications.

Holy *could it be him?* no way.

The voice had been so garbled sometimes. Or too low or too high. But always there. I should've known Trek couldn't do that. He was still in school—and he hadn't missed a class in forever.

"You're the assistant? You've been in my head?"

A flicker of movement turned his lips upward. "Me. Or Starr, who I finally managed to secure as my protégé at the end of last term. She's in line to Think over Rise Twelve should anything happen to me."

Starr. Oh my hell, *Starr*. My head spun with all they might have seen or learned over the past couple of weeks.

"What about Trek Whiting?" I asked.

Thane half-smiled. "He doesn't live out in the camps for fun. He has more tech out there than we've got in Twelve. A whole communication hub. But he only helped a couple of times, right at the beginning."

I didn't want to talk about Trek *he's so awesome* Whiting. "Why Starr?"

"She's your match, and then when she came on board with me, Van wouldn't think twice about her comm-ing you all the time. We were able to cover up the most serious of your protocol issues. With her set to Think over Rise Twelve and your voice, we were ready to begin the overthrow. It was perfect."

"Perfect," I murmured, my brain simultaneously full and empty at the same time. Thane must have sensed that, because he gave me a few minutes to process.

Thane = the Insider-sympathetic Thinker of Rise Twelve. Holy heavy.

Starr = helping me sneak out to meet Raine or break into

the Confinement Rise for a quick chat with Jag. No wonder she'd been so angry with me and my rash choices. We really were in this together.

"So now that you know all this," Thane said, his voice lowering and finally a wisp of sadness emanating from him, "I'll need you to do something for me."

For some reason I was nodding. "Name it."

"After we get to the farmhouse, after you have the journal, you'll need to tase me."

Raine

My name is Raine Rose Hightower. My name is Raine Rose Hightower. I am seventeen years old. I live in the city of Freedom. My best friend is Cannon Lichen. I am in love with Gunner Jameson.

My name is Raine Rose Hightower . . .

I sat on my bed, my knees drawn to my chest, rocking back and forth. As the sun settled into the ocean, I repeated the facts of my life over and over and over. I felt like if I didn't, my vitals would slip away into oblivion.

I'd forget.

The truth would be erased, just as I'd seen so many other things in my life wiped away.

In the kitchen, Cannon bumped around every now and then. I almost called out to him just so I wouldn't have to endure the silence of my bedroom alone. He'd come. He loved me in a different way than Gunn did, but it was love nonetheless.

And I loved him too, the way only two people who know each other's every secret can. I'd watched him pour the post-drain meds down the drain. He'd tucked me in bed with another apology and said he'd be here whenever I wanted to talk.

I didn't want to talk. Not yet.

My flatmate's name is Violet Schoenfeld. Her match is Zenn Bower, but she's in love with Jag Barque.

My name is Raine Rose Hightower. I am seventeen years old.

My name is Raine Rose Hightower . . .

Gunner

41. Fifteen silent minutes later, with the sun cresting the mountains in the east, the transport halted a safe distance from a lonely farmhouse.

I got out. "So I'm going to tase you?" I asked Thane, who stood on the opposite side of the craft, looking toward the tall buildings smashed against the horizon.

"Above all, Van must think I'm with him. And besides, I've already reported you to the Greenies." He turned his attention to the house. "Come on, we don't have much time." His boots crunched on the snow. "I'll take the basement; you search the main floor."

I approached the building with caution. I wasn't sure

what I expected to find. Trails had been tamped in the snow leading from the back porch to a sagging outbuilding. A clothesline stretched from the leaning roof of the smaller building to a leafless tree. A sense of peace I couldn't describe accompanied the scene.

I followed a path in an indirect route to the back door so I wouldn't leave footprints. I didn't knock, just went inside with Thane right behind me. The little kitchen where I stood looked functional yet not extravagant, just like all controlled societies.

"Find the journal," Thane whispered as he passed me and disappeared down a dark stairwell.

A single glass sat on the weathered table, half full of cloudy liquid. The living area appeared neat and tidy, with a homewoven blanket tossed over the arm of a rocking chair. Down the hall, one door lay closed on the right, but an open door on the left revealed a bedroom with an already made bed.

I didn't question whether the bed had been slept in or not. The house felt alive. Someone definitely lived here, took care of the place.

Another door stood ajar in the corner of the bedroom, revealing a small anteroom stuffed with papers and books and letters.

I went in and simply stared for a few minutes. The existence of all this paper felt like evidence that this house belonged to someone in the Resistance.

Had my dad owned a room like this once?

I fingered a long instrument, obviously used for writing, what with the sharpened tip. I measured the weight of it in my fingers. I breathed in the scent of old wood and something that smelled sharp, colored. When I uncorked a flask of black liquid, I found the source of the smell. Ink.

So wrapped up in the joy/love/beauty of the papers and books and writing supplies, I didn't notice anything. Until my eyes landed on a brown leather book. A tremor of excitement zipped through me. Fear accompanied it, as I remembered the dream where I'd opened the journal to only blank pages.

I reached for it, and it seemed to take forever for my fingers to brush the cover. I lifted it, registered the weight of it in my hand, made to open it.

"Who are you?" someone asked in hard, even syllables.

I turned around slowly. I slipped the journal into my back pocket, disappointed and relieved I hadn't been able to look inside.

Jag stood there, gripping a shovel. His bright blue eyes burned with liquid fire. His hair stuck up at just-slept-on angles, but he wore clean clothes and a thick bandage around his right arm.

"Oh, hey Gunner," he said, like nothing had happened between us. Like he hadn't left me clipped into a nourisher, alone in the unknown city of Castledale. "You could've just knocked. I'd have let you in. Did Indy tell you where I was?"

I took in the sharpness of the shovel before speaking. "You left me in Castledale. What gives?"

He half-smiled and propped the shovel against a dresser, where it fell to the floor. "Sorry. But Fret took care of you, yeah? He said he would."

"That's not the point." I folded my arms, but before Jag could explain properly, footsteps behind him caught my attention. Jag bent to retrieve the shovel as Thane stumbled into the room.

"Leave it," Thane commanded. He took a step to the right as if circling his prey, never once looking at me. I swallowed hard, wondering how long we'd have to play before the Greenies showed up.

Jag straightened, shovelless. "I would *not* have let you in," he said to Thane.

I made to move, but Thane held up one hand. "Better stay there, Gunner. We don't want any of these barbs to hit you, now, do we?" He raised a taser, activated it, aimed it at Jag.

I looked at a point above Thane's shoulder. He had the taser, but I needed it if he wanted me to zap him.

I couldn't detect any emotion from either of them. They both buried their true feelings deep, deep, deep.

Thane took another sideways step, taser still locked onto Jag's chest. "So."

Silence followed. Thane licked his lips as if he didn't have his speech prepared and wasn't quite sure what to say next.

So maybe I should speak first. "Drop the weapon, Thane."

The taser fell to the floor, sparked, sent techtricity up Thane's pantleg. He bent to retrieve it.

I worked up a mouthful of saliva and tried to swallow away the tightening in my throat. Jag's left hand flicked toward the door, a gesture meant for me to leave.

Like that was gonna happen. I'd spent the last three weeks running away from people when they needed me most.

Instead, I glanced toward the doorway to judge how far Thane had migrated.

Jag wore a look that scared me enough to take a step backward. "Thane," he said. Then before Thane could even turn around, Jag nailed him in the nose with his fist.

Everything else in the room faded into the background, a blur of black and blue and white. All I saw was the silver taser flying in a perfect arc toward the bed. It hit the floor with a loud *clack!*

Around me, too many things to catalog happened. Grunts,

curses, a scream, the scratching of furniture being slammed around.

I dove for the taser, wrapped my fingers around it.

When I stood up again, I simply stared at it for another moment.

"Gunn! Help me out here!" Jag's voice came out muffled.

I looked up from the silver object of death in my hand to find him on the floor. Thane knelt on his spine, twisting both of Jag's arms behind his back. The hurt on Jag's face made me ache.

I pushed a button to activate the taser. "Release him," I commanded Thane. "Release him now. Stand up. Move to the window."

My voice came out in a tone I'd never achieved before. Barely suppressed anxiety skipped through my bloodstream. What I might say scared me, scared me, scared me.

I didn't know how much Jag knew. I didn't know how much I could say.

But I did know we all heard the distinct buzz of hover-copters.

Raine

42.

"Cannon?" I called.

He appeared in the doorway. Exhaustion lines crowded around his eyes, deepening when he smiled. "Hey."

"Will you—will you sit with me?" I hated how weak my voice sounded, but it matched the quivering in my muscles and the uncertainty coursing through my veins.

"Of course." The guy (what was his name again?) moved to the other bed (other bed?) in the room and sat down. He didn't speak, and I didn't dare, because every fact in my head had just disappeared.

A shiver stole across my skin at the inquisitive look the

guy gave me. Like I should have something important to say to him, or something crucial to show him.

But I couldn't even remember my own name.

I rubbed my hands over my sleeved arms, frantically searching my memory for the name of the person who slept in the other bed.

A hole gaped in my soul, reserved for someone special. Maybe the guy in front of me, the one watching me like I might leap across the gulf between us and hold him close. Maybe I should.

Acting irrationally, because all rationality had already fled, I did just that.

The guy caught me around the waist, emitting a soft grunt. But then he settled me on his lap with my cheek pressed into his chest. The hole filled and filled and filled with the touch of this boy. With the gentle way he stroked his fingers over my back. With his soft murmurs of apology and reassurance.

Dark shapes swam behind my closed eyes, but I didn't pay attention to them. I still didn't know his name. Or mine.

"Raine," he whispered, and I seized on the information.

My name is Raine. My name is Raine Something. I have a last name. It's . . .

Instinctively, I knew we'd hurt each other and were both desperately trying to make up for it.

"I'm sorry," I said, not knowing why, but sure the apology mattered to him.

He didn't say it was all right, because it wasn't. Deep down, I felt like I could trust him, that he wouldn't freak out on me if I asked him a potentially insane question.

"What's your name?" I asked, going for nonchalant and ending up sounding scared as hell.

Across his face, horror warred with fear, which fought against a rising tide of panic. "My name?" the boy choked out. "What's *your* name?"

"It's—" I stopped, because I'd forgotten again. Tears of frustration welled in my eyes, and I let them spill over. "I forgot. I knew, just now, and I've forgotten." I looked at the boy, desperate for his help. "Is this normal? Do I forget things often?"

Sadness painted every line in the guy's face. "No, Raine. You don't forget things often."

"Raine!" I said. "My name is Raine."

Before the still-nameless boy could answer, the door to my flat opened. Two people entered, talking. One boy, one girl. Their conversation didn't carry to me in words, just sound. I slid off the boy's lap and went into the living area.

"Hello," I said.

The girl had ultra-black hair, cut in a stylish mess of spikes.

She full-out stopped when she saw me. "Raine, you're awake." She crossed the room quickly and wrapped me in a hug.

"You live here, right?" I asked.

She jerked backward as if I'd burned her with my question. Then she looked at the guy with whitewashed hair and almost transparent blue eyes. "Zenn, she can't remember anything. Oh, no."

"So, he's Zenn?" I looked at the girl. "Who are you? And who's he?" I indicated the guy who still sat resolute on the bed behind me.

The girl grabbed my wrists. "I'm Violet. And he's Cannon, your, well, your best friend."

No wonder hugging him felt comfortable. I smiled over my shoulder at him. "And I'm Raine."

"Yes, you're Raine," Violet said, like I was four years old. Maybe I was.

"You're seventeen," Violet said. "And you've been brainwashed. Cannon," she addressed the guy in my bedroom, "I need to talk with Raine alone. Maybe you and Zenn can—"

"No problem," Cannon said. He trailed his fingers across my shoulders before leaving with the guy called Zenn.

Vi led me back into the bedroom. She lay down with me on the same bed, just staring at the ceiling. I'd almost forgotten she was there when she said, "Sing with me, Raine."

She began to hum a melody, soft at first, rising and falling until it settled into a rhythm on her tongue. She sang the lullaby through once, and something stirred inside of me. When she started again, I chased her voice with mine.

We finished, and everything came rushing back in a tidal wave of colors and sounds. Starr. Gunn. The Insiders. My father. My mother. Jag. Cannon.

Everything.

I struggled to breathe. "Vi," I gasped.

"It's okay," she soothed. "He smothered you, that's all. It won't happen again."

But she was wrong. My father had broken me. And I couldn't be put back together. Even if I could, he'd just smash me again.

"No, he won't," Vi said, answering my thoughts. I remembered that she could do that now. How could I forget that? How could I forget Gunn?

My mind felt numb, yet a million thoughts whirled around in there, trying to combine into one cohesive sentence.

"My dad knows about the Insiders," I said, barely audible.

"I know." Vi's voice wasn't any louder than mine. Before I could reply, something beeped in my head. My cache. Incoming file.

It bore the label *Known Insiders*. Upon opening it, I

wanted to throw up. Name after name after name, most of them my friends. All of them my colleagues.

Half of them dead, documented carefully by *(deceased)* after their name.

Zenn burst into the bedroom, his eyes wild. Cannon followed, his mouth set into an accepting line.

"Yeah, we got it too," Vi said, her voice filled with sharp edges.

I hadn't seen my name yet. I scrolled further until I did. Grouped together with Cannon Lichen, Violet Schoenfeld, and Zenn Bower, it sat under the label *Dangerous: To Be Modified Immediately. Retrieve and relocate to the Evolutionary Rise.*

Gunner

43. The sound of the hovercopters filled the room, getting louder and louder, punctured only by Jag's ragged breathing.

He lay on the floor, chest heaving, for a few seconds. When he stood up, he favored his bandaged arm so much I thought it must be broken. His skin glowed a dull gray, beaded with sweat.

"Tase 'im," he slurred.

My gaze volleyed between him and Thane.

"Gunner," Thane said, "please." I knew what he was asking, but when he continued, the breath left my body.

"I knew Jag was here. I know you swam in the ocean. I know you love Raine Hightower."

I wasn't sure what he was playing at. I already believed him about his involvement in my life these past three weeks.

Jag stepped next to me, his eyes still cutting holes in Thane. "Don't listen to him, Gunner. You can't believe anything he says."

Thane didn't answer him, but he leveled his gaze on Jag. "I crashed into the Confinement Rise."

I felt like this coded conversation was crucial. Suddenly I realized Thane wasn't trying to convince me, but Jag.

"Liar," Jag breathed. He put his hand on mine, bumping the taser lower. "Gunn, don't let yourself get sucked into his voice. The man's a monster. He killed his own daughter."

I looked at Thane, the pieces of a very complex puzzle wafting through dark space. I looked into Jag's eyes and felt the depth of his anguish, saw the sincerity in his soul.

But just because he believed his version of the truth with every fiber of his being didn't mean it was true.

"He killed Vi's sister. I watched him do it." Jag gripped my shirtsleeve now. "You can't believe him. You have to tase him, Gunner."

Thane relaxed against the window frame. The buzz of hovercopters descended. "Gunner, please." I knew what he was saying: *Tase me already!*

Jag opened his mouth, but I cut him off. "Shut up. All of you, just shut up! I need time to think."

I held the taser at my side, activated, ready to fire. Jag didn't speak—he simply glared at me, waved his hand like, *Think away, thinky thinker boy.*

The hovercopters were so, so loud. I closed my eyes and tried to find that place inside myself that would tell me what to do. My gut or whatever.

I heard the floor creak. I heard the wind blowing outside. I heard the steady rhythm of Jag's breathing.

I didn't hear anything from my gut.

Each second that ticked by felt like a decade. Jag's frustration rocketed through the roof. I felt nothing from Thane. *Nothing, nothing, nothing.*

I opened my eyes, surprised at how bright the room appeared.

"Gunn—" Thane took a step forward.

I swung the taser toward him, moving in slow motion.

I

      pressed

            the

                 button—

Four barbs pierced his chest in a perfect box formation; techtricity lightninged into his body.

He shrieked, clawed at the tethers, slumped to the floor with smoking clothes.

I stood there, shocked, as the consciousness drained from his eyes. As the Greenies buzzed closer and closer.

The earth spun faster, bringing me along with it. Jag said something to me, but nothing registered.

I stood there like a raging loser, holding the taser as if it were my lifeline.

44.

I adjusted the straps on the backpack Vi had given me while Cannon watched. "You could come with us," I said. "Zenn could bring you a backpack."

Vi, silent and observant, ordered another bottle of water from the dispenser.

Cannon shook his head. "My parents, they're—" He cleared his throat. "They've been moved to Camp A until this is resolved. Who knows what will happen to them if I leave?"

I nodded, fighting back tears. I didn't have parents to torture or threaten.

Vi finished packing her backpack, and I moved to add a handful of vitamin packets to mine.

"I'll be okay," he said. "I'll get a new name and a new flat, and hey, maybe They'll match me with Flare Riding." He almost smiled, so I almost returned it.

"You'll be okay?" I zipped my pack closed and looked at him.

His chair scraped as he stood. He wept as he drew me into a hug, touched me carefully, like I might shatter, just as he always had. He leaned his forehead against mine, and that gesture of skin-to-skin contact spoke more than voices ever could.

He squeezed my gloved hands. "Be careful out there, Raine."

That's it. No "Come back if you can," or "I wish I was going with you," or anything.

I didn't know how to be careful, but I nodded like I did. Then Zenn entered the flat with his bulging backpack, and it was curfew, and Cannon was leaving, and all that remained was the knowledge that I might never see my best friend again.

We abandoned the flat just after midnight. We used our feet for transportation, because our hoverboards had been confiscated.

Worry gnawed at my insides, but I couldn't quite identify why. No particular topic occupied my mind. I simply couldn't make it settle down.

I focused on putting one foot in front of the other, concentrating on taking another step toward freedom, and then another. I made the turns without consideration. Vi and Zenn followed without question.

I knew where to go. The same apple orchard where my mom had met Gage. Where she'd died. I knew what would happen when we arrived.

We'd go through the wall.

Breach the barrier.

I swallowed hard at the thought. "I can't," I said so softly the sound evaporated the second it left my mouth. I froze.

Vi pushed me forward. "Yes, you can. I came from out there. It's fine."

She was right; I knew it in the rational section of my brain. But so much of my mind had been taken over by the irrational, and right now, that part screamed louder.

The surrounding buildings shortened until they leveled out into Blocks. The sidewalks narrowed, and I noticed cracks for the first time. My city wasn't perfect, no matter how hard my father tried to convey that it was.

I replayed the good-bye with Cannon. "Be careful out there, Raine," looped through my mind.

"He'll be all right," Vi murmured. "Don't worry about him."

I kept my eyes on the cracks in the sidewalk. "I'm not worried about him." And I wasn't. He wasn't scared of Modification; he actually wanted it.

I wasn't sure what I was re: Cannon. Angry I couldn't seem to protect him from my father? Disappointed he hadn't wanted to come with me? *Something* that I hadn't done *something*?

Well, I could do something now. I took whatever was raging through my bones, through the empty spaces in my body, and poured it into my footsteps. The cement turned to dead and crinkled grass (dusted with snow) as we entered the orchards.

I would get Vi and Zenn out of this soul-sucking city. I would find Gunner. I would not let my father reprogram me, give me a new name, a new identity. He would not get to clone—

"Hello, Rainey."

My heart leapt into my throat. Anxiety thrummed under my skin. My step faltered. It took me a moment to locate my father through the inky night, leaning against a bare tree trunk.

"Hey, Dad," I said casually, like we'd go sit down to dinner in a few minutes. Like we'd have a polite convo and retire to our beds for a mandatory rest period. I recovered from my hesitant step and tried to move past him.

A buzzing noise filled the air, along with the smell of overworked tech. A force field encompassed me and him, trapping us in a clear bubble with Vi and Zenn.

"Where are you off to?" Dad took in the backpacks, the winter clothing.

"Nowhere," I said.

"Let us pass," Zenn said, his voice full and rich, seeming to echo with varying tones of high and low.

Vi and Zenn stepped to either side of me, each of them linking one arm through mine. We stood as a united front against my dad—the person who had authorized the murder of my mom. The reason I'd killed Gage.

I let the suppressed rage, decade of loss, and overwhelming sadness fill me again and then again. I felt stronger when I could feel. It was not feeling that scared me.

"I knew I made a mistake," Dad said in a voice I'd never heard before. It lilted into the air, as if dancing with an unseen current. "Letting you two come here. I never thought my daughter would allow herself to be corrupted."

My heart pulsed twice before I realized he was talking to Zenn and Vi. I cut a glance to Vi and found her practically glowing in the darkness. She exhaled, her breath escaping in a dense cloud.

She terrified me.

But not my dad. He glared right back at her. "We're cut from the same skin," he said to her, almost desperate now. "You should let me train you, Violet." He took a step forward, admiration skating across his face. "I've never met one such as you."

"Don't touch me," she growled, and my dad pulled back the hand that had been reaching for her.

He seemed to snap back to his senses. "Of course, except for Raine." For half a breath, his eyes softened. They marbleized again so fast I couldn't be sure anything had happened at all. "She's been quite helpful all these years." He grinned at me in his predatory way.

My legs felt incapable of holding my weight. Thinking about the countless lives I'd ruined made my heart twist. My stomach squirmed. My life had turned completely inside out.

"Let us go," Zenn commanded again, his voice fully employed.

"You're not going anywhere," Dad hissed without missing a beat, like Zenn's words hadn't had any effect. "My barrier will not be breached again. You want to leave Freedom, you die."

Vi's arm against mine tightened. One look at her, and I thought, *Why can't you brainwash him into letting us leave?*

She gave an almost imperceptible shake of her head. I took that to mean *Doesn't work that way*, or maybe *He's blocking me*, or some other thing that meant *We're screwed.*

Zenn's voice: out.

Vi's mind control: useless.

"There now," Dad said, his tone falsely bright. "Let's all get back to bed. It's too late to be out." He shivered and smiled. "And my, it's cold tonight."

"I'm so sick of you telling me what to do," I said. Then I did the only thing I could think of, even if it ended up killing me.

Ripping my gloves off, I lunged forward and gripped my father's face in my bare hands. He tried to jerk away, but I held firm.

Pain sliced through me like a roto-blade. I managed to stay on my feet and keep my fingers digging into my father's skin, even as he tried to get away.

The force field went down.

"Run!" I screamed. At least I think I did. The word came from somewhere, possibly everywhere. It echoed through the bare branches and filled the starless sky.

Run, run, run runrunrun!

447

Gunner

45.

Endless plains stretched before me, behind me, around me. After crossing the mountains—which I totally didn't remember doing on the way into the Goodgrounds—only waving grasses existed.

Jag's voice floated around me. When I had to, I gave noncommittal, one-word answers. The transport hummed, relaxing me into an almost-sleeping state where the words being said sounded more substantial.

"You'll be okay," Jag said. "I remember the first time I tased someone." He chuckled. "Rough day. Still . . ." His voice trailed off, and I could feel his eyes on me. "You can't lapse for long."

A spike of irritation flashed through me. "I'm not lapsed," I mumbled, not sure why that word bothered me so much.

"You should sleep while you can," Jag said, his tone soothing and feathery.

I didn't want to sleep. I needed to read my father's journal. I gripped it in both hands. Just like I had as we'd sprinted into the basement of the house. Footsteps had pounded overhead as Jag ushered me into a hole in the wall and then heaved a bookcase in front of the opening.

In the resulting darkness, I'd held the journal so tight, afraid it would disintegrate if I didn't.

We'd exited from the tunnel a mere ten feet from where Thane had parked the transport. I'd squeezed the journal as we piled in and put the Goodgrounds behind us. I squeezed it again now, just to feel something solid.

"Really, Gunn. Go to sleep."

Jag had used his voice, but I didn't care. I slept.

When I woke up, Jag leaned against the window, seemingly asleep.

"Hey," I said, hesitant, unsure.

"Hello," the transport said. "Manual control?"

"What? No, maintain." I looked out the windows at the deep darkness. "What time is it?"

"One fifty-two a.m."

"Location?"

"Nearing Freedom now. Four minutes until coordinates are reached."

I elbowed Jag, who muttered an obscenity. Two more jabs and he sat up, rubbing his eyes. He peered through the window at the dull glow—Freedom—a few miles in front of us.

"Damn, I hate that city," he said.

"Me too," I said, and everything broke. The tension. My guilt. I laughed along with Jag, wondering why I'd ever felt anything but completely relaxed around him.

"So the Insiders have an underground fortress a few miles away from the border of Grande, a city in the southern region," Jag said. "Indy said she'd do her best to get her people gathered and there by mid March."

"She's gonna be so pissed at me," Jag continued, more to himself than to me. "You wait, she'll punch me." He gazed out the side window. "And I deserve it."

"Yeah, okay." I had no idea what that meant, and I wasn't sure I cared. I was still trying to figure out how Jag knew every intricacy of the Insiders. The guy seemed to know everything despite his absences and lack of implants.

"You have the journal, right?" Jag asked.

"Yeah, and the letter from my dad," I said.

Admiration filled the transport, all of it beaming from Jag. Or maybe I was hallucinating again.

"You know, Gunner, my uncle knew your father." He shot me a glance out of the corner of his eyes. "He mapped every city in the Association," Jag said. "And made detailed instructions for us to unite the Insiders for an attack on Freedom."

I fingered the journal and opened it when Jag remained quiet. Written in the same slant as the letter, the first page launched into a list of names.

Javier Benes—Harvest

Greene Leavitt—Cedar Hills

Phillip Hernandez—Lakehead

Laurel Woods—Grande

The list filled the whole page. I flipped to the next page, and found a map of the Union, bodies of water labeled on the east and west. Above and below the Association, the land on the map simply said *All dead.*

A chill started at the top of my head and ran down my spine.

I fanned a few more pages. The words *West End Lakehead Treatment Facility* sat at the top, and a few lines of instructions followed. A number—*4*—was circled in the corner. The order in which to visit Lakehead and find Phillip Hernandez and install a false feed?

Jag put a finger on the journal. "I've been to Lakehead. Tiny little city. Mostly water purification."

I grunted, feeling like this conversation wasn't real.

"Finally," Jag said. "All the pieces are coming together."

I flipped another page and had started to read about Greenhouse Eighty in Cedar Hills when a bright-bright-bright strobelight bled onto the paper. I looked up—Freedom flashed before me. A few seconds later I heard the screaming siren of a wall breach.

"Sector fifteen, southwest corner, speed: ten," I said.

The transport zoomed forward, careening toward the corner where Jag and I had escaped. I held my breath during the twenty-second journey.

When I saw Zenn's white-blond hair in the distance, I released the stale air in my lungs.

"Pick up," I ordered. "Accommodate for three additional people."

While the transport calibrated, only two people sprinted away from the city and toward us. Vi + Zenn.

No Raine. Raine wasn't with them. Why wasn't Raine with them? *Raine is supposed to be with them.*

"Two additional people," Jag amended, his tone flat, accepting.

"No," I said, barely recognizing my own voice. "Where's Raine?"

We hovered a few feet above the ground while Freedom wailed and flashed and lost two of its most important Thinkers. Not three. Two.

Jag remained oddly quiet. An awkward vibe filled the cabin, and I felt numb all over.

Zenn climbed in first, then turned to help Vi. As soon as she was in, the emotions went from awkward to so tense the air became unbreathable.

"Hey, Violet," Jag said, his voice so soft she surely wouldn't hear him.

But she said, "Hey, Jag," with that same reverent tone.

Thousands of words went unspoken. Ten seconds became twenty as they gazed at each other. I sorta wanted to get out of the transport and walk to the hideout so they could have their reunion in private.

Especially when they started kissing. It wasn't the *groan*

and look away kind of making out, but more like the *we love each other and have been apart way too long* kind of kissing.

Jag gripped Vi's shoulders like he couldn't believe she was real. She slid her fingers through his hair, along his back, and down his arms. When they finally broke apart, I found that my heart was beating double-time, thinking about Raine and how I could kiss her like that when we were reunited.

"Told you I'd find you," Jag breathed.

"Yeah, I think I found you," Vi responded, a smile growing on her lips.

Before they could start kissing again, Zenn's hand came down on Jag's shoulder, waves of pain/anguish/hope pouring from him. "Hey, bro."

Jag looked away from Vi, and the mood in the transport broke.

"Where's Raine?" I asked immediately.

Vi untangled herself from Jag and wrapped her arms around me. She gave me exactly what I needed: a hug.

"Raine saved us," she whispered in my ear. "She made it so Zenn and I could escape."

I closed my eyes, trying to draw strength to speak. "She was good at that."

"Is," Vi said, releasing me. "She *is* good at that. We'll get her out."

I wanted to believe her. I wasn't sure I could. I cleared my throat and returned my attention to the journal. Jag kissed Vi again before saying, "Get us out of here," nothing but determination in his words and fire in his eyes.

As he directed the transport south-southeast toward the city of Grande, I watched the barrier of Freedom flicker from purple to blue to green to silver, clinging to a thin thread of hope that Raine would come running, flag us down, sit next to me, and hold my hand.

She didn't.

Raine

46.

Run, run, run runrunrun!

The shriek became one constant loop in my head. Darkness blinded me, pressed in on all sides. My hands seemed welded to my dad's face. His cries melted into the cacophony of sound surrounding me.

Shapes formed, dark and dangerous. My heart beat so, so fast. Surely it would flop out of my chest, leaving me with an empty slot where my vital organ should be.

Yet I held on. I didn't push the images back as they rushed forward even though I had zero desire to see what my dad wanted most.

But if it meant Vi and Zenn could get out . . .

If it meant Gunn would have a chance to regroup and launch an attack . . .

If it meant Cannon wouldn't be punished . . .

White-hot lightning bolted through the darkness. The sky split with an ear-blasting wail. I couldn't be sure if it was the siren signaling the barrier had been breached or if the sound came from my throat.

Scream upon scream beat down upon me. In the air, in my head, on my vision-screen. Because what my dad wanted most was to dominate every Citizen in the Association. Directing the most powerful city (and the surrounding cities) in the union wasn't enough. He wanted more.

He wanted to be the General Director. And to get what he wanted, he needed Gunner's voice. He needed my touch-and-see ability.

He needed Violet's extreme mind control.

He needed Zenn's allegiance, his ability to play both sides.

He needed the loyalty of powerful people. Thane's face flashed across my vision-screen.

My dad couldn't have any of them.

Icy tendrils of wet snaked up my legs. Somehow I'd fallen to my knees. My dad writhed on the ground next to me, panting and still trying to escape the death grip I had on his face.

I felt my grasp weakening as the strength left my body.

My muscles burned. My throat throbbed with pain.

Rivers of hurt and anger overflowed. Light the color of blood splashed across my vision-screen. It wasn't until the metallic scent hit my nose that I realized it wasn't light, but real blood.

I tore my hands from my father's face, but it was too late. They were covered in blood. Mine, his, didn't matter.

I wiped my face, feeling the slickness of it, my stomach twisting with the cloying scent. I twisted away from his ruined face and my welted hands, and retched. Again and again, until my abdomen felt tight and I coiled into a ball.

Gunn, I thought. *I miss you, miss you.*

Then I started reciting my vitals again. *My name is Raine Hightower.*

The night wore on, and still I lay there, bloody and wet, a man I thought I should know gasping for breath only a few feet away.

My name is Raine . . .

Even when the sky opened up and the rains came, they couldn't wash me clean. Nothing could restore what had been taken from me.

My name is . . .

Gunner

47. The transport vibrated, making my legs seminumb as we flew south toward the safehouse. I sat among the others, watching Zenn eye Vi and Jag as they whispered to each other.

I wished I could talk to Raine. I settled for imagining a conversation in my head.

Are you going to pine away forever, Gunn? she'd ask.

No, I'd answer, sullen, defensive. *Just for today,* I'd think, but not allow to leave my cache. *And maybe tomorrow. Or until I learn to live without you in my life. Yeah, okay, forever.*

I would never learn to live without Raine Hightower.

Sure, sure. So the past twenty-four hours have been . . . what? Gunn's Pity Party?

Shut up.

That's nice, Gunn. What a way to talk to me.

I'd ignore her sarcasm, of course. *Raine, I'm—*

Don't, Raine would chat. *I know you are, but apologies won't do a whole lot here, will they?*

A slow tear edged its way out of my eye. I let it fall, knowing a whole flood would follow. At least Raine wasn't here physically to witness it.

I miss you, I'd say.

That doesn't help either, Gunner, she'd chat back. Raine never was one for crying, despite that one episode.

But it's true.

I felt someone in the transport watching me, probably Vi. I wiped my face real quick, fake-chatted to Raine, *I gotta go. Chatcha later.*

As the transport slowed, I swear I heard Raine chat, *I miss you, miss you.*

We landed behind a single tree, gentle swells in the landscape darkening the night sky surrounding us.

"We have to walk in," Zenn said. "This way." He moved off toward one of the rising hills.

"How do you know?" I asked, falling in step beside him. I figured Zenn would be better company that Vi and Jag, who couldn't seem to keep their hands off each other for even a moment.

"Not all of my training took place inside the city walls," he said.

"But . . . but how did you get beyond the wall?"

"Thane," Zenn said, effectively stunning me into silence. I put my hand in my back pocket, felt a slip of paper there. After pulling it out, the moonlight helped me make out *Jag* written in loopy writing.

I turned around and thrust the note toward Vi and Jag, who walked behind me. "Here. It's a note from Indy."

Vi took the note even as Jag reached for it, coils of shock emanating from her. "Indy?"

"Yeah. Dark skin, pink hair—"

"I know who Indy is." Vi stared at the note like it might bite her.

"Well, super," I said. "Can you give that to Jag?"

Vi looked at Jag, who wore a shadowed expression of half horror, half amuesment. She pocketed the paper. "Yeah, sure. Sure I can."

When Jag chuckled and pressed his lips to Vi's temple, anguish poured from Zenn.

"Thanks," I said. I wanted to feel sorry for Zenn, but at least Vi was here. Everything seemed muted and colorless without Raine.

After crawling through another hole and walking down another long tunnel, I emerged into an empty cavern big enough for a table and chairs. The few people sitting there halted their conversation when we arrived.

A petite girl with long blond hair stood up. "Zenn?"

"Saffediene. We need everyone out here now."

She nodded and hurried down another corridor.

"Is my brother here?" Jag's voice came out husky, hopeful.

A man with long silver hair appeared in a doorway to my right. In the next second Jag was sprinting toward him. He yelled, "Pace!" before they collided.

The meeting Jag had called wasn't due to start for a few minutes. I laid on a lumpy couch in a tiny cavern, obsessing over Raine. I seriously felt like I could sleep forever, that I didn't give a damn about what happened next.

Jag was right. I was lapsed.

What unlapsed me: Zenn.

"Can we talk?" he asked, filling the doorway with his tall frame.

I scrambled to sitting. "Sure, come on in." I wiped both hands over my face, hoping to force myself to stop thinking about Thane-and-Raine-and-Starr, Starr-and-Raine-and-Thane.

Like that worked. They all bounced around inside my head, demanding explanations.

"I know what happened with Thane," Zenn said. He settled on the couch next to me, careful to leave an unassuming gap. "You did the right thing for him back there."

"He said—" My breath shuddered on the way in. I studied the uneven stone floor of the cavern. "He asked me to tase him, leave him for the Greenies. He said Director Hightower wouldn't be able to blame him that way."

"You did the right thing, Gunn."

We sat in comfortable silence. My mind buzzed with questions, and the one that came out was, "How come Jag doesn't know?"

Zenn studied me as if I should've worked this out for myself. "Jag—the known leader of the Resistance—shouldn't know anything about the Assistant Director of Freedom. Can you imagine if Jag got caught, interrogated?" He shook his head. "No, he couldn't know. He probably still doesn't believe it. Jag's not what you'd call forgiving."

I followed his logic. If Thane got caught, he couldn't know

incriminating things about Jag either. Still, their obvious hatred of each other felt very real.

"Do you think it's worth it?" I asked.

Zenn took his time thinking about it. "Some things are worth fighting for." He was right. I'd fight for freedom. I'd fight for choice. I'd fight for Raine.

"Hey, you guys ready?" the girl Zenn had called Saffediene asked from the doorway. "Meeting's about to start."

Zenn stood, sighing heavily. "Let's get this Resistance started. Bring that journal, Gunn."

As I tucked the journal in my back pocket and followed them out of the cavern, I couldn't help thinking:

We're here.

And we're ready.

48. I wake to a preset alarm in my head. I stretch and glance out the sliding glass door. Winter has finally broken. The temps the last few days have been reasonable, and the sun shines hotter every day.

I check my cal: March 16. Midterms start today. I jump up and dress quickly. Dad will be angry if I'm late to breakfast.

"Hey," I say breathlessly as I enter the dining room just in time. Something about the glass and chrome table bothers me, but I can't pinpoint what.

"Good morning, Arena," he says. "Exams begin today?"

"Yes." I check my meal plan and order the mandated two-egg breakfast.

"Are you ready?"

"Ready enough," I say.

He watches me with those sharp eyes. Long scars run from temple to chin on both sides of his face, still pink and raw. I can't remember where he got them.

I can't remember a lot of things.

I am Arena Locke. I am sixteen years old. I—

I cut off my thoughts, somehow feeling like I shouldn't finish that sentence. At least not in the presence of my dad. I'm not sure how, but he seems to know everything, even things I don't say out loud.

He gestures toward me with his fork, as if to say, *Go ahead.*

I know he means to get a move on and eat already. But what I do instead is finish my thought.

I shouldn't believe everything I hear.

A rush of memories floods my mind. I used to have white hair. My own flat. A roommate with spiky black hair. A best friend. A guy who loved me, and I loved him.

A different name.

I used to be called—

"Your name is Arena Locke," the man across from me says.

I look up slowly, as if my eyes aren't attached to my head. "Who are you?" I ask, which sounds ridiculous because I don't even know who I am.

"I'm Van Hightower, your guardian."

The name sounds right, settles in my mind into a familiar slot. But the word *guardian* holds no meaning.

Don't believe everything you hear echoes through my mind again in this strangely robotic voice.

I blink and see a city burning. Tall buildings crumble under the weight of smoke and flame. Silhouettes rise through the midnight sky, outlining people riding hoverboards. The wind swirls, spreading the fire.

Another voice speaks: "About time, Gunner." It's a girl, and I swear I know her. Maybe I am her.

I'm brought back to reality when my guardian says, "Time for school, Arena."

"Arena," I repeat. The name doesn't fit, but I don't have anything else.

I am Arena Locke.

I am sixteen years old.

I have midterm exams today.

Three hours later I settle into the ergonomic in lab seven. Unused tethers hang from the armrests. Inside, a quiet flurry of excitement rides underneath the blatant fear screaming through my blood.

I hate the practical exam. I hate touching other people

and regurgitating their deepest desires onto a projection screen for the world to see. Most of all, I hate that they're strapped down and I'm not.

Before I can dwell on that too much, the door in the corner opens. Van enters, a small smile playing on his mouth. Next to him strides a man I've never met, with black hair that's turning gray. He moves with power, his shoulders square and his eyes already locked onto mine.

"Is this her?" he asks Van.

"Yes, General. This is Arena Locke." He stops a few paces away. "Arena, this is General Director Ian Darke. He's here to"—He exchanges a look with the General Director—"observe your exam."

Behind them shuffles another man, badly injured judging from his walk.

As Van helps him onto the table, I want to look away but find I can't. The other man, clearly as old as Van, isn't wearing a shirt. His chest bears four identical wounds (halfway healed), that if connected, would create a perfect box.

"There you go, Thane," Van coos. "Just lie nice and still." He nods to the physician on my left, who reaches for me.

I usually let him paint on the perma-plaster willingly, but today my hands stay fisted in my lap.

"Arena," Van warns, casting another glance at the General

Director. I detect a glimmer of fear in Van's expression.

I have to pass my exam, but I watch Thane, ~~hoping praying~~ needing him to speak.

"Don't believe everything you see," he gasps out, looking only at me. It sounds like he's giving me permission, like it's okay for me to touch him, drain him.

I raise my hand and uncurl my fingers. The physician slops on the connective tech and places my hand in Thane's.

Then the show begins.

acknowledgments

It has been said that the second book requires much more work than the first. I don't know if that's true, but it's at least equal—and in a much shorter amount of time. I think that's what almost killed me: writing and editing *Surrender* in under four months.

Of course, that would not have been possible without a great many people. My husband, Adam, whose enthusiasm to play taxi driver and eat too many Baconators was contagious. My son, Isaac, never complained about babysitting and/or riding his bike to activities so I could get more words written. And my daughter, Eliza, set aside games of Guess Who? and waited patiently for me to finish the chapter before I could watch her latest dance move.

Not only did I dedicate a solid chunk of time to this book, but *Surrender* would never have made it out of the embryo stage without the keen eyes of Christine Fonseca, a cherished friend and genius beta reader. She's also terrific at late-night chatting, bringing treats to the ledge, and driving long distances for launch parties.

Let's not forget Ali Cross, who feels like my right hand—and my left. Nothing I do gets done without her stamp of approval. A hearty dose of gratitude also goes to Michelle McLean, who donated her time to make me a better writer and storyteller. Talk about sacrifice.

I'd deserve to be whipped if I didn't mention Bethany Wiggins, who read *Surrender* and kindly told me all the problems it had. Her advice opened my eyes to new avenues for the book. Ditto for Jamie Harrington, who clued me in to one of the most precious moments in the novel (can you spot which one it is?)—or at least what it should've been. I hope I did it justice.

Last, but certainly not least, Shannon Messenger did what any good crit partner should: She shredded me. I covered up all the bleeding wounds, opened the document, and performed CPR.

In addition to my beta readers, I need to thank my debut buddies, who helped to make 2011 one of the greatest years of my life. Lisa and Laura Roecker. Beth Revis. Jeff Hirsch. Angie Smibert. Julia Karr. Gretchen McNeil. Kirsten Hubbard. Myra McEntire. Matt Blackstone. Carrie Harris. Jessi Kirby. John Corey Whaley. Michelle Hodkin. Tyler Whitesides. Amber Argyle. Jessica Martinez. Stasia Ward Kehoe. They each helped in more ways than they know, from angsty e-mails to friendship to phone calls that brought me back from the brink. So yeah. Thanks, Team 2011!

My life would not be the same without the WriteOnCon Underbelly, who provided not only the best writer's conference out there—for free!—but a safe place for me to be, well, me. Thanks to Casey McCormick, Jamie Harrington, Shannon Messenger, Lisa and Laura Roecker, Carolin Seidenkranz, Nikki Katz, and Dustin Hansen. And for the many thousands who attended and provided services for the con: We love you!

A special thank-you to Ally Condie, who always makes me feel like the most important person in the world. And one for Nichole Giles, who is surely tired of riding with me to signing events. And a final vote of gratitude to Heather Lyman, who continually asks about my books like she really cares.

I swear I'm almost done. These people are gems of the highest quality: Sara Olds; Stacy Henrie; Jenn Wilks; Heather Moore; Paul Greci; James Dashner; my blogging buddies; and all of Mr. Johnson's sixth graders, past and present.

Everyone knows a book isn't born by itself. Anica Rissi and her team of Freaking Smart People (Bethany, Michael, Mara, Carolyn, Matt, Jen, Anna, Dawn, Siena, Paul, and Laura, I'm looking at you!) at Simon Pulse deserve all the credit for making my words shine; Angela Goddard gets major props for the graphic genius that is *Surrender*'s cover; Beth Dunfey provided brilliance I never would've come up with on my own; Katherine Devendorf and the dedicated team of copyeditors at Pulse deserve praise for their tireless efforts to make the story look beautiful on the page. Thank you, thank you, thank you.

A million + one thanks to the best agent on the planet, Michelle Andelman. She believes, and because she does, I work harder. Thanks, M.

I'm additionally grateful for my parents, Jeff and Donna Watkins, and to my sister, Jessica (and Paul) Cottle. As if they weren't already the most fabulous family a girl could ask for, I also have the best in-laws in the known universe in Chris and Carol Johnson, Keith and Lisa Johnson, Mary and Ryan McBride, Curtis and Alisha Johnson, Amy and Ryan Harris, and Bill and Janelle Johnson. Their undying support of me as a real, live person means more to me than their support of my books (which they also give freely). Love you guys.

And who does an author write for? You, the reader. I've received so many e-mails that have made me smile, brightened my mood, and encouraged me to keep writing this series. Thank you. I hope you enjoy!